Journal of a Cavalry Bugler

by Georgiann Baldino

Published in the United States

A Pearl Editions, LLC Production
Naperville, IL 60564

Copyright © Georgiann Baldino, 2014

Publisher's Note: This is a work of historical fiction. Apart from the well-known actual people, events and locales that figure in the narrative, all the names, characters, places and incidents are the product of the author's imagination or have been used fictitiously. Any resemblance to events, locales or persons, living or dead, is entirely coincidental. The autobiography and correspondence of Charles Henry Dickey provides a sequence for this story. Dickey mustered into the 4th Illinois Cavalry August 12, 1861, served as a bugler, member of General Grant's escort and fought alongside African American troops. However, Dickey was not present at all of the engagements depicted in this novel. This story expands the timeline of his service; adds incidents; invents scenes, relationships and dialogue; and expresses feelings Dickey did not articulate. To write a historical novel, an author recreates voices and emotions appropriate for the time period.

ISBN   9-7809-8591-233-8

"If there be those who would not save the Union unless they could at the same time save Slavery, I do not agree with them. If there be those who would not save the Union unless they could at the same time destroy Slavery, I do not agree with them. My paramount object in this struggle is to save the Union."

Abraham Lincoln, August 22, 1862

Journal of a Calvary Bugler

By Georgiann Baldino

One side is not braver than the other. Bullets fly, and men get swept away. They rush into the thick of fighting, and 'kill' is written on every face. In a battle the commander who has more men—not afraid to die–drives his opponent off the field and declares a victory. Charlie Dickey, May 19th, 1864

Chapter One
Charlie Dickey, April 15, 1865, Good Friday
Ottawa, Illinois

The series—dash, dot dot, dash dot—clicked louder than the chatter of people in the offices of the Caton Lines. I hoped to get work as a telegraph operator, but before I introduced myself to Mr. Henning, the Superintendent, the sounder began to click. Peter Crego bent over to transcribe the message, and the desk lamp cast his face in shadow.

A mental translation told me the message concerned President Lincoln.

Peter's posture sagged.

Mr. Henning chided him, "Peter, you slippery critter, what's wrong?

Peter drew a breath, and his lips moved in silent rehearsal, but he could not say the words. Instead he passed the transcription to Mr. Henning.

"President Lincoln assassinated. Seward attacked the same night now mortally wounded."

Peter was a hulking fellow, tall, loose and heavy. He staggered to his feet and tramped out the door.

My heart jumped to my throat. No one spoke a word. Surely, the South was not foolish enough to murder the President.

Mr. Henning passed the message to the rest of us. When it came to me, I could not take the page because a transcript made the news official. Mr. Henning's voice quivered. "Secretary of State Seward also attacked. My God, is this a scheme to topple the government?"

Just days ago we had rejoiced over military victories, but General Joe Johnston still commanded rebels in the field, as did three other Confederate generals—battle-hardened men all, unwilling to concede defeat.

Mr. Henning became pale. "Lincoln gone? His death could renew the fighting. What shall we do?"

Someone suggested, "Let's gather at the courthouse."

I inched forward and stumbled into the seat Peter had vacated. Mr. Henning knew my father, Colonel Dickey, and apparently trusted me to assume control of the telegraph because he rushed out with the others.

Hooves and wheels of carriages outside hardly made a sound. The world moved in secrecy. Evening fell, quiet but unprotected. My thoughts churned. I remembered fierce battles fought over unimportant patches of ground. When we ceased fire, one side or the other held a piece of turf, but what fields they were—banquets for flies and maggots. Only infernal luck kept me from being blown asunder. Men, even ones I knew to be pious, family men, had descended into bloodthirsty rage. Shot and shell did not check them. They rushed at each other with heathen screams, echoing down the line.

Now Mr. Lincoln counted among the fallen. With the President assassinated, the worst was confirmed. His murder reopened wounds not yet healed. At the moment of Mr. Lincoln's reward—bitter defeat. Did it mean war had become a thing of permanence?

Chapter Two
Ella Linsley, Ottawa Mourns
Easter Sunday, April 16, 1865

Ella had watched workers drape public and private buildings with mourning, and she struggled to believe the Almighty's judgment was great. Church bells tolled every hour. Pews filled fuller than any time in her memory. From the pulpit, the minister cried for vengeance against the slave-holding South. "We have no need of evidence. The South is guilty of assassination," he thundered.

The congregation cried, "Amen!" No one voiced moderation.

The deacon decreed, "The Almighty removed President Lincoln because he was too merciful towards the South."

Late into the evening, the streets remained crowded. Officials made speeches in the town square. Veterans who had survived war's horror huddled together. Two old soldiers, Myron Kingsbury and Paul Staley, could not talk about Mr. Lincoln's death. Paul bowed down in grief and wept.

Myron cried, "No one stood guard over Mr. Lincoln."

Ella went forward to comfort him, but her father held her back. "I am taking you home."

"No," she insisted.

He pulled her closer. "This loss outruns comprehension—no telling what may happen."

"Before the assassin attacked," she said, "we comforted ourselves with stories of glory and heroism."

Wanderers packed the streets. Irate voices echoed. "The South resorts to murder."

Father took her arm and led Ella away. "Lincoln's death comes on the anniversary of a day, four years ago when our country's flag was lowered at Fort Sumter."

"But surely people remember how the President walked into Richmond just days ago—humble, not triumphant. He asked us to have malice for none."

He steered her past St. Columba Church. "Let's go home."

Mourners filled it to capacity and spilled onto the steps. A little girl drew her skirt over her head. Neighbor women swayed, backs twisting slowly, hands kneading the air, eyes heavenward, urging the spirits to visit. Their weeping made the little girl cry.

Father hurried along. Few people knew Abraham Lincoln the way he did. Their friendship went back to the 1840s when Mr. Lincoln rode the Eighth Judicial Circuit.

James Cummings ran up. "Mr. Linsley, what can we do?"

"It is too soon to tell."

"General Grant has to be crazy for vengeance."

"We don't know that."

Cummings turned toward the tavern. "I hope the Confederates refuse to surrender, so we can teach those rebs once and for all."

Father's expression looked sadder than she had ever seen him.

"We can no longer look forward to a visit from Mr. Lincoln," he said. "I am selfish about this. Now more than ever, the country needs Lincoln's wit and humor, story and laughter, bubbling up from inside."

Father seemed years older than just yesterday. She also worried about Charlie. The thought he might return to the army made her stomach churn.

Chapter Three
Ella Linsley
April 23, 1865
Ottawa, Illinois

Ella thought she ought to summon the doctor. War service had left Charlie painfully thin. The way he wavered on his feet concerned her, but he put his hand on the small of her back. Feverish warmth spread through her clothing. Ella's parents had gone out to a town meeting. Though they had no chaperone, Charlie steered her inside.

"Let me get you some water," she said.

"Just come and sit with me." Blue-black rings encircled Charlie's eyes.

Ella followed him to the settee.

His hands shook. "I intend to make up for lost time."

She steadied his hand. "I'm glad to hear it." How unlike Charlie to stay inside. The Charlie she knew loved to wander, itched to run, swim and ride horseback. They had tramped outside in all kinds of weather since they were children. Growing up with Jennie, John and Cyrus, they hiked the woods, ate outdoors, raced. Outdoors meant freedom, and today the sun warmed the ravine, a perfect day to be out.

He eased his injured left arm onto his lap. She nearly pulled him around to face her, but a lady must not do such things. She must settle for tugging at her hoops to straighten her skirt.

His voice wavered. "I was hoping to talk to your father."

"He went to the meeting to hear what authorities want to do."

"On my way here," Charlie said, "a young man who favors the South insulted Mr. Lincoln." His expression hardened. "The mob wanted to beat him to death."

"Dear Lord—someone we know?"

"Just a boy, repeating what his elders say at home."

Just a boy. Similar to Charlie four years ago when he ran off to war because his father and brothers did. Ella brought her face close to his. "And you stepped in?"

"Someone had to." His words tumbled out. "Just a boy."

"You must be more careful," she whispered.

That made him smile. Not exactly the Charlie she knew, but a glimmer of the man she loved.

"Do you know when your father will return?"

"Should I tell him why you want to see him?"

His smile broadened. "It is up to me to tell him I want to marry you."

For years she had longed to hear Charlie say that, but something felt terribly wrong.

Embarrassment softened his voice. "My finances are not yet assured, but the prospects will improve."

"Father knows you will make a good husband."

He examined her closely. "Contrary to what civilians think, army life does not ruin a man's character."

She looked down. When the war started, Charlie had ridden off, eager to rattle a saber, nearly got himself killed. When he came home, Charlie was a different, dispirited man. This morning, she wasn't sure who he was. His breathing quickened, but she did not know what to say.

"What's wrong?" He stuck the good hand in his pocket. "I have a ring."

Doubts made it impossible to answer. Charlie wanted someone to marry—but did he want to marry her? She left his side. "When you were sick, you said things—"

"In delirium."

She looked out the window. Today should be the happiest day of her life. "Charlie, you called out for another girl."

"When I was gripped with fever? Surely you don't place importance—"

"A woman who seduced you."

"No one—"

"You called out repeatedly for some girl named Leah."

The color drained from Charlie's face.

***

"Take it." Charlie thrust one of the books at Ella.

The back felt uneven. When she turned the journal over, Ella nearly dropped it. "Oh, my Lord." The cover had a bullet hole. She raised the book toward him, as a question. "Did this journal save your life?"

Charlie waved that off. "The Hand of Providence saved me."

"Are you angry with me?"

He shifted from one foot to another. "I started keeping a journal when John and I went away to boarding school. By the time war came, the habit was well ingrained, so I decided to make a personal record. Serving in Grant's escort put me in a good place to observe." He searched her

9

face. "But then we got caught up in horrific events, and the sights out-stripped reason. As casualties mounted, a record grew vital, the strife in camp, conversations between ourselves and southern sympathizers, the plunder and waste, and yet my ability to find proper words failed. I didn't want to disremember or diminish one thing."

"Did you write about her?"

Charlie looked surprised and hurt—as if she slapped him.

"Is there a reason you don't want me to read?" she asked.

Words caught in his throat.

Charlie's older brother, Cyrus, had been killed somewhere near Mans-field, Louisiana. Charlie's brother-in-law, Will, died from wounds received at Shiloh. Countless of their friends had been cut down—tremendous losses. Ella lost a cousin at Shiloh. Sorrow shared became sorrow magni-fied. A terrible, unfamiliar, pleading look on Charlie's face made Ella re-pent. After what he had suffered, wartime dalliance with a rebel woman paled by comparison. Ella handed the journal back, but now he refused to take it.

She wanted to wrap her arms around him, but he took a step back-ward.

His voice trembled. "I brought all the journals. The first volume is about growing up, even has my early memories of Mr. Lincoln." A wry smile brushed Charlie's lips.

Ella's knees buckled.

He pushed a stray lock of hair from her forehead. "Battle scenes are not meant for a gentlewoman to read."

"Women are stronger than men allow."

"No matter what you read, always remember, I asked you to be my wife." He inched away. "What you want to know begins in volume three."

"Will you kiss me before you go?"

Charlie acted as if he did not hear and hastened down the walk.

Had he kissed that woman? Were they lovers?

Long strides carried him away—without a word or backward glance.

Chapter Four
Ella Linsley, The Nation in Mourning
President Lincoln's Funeral, Chicago, Illinois, May 1, 1865

The train halted at Park Place, the coffin was withdrawn and the remains borne to the hearse beneath a stately, gothic arch. Emblems of bereavement draped the streets from every roof, window and lintel. Flags at half-mast were all edged with black crepe. Temporary seats filled doorways, windows, roofs, sidewalks. Thousands of people came to look at the coffin, hoping to see more. At length, amid the firing of guns and the sad tolling of bells, the coffin and dais began to move.

The procession inched along Clark Street toward the courthouse. Leading the parade Colonel R. M. Hough and General "Fighting Joe" Hooker. A strange gray, cloudless sky made the whole occasion somber and unreal. Slow movement of the horse-drawn hearse made it seem Lincoln's funeral procession might never reach the courthouse.

John Dickey escorted Ann Wallace, Belle Dickey and Ella as they waited in line. From the size of the queue, they realized they had to stand all day if they wanted to view the President's remains. Colonel Dickey had been among the dignitaries on the platform when the train arrived in Chicago, but the Colonel was not well, and Charlie had taken him to the hotel. At 12:45 p.m. the guard carried Lincoln's body to the rotunda.

Behind Ella two gentlemen spoke in harsh tones. "Confederates still have troops in the field."

"How many?" his companion asked.

"One is too many." The voice rose in agitation. "Rebel Generals Taylor and Kirby Smith are dangerous men, ready to renew the conflict."

"Pray God, they do not!"

Yes, Ella thought, pray for peace. She turned toward John. "Does the President's death mean Charlie and Colonel Dickey have to go back to the army?"

His back stiffened. "Father isn't well enough, and I doubt Charlie is either. The wound in his shoulder still weeps fluid."

"I worry more about his mental distress."

"If peace holds, Charlie has no reason to go back. If armies renew the fight—let's not think about that."

At 4:00 p.m. officials opened the doors to the public. The queues moved forward one foot an hour, the crowd sluggish in its grief.

11

Close to midnight, Ella and the others entered the rotunda. Her feet had become numb, but she refused to give up. She wanted to tell Charlie she paid respects to the martyred President. Citizens in line looked with indescribable sadness on the body, resting beneath the rotunda dome. The dais sat on an angle to make the remains visible to viewers with the President exposed to the public. No one spoke. Ann cried softly. Ella struggled to remain conscious.

***

The next day, Ella ran her hands over Charlie's first journal. The book had thick, weathered binding and well-ruled pages. It was the largest volume. Knowing Charlie, he had captured family memories, but with himself in a starring, central role. Volume two was smaller and the binding nearly worn out, apparently battered in the field. She arranged all the books on her bed and flipped through a succession of pages. The penmanship changed over time—first it was small, conservative script, then he wrote an elegant, mature hand and finally hasty, chicken scrawl. Each book was a different size. The ones he carried during the war were small. Volume six, smallest of all, fit in the palm of her hand.

Charlie must have gone to a great deal of trouble to preserve the journals.

She opened the first volume and read half a page. Pangs of guilt hit, but then Ella reasoned she had a right to know the man she married. A married woman had no rights, other than those her husband allowed. He could sell her property, indenture their children, lock her away. A woman needed to choose wisely. She hoped she could choose Charlie.

The first pages made her smile. Endeared him even more than before.

Once she got well into Charlie's story, Ella holed up indoors, fed the fire when it rained, barely noticed when fog opaqued the windows. She became a hermit. Charlie's words drew her in.

Charles H. Dickey, Journal
Volume One, Early Years 1842 to January 1862
Growing up in Ottawa, Schooling, Mustered into the army.

I couldn't wait to come into the world. Mother said waywardness started the first day of my life. I entered with none of the comforts or safeguards of home. My parents had taken a buggy trip to spend a week with neighbors. I decided to be born early while they gathered blackberries. Mother disapproved of giving birth in a ditch, the first of what she called 'Charlie's misadventures.' I hollered the moment my mouth pushed out, shattering the peaceful countryside.

Father always frowns on antics. Mother softens the verdict. "God made Charlie this way to compensate for a consumptive chest." Whatever the cause, I thrust those who love me into difficulty, but never more danger than I bring down on my own head.

We can trace Dickey ancestors to colonial times. All Scotsmen, persecution drove them to northern Ireland. My great-great-grandfather emigrated to South Carolina in the seventeenth century. They say I inherited a high-strung nature from him. Five forefathers fought as patriots in the Revolutionary War. Grandfather trekked across the mountains to Kentucky. Father married a Welsh girl and moved further west to the new frontier in Illinois. Back then scurvy, typhoid and ague fevers took a great toll.

By the time I dropped into the world, the family had moved from a log cabin to a frame house in Ottawa, which stood in the center of town. Father taught school but also studied the law and began its practice. From the first, I showed a talent for mischief. My squeals stole attention from everyone else: big sisters, Martha and Ann, and big brothers, Cyrus and John Jay. Even before I could talk, I demanded they take notice. When Belle joined the family after me, her delicate chatter was no match for my shouts.

A fondness for adventure grew faster than Mother's and Father's ability to control me. When I started to crawl, the family went on a picnic. Mother spread out a lunch of chicken and biscuits. Everybody loved her cooking and enjoyed the feast while I crept to a ravine and fell into the stream, wailing as I went over.

A loud splash told them where. "Oh, my lord," Mother cried. "Save him."

Big brother Cyrus jumped in and pulled me out, wiggling and coughing. Mother tried to comfort me but failed. After hearing her tell and retell the story, I can picture it. Mother dried my tears and distracted me with a biscuit and chicken bone to suck on.

The winter of 1844 William Wallace landed downstate in Illinois to study law with Messrs. Logan and Lincoln. On a stagecoach he fell in with Father, now also an attorney, and Father lured him to Ottawa. Will studied for a year, was admitted to the bar and practiced with Father instead of Mr. Lincoln. Father had something Mr. Lincoln did not, a beautiful daughter. Ann captivated Will from the start.

When war came in 1846, Father raised a company of infantry, and Will went with him to fight in Mexico. Father's company became part of Colonel Harden's regiment, but sickness hit and Father missed the battles. Though fighting continued, Will brought Father home.

Will acted like an elder brother but took a special interest in my sister, Ann. She had a warm disposition, ready for fun and frolic. She rode horses bareback and could have developed a real talent for horses, but as the eldest daughter of an invalid mother, household duties fell to her. Will came back from Mexico to find Ann, a charming girl fifteen-years-old. Noticeable softness came over Will when he looked at Ann.

Soon after their return, Father received an appointment as a judge of the northern circuit of Illinois. Chicago was just a small village on the circuit. Our family moved into a new, brick home on an Ottawa bluff, but Father spent four months each year traveling the judicial circuit. Abraham Lincoln and Stephen A. Douglas tried cases in his court.

In 1847 Lincoln's towering figure approached our home on Worth Bluff. I was five years old, too early to remember all the details, but others told the story many times, eager to claim Mr. Lincoln's friendship. I had lined toy soldiers along the floor for battle, but then huge feet pounded the boards and the burden of Mr. Lincoln's weight made the porch groan. He jerked off a stovepipe hat, and a thick bush of black hair sprang ungovernable in every direction. High bones, hollow cheeks, prominent nose and a sleepy eye made me run and hide from the ogre.

"Abraham, welcome." Father motioned me to come forward. "Charlie, come and greet our guest." I hid behind a bench, and Father excused my poor showing, "A skittish boy but his mother's favorite."

The giant came closer, bent long legs and lowered his nose to mine. A smile lighted his eyes. "Charlie, is it? Or shall I call you Charles?" His high-

14

pitched voice did not match Mr. Lincoln's large size.

Father folded his arms across his chest. I could not move, even to please him.

Huge hands lifted me up. Dust from the road flew off Mr. Lincoln's coat, and I sneezed an uncouth greeting.

Though he said, "Bless you," I squirmed to get down. "My own son, Robert, is your age."

Father reassured me. "Mr. Lincoln is partial to boys."

Laughter rattled Mr. Lincoln's chest. "Herndon says I'm too partial to boys; he gets cross when Tad and Willie turn our law office topsy-turvy." He carried me into the front parlor, as though I were fine porcelain. I twitched to escape, but his gentle touch bade me stay.

***

The family had a mare with a colt, which I named Rhoderic. Cyrus broke Rhoderic to harness and made him a pet. With the mare to steady Rhoderic, Cyrus hitched the pair to a wagon. When Cyrus went back to the house, he let me hold the reins. John came out with an umbrella, which he opened in front of the colt, and Rhoderic bolted.

I dropped one of the reins, pulled on the other and made the matter worse. Over a sheer drop we went, boy, horses, wagon.

My brothers ran to the edge of the bluff but saw nothing. The horses, still tied to the front wheels, ran up the other side of the ravine, leaving the wagon bed behind, upside down on a stump. I cried out, and Cyrus and John shimmied down.

John examined me. "No broken bones."

Cyrus looked in my eyes. "Why are you crying?"

"My new straw hat is spoiled." The hat was indeed ruined. "It cost ten cents." The more I gulped, brayed, yelled, the more Cyrus laughed.

***

Will Wallace became a fixture in our home. Although he was 11 years her senior, in 1851 he asked Ann to marry him. I spied on them as he proposed. Ann looked beautiful by candle glow, wearing a turquoise shawl.

Will spoke in a clear voice. "Your father said I may ask for your hand—"

I piped up. "Ann, if you turn Will down, the rest of us will never forgive you."

"Charles Henry Dickey," she said, "mind your manners."

"Yes, but—" Before I could say more, Mother pulled me away for

15

further "instruction" at Father's hand.

My parents did not send me to school until age seven. Instead Mother gave me an old Bible. I opened to The Book of Job and tagged after her. "What does this spell: U-p-r-i-g-h-t?" I gave her no peace till she told me. "And what does it mean?"

"Wholehearted obedience to the will of God," she answered, "no matter what difficulties come along."

"How can a boy obey with his whole heart?"

"Through God's grace. The Almighty is aware of everything that happens. Even the hairs of your head are numbered." She pushed curls out of my eyes.

"My hair is sparse, but Belle's is a tangle. God counts her hairs?" Seemed like wasted time.

"Satan struck Job, persecuted him to test his obedience, but Job remembered that God knew everything, especially what was in his heart." She went on with her work, but I continued to plague her with questions. When I finally went to a country school on the edge of the prairie, *McGuffey's First Reader* was easy for me. Job's story remained a favorite, a warranty the Almighty cared for righteous men. Trials here on earth brought reward in heaven.

Also when I was seven, Mother got some currant cuttings, which she planted in the garden. They looked spindly, and I asked if they would grow. "Certainly," she said, "they will take root in a few days and become bushes." Two weeks later she remarked to some visitors her currant slips had failed. "They have not taken root."

I volunteered, "No roots yet. I pull them up every day to see." She sent me out for a hazel switch, which she applied to my backside to impress on my mind the importance of leaving her garden alone.

Father built our next home on Ottawa's north bluff, the best place in the county to take walks, play and gather wildflowers. The ravine gave us a fine view of the city. A girl name, Jennie Linsley, lived next door. Jennie had a thin face, framed with tight braids that her mother used to tame curly, red hair. Her body consisted of angles, too sharp to be pretty, but when she grinned, broad, white teeth flashed. Her cousin, Ella, often came to visit. Ella looked like a porcelain doll, her hair wavy and the color of sun-bleached wheat. Startling blue eyes looked wide, as she marveled at the view.

Jennie and Ella, John and I played four musketeers and staged battles.

16

Jennie was gay as a lark and not any bigger. Ella played a beautiful hand-maiden in need of rescue. Her face inspired adventure—high, arching brows, wide mouth, generous lips and straight nose. One day I hoisted Ella over my shoulder and carried her away. She made a sound, part squeal and part laugh. Her body twisted, trying to free herself, so I grasped her legs more tightly. Holding her was a jolt of realization that felt like more than a child's game.

Jennie rushed to Ella's rescue. "You, devil! Unhand her or face my wrath." John joined in the defense, and we fought a three-way duel to possess Ella. Jennie won Ella's freedom, but only because I let Ella go and ran away—to hide my growing feelings of intimacy.

Then Ella took us for a stroll along the ridge. May was a particularly beautiful time; the hillside full of wildflowers.

"What flower is this?" Jennie asked.

"Blue-eyed Mary," Ella answered. Three petals of the flower paled next to her blue eyes.

I picked yellow buttercups for her. John added deep purple flowers to her bouquet. "Larkspur," she whispered, breathless over the color.

I wished I had put them in her hands. Her expression was the sort one wants to study, learn well, a face transformed by joy.

***

Father sent John, Cyrus and I to a number of private schools, shifting from one school to another because Father believed boys learned mischief from each other once they got well acquainted. It may have been good in theory, but it provided a queer education. I studied the third reader half a dozen times. In each new school the teacher asked what reader I was in. When I answered the third, he or she put me in a class just beginning the book. Eventually I knew *McGuffey's* by heart.

The courthouse where Father worked was a mile away from the house, near the junction of the Fox and Illinois Rivers. In the spring of 1854, when I was eleven, the whole family except Father went to South Salem, Ohio, where our maternal grandfather, Isaac Evans, had a home. Not to burden Grandfather, we took a small house in town, and we three boys attended the South Salem Academy, then in charge of James Alexander Irwin Lowse. Settlers were pouring into the Northwest Territory, but not many towns provided education. Father gathered John, Cyrus and me together. "Consider yourselves fortunate. Many other young men have strong natural abilities, but few have an education to equip them for the world." The exacting course of instruction produced well-rounded men, or so they claimed. The headmaster gave classical and mathematical training, all the things a man must know. Facility speaking came easily to me, as did composition. The headmaster also stressed moral instruction, so when grown we could lead useful lives.

We had our first classes in Latin and felt proud of ourselves. Then Father visited. With two questions he discovered how little we knew. Father took us back to the beginning of Latin grammar and put us through a rigorous course of his own design. Each day he made us recite from the beginning to the point we reached the previous day. Before vacation ended, we knew the last regular verb. Back in school, our fluency amazed the teacher.

A fine maple grove grew near Grandfather's place. When the right time came, we went from tree to tree, removed sap and carried it to boilers. Caramel smell filled the barn. When the sap cooked down to thick syrup, we made candy. Grandfather threw a party to celebrate the season. My youngest uncle, Stuart, was only a little older than I and became a playmate. Grandfather, however, thought of games as evil. One day he caught Stuart and I behind the barn playing marbles, gave us a good thrashing, confiscated the shooters and target marbles and sent us into the house to contemplate our sins.

Whenever Mr. Lincoln came to Ottawa to practice law, Father made him welcome in our home. Mr. Lincoln's appearance had grown rougher since I last saw him. He never brushed his well-worn suit. The cloth fitted his angular frame like an outer skin. I doubt he owned a comb or hairbrush. Strong lines cratered his mouth. Many times he disagreed vehemently with Father, yet always remained patient with me. I didn't understand what he said and yet lingered in his company. It was unnecessary to take his full meaning. Kindness and humor drew me near. His arms and legs were ungainly to an extreme; his words never so—he never got angry or impatient. While seated in our parlor, Mr. Lincoln told story after story, crossing and uncrossing his legs, sometimes tying them in a bow.

Problems disappeared in Mr. Lincoln's presence. If a man like him succeeded in the world, with plain clothes, no part of which fit him, homely face, any man had the same hope. Mr. Lincoln lost his mother at an early age. And when he spoke of it, his face looked so sad my own troubles seemed small by comparison. I had the blessings of good food, clothing and comfortable home, while Mr. Lincoln had gone hungry. Sad and yet happy, uneducated yet smart, grotesque yet warm, Mr. Lincoln drew me in, now more than Job.

Father and Mr. Lincoln had spirited discussions on what to do about slavery. Father worried about disunion. They spent long hours debating the Kansas-Nebraska Act. The day Congress passed the law, they argued half the night. Long after Father sent me to bed voices filtered upstairs, at times whispered and conspiratorial, other times piercing (Mr. Lincoln) and wild (Father in anger.)

Early the next morning, Mr. Lincoln's voice came from Father's room, and I snuck out to see. Lincoln sat on Father's bed. "I tell you, Dickey, this nation cannot exist half slave and half free."

"Oh, Lincoln! Go to bed." Father pulled the covers over his head.

In November of 1854 Father wrote Mr. Lincoln, "I want you to be a U. S. Senator from Illinois." On a cold Thursday afternoon in Springfield, when members of the Illinois General Assembly met to elect a Federal senator, Lincoln collected 45 votes on the first ballot—more than anyone else, including the incumbent, Democrat James Shields—but five votes short of the prize. The hours dragged, and no candidate secured the required majority. After nine ballots the factions still had not selected a candidate. Mr. Lincoln then released his supporters to Lyman Trumbull, a prominent anti-Nebraska Democrat, and broke the deadlock. Mr. Lincoln sacrificed political ambition for the cause of free-soil. It had to be a great blow to his ambition because he told Father, "I would rather have a full term in the Senate than the presidency."

That winter we moved to Chicago and took a house on Lake Street. Hannah Collins, a friend from Aurora, kept house for us and later Sarah Ryan came and took charge although no matron ever lived up to Mother when she ran the house. Our home was a block west of Union. An omnibus ran down Lake Street to take us to and from the city. One of my daily chores was to milk the Durham cow. I detest milking, but faithfully kept her from going dry. Miss Gere gave us music lessons, and I got far enough along to play the rolling notes of "Monastery Bells."

When I finished, Belle whispered in my ear, "Be sure to keep that piece in your repertoire."

"Why are you whispering?"

"It's a courtship song."

"Oh." I must have looked confused because she pulled me aside to explain.

"Courtship takes place around the piano. Songs like 'Monastery Bells' are respectable and yet hint at desire." She said it in a conspiratorial tone, and I wondered how my younger sister had become so worldly.

Another chore became the marketing, a job I enjoyed as long as I could ride on the top of the streetcar because it made me sick to ride inside.

One day I needed money to shop and went to find my father in a courtroom, where he prosecuted a case. Mr. Lincoln stood for the defense. While Father made an argument, Mr. Lincoln walked up and down with his chin in his hand, twisting one way and then the other, a comical sight and not at all handsome, but apparently a necessary part of his concentration. I wanted to stay, but Father pushed me along.

The spring of 1855 we returned to Ottawa. For some reason I do not remember, I did not come with the others but my uncle, Marcus Evans, who had just married, brought me home. I was small for my age and I learned afterward the railroad conductors passed me right along as being under age. I remember running up to the front door and straight through to the woods, eager to be back on the bluff after a year's absence.

To welcome us home one of our mares, Aurora, gave birth—my first experience with this miracle. Cyrus showed me how to prepare a stall with dry straw. He led Aurora in; I followed but Aurora disliked my company.

Cyrus said, "It's her first time. We must stay clear unless she needs us."

Aurora went down, cried and pushed to expel the baby.

"It's bad," I said.

Cyrus consulted his pocket watch. "This is how hard it is for a creature to give birth. If Aurora goes 20 minutes and the legs haven't appeared, then she needs help."

I held my breath. The foal's front hooves appeared first, one slightly ahead of the other, covered in a protective sac. Then the front legs came out to the knees, nose and head appeared and Aurora birthed all on her own. Adeptly she cleaned her baby.

We did not get to enjoy the new colt, however. Cyrus went off to Oxford College, near Cincinnati, while John and I headed to German boarding school in Oakfield, Missouri. Father made it sound like fun. "You can learn to talk German and play the fiddle." I pleaded to stay home. "Let me train the colt, so it gets used to my touch." Father thought more of education than horseflesh. Request denied.

Evans Walker, the son of a neighbor, went to school, too. The headmaster who welcomed us had a cancerous sore on his left cheek, repulsive in appearance, but he talked fluent French, German and English. Ignoring his deformity was the only way to get along.

The first week felt like a picnic, compared to what came next. Ironclad discipline descended. We could not speak anything except German after noon. Each infraction meant extra German penmanship. Few infractions escaped the headmaster, and my German vocabulary blossomed.

Miserly rations meant John and I suffered continual hunger pangs. We got a piece of cornbread with molasses for breakfast. No coffee. Mother used to let me drink coffee at home. She ground the beans by hand, brewed them with an egg in the pot, filled a cup mostly full of warm milk, added a spoon of brown sugar and then just enough coffee for a steaming mocha. She allowed me one cup each morning. If I begged and promised no mischief, I got two. Students at German school got no coffee, only the staff, although we could smell the aroma as it brewed. At noon the matron served meat and vegetables, but I never left the table satisfied. More cornbread or sometimes a biscuit served as supper. Portions of fruit equaled one mouthful. Lucky for me, an orchard grew on the grounds. When fruit ripened, the crop lured me outdoors in the middle of the night. Juice from clingstones ran down my arms until I couldn't eat more. I washed the telltale smell of peaches off in the horse trough and climbed into bed wet but satisfied.

We complained about starvation in our letters; Evans Walker did the same, and when the accounts matched, Mr. Walker came to investigate. He found us in perfect health and so left us to suffer. Once when Ann visited, she left me some coins. The moment she left I walked five miles to a village and bought ten cents' worth of soda crackers. I devoured the whole lot in the woods on the way back and for one day my stomach stopped grumbling.

A boy named Clarence had an old pipe, and we trekked off into the woods to light up. After a few puffs, however, strange feelings hit.

Clarence grinned. "Your face is green."

I persevered and created billows of smoke. Then lost my breakfast. "Your tobacco is not to my taste," I murmured and gave Clarence back his pipe.

***

21

Early in December we received word Mother's health had worsened. When we arrived at home, the family gathered at her bedside. Her stark white face alarmed me. Also worrisome, her long, gray tresses were unpinned, a sight I was seeing for the first time. She asked Father to leave and waited until the sound of footfalls confirmed he had gone downstairs. She looked from one child to the next. "Be good and kind to your father, and watch out for each other."

Ann protested, "You will recover."

The rattle in Mother's chest said otherwise. "When troubles find one of you, the others must help."

Six children joined hands.

"Treat the world with kindness," Mother whispered.

Ann arranged her covers. Belle cried.

I offered the Creator my life for hers, but she passed away on Christmas Eve. I had attended many funerals—for babies just born, cholera victims and farm accidents. Death always lurked nearby. No one in our immediate family had died, however. We had lived blessed lives. Until now.

The minister intoned, "Heavens laws are inflexible and do not bend to our tears. Whatever God doeth, it shall be forever, so that mankind will fear Him." Who would answer all my questions now with Mother gone? I went back to the Book of Job. Mother had encouraged me to take the story to heart, but now Job failed.

Father sent John back to Oakfield but kept me at home, a strange departure of discipline. The morning he left, John whispered, "Behave, Charlie. Always make sure your conduct consoles Father. Give him no reason for sadness—no *other* reason that is."

My sister Ann stepped into Mother's role as mistress of the house, which included taking care of Belle and me. Though she mourned, too, Ann gave us steady assurances. My tears hovered just below the surface, like I was still a toddling child.

Father's friends, Mr. Lincoln and David Davis of Bloomington, each offered to take a child for a time. To my surprise, Father accepted their offers, agreeing to send me to Mr. Lincoln and Belle to Judge Davis. Belle and I were not consulted about the arrangement. When we were ready to start, however, plans changed, and we both went to Bloomington. Mrs. Lincoln had one of her attacks of brain trouble and could not tolerate another boy under foot in Springfield. I rejoiced at staying with Belle but felt disappointed at the loss of Mr. Lincoln.

I attended a farm school seven miles from Peru, Illinois. Hour after hour, in good light and bad, I pressed my nose into books and became rundown, so Father sent me 20 miles farther west, not to school—but to keep me away from books. He forbid me to read on weekdays except the Bible; instead I helped old man Hutchins. I took piano and dance lessons but had to leave books alone. I enjoyed music more than any other program of study. Natural ability allowed me to play piano pieces by ear. I delighted in picking out tunes but did not like to practice. When I returned to Ottawa in the fall, I could play the polka, schottische, vasouviene, mazurka, waltz and cotillions, as well as dance the steps.

Belle and I spent the winter of 1856 with Ann. Thanks to my urging, she had married Will Wallace, Father's law partner. Ann had tiny, delicate stature, but a rock solid spirit. Her best feature has to be large brown eyes. Belle practiced piano while Father condemned me to read *Hume's History of England* two hours a day.

Brother-in-law Will became a candidate for Congress and preached peace between North and South. Ann said that he stood in a terrible current. In June of 1856 Will wrote from Philadelphia, "I have been here since Sunday but too busy to write. We just concluded our business here by nominating Col. Fremont for president. I don't feel altogether satisfied but hope for the best. I think of you often, wish you all were here, and then again am glad you are not."

A political tornado hit the country when free-soil and slave interests exploded in Kansas-Nebraska Territory. The Illinois congressional convention met in Ottawa and nominated Rev. Owen Lovejoy, a rank abolitionist, for Congress. Half the delegates bolted and called another convention to nominate someone who could defeat Lovejoy. The feud didn't make much sense to me because both sides opposed slavery in Kansas. The only difference was the second group said the South had the right to capture runaway slaves, touting their platform as a spirit of friendship toward the South.

Father said they hated Lovejoy because he called for immediate abolition.

Kansas became a battleground. Slavery proponents rushed southern settlers into the territory. Northerners also brought settlers in and vowed to make it a free state. Factions murdered each other and harassed the other side's settlers. So Father assembled the family to give firm instruction on the slavery question. "We do not condone going to war to free slaves, but make no mistake, God's grace includes the black race." Although southern born, he opposed the extension of slavery to the west. He had inherited slaves, but freed them even though he had debts. Money from the sale of slaves, while acceptable, was not agreeable. Father hated the notion of driving people like cattle.

"What worries you," John asked.

"Lovejoy's demand for negro equality."

Father said, "These murders in Kansas mean no one is safe. White men have died. Opposition grows stronger than a desire to compromise. Both sides go too far."

The election solved nothing. Will ran on a platform of compromise and said he could vote to uphold slavery further. A few people who supported a fusion platform voted for him, no matter how horrid slavery, in order to preserve peace, but America had two minds. In Ottawa people rejected the institution of slavery. In politics, however, one side refused to compromise with the other. Will tried to ride a current of peace, but the South became harder to console. They demanded slavery be allowed in Kansas and other territories; anything less became provocation. They threatened to secede. Moderate men like Will got struck down during the campaign. The extreme abolitionist, Reverend Lovejoy, won the congressional seat.

Slavery bothered all minds. Southern newspapers outlined plots, insurrections, claimed slaves poisoned masters. Terror threw southerners into a state of war before anyone fired a shot. Turmoil ruled. Both sides ranted. Angry speeches filled the halls of Congress. The Republican Party came into being with the object of excluding slavery from the territories.

***

For some years Ann suffered from rheumatism, and in 1857 it left her helpless. Ann blamed her inability to conceive a child on the illness and was eager to find a cure. Will took her and Belle to Hot Springs, Arkansas, a formidable series of travel connections. Ann wrote, "He carried me in his arms to the spring." Will then left Ann and Belle at Hot Springs and returned alone.

In the spring of 1858 I became a farmer. Father gave me a piece of ground to raise a crop of potatoes. I turned the soil by hand.

Ella came over but laughed at my skill with a spade. "You need some help?"

"No, thanks. I am a prairie farmer."

"You have a muddy face." She brushed the dirt away.

I leaned into her touch. "I'm like a pioneer."

"I'll reserve judgment until the harvest is in."

That October I sold my yield at forty cents a bushel—and became a wealthy man, who could treat Ella, Jennie and John to a trip up the Fox River to visit friends at Oswego, Aurora and Geneva.

***

That year the great Lincoln-Douglas debates came off in Illinois. Mr. Lincoln asked Father's opinion about the speech he planned to give to open his campaign.

Father raised his voice. "The first ten lines of that speech will defeat you for the Senate!"

Always one to value other opinions, Mr. Lincoln asked, "Why do you say so, Dickey?"

"It's a damned-fool speech—not enough for abolitionists—way too much for the rest of the country. My god, you say our government cannot last part slave and part free. Nonsense. It has done precisely that for four generations."

Mr. Lincoln thought for a time. "But if I stand by the speech, I will ultimately find myself in the right place."

Both Father and Mr. Lincoln believed in the gradual emancipation of negroes, the government to stand the loss. Despite Father's advice against it, Mr. Lincoln used his damned-fool speech to accept the nomination. Some embraced the power of Lincoln's House Divided platform, but it turned Father against Mr. Lincoln, saying "abolitionists shanghaied him." Father had stayed out of politics for many years, but when Douglas started the Conservative Democratic Party, Father joined—vowing to oppose Lincoln.

The Lincoln-Douglas debate at Ottawa, the first of seven, became a much anticipated fight. Excitement prevailed everywhere, not just in Ottawa. The Parties rallied, but no one centered on Republicans or Democrats; everyone rallied for Lincoln or Douglas. People came long distances to hear the battle of titans. Coaches, buggies and wagons of all sizes clogged the roads. Axels groaned under the weight of passengers. Countless more citizens came on foot, raised clouds of dust and covered the city in a brown haze.

Ann still suffered rheumatism, so Will and I watched over her. Early that morning we took a position on the grounds of William Reddick's mansion. Fortunately we got there early because other spectators clambered onto the roof, custodian house, horse barn and carriage house to get a good look at the debate stand across the street. By noon an immense crowd inundated the speakers' platform.

At two o'clock the candidates emerged from the mansion. Lincoln patted me on the head. "Rub against people. Learn from them. Don't be afraid if they are larger." I had celebrated my sixteenth birthday nine days before, but still had to look up into his face.

Mr. Lincoln nodded toward Senator Douglas with cool politeness. The Senator reciprocated with aloofness. The two failed to shake hands.

Ruffians fought over the stage. I lunged forward, but Will held me back.

"I can't see."

Will's grip tightened. "The situation may spin out of control. Help me protect your sister."

It took 45 minutes for the sheriff to stop the brawl and restore order.

Senator Douglas, short, broad and red-faced, spoke first in remarkable contrast to Mr. Lincoln. Douglas had a deep bass voice, which carried well, but his enunciation became gruff, and only people within a hundred feet understood, while the sea of constituents extended several blocks.

After Senator Douglas finished his opening speech, I asked Will why Father supported Douglas.

"Mr. Lincoln's platform is radical—your father worries prohibiting slavery in territories will lead to more murders like the ones in Kansas Territory."

When it was Mr. Lincoln's turn to speak, the crowd murmured, "Black Republican." His high tenor voice and distinct enunciation allowed people to hear at a greater distance. As a musician, I appreciated the tempo and Kentucky modulations in his speech, but it wasn't just his voice. Lincoln was my favorite.

Reporters took down the speeches word-for-word and put them in print for the entire country to read. Lincoln started his campaign as a country lawyer, little known outside our state. Douglas sat in a position of power in Washington. People expected him to be the next president of the United States, but slavery blew the contest sky high. Douglas claimed political decisions like slavery should be decided locally while Mr. Lincoln said something as brutal as slavery should never be subject to majority rule. Together the two men split the nation's seams wide, and a house divided sounded prophetic. Father's worries grew so strong he campaigned in the central part of Illinois for Douglas. The election would be won or lost in the center of the state, where voters remained undecided.

A cold rain struck most of Illinois on election day. Reports of men unable to reach the polling places came in. The tally of popular vote put Illinois in the Republican column for the first time and won some races, but Douglas retained his seat in the Senate. Democrats exulted. Supporters went wild with excitement. Bands played. Whiskey flowed. Senator Douglas proclaimed, "Let the voice of the people rule."

Defeat made me bitter. Father saw my hangdog look. "Lincoln did it to himself, Charlie. I told him to retract the House Divided speech. His own stubborn determination to stand by it did him in."

Some weeks after the election Mr. Lincoln came back to Ottawa on court business. He did not show the slightest ill will toward Father for opposing him in the campaign, instead showed his customary kindness. When Father asked him to tell a story, a mischievous glint lit Mr. Lincoln's eyes. "This occurred in the early days of my legal career when my colleagues and I took pleasure in athletic sports. One day at circuit court in Bloomington, Illinois, my partner Lamon wrestled some local boys near the courthouse, the very ones who challenged him in the trial, and in the scuffle made a large tear in the rear of his trousers.

"Before he had time to change, court was called into session. Lamon, being the Prosecuting Attorney at the time, got up to address the jury. Wearing a short coat, his misfortune was apparent. One of the lawyers started a subscription, which passed from one member of the bar to another to buy new pantaloons for Lamon. 'He being,' the paper said, 'a poor but worthy young man.' Several colleagues put down their names with ludicrous subscriptions, and finally someone laid the paper in front of me.

"I wrote after my name, I can contribute *nothing* to the end in view."

Whenever he came to Ottawa, storytelling tournaments occurred. If Mr. Lincoln walked into a tavern, it filled to overflowing, and he undeniably enjoyed a reputation as the best spinner of yarns around.

Later that year I also got to know Mr. Douglas. Father took John and I to a race in Chicago between two legendary horses, Princess and Flora Temple, a little, rough-coated bay mare with black mane, legs and bobbed

27

tail. I fancied I knew all about horses. Every time visitors arrived at home, I raced forward to care for the horses. I washed, brushed and fed, not like working at all, and so I considered myself a good judge of horseflesh. "Flora does not look like a racer," I declared.

Senator Douglas pulled me forward to debate the issue. First, he pointed out Flora's qualities. "See the well-set neck, firm shoulders, strong, straight back, powerful forearms and short cannon bones?"

The men in attendance agreed. Nobody took on the Senator. Nobody dared, except Mr. Lincoln.

Senator Douglas bet on her to win. "Until she was five years old, Flora was willful and flighty. Then George Perrin bought her. He has a special eye for horses. With hard training Flora became a stepper with a clean, locomotive stride." In these days races lasted many heats, and Flora Temple defeated her competitors in good style. While we watched, Flora Temple became the first trotter to finish faster than 2:20.

That winter Father took an office on Dearborn Street, Chicago; Cyrus opened an office in Bloomington; John started college at Normal and I went to Jacksonville to be office boy for Rice Smith. A complete breakup of the family.

In 1860 Father sent me back to school, this time in Kentucky. I lived with my old Aunt Ann Gass a mile from town. When Belle came to Lexington, we spent happy weekends together. Aunt Ann, her husband and children lived on a farm on the Winchester Pike. I went to school with my cousin Hope and slept with Cousin Tom, who was six years older than me. I learned more in that school than any two before because I liked the teacher and studied hard for the first time. The school was in the middle of its session when I joined. I wanted to study geometry, but the teacher said, "Impossible. The class is made up of bright boys, and you cannot catch up." I kept after him, however, and he finally agreed to let me try. I sat up till after midnight and mastered the first theorem. The next day I attacked another and did this for a week. Then the class came to a problem they did not understand. I had the matter at my finger ends, and the teacher called me to the board. When I solved it, faces showed surprise. Suddenly I became a full member of the class.

I learned about the South as well. The sons of planters provided an education, not found in books. Every one of these fellows had excellent billiard and sporting skills, never worked as manual laborers and disdained anyone who did. Full of froth, rich in self-esteem and aristocratic assumptions, they were the best riders in the world and excellent marksmen. Cousin Tom spent a great deal of time practicing with dueling pistols. "Could you face a man and aim to kill?" He handed the pistol over. "You try."

I missed completely.

From 20 paces he hit the target's center. Then he looked at me with a cold expression. "Gentlemen fight to defend honor."

During the rest of the visit I kept all observations about the South, her institutions and culture to myself.

Father came through on his way to attend the Democratic convention at Baltimore. He told me, "I hope the Party will unite on Douglas for president and avoid war between North and South."

What about Mr. Lincoln, I wondered, but did not have the courage to ask because Father looked worried. "If Democrats fail to do this and nominate an extreme southern candidate, and the Republicans pick someone opposed to slavery, it will plunge us into war. The North does not understand the South, and the South does not understand the North. Each thinks the other is bluffing and will not fight if the time comes."

When he thought I was asleep, he told Aunt Ann, "If war comes, it will not be settled in a few days or months."

"Pssh-taw, everyone says it will be over before it starts."

"Fighting could last for years. Each side will find the other has brave people." The tremor in his voice matched the worried look in his eyes. Father pressed on to Baltimore, but his efforts and those of others failed. The Democratic Party split.

Belle and I returned to Ottawa in the winter of 1860. Our family was once more united. But for how long? Political distrust grew daily. I became interested in religious matters and joined the Episcopal Church, where Ann belonged.

I went into my father's law office as an office boy where he practiced with Will. I began to study law but also spent time in Judge Caton's office, learning telegraph signals. The Judge owned the Caton Lines, covering Illinois and adjacent States, and my brother John worked as his private secretary, the operator and railroad agent. John let me take his place one day, and I managed to get along, as they used a paper telegraph machine. Practice improved my manipulation of the telegraph key, but I had little chance to practice transcribing by sound.

Brother Cyrus practiced law in Memphis, Tennessee, and wrote about growing unrest. "The Union occupies everyone's attention here, but Union men have little hope of its preservation. A call went out for a torchlight procession of those opposed to secession, so last night I marched for three hours. The band played the "Star Spangled Banner" and "Hail Columbia." I never before marched in a procession. We drew all sorts of curses. The procession covered two miles, nearly spanned the whole city. People got perfectly wild with enthusiasm. Torches lit. Stars and Stripes waved everywhere. Drums, fifes and brass instruments clamored. The march inspired confidence the South will not secede, and Union may yet be restored. Then fights broke out along the route and dashed those hopes."

When he read this, Father paced the floor. "Southern sentiments may develop into treason."

The presidential contest of 1860 blew the country apart. Bickering divided the nation, and four candidates each professed varying shapes of the central question—slave versus free-soil—a house divided. Extreme southern Democrats nominated John C. Breckenridge of Kentucky for president, while northern Democrats nominated Stephen A. Douglas. The same Senator Douglas, who knew horseflesh.

This second contest between Lincoln and Douglas captivated me, as much as when I stood in the audience the first time the two men squared off. Father expected Douglas to spoil Mr. Lincoln's chances again, but owing to the destruction of the Democratic Party, Douglas did not win. His stature brought a large number of voters to the polls, but this time he lost. In a four-sided contest Mr. Lincoln rose to the pinnacle of power.

To keep the nation out of war, Stephen Douglas spoke out against secession. "You will not be true to your country if you seek to make political capital out of disaster."

But fear spread. As president, Mr. Lincoln could appoint marshals and postmasters in southern states and, if he chose, put abolitionists in place. South Carolina seceded, and we called it "treason." America was a sovereign nation and must remain so.

Governor Richard Yates of Illinois declared, "Not for one minute will I consent to the Mississippi flowing hundreds of miles through foreign land with Illinois compelled to pay arbitrary taxes and exorbitant duties."

Rebellion spread. Other states followed South Carolina—and prepared for war.

Will feared for Mr. Lincoln's safety and went to Washington for the inauguration. He wrote, "The political cauldron is a dreadful boil. A peace conference brought conservative men of all parties together. These good men considered the country. I saw Mr. Bell of Tennessee, Governors Hicks of Maryland and Pollock of Pennsylvania, Mr. Gilmer of North Carolina and Thurlow Weed of New York—men of different parties, all content to surrender dogma if it retains the Border States in the Union. When the conference ended, Governor Hicks of Maryland called the legislature of his state together. Mr. Bell asked for support to keep Tennessee as part of the Union. I trust these efforts may restore peace."

Will got an invitation from Henry Winter Davis of Maryland, and the two of them watched the crowd assemble from the eastern portico and saw Mr. Lincoln sworn in. "An honest man stood before his countrymen and the civilized world. Without reservation Mr. Lincoln vowed to protect the Constitution and kissed the Good Book. The Marine Corps brought forth triumphant strains of music mingled with joyous shouts from the crowd. Our country passed her darkest hour and a happier day dawned. Conservative men approved the spirit of the President's address and its direct and honest tone."

After the inauguration, Will called on Mr. and Mrs. Lincoln. "Mr. Lincoln seemed perfectly at home—awkward in appearance as always, but just as sociable in the White House as in Illinois."

***

Father, John, Will, and I worked in Judge Caton's office one April evening when a telegraph came. The Judge read it silently. When he finished, his hands shook. John rushed for a chair and helped the Judge sit down. Fort Sumter had fallen.

Will reread the message. "Even with this news, I am disinclined to prepare for hostilities against southern states."

Judge Caton's back stiffened. "Disloyal states have stolen from the country. We must give them more *ammunition* than they bargained for."

Will shook his head. "Demagogues too old to enter the army denounce the North as cowards and aggressors against the South, but surely other southerners understand the risks. Reasonable men will prevail."

Father disagreed. "The Federal government has great material wealth now in the hands of marauders. We must rescue it."

"They pursue a wild course," Will said, "but we must regard southern

31

people as brothers."

Father planted his feet wide apart. "They attacked the flag."

The Judge raised his voice. "They spat in our face! The North must reclaim Federal property and revenue."

"That will take great use of force," Will said.

"What other course is open?" John asked.

Will spoke from the heart. "We ought not force our institutions upon unwilling states. We are stronger than they. They cannot truly hurt us and, if possible, we ought to prevent them from hurting themselves."

Father folded his arms across his chest. "The South thinks they can slap Yankees in the face, and we will sue, not fight."

Will's gaze wandered. "We could stand like the Forefathers, calm amid a wild storm, pursue an even course without being provoked, resist the threat of our own passions. That way, a stronger, more fraternal union can emerge." He covered his eyes with his right hand. "But if the war spirit of the South grows, if attacks are made on any of the loyal states—" His voice trailed away.

Under his breath, Father said, "I reject rash anger as you do, but we must brace for a great struggle."

Will leaned closer. "Should military force become necessary I will serve with you."

"Father," I pleaded, "include me."

He ruffled my hair.

"Fort Sumter fired on!" I said, "I must go, too!"

His mouth smiled, but his eyes did not. "We'll see."

I could not question him—but in Ottawa everyone knew who volunteered and who did not. Derision soon started; those men who declared they must stay home found themselves targets of scorn. People said it was a man's duty. If I didn't volunteer, what would Ella and Jennie think?

One afternoon when the three of us walked, I touched the subject. "Father and Will are veterans. They have to go."

Ella halted. "Are you going, too?"

Jennie pulled her along. "Of course, he is."

Ella looked so strange I didn't answer immediately.

Jennie's back stiffened. "Charlie doesn't have a wife and children to hold him back."

Ella's lip trembled. "He doesn't belong in the army."

No one, not even Ella, could make me out a yellow-belly. "If Father refuses to let me enlist, I'll find a way."

Ella avoided my gaze. So I made a silent vow to prove myself in combat.

Cyrus rushed home. Tennessee's largest city became a hard place for a Union man. Residents of Memphis celebrated the fall of Fort Sumter with fireworks, cannons, speeches and endless displays for the South. Suspicion now focused on "northern men." The fatal shots in South Carolina began terrible strife. Intense feeling surrounded the assault. We enjoyed the peace and prosperity of a united country all our lives. Treachery made some people angry and others contemptuous.

War caught the State of Illinois woefully unprepared with no armed militia.

On Sunday Reverend Eddy told our congregation, "Union is assailed, and war begun." His voice rang clear and strong. "No single thought proves more provocative than dishonoring the flag, the symbol of majesty, emblem of authority and protection. It is honored on all seas, afforded sanctuary in all lands, but now hauled down by home conspirators." He screamed, "Where the flag? Defend the flag. Rally to the flag!"

Mottos appeared all over town. 'Avenge Stars & Stripes!' Old party lines went down, and we united for national salvation. Ministers declared what God has joined together let no man put asunder. "The Almighty created great rivers of the continent to link the states of the cotton, rice and sugar with those of the wheat, corn and barley and the spindles of textile industry."

The press became more active than ever. Newspapers were cheap and common; everyone relied on them. Political, secular and religious life made appeal after appeal to defend democracy. Oratory played its part, addressing masses of people with one great purpose—Save the Union. The country plunged into a life-and-death struggle.

Even womenfolk, who faced the absence of husbands, sons, brothers and lovers, said the nation must be preserved, no matter the cost. Everyone turned to the national capitol. What could President Lincoln do?

On April 15th he issued a proclamation, calling out state militias to suppress the rebellion. Simon Cameron, Secretary of War, also called on the governor of Illinois. The next week Governor Yates convened the legislature to call for troops. Everyone talked about the traitorous attack on the government. What measures could suppress the outbreak? Men offered themselves by the thousands, but southern secessionists seized firearms, stored in Federal arsenals. They raped the North.

It took just four days, until April 19th, for the first volunteers to arrive at what they christened Camp Yates in Springfield. Soldiers went by foot, wagon and rail.

Excitement in Ottawa reached fever pitch. John and I decided to sign up. We reckoned without Father, however, for when he heard he took John and I for a walk in the cemetery. He approached a grave in silence. The plain marker showed 'Michael Kelly Rooney, 1827-1849.'

John asked, "Is this someone you knew?"

Father removed his hat. "He served in the Mexican War."

John removed his hat and mine, too. "And he died from a wound?"

"I refuse to let you join. Because of what happens to young men like Michael." Father faced me, rather than John, who had just gotten married. "This boy died from the 'private disease.'"

I started to ask what that had to do with us, but John shuddered, a clear warning to hold off.

Father's voice dropped to its lowest register. "John, your first duty is to your wife. Charlie, I refuse—"

"The recruiter claims fighting will be over in 90 days," I protested.

"The South has more determination than that," Father said. "I'll take a hand in it myself. The army needs men with the experience of Mexico, but—for you—the subject is closed."

When Father walked away, I made John tell me what he knew about the private disease. He spoke in my ear, as if unwilling to let anyone hear his warnings about women of ill-fame and the ailments of Venus. "Michael Kelly Rooney should have kept his penis in his pants." John turned bright red. "Doctor Figley can tell you more if you want to know, but the treatment is hard for a man. Wait until you marry to be with a woman. Let a wife fulfill you. That way you keep affection pure." Quick, shallow breaths closed the subject.

"All right, I must avoid the private disease—but why stay home?" When he shrugged, I declared. "I will be a soldier, sooner or later." Like Father, John ruffled my hair.

The newspapers encouraged patriotism, but no one needed to stoke fervor. "The Star-Spangled Banner" raged furiously, bands played it, young men whistled its tune, people in theaters sang, small boys hammered it on pans. Only if dogs barked the national anthem, could it reverberate more.

My friends enlisted to protect community and family, for fun, glory or to avoid being branded a coward. We all thought of toil and danger as pre-requisites to manhood. No one said he wanted to end slavery. My friend Alvin Chapin voiced the opinion many shared. "I'm not fighting for free-soil or slavery. I'm fighting *against* the Union breakup." Alvin was tough but not aggressive, forthright but able to take a joke, a man of good talents in his own way. From his conversations, no one ever thought he learned more than to read and write and cipher to rule of three, but Alvin showed great concern for his manly stature. The pressures on a young man's pride weighed heavily. Friends urged friends to enlist. Fathers gazed toward rifles on the wall and lamented being too old. Sweethearts demanded if fellows wanted to court them they better sign up. Song lyrics proved it. "I am Bound to be a Soldier's Wife or Die an Old Maid."

Not Ella, however, she trembled at the idea I might go.

I secretly swelled with pride at her concern. "Don't worry."

"Charlie, you have lived so much of your life with books and music. A gun does not suit you."

"But it does. I am a good shot." Nothing I said or did convinced Ella I'd make a good soldier. I had to prove it to her.

Some young men enlisted just to have a change of scenery. The army promised more adventure than struggling behind a plow or scribing behind a desk. An adventure, the great adventure of our generation, filled with glory, excitement, new places to see. Most of my friends had never been outside LaSalle county, and the army promised to take them across country. Even men who had traveled wanted to go. John Benson was forty-six years old and a veteran of the Mexican War, but he enlisted. John said it was the right thing to do. I had heard Father's stories of cavalrymen riding into battle, reins in their teeth, pistols blazing from both hands, the rest of the friendly force 100 miles away, a merciless foe ahead, doing their all to protect the infantry.

The national crisis deepened, so Father allowed Cyrus to enlist. He became a private in the first company Ottawa raised. The company became part of the 11th Regiment, a magnificent-looking body of fellows, ruddy faces glowing with health. Four companies carried flags, which fluttered in the breeze, while the regimental band played patriotic tunes. We never saw the like before.

Will offered his services despite the personal sacrifice of leaving home and a lucrative law practice. He and Ann had taken two years to build a beautiful home, overlooking Ottawa, and enjoyed but one year in it when the war came.

"Must you go?" Ann asked. "Is it better to serve your country at home?"

Nine days after Mr. Lincoln's proclamation of war, Will enlisted. When it came time to say goodbye to Will, Ann consecrated his sword with a kiss, smiled farewell, but when he was gone, went to her room and cried through the night. From Springfield Will wrote, "feeling here is tremendous about sustaining the government. Stephen Douglas is expected tomorrow morning, and he will make things unanimous. Troops will be needed immediately for active service."

When he left, Cyrus rode with 400 men in open coal cars, floors covered with several inches of coal dust. Planks became seats. The train pulled out, rocked and belched across the prairie. Smoke and cinders from the locomotive blew into soldiers' faces, and the coal dust rose into noses and eyes. They rode all night, and when they arrived in Springfield, it took half a day to assign rations and cooking utensils, so they could make their first meal.

Cattle stalls, ripe with the smell of animals, served as their barracks. Men tacked up curtains or sheets as makeshift doors, and wind blew campfire smoke into the stalls. Cyrus rolled up in a blanket but found sleep impossible.

Even though Will got positive assurance from the governor their regiment would muster next, Captain Pope, the mustering officer, left camp before completing the paperwork. Will's regiment did not muster until April 30, and the men promptly elected him colonel, saying 'We want a colonel whose whole soul is in this fight.'

From Springfield Will and Cyrus headed for Cairo. No one anticipated an attack on Cairo, but if Missouri seceded, rebs might surprise them. Nothing much happened, however, and at the close of 90 days' service, the regiment reenlisted for three years, although everyone doubted the South had that much determination to fight. This time Cyrus became adjutant.

When would Father let me go? I continued practicing telegraph and reading law, filling in as a telegraph operator when needed. Perhaps skill with a telegraph was a way into the army.

Father went to Washington and offered his services to Mr. Lincoln.

The President asked Father what he would like to do, and he replied "raise a regiment of cavalry." The idea pleased Mr. Lincoln, so Father pressed further. "I want you to give me orders for manufacturers to furnish arms, uniforms and other supplies necessary before I raise a man."

President Lincoln asked, "How do you know you can raise the men?"

"Not one particle of doubt on that," Father said. "I can raise any number of men."

"Then I agree."

Father traded on their long-time friendship. "I also want authority to appoint all the officers and a major from the regular army to train these officers."

"I see no objections," said the President, and so it was arranged. Father went to the manufacturers before returning home. He posted advertisements in the newspapers to raise a cavalry regiment from companies all over Illinois. Nothing felt more natural to him than defense of the Union.

Offers to provide cavalry companies poured in, not only from Illinois but the entire country—but with severe caveats. Volunteers prized liberty above everything else. It never occurred to them they had to give up personal freedom to become soldiers. A charismatic leader might lead them—if they liked him—but rank or stature was not sufficient. To lead volunteers, a commander had to be popular. The messages Father received made this clear. "Hampshire, August 21, 1861, Dear Sir, The boys got together here last night & talked over the volunteering business. They are unwilling to volunteer under any person unless their wishes are consulted. The enlisting line waits for your answer." W.D. Wardlaw.

Companies contained blood relatives or fellow townsmen, bands closely tied like brothers, and favoritism played a huge role. Most of the time soldiers elected the officers, and the governor then issued commissions. However, men used chicanery and petty tricks to gain rank.

Messages poured into the Caton Lines Telegraph Company. Men wrote to obtain special favors. Because Father had the authority to appoint all his officers, they felt sure he must pick them personally. One fellow cited his "considerable experience" as "seven years of drilling with the N.Y. Militia." Every man who knew Father, and hundreds who didn't, wanted a post. Men attached to state militias no matter how briefly considered themselves, "competent to discharge military duty."

Some applicants wanted safe jobs as noncombatants. Nathan B. Dodson wanted a "situation" in the commissary or supply department.

Recommendations also poured in. "I wish to give you a word of description of Mr. F. although my knowledge of the military is sparse. He may not be a man you approve. He has no military experience, is not commanding in appearance, but these are the only objections to him. I have known him several years. He is a citizen of first-rate standing, prompt in thought, sound in judgment, a judicious manager," and on and on for two more pages, qualifying Mr. F. as a friend without one morsel of military experience.

If Father offered a position not exactly to someone's liking, curt telegrams came back. "I cannot accept your proposition." If the offer had sufficient importance, the telegraph said, "Will see you tomorrow or Saturday."

In just two weeks Father had enough men to make three regiments, an indication of how well he was known throughout Illinois. As a result he could be selective and take on companies where he knew the commander was a good officer.

At first, Ann wrote Will gentle letters that did not make it hard for him to be away, but then changed. "Being homesick will make him a better commander. Besides," she said, "I am selfish enough to want my husband thinking of home, and if he cannot bring our troops back, regret it."

Will sent a havelock pattern and asked Ann to buy linen and recruit ladies in Ottawa to make these cloth cap covers for his command. Separation was very hard for Ann. She confessed, "I want to be a true soldier's wife and take part in the work but cannot keep the danger out of my mind. Longing comes naturally to a soldier's wife." Then news of Bull Run arrived. Union men had failed, and rebels ran them off. Heads hung down in shame. Surely, defenders had more power than that. If a unit held together, how could the enemy dislodge them? Bull Run gave loyal people a terrible awakening, crushing disappointment and bitter mortification. If it had been a stunning Union victory, fighting between North and South might have ended right then.

After serious discussion whether I could deny my flighty nature, Father gave me permission to enlist. I mustered into the service on August 12, 1861, my nineteenth birthday, and felt like quite a man. Imagine: me as a private in the cavalry. Henry, my friend in town, was only fourteen-years-old but desperate to go and kill a reb before the supply ran out.

A large cavalry force makes a fine sight. When Illinois troopers assembled, mounted bands rode at the front and played heart-jumping tunes. Next came the principle officers, then company after company, a war cavalcade and gay show. A thunder of hooves and sabers clanking, men in full control of their destiny, gallant, bright-faced, eager for the field. Men with fine seats, weight and balance in their legs, tall in the saddles, inspiring to see.

People also cheered when infantry passed, rifles at the right shoulder, marching smartly along. Everyone felt the war as good as won. I anticipated going straight into battle.

When fellows signed up, they became like generals in the eyes of their families. Mine, however, expressed no eagerness for me to go, a circumstance I laid off to being the youngest son. When I broke the news, Sisters Ann and Belle peered down at the floor. After a prolonged silence, Belle hugged me, and Ann whispered, "God go with you."

Ella refused to talk about it. Jennie jumped for joy.

Father provided my first horse, saddle, harness and tack. The government reimbursed him forty cents a day for the use of the horse, supplied the feed but only paid the appraised value of an animal if it got killed in battle. If it died of disease, starvation or overwork, Father must stand the loss. "Trust me," I promised, "to take care of him."

I owe Father many debts. He sent me off well equipped for war, but he also prepared my mind. His care of my education and his military service inspired me. When I look in a mirror, I do not see his slender features or curly hair, but I am stronger because of the way he raised me. He also directed my military training. "Cavalry usually travels four miles an hour," he said, "but even that pace severely tests horses. To cover 40 miles takes 15 hours—a trifling for men, who can remain well despite wet, cold, heat and sleeping on the ground, not so for horses. They suffer. A trooper needs to be as much horse-doctor as soldier. Long marches break horses down and leave the officer with two choices, both bad. He can send fagged horses to the rear, which strips him of his command, or force horses to go on until they drop, hoping he can steal mounts along the way to keep up the strength of the unit." Father crossed his arms across his chest. "If you lose the horse, Charlie, you have to transfer to infantry."

"I promise."

"It will be hard—water, feed, stable, water, groom—utter drudgery. At times food and water will be scarce for you and the mount. The horse will get sick, need shoes."

"When have I failed to take care of a horse?"

He smiled. "See that you continue."

I named the horse Rhoderic, after our pony from childhood.

***

Real fighting commenced in the west on September 4, 1861, when Confederates under Leonidas Polk seized Columbus, Kentucky. The enemy camped on high ground two-and-a-half miles from the landing, protected with artillery. Fighting raged from the landing on the Federal side up to the enemy's camp, which the Union took but could not hold. Federal soldiers fell back to their boats, fighting all the way. The secesh fought with vigor. In the end the Federals called it a victory, but General Grant received severe criticism. If all victories turned out this way, the war could go on for decades. The Union gained no ground, and both sides lost nearly equal numbers. General Grant, like his troops, narrowly escaped capture. Was it a victory?—yes. General Grant fought. Proved he was not afraid to fight with the troops he had on hand, not delay, cower or call for reinforcements. Men who served that day gave General Grant high praise.

Afterward, Confederate Lieutenant Herndon came in bearing a flag of truce and proposed to exchange prisoners. He was a gentlemanly fellow, and the officer of the watch treated him as such, gave him dinner and detained him with polite conversation while Will went to consult headquarters. They decided to exchange man-for-man, equal ranks.

During the exchange, a Confederate officer asked if he could write to a soldier not included in the exchange, only to inform him about his friends. Will allowed it, promised to see it delivered and sent Cyrus to find the prisoner. He located him in a hovel the government called a hospital. Slender-framed iron bedsteads, narrow and plain, lined the inside. On either side of the central passage a row of beds, feet toward the aisle. Evergreens tacked to the walls masked some of the smell. Cyrus took in the whole view at once because there were no partitions. Sounds of suffering came from the cots, but on the whole was quiet and absent of demonstration. Pallid faces, dull eyes, moist lips told the story instead. Half were sick; half hurt. Young fellows, farmers' sons largely, fine large frames, proof of formerly strong constitutions, but now a sad collection, representatives from all cities and states, entirely without friends or acquaintances here, no familiar faces, hardly a kind word, no cheer. Cyrus learned to be careful where he looked. A local man came to the ward to satisfy his curiosity, stopped where doctors probed a wound, turned white and fainted.

One boy had a desire for homemade rice pudding, but his stomach

40

was weak. The doctor said, "Nourishment will do more harm than good."

However, a local lady heard his wish and circled round after the doctor moved away. "I shall make you some pudding."

Cyrus prayed the boy lived long enough to eat some.

One young man had an amputated arm, and he called Cyrus over. "The stump is healing well. When a surgeon cut it off in the field, I was unconcerned, munched a cracker with the other hand while still wearing the bloody uniform." Then his eyes clouded. "I will recover but doubt I can kill more rebs."

Cyrus resisted the next wounded man's call, found the right fellow and delivered the letter. The recipient trembled with excitement and pressed the envelope to his breast.

***

Father organized a camp in Ottawa called Camp Hunter. He designated an old friend, Mr. Townsend, as captain. John Wallace, Will's younger brother, became one of our lieutenants. George Walter became the adjutant, and Andrew Haynes, sergeant. Because I write with a fair hand, regiment headquarters detailed me to help them. We had a saddler sergeant and a chief farrier, both men skilled with horses, but I also inserted myself there and helped care for livestock, especially when it came to doctoring them. An animal knows when a fellow wants to rescue it and keep it from being worked beyond endurance.

In September another company arrived at Camp Hunter. New recruits should have received smallpox vaccinations, but some skipped out because of its disagreeable execution. I waited my turn in line. A doctor cut under the arm with a knife and put liquid from a cow infected with pox into the wound. Cutting my armpit left me sore for 10 days, a small cost if it protected me from smallpox.

We remained in camp many weeks, getting ready for the earnest work everyone expected to perform at any moment. I donned my uniform October 26, 1861.We drilled daily, both mounted and dismounted, but leisure time sat heavily, everyone wanted to get on with fighting. A few men had copies of Beadles DIME novels, which we read and passed along until the bindings fell apart. In the evening we used sabers to roast rabbits for supper.

A squabble broke out over who became second lieutenant, another man tried to displace B. F. Hyde. Their company officers made quite a stir and decided to withdraw and join the 8th Cavalry, which was organizing at

41

St. Charles. As soon as Father heard this, he sent word for us to keep our organization as it was.

When bugles arrived, not enough men could blow them, so I offered myself as a bugler for the company.

John Wallace took me aside. "Are you sure you want to be bugler?"

"I can learn—"

"It's not your ability that worries me." John's dark eyes narrowed. "In a battle the enemy aims at buglers."

"Surely they have more important targets."

"Yes, they aim at officers first. Then the color bearers—because those men guide regiments forward. But buglers become a target, too. If they hit the bugler, the enemy stops calls heard over the clamor of battle."

I raised myself to my full height. "I love my country as much as you do, *Lieutenant.*"

John shook his head and said no more.

After I received a bugle, I had the painful task of learning to play. Lips controlled the pitches, but mine created sour notes. So bad, other soldiers banished me to the woods.

For days I trudged up and down scales, struggling to train my lips. It seemed I'd miss the war entirely, but eventually I conquered all the calls—Drill; Fatigue; Guard Mount; Boots and Saddles, meaning get yourself and your horse equipped; Stand to Horse, formation; Forward, Right, Left, About, Wheel, Trot, Canter, Charge, Commence Firing, Cease Firing, Retreat, Rally, Dismount and Fight on Foot. Each regiment had one chief bugler and more with each company. Leonard, our chief bugler, blew the finest notes heard in the army, such an excellent musician that even reveille elicited applause. He gave concerts in camp and whenever the regiment marched on parade, he led. His favorite tune was "John Brown's soul goes marching on" in honor of the abolitionist, executed in 1859. I longed to play half as well as Leonard. He made a bugle sing.

For now, I satisfied myself with making the vital calls recognizable. Privates had only vague notions of the machinery of battle and relied on bugle calls. I began the motion, arm raised, mouthpiece to lips, and officers spurred their horses from a three-beat canter to a four-beat gallop. Clear notes issued commands. Other times, slow notes would give heartbroken tribute to a fallen man. In either case, the bugler must not hurry. The sound must be firm and faithful, no matter the faintness in my heart or head—although here and there I allowed myself the pleasure of a long-drawn out note, the kind Leonard blew so well.

Supplies came in haphazardly. Newer recruits lacked guns and drilled with corn stalks on their shoulders. Horses became unfit for service due to a lack of horseshoes. Some regiments lacked haversacks. Everyone lacked cartridges. The ones the army supplied shook to pieces while riding, and at the end of a march we had jumbles of powder, ball and papers.

For some units, rifles provided the supreme disappointment. Troops received old guns in poor condition, huge, heavy, some 69-caliber. Attempts to learn the manual of arms with a big, awkward weapon shook a man's patriotic fervor.

Elementary maneuvers proved difficult for the infantry. Many recruits did not know left from right. Drill instructors tried to solve the problem by making the men attach a piece of hay to the left shoe and straw to the right. Then called out "hayfoot" or "strawfoot" instead of left or right. Good as far as it went, until a sergeant yelled, "Right face." Instead of turning in unison, faces met other faces in great confusion.

As punishment, the drill instructor assigned extra drills. Just lifting a heavy Springfield rifle into straight-out firing position takes muscle power. If one man in line failed to hold steady, the drillmaster sauntered up and down, adjusting muzzles until every barrel lined up perfectly. Loading took nine steps, and units went through the motions without live ammunition to learn. Even after soldiers knew how to load, they rarely got permission to fire. Target practice was not part of the training, but a few small groups snuck off to shoot. The result: accidents. Inexperienced soldiers shot each other, lost eyes and fingers. It got so bad commanders refused to issue ammunition.

Organizing the army into divisions and brigades delayed us. Seemed we wouldn't move before the rainy season caught us. General Logan boasted we could end the war in 40 days. "If we can't subdue the rebellion, the next best thing is for all to go to hell together." Countless soldiers shouted, "Hurrah! We aim to slap General Johnston's back and yank his whiskers."

We spent six weeks drilling daily at Camp Hunter, both mounted and dismounted, until orders came to march to Springfield. When I told Ella, an ugly look spread across her face. She brushed dust off my shoulder, brushed again and hesitated to take her hand away. Her lips pouted, so I kissed them. Tears pooled in her eyes, and I blinked back a few of my own.

The day we left, townspeople lined the road. Father doffed his hat in farewell. "Our country calls for us, and we leave all we hold dear on Earth and freely go to her assistance, knowing we embark on an honorable cause." Girls wore red, white and blue ribbons in their hair, waved little flags and looked sweet. But where was Ella? I could not find her in the crowd. We swung our caps, whooped and hurrahed. Ann and Belle came out. The band played "Glory, Glory, Hallelujah." The women of Ottawa sewed flags and presented them, and we stopped to pay tribute to patriotic women. In every direction ladies and men waved handkerchiefs and children ran. I could not hear my own thoughts for their shouts. The troops looked sharp in new uniforms. The drums roused the crowd, but raised the realization we were leaving families behind. Women, children and even men choked back tears at our passing.

When we cleared the last street and turned south, Ella stepped out from behind a tree. Too late in the season for wildflowers, she held a bower of evergreens. When I accepted her gift, our hands met, and she held mine fervently. 'Come back to me,' she mouthed, and I promised. "I will."

Charles H. Dickey, Journal
Volume Two, Fall 1861 to January 1862
March downstate, Encampment at Cairo, First Glimpse of General
Grant, Western Kentucky campaign, Victory at Fort Henry, Tennessee

On November 4th we broke camp and marched in the direction of
Springfield. Other regiments traveled to the Capitol by train, but Father
got permission to march to the rendezvous. He promised headquarters we
could march as cheaply as go by rail. This also gave us time to hone our
skill in the field. Our first camp was on a plain north of Starved Rock,
west of Ottawa. Thereafter we camped near any other company as it was
raised. When locals gave their men sendoffs and feasts, townsfolk invited
us to join, saving the cost of rations.

On the trip downstate we marched several miles each day with plenty
more drill time, mounting, dismounting, marching, raising and striking
tents. Leonard called the midday meal by playing "Roast Beef." Following
the meal, more drill with late afternoon devoted to tent inspection and a
second watering of the horses. I curried Rhoderic and rubbed him daily,
washed his legs and kept careful watch for any injury or disease. The best
army farriers did not do a better job of caring for a horse than I did.

Drills brought misery, embarrassing privates and officers alike. Infantry looked like yokels. Nothing in life prepared volunteers to march in
lockstep and respond to shouted commands, and few officers possessed
the skills to teach them. Some commanders understood drilling but not
how to give orders. Other officers started from scratch, learned the commands and struggled to get men to listen. A bewildering array of orders
needed to become second nature. If men failed to understand in battle,
they would die. Privates stumbled over one another; formations collided;
frantic officers shouted more bewildering instructions and struggled to
untangle troops.

Cavalry performed poorly, too. Mounted drills nearly got people
killed. Some horses had hardly been broken; they turned round and round
or backed against each other. Even tame horses had never exercised in
formation. Riders were as green as the mounts. Add to this—recruits carried sabers, belts, carbines and slings, pockets full of cartridges, horse-nose
bags, haversacks, canteens, spurs, frying pans, cups, all of which rattled
and jingled in ways horses cannot bear. How could we attack like this? The
rebs must hear us coming miles away. Men cursed, as I never heard. Blan-

kets slipped from under saddles, or slipped backward onto horses' rumps. Horses ran, kicked, reared. Unless they held on with both hands, riders plunked on the ground. The drill instructor screamed, "Close up!" to no avail. As equestrians the cavalry had a way to go before we could meet an enemy.

I was grateful for the time I had spent in Kentucky, where horses are like religion, studied and part of a man's upbringing. No better training than living among southerners existed. Men born to the saddle taught me to hunt and steeplechase. My southern cousins oversaw planting and conducted business on horseback. They found pleasure, too, on horseback. The skills I honed among them bolstered confidence. A fence or a ditch cannot be jumped by careful study. It requires dash.

I found a large piece of paper, folded it in fourths and started a letter to Ann. I did not have a private place for writing but sat down on a box with a board for a desk. Raucous drinking on one side and fisticuffs on the other created powerful distractions, yet I wrote. Thoughts of Ann and Belle comfortable at home increased the loneliness. I filled the paper completely, more than a week of details before affixing a stamp and sending it off. Thankfully, Ann didn't wait to get my letter. When the first letter reached me, my hand trembled so badly I tore the envelope. She wrote gossip, reports of the weather and her health, which had improved. Reading soothed like balm. Mail from home made me want to skip with joy. Another letter from Ella made me ache with longing. She filled the page with goodness, like an angel whispering in my ear. I sheltered in my tent, while rain poured torrents outside. Wind drove water through the canvas, and the ditch outside did not carry water away fast enough. A stream flowed and puddled inside, and a single rubber blanket separated my backside from the mud.

Rain brought feelings of gloom. Soldiers are not heroes only if they fight. They live in poor shelter, drenched by rain, scorched by sun, tormented by lice, tainted with fever, shaken with doubt. It helped to think I protected the women at home—Belle at the piano, going to a bed on a downy mattress, covered with a quilt, oblivious to the chill outside. When I wrote back, I told Belle and Ann their letters raised my spirits. Told Ella her letter made army life bearable.

The 4th Illinois cavalry attracted elite men from all over Illinois and as far away as Massachusetts. Other northern cavalry units consisted of clerks, tailors or farmhands, but Father had enlisted men comfortable in a

46

saddle and then outfitted us with matching shell jackets trimmed in yellow, blue kepi, regulation sabers, sky blue pants and carbines. We had to dismount to fire these accurately, but .52 caliber rounds created a fearsome ruckus. Even our spurs and black leather belts were regulation issue.

Arriving in Springfield, we camped on the Sangamon River. Vermin infected the barracks of men who stayed in town, so we slept on the outskirts. Soldiers nicknamed the vermin greybacks because bugs plagued them like an enemy. A merchant set up a saloon near camp and enticed soldiers until Lieutenant Hapeman took a squad and cleaned the place out, spilling all the booze he could find. Indignation rolled through the ranks, especially when soldiers realized they needed passes to leave camp and could not visit saloons at will.

Card games such as poker, twenty-one, faro, euchre and whist helped pass the time, and only a rare game did not involve betting money. One game was called chuck-a-luck. Boys set out numbers from one to six and placed their bets. One man rolled three dice; payoffs were one-to-one on singles, two-to-one on pairs, and three-to-one on triples. If a player bet on six, and someone rolled two sixes, it paid two-to-one. A tempting, simple game, but in one night I lost all my cash.

When no other entertainment offered itself, soldiers raced lice. Each man placed a louse on his tin plate, and the first louse to move off the plate won—a popular sport until we discovered Private Johnson heated his plate before a race. The men banished him from this and all future games for cheating. Johnson stomped away. "I am anxious to get down into seceshdom and clean them out. Won't we have gay times, though?" His enthusiasm made men repent and call him back. With the stipulation he raced his lice on a cold plate.

Commissars failed to clothe most regiments. Blankets were luxuries. Many fellows had no change of clothes. Soldiers spent time brawling and betting on anything they could turn into a contest. Whiskey was not supposed to be allowed, but women showed up and sold it from special tins, hidden under hoop skirts. Hard liquor, called tangleleg, had a predictable effect. A fiddle player gave us lively tunes. As more liquor went down gullets, we hollered and whooped. One private slurred his words. "I do not know any southerners, but hear from those what do—rebs are lazy, cruel taskmasters."

"Peace-loving citizens such as us," came the reply "have ta teach secesh to leave off villainy."

"Yeah, we'll whip Johnny rebs."

"Think they can fight?"

"Nothing we cain't handle. Whip them surely."

Some women heard the revelry, dared to come near and became the center of attention. They joined the spirit of festivities. After significant whiskey and dancing, the girls shed some of their clothes and offered their bottoms. One plump girl took dozens of men and, as each one entered, squealed with delight. Alvin pulled me toward the line. "Let's have a go."

My loins said 'yes,' but I looked around. I could rely on Alvin's discretion, but not other men. Many knew my father and brothers. While Alvin coaxed me forward, three boozers fired off guns. Provost guards took a dim view of shooting up townsfolk, collared those soldiers and drove the rest of us back to quarters. The plump girl raised her skirts to wave good-bye and reminded fellows how to stray from the path of duty. Thereafter headquarters ordered a strong picket posted to discourage booze and big-bottom women.

Will Wallace received second-class guns for men of the 11th Illinois. Even worse, he had no cartridge boxes, cap boxes or belts to give them. Complaining did no good. Other units received ancient flintlock muskets, which were only fit to drill with.

Volunteers showed up in all sorts of uniforms. Some units dressed in gray, the standard issue for state militia. That caused great worry. If they went into battle wearing the same color as the enemy, other Federals might shoot them down. Each private should have a frock coat, trousers, wool forage cap, belt, cartridge box, percussion-cap box, bayonet and scabbard, but few got all the equipment at once. Many fellows got clothes too big or too tight, so a trading post opened where fat fellows bartered for large clothes and thin men gave them up. Still, proper sizes were hard to come by.

Governor Yates appointed Ulysses S. Grant a colonel of volunteers. Grant had graduated from West-Point and served in the Mexican War but had not earned a good reputation. Worse still, Colonel Grant did not look like a man worthy of confidence. He arrived in Springfield wearing an old army coat, worn-out at the elbows and a stained felt hat. His chin was square, jaw straight, forehead broad and high, hair brown, eyes hesitant, mouth set in a determined line. But his standing rose with me the moment I saw the huge, peevish horse he rode. Grant was small, only five feet and seven, too small for a fiery mount—but a daring horseman. He named his stallion Jack—cream-colored with black eyes, mane and tail of silver white, which gradually got darker toward his feet, an intelligent, high-spirited horse, the sort other men do not approach. Dismounted, Grant became a much different fellow. He leaned forward when he walked—the best way to describe it is to say Grant toddled.

Gait aside, Grant was a military professional. A lack of trained military men hobbled the Union. Campfire discussions about strategy revealed commanders' ignorance. Their talk filled experienced military men like Will with dread. Governor Yates appointed undeserving civilians to posts, and raw-recruits got elected as officers. When farmers volunteered, they rejected military discipline and elected popular fellows to lead—that is men who allowed them to run lose. Some commanders didn't know what to do or how to do it. Their hesitation, in turn, infected the men.

Cairo, a hellhole where U.S. Grant Assumed Command

We began to march toward Cairo, but after three days received orders to board a train, as Grant needed us. Some men had never traveled more than a few miles from home. Now the horizon expanded. We embarked at Vandalia and arrived in Cairo in a few hours. We stepped off the cars and wanted to step back on again, for Cairo was a wretched, flat morass, strewn with fallen timber. The day we arrived, infantry volunteers mutinied over bad bread and burned down a guardhouse. The town sits at the junction of the Ohio and Mississippi Rivers. Levees meant to hold back water failed. Steam-driven pumps worked day and night—but a slip off a boardwalk meant plunging into mud waist-high. Streets existed, but hidden beneath a foul, stagnant swamp. Good earth had disappeared under slime. Trees were gnarled or weed-like. The bloated remains of mules and horses floated in currents, snagged on submerged vegetation and filled camp with putrid odor.

Although Grant had been promoted to brigadier, he arrived in Cairo in civilian dress. When he approached headquarters to assume command, the duty officer ordered Grant arrested, but something made him pause and rescind the order. Grudgingly he saluted, and Grant took command. Rowdies, who refused to take orders from others, started to show respect. Grant had a knack for calming excitable men. The rumor was Grant's father had an explosive temperament, which taught him how to survive confrontation. An unassuming demeanor reportedly came from his Calvinist Mother. However he acquired a talent for listening, Grant was well-suited

49

to leading ragamuffin volunteers.

I also heard while still a boy, Grant tamed horses, forded swollen rivers and traveled alone. He won any horse race he entered. His talents as a rider put the cavalry's best troopers to shame. But he earned respect even from men who didn't give a damn about horses. In a few days he set the camp in good order. Volunteers halted destructive ways. It is hard to capture why, but Grant influenced the lowliest privates. When he put on the uniform of rank, he still didn't dress properly. Grant's coat remained unbuttoned. If his clothes got spattered with mud, he took no notice.

An incident in Cairo earned Grant even more admiration. When a wagon stalled in the mud, a teamster driving swore and smashed the horses' faces with the butt of a whip. Grant dashed forward. "You scoundrel," he cried, "stop beating those horses!"

The teamster looked at him coolly and delivered another blow.

Grant shook his fist in the man's face and called the officer in charge. "Take this man and tie him to a tree for six hours as punishment." As they pulled him away, the teamster showed no remorse, but Grant spoke of the incident for several days, showing how much it angered him.

Half the soldiers in Cairo had no firearms. Those who did carry guns had seven different patterns of muskets, three American-made and four from Europe. Green troops spoke a Babel of dialects. The styles of dress made me laugh—every man who possessed some sort of military garment brought it along. Militia uniforms came from many states, some from Europe. One private wore his grandfather's coat—that of a colonel. Another had a highlander's hat. Patterns, colors, even tinsel dazzled the eye.

I filled the vacant hours writing to Ella, Jennie, my sisters and in my journal. Sameness made the days drag, but writing captured feelings. How much pleasure I got from that word, home. Now I fully appreciated the indulgence of Mother and then Ann, care I disregarded in the past and planned to appreciate when I returned—home.

Refugees from southern states arrived. Some had been beaten blue. Ten men from Memphis got lashed until their backs had bled. One loyal Union man showed up with half his head shaved, one-half his heavy beard gone, lips cut from club blows and two teeth knocked out. Neighbors drove him from his home because he supported the Union.

Troops spent several months drilling until we looked more like soldiers. Our gunstocks were oiled and bayonets bright. I wondered if I had chosen the wrong branch of service. Artillery batteries intently studied their craft. Here, finally, a way to use geometry. When in school, I begged to join the advanced class. Could I now make the grade as cannoneer? They calculated angles and measured precise fuses to explode amid enemy lines. Man is God's deadliest creation; a cannoneer the military's.

A box arrived from home, brimming with gifts from the women of Ottawa. The ladies knitted stockings, each pair held a personal note, written in a different female hand. The pair I received said, "Brave fellow, I pray for your safe return." Though they were too big, never ever did socks feel this good.

The low, mud-filled ground in Cairo made life disagreeable, but the confluence of the Mississippi and Ohio Rivers gave it great strategic importance. The Union positioned several thousand men here, threw up earthworks and mounted heavy cannons.

When my skin turned yellow and I lost my appetite, the regimental surgeon dosed me with tincture of camphor for three days—the fourth day I avoided the good doctor.

To escape the monstrous surroundings, an officer named Ben Whiting read novels. He always had a book at hand, often a romance. Ben poured over stories while he rode and often became so curious how the hero extricated himself, Ben failed to watch where his horse went. He could live without a blanket or enough to eat, but not without books. He took it for granted everyone else wanted to devour the latest novel, too. When he received *Les Misérables*, he anglicized the pronunciation. "Have you seen 'Lee's Miserables?'"

Thomas Bail never had formal schooling. "I hope Lee's miserables are a good deal worse than mine."

Army and navy both occupied Cairo. Admiral Foote launched naval missions from here, felt his way into the conflict, probed the Tennessee and Cumberland Rivers, patrolled the lower Ohio and reconnoitered the Mississippi. One of Foote's gunboat commanders, Lieutenant Phillips, reconnoitered the Tennessee River aboard the *Conestoga* and returned with intelligence about Fort Henry.

Many soldiers envied river-borne warriors. Not for the rickety boats they rode, but because navy personnel got grog rations. Envied, that is, until Admiral Foote organized a temperance society. Men aboard the frigate *Cumberland*, officers and crew gave up booze. Foote had strong convictions about temperance and offered cash payments in lieu of the liquor ration.

At this point my company got rewarded with scouting parties to Kentucky. Confederates had invaded Kentucky and turned a neutral state into a battleground. They built two forts in Tennessee just below the Kentucky border. The high ground we traveled challenged the horses. The low ground did too, subject as it was to flooding. Such places are even harder for footsore infantry and artillery to slog through. Waterways made it much easier to move men and equipment, hence the importance of forts along the rivers.

By the first of December, Will and Father got discouraged. The government seemed unequal to the emergency. The War Department should adopt measures to crush rebellion. Instead they rewarded political favorites and enriched contractors. The Union high command constantly changed generals and plans. Men, not qualified to be sergeants, gave orders to thousands of soldiers. With such men in charge, prospects looked doubtful. Because Will's letters became so sad, Ann left home and traveled nearly 400 miles to join him. Father knew about her trip but became ill with miasmic fever and could not meet her. Father's care fell to me, so I did not see Ann either. Army troop movements fouled transportation, and she could not come to us. Father recovered—but I found it hard to console myself about missing Ann.

On Christmas Day—as our present—commanders allowed target practice. Not much of a Christmas celebration without turkey, pot-pies or claret, but we contented ourselves. The target was a life-size image of a man—Jeff Davis we called him—painted on a board, 200 yards distant. Each captain detailed 30 of his best shots. The 1st Battalion came forward first. Company A fired a volley but missed the board entirely. The next company had ancient rifles with the tendency to fire while being loaded. A gun went off accidentally; the round passed through a soldier's wrist and left a nasty hole. From the look of it, the man's hand got ruined for life. The injury inspired a mutiny. The company stacked their rifles and refused to take them until their colonel yelled, "I'll court-martial any man without a weapon." The anger in his voice caused them to relent. Their best company hit the target six times, none in a vital spot.

The next day the 2nd Battalion fired, and the best record of any company was seven shots to hit the target. On the 27th, the 3rd Battalion took its turn, and our company hit the target eleven times for the winning score. Major Bowman complimented us. "You came on the ground, loaded, fired in good order and made the best shots." He did not know, however, we had found powder and lead pipe and made up a extra cartridges to shoot at snags in the Mississippi River, practice other companies lacked.

Because of this stellar performance headquarters assigned our company as General Grant's bodyguard, a surprising reward for cheaters. Even under close scrutiny, Grant appeared commonplace. When scouts brought Grant information about enemy positions, he listened but seemed to take little notice. If they reported the enemy had moved, General Grant showed no excitement, merely sat down to write orders. The General might continue writing for an hour, occasionally stopping to think a moment, but not asking for added information or advice. When he finished writing orders, he relapsed into his usual, quiet state, but the orders showed he knew the location, strength and effectiveness of every unit in his command. While he had listened to scouting reports, Grant envisioned physical barriers. He also knew the capacity of each officer to command troops and where to place him to get the best service. People who did not witness the depth of his grasp saw him as a man destined for obscurity, but soldiers who served him felt otherwise. If other officers did as well, we were confident of victory.

An expedition into West Kentucky became our regiment's first active duty. Columbus was a valuable prize. When Confederates invaded Kentucky, they became aggressors in the eyes of neutral citizens. We went out on reconnaissance. This trip turned into a "mud march" because sleet was the prevailing weather. Infantry marching by were all ages, many boys younger than me. Rain plagued us. Wagon wheels churned the roads. Haversacks grew heavy. The boys endured countless halts and delays and no longer sang or laughed. I stood guard one night, just for fun, as I was not required to do it. We never encountered armed enemy but captured two Confederate couriers.

One day I cooked for headquarters, dug up sassafras roots and made them into tea. Just as we started to eat, General Grant rode up and joined us. He ate what we did, and I had the honor of serving him bacon, hardtack and tea.

The navy had a fleet of gunboats nearby but not sufficient sailors to man them. Unwilling to wait for enlisted men, the Admiral asked for volunteers. Sufficient numbers did not step forward, so Captain Stewart detailed men he could spare, Norwegians and Germans who hardly spoke English. He told them they had to go, and they went.

General Grant occupied Paducah and Smithfield at the mouths of the

Tennessee and Cumberland Rivers and then devised joint army-navy assaults. Amphibious forces—fleets and armies—had to be combined. No use in parading up and down the river, however triumphantly, for sailors could only hold the channel within range of a ship's guns. If they drove Confederates off the rivers at any point, the army must prevent them from coming back. Grant planned to do just that, seize and hold strategic points.

I fell in love with Paducah and thought it a nice place to settle when war ended. Pretty women filled the streets, plump, smooth-skinned, small-boned and high-bred. Of course, at the sight of Union soldiers they called, "Hurrah for Jeff," so settling down there would require tact and patience.

One captain named William J. Kountz decided to make a nuisance of himself, barged in and demanded. "I must see General Grant." President Lincoln had appointed Kountz commander over merchant boats the army used, but even I could see that Captain Kountz burdened the General with matters he should have decided on his own. He insisted on interrupting General Grant about plans for Fort Donelson. Grant expected him to handle such matters and sent him away to decide.

Then the boatmen came to complain. "We captains all came together," their spokesman said, "and refuse to work with Kountz." In addition to the hatred of river men, Kountz denounced everybody connected with the Government as thieves and cheats, which made the job of getting crews and boats to move troops nearly impossible.

General Grant chewed an unlit cigar. "Your boats are indispensible." Although still unhappy about Kountz, the boatmen, under threat of arrest, agreed to continue.

The cigar became a legend. Grant smoked, but only on occasion until a reporter spotted him holding one unlit. Soon ten thousand cigars arrived for General Grant. He gave away as many as he could, even to lowly buglers like me, but the rest developed into a continual smoking habit.

When Mrs. Grant came, she was a constant, yet unobtrusive companion. Any fool could see the Grants relished each other's company. After years of marriage and in a theater of war, an otherwise passive Grant escorted her on strolls and bent his head to catch her whispers. His looks said, *What a joy—to find a woman of sturdy health, loyal, ready to share harsh conditions.* Her presence eased the burden of command decisions pressing down on the General. Mrs. Grant looked as comfortable in a saddle as in a drawing room.

When Kountz continued to plague Grant on minor matters, the General retreated to the privacy of Mrs. Grant's quarters, where Kountz could not go. He stomped out of headquarters. "Grant's withdrawal is an intolerable affront." Half the army heard him rant.

On January 2nd, Father received orders to take out two companies with two days' rations. He read the order in a matter-of-fact tone, and then his voice softened. "Men, in a crisis it is impossible to say how each of you will react. When that time comes, look at me. You can rely on me to hold fast."

On the way out we passed General Sherman's Division. A close-up view of Sherman made the march feel like a life-or-death matter. Tall in the saddle but slightly bent, Sherman had a striking posture. The General's piercing eyes gazed eastward. Though he sat immobile on a black horse, he showed intense energy like a compressed spring ready to let go. His scowl forewarned the weight of what lay ahead.

We rode off southwest toward the rebels. After all we endured to get into action, we wanted to make a name for ourselves. Show the nation western pioneers could suffer more, ride farther and strike as deep as any troops.

Our time had not come, however. We got close, could smell unwashed bodies on the wind, but never met the enemy. Someone had dropped a copy of *The Memphis Avalanche* newspaper, and I salvaged it. The articles had scant war news, just urgent rhetoric, military details replaced with extravagant rumors of McClellan's army cut to pieces and Jackson bombarding Washington City. The editor did not report the high cost of waging war, but losses showed nonetheless. Page after page contained notices of concerts and benefits to provide for widows and orphans.

By the middle of the month General John A. Rawlins, who ran Grant's HQ, confronted Captain Kountz and chided him for driving General Grant out of the office. Before John Rawlins became adjutant, Grant's staff consisted of roistering, hard-drinking men, who took advantage of Grant's quiet nature. Rawlins had black hair, deep eyes and a tubercular cough, but he ran headquarters like a zealot, came down on worthless or vicious men, fired the worst and made others buckle under. However, Rawlins could not rid the army of all its featherbrains.

To retaliate, Kountz spread a rumor Grant got drunk. When Colonel Hillyer on the staff heard this, he had Kountz gagged, arrested and thrown in the guard house. Although he deserved it, Mr. Lincoln had appointed

Kountz and more tact was called for. When Grant learned of the arrest, he ordered Kountz released. "We must bear this man. He is just overzealous in doing his duty."

Rawlins preferred to let Kountz rot but had him released. Whatever else happened, Rawlins protected Grant's military ability and vulnerable nature—from himself and others. Anyone who knew both Grant and Rawlins understood Rawlins's ardent, opinionated, profane style complemented Grant's taciturn, kind heart. Together the two men constituted one purpose.

After his release, Koontz grew malignant—he interrupted telegrams between Grant and General Halleck. The breakdown of communication put troops and the nation in jeopardy. Even Kountz's friends described him as overbearing, devoid of tact and oblivious to military chains of command. He used his appointment to punish riverboat operators he disliked and secure government business for boats he had invested in. Grant lodged no charges, which would embarrass the army. Instead he got Kountz assigned elsewhere.

One upheaval followed another. Soldiers pilfered a cartload of vegetables and chickens, and the two slaves who owned the goods came to complain. The pair had close-curled wool hair, great black and white eyes, dressed in ragged cotton, I presume yellow in color—the clothing was not clean enough to tell. Neither slave bore marks of punishment, were not crippled from club blows to the ankles or knees, had no purple scars on their arms where whips had cut. Still their heavy movements told a tale of woe.

The duty officer feared negroes who came and went without restraint, so he turned them over to the public guard. The guard led the negroes away, but only moved a few yards when a white man ran up. With one whack of a Bowie knife he slit a slave's neck, nearly severing his head. At first, no one detained the murderer. Then the duty officer, who had detained the negroes, saw me standing there, a witness to murder. He knew me as Colonel Dickey's son and someone with access to General Grant's staff. "Halt," he cried. "Detain that man."

Once they had the culprit in custody, I turned away from the horror. A telegraph tent offered the closest escape, and I plunged inside. At that moment, the operator had no business to handle, so he welcomed the company. "We pride ourselves no orders ever have to be given to establish the telegraph. The moment troops establish camp, we put up wires."

It surprised me the operator wore civilian clothes, had no rank or corps affiliation. "Who do you work for?"

"A civilian bureau attached to the Quartermaster Department."

"At times I worked for the telegraph office at home."

He offered a pad and pencil. "Make a key for the army dots and dashes. No telling when a shell might blow me to kingdom come and demand a replacement." Military messages got converted to complex ciphers, and the codes changed often to prevent Southern spies from understanding messages. Therefore, only men with superb skills worked army telegraphs. Though it seemed unlikely, I made a key and tucked it inside my blouse, in case I got a chance to send or receive telegrams.

On January 8, 1862, orders came to march at ten o'clock the following morning, which put us all in fine spirits. The prospect of having something to do, besides drill and camp duty, made it hard to sleep. Here was a taste of real soldiering. General John A. McClernand, in temporary command, wanted to penetrate the interior of Kentucky. When President Lincoln appointed Major General John A. McClernand, Grant showed a rare display of temper. The rumors said McClernand wanted to be President of the United States and needed a military record to further his ambition. If McClernand's political goal was the source of General Grant's displeasure, Grant never let on. McClernand took six regiments of infantry, two batteries of light artillery and eight cavalry companies. Cavalry rode in advance, crossed the river and marched to Fort Jefferson. Captain Stewart sent small groups of men forward as pickets to guard the pass at Elliott's mill and other approaches from Columbus. Pickets were the army's watchdogs.

We scouted the area, encountered no armed enemy but interrupted two southern captains having a party in a tavern side room. A girl by the name of Sarah was in bed, had been paid and made ready, but unused. Several troopers decided, "We're too much gentlemen to leave a lady in this distressing condition," so each took time to 'comfort' Sarah. When my turn came, Sarah had been well used, and for me it was a hard come.

Rations ran out, instead of five McClernand stayed out 13 days. The weather stormed and made roads horrible. On the whole a rough introduction. Although we had no fighting, General McClernand felt we could have been attacked any time.

On January 16th, Father had a chill but sent six companies of cavalry east to Maysfield with General McClernand. McClernand squinted against the glare of snow. His unshaven face looked weather-beaten. He wore an unbecoming regulation wool hat, hooked up on one side. Thin and below average height, he sat too far back in the saddle, and his posture stooped. Cold and snow made travel bitter. Floating ice clogged the river. Going out, not knowing where or under what mission, made it hard to put myself in the hands of over-ruling Providence.

A detachment of infantry encountered two mule teams, hauling flour for the rebel army. Our soldiers allowed the haulers to load, then drove them inside our lines and confiscated everything. We made slapjacks out of the flour—with a disagreeable outcome—flour, salt and water slapjacks turned to lead inside my gut.

Infantry slept that night in the fence corners at a railroad crossing. At daylight two companies escorted General Sherman into LaGrange, a railroad station of good buildings, quite modern, an attractive town—that is until armies defaced it. Fences vanished in order to boil coffee and fry bacon. In town soldiers found a quantity of Scotch ale. As liquor disappeared a great deal of robbing began.

The cemetery grounds of LaGrange had tasteful displays of evergreens, hollies, dwarf pines and bushes of all kinds. The inhabitants of LaGrange showed themselves to be bitter rebels. No way to tell which citizens spied for the enemy—perhaps all of them. People talked of secession boldly. Ladies treated us with contempt. If we turned our backs, vulgarities and vegetables pelted us. When a beautiful woman shouted her rage, derision made my face burn. The provost guards closed our post. The North has a huge fight on its hands. Harsh words dashed hope of a quick end to war. Their scowls forbid negotiation. Southerners hated us, and feeling ran deep. One side will have to be annihilated, and democracy becomes the loser.

We camped on property belonging to Mr. Mickley, a wealthy planter, who owned thousands of acres and 200 slaves. When soldiers set a barn ablaze, he rushed out, waving a Colt Dragoon in his left hand and Enfield musket in the right. "God damn Yankees, get off my property."

Henry Engle lassoed him. "You need to recant rabid, rebellious ways." Henry cinched the rope tight and toyed with Mr. Mickley, as if to drag him behind the horse.

The planter did not flinch. "I say Yankees are the Devil's spawn." Men like Mickley are brave, bold to rashness and dangerous in every sense, the most dangerous men war can turn loose, but this gentleman was not an imminent threat to us, so we disarmed him and convinced Henry to let him go.

Mickley's voice reached higher notes. "A number of our citizens have skedaddled, not me ever!"

We moved on before Henry killed him. His slaves moved on, too. I saw them running like rabbits chased by dogs. A few carried bundles tied up, but they couldn't tote much. The women carried children wrapped in blankets and nothing more. As soon as Yankees came, slaves ran. Went by the hundreds.

Gunmetal clouds stacked the sky and left no opening for the sun. However, our men had good spirits and withstood duty better than in the summer. At night we slept on terrain overlooking the river. The 4th Cavalry got the job of scouting country as far as Columbus. Three inches of snow covered the ground, but the weather moderated on January 17.

I had guard duty until 2 a.m. This clear, moonlit night I could see all the way to Holly Springs, twenty-three miles in the distance. I sat down on a high bluff and inhaled the forest scent, originally the place had been a Chickasaw Indian village named *Itey Uch La*, meaning Cluster of Pines. To stay awake I composed a letter in my head. *"Dear Ella" but what to say, how to say it and not sound like a trembling child?*

Then the sound of musketry.

I faced the retort and trembled for real. Again. *Crack!*

Now I picked out the assailant—nothing but a falling branch.

***

By January 19th Father was not well, and the doctor confined him to camp at Bird's Point. One man belonging to our regiment died from measles, the first death from childhood disease. When he heard, Father said, "He was a good soldier." I did not tell him four other men had fallen dangerously sick. Rural boys had never been exposed to children's diseases like those of us from town. One case of measles spread and, because of poor shelter and food, became deadly to grown men.

When the ground thawed, it got fearfully muddy. Cyrus and Will embarked with 712 men and officers on a steamer. Now the government provided light, short barreled carbines. As orderlies handed out guns, the ordinance chief trounced along the line, giving a speech. "Carbines have an effective range of 450 to 600 feet, more than enough for the close-in fighting horse soldiers must do. It's breech loaded and fires three times faster than the infantry's Springfield." Some men wore unsettled expressions as they took the newfangled weapons.

Though they left in an ugly, February sleet storm Will did not get ruffled. His fine appearance impressed any rational man. He rode a black steed, named Prince, moved from one point to another, directed maneuvers as if on dress parade. Officers and privates alike snapped to attention. I mouthed Ann's prayer. 'God own him and protect him this day.'

The rest of us prepared to leave camp soon after. I felt truly a soldier with saber at my side, knapsack and cartridge box.

Charley Walsh got himself arrested for drunkenness and attempting to kill Lieutenant Hapeman. The command gave him the privilege to volunteer for service on a gunboat or stand a court-martial. He chose to volunteer.

Martin Wallace was one of our majors, so we had three of Will's brothers in our division. As he boarded a transport, a swinging beam hit Matthew Wallace, another of Will's brothers, and threw him into the river. In the fast moving current, no one recovered Matt's body. *Pray that our family's first loss will be our last. It goes down especially hard because we have no remains and cannot give Matt a decent burial.* Adding to the sorrow, the loss had no gain, not a glorious death in battle. Martin took no time to mourn, however. He went on with a commander's duty.

When we became part of a joint navy-army expedition, we made history. General Grant's army boarded boats headed up the Tennessee River. Riding swollen waters is not my preferred method of travel. Naval transports dropped us 17 miles above Paducah and returned for more troops. Fort Henry sat on low land adjacent to the river. It had no ramparts or imposing structure—just a squat, muddy affair. The stream ran high, and water largely submerged the fort. To get near Fort Henry by land meant moving through wild, hilly country full of heavy timber.

Navy gunboats also came upstream—an armada never seen before— boats specially built to wage war on rivers, 175 feet long, 50 feet in the beam, flat bottom, sides angled at forty-five degrees, iron-clad above the waterline.

Fort Henry sat 12 miles distant from our landing point, but it took us two days of hard marching to get six miles. High water backed up into bayous and forced us on a circuitous route, twice as far as a direct line. The forest foliage had not yet bloomed, but mistletoe hung in bunches and made the trees appear green.

General Grant put cavalry in the advance. He rode up one morning with Lieutenant Colonel McPherson. Then Grant joined Father, which left

McPherson beside me. In that order we rode the rest of the day, a splendid station. McPherson was Grant's Chief Engineer, but McPherson trusted me to measure the route by counting his horse's steps.

A Union force of 15,000 approached the Confederate stronghold. On the eve of the assault, a storm swept through, and more water rose where the army bivouacked. Our objective looked like a hog pen, but officers assured us the earthen walls created strong defenses. My heart rose into my throat. I wished to be back in Illinois but didn't dare halt. All my friends watched. I could count on them to tell the story of my conduct back home. If I shirked, I could never live it down.

One gunboat got caught in a mass of debris that swept it down river. The storm tore torpedoes rebels had planted in the water lose from moorings and sent them bobbing like bears. Union sailors crawled into lifeboats and plucked torpedoes out, so gunboats didn't get blown up.

Will commanded a brigade, which included the 11th, 20th and 48th Illinois regiments, Father's 4th Cavalry and two artillery batteries. When we approached the skirmish line, the horses slowed. I wrestled mine forward but then heard cannons boom. Rhoderic realized before I did that artillery was close. Missiles shattered the air. Shouts of commanders ranged out of pitch and tone, unlike human voices. Each man had a unique way of entering the battle. Some soldiers became so agitated they did not know what they did. Some exhibited numbing fright. Others, eager to fight, helloed, sang, laughed, swore or whistled on impulse.

But this was not General Grant's battle plan. Admiral Foote was supposed to wait until land forces got around the rear, so Grant could capture the garrison. Floodwater flowed across the line of march and held infantry back. The gunboats opened up too soon.

I had full view of the furor. Fort Henry was half under water. The fort had a terrible design, but nine Confederate guns still fired on the fleet. Gunboats steamed to within 600 yards. Thunder from the navy roared through the valley. Shells ripped huge holes in the earth and sent up plumes of dirt and splinters.

By one in the afternoon, infantry had only gone four miles but pushed on, desperate to arrive in time to cut off retreat. Our cavalry regiment had to hold back, waiting for infantry and artillery. The ironclad *Carondelet* received fire from the enemy's guns. Confederates hit the *St. Louis* seven times and the *Essex* with a 32-pounder, which penetrated the bulkhead above the boiler. An eruption of scalding steam blasted men on the forward deck, including pilots and captain. The disabled vessel drifted downstream, forced out of the fight.

Still, the fort took a heavy beating. Our sailors aimed with devastating accuracy, smashed through earthworks, dismounted the fort's heavy guns, crumpled buildings or set them ablaze, toppled trees in the compound and rained shrapnel down on the defenders. Stinking sulfur filled the air.

Rebels took off on a cross-country hike, leaving one artillery company behind to fight the gunboats. Confederate infantry, some two or three thousand, moved rapidly down a long slope and disappeared into the heavy forest, headed eastward. Forty-five minutes after the navy assault began, the Confederates lowered the flag and raised a white one. Crewmen on the water broke into wild cheers, for it was their victory.

Sergeant Jeremiah B. Cook dashed into the sally port of the fort and pulled down a Confederate flag. He could take great pride in being the first man of the Army of the Tennessee to occupy enemy works and capture a Confederate flag. When inside Fort Henry, Sergeant Cook sent word to Colonel McCullough they were in. Twenty minutes later the Colonel drew his saber for a charge, at first a trot, then a gallop and finally a run, bodies leaning forward in line with horses' heads, sabers at the front point, ready for the shock of contact. Naked swords flashed, and the reflections created silver patches on the ground, but rather than a fight, the Colonel found his advance guard eating a hearty dinner of ham and biscuits, which Confederate soldiers had prepared for themselves but left behind.

At three o'clock General McClernand ordered cavalry to make rapid pursuit. Under command of Lieutenant Colonel McCullough, we overtook the enemy's rear guards, met effective fire but came steadily up the slope, over and down, double quick. Never wavered. The rebels skedaddled in disorder and exposed their backs as targets. One man hid behind a tree, too small to protect him. He loaded to fire but fell, hit square in the head. The force of the blow twisted him like a screw, and he fell with one leg doubled under the other, torqued out of place. Captain Brown showed coolness equal to the crisis, lifted his sword and shouted, "Company E on the right by file into line!" But a bullet passed into his open mouth, forever silencing his voice. We did not get around the rear or cut them off, although if released earlier we could have made it.

Sergeant Cook again led the advance. Three miles out, rebel stragglers filled the road. By this time we had to dismount and wade through mire to get the horses through. Because animals and soldiers were exhausted, Colonel McCullough relieved us from the advance guard. He drove the Confederates across a deep creek but then abandoned pursuit and took the regiment back to Fort Henry.

Some Union men broke into houses and took what they liked. The Colonel rebuked them as Goths and vandals and ordered punishments. However, these men showed no remorse. "We are victorious and entitled to spoils of war."

A letter nailed to a tree caught my eye. "Yankee Occupants, We retired down country for a spell to recruit our health and give you an opportunity to satisfy yourselves as to our defenses. We trust a short residence in a place occupied by honorable men will instill courage in your breasts and allow you to come within range of white men forthwith. Advise Grant to keep sober, and your Congress to hunt up millions of specie to pay the debt you incur. As you move south you earn the contempt of every man, woman, child. If you think you are coming to Richmond, it is a score we will settle with you to death. If you rise on the scale of created beings as high as African baboons, we will allow you to associate with our negroes. The only dealing we will have with you is to whip you on any equal field."

They found four dead Confederates in the fort, all killed when one of the cannons burst. Infantry killed another man and captured 38 prisoners. A glancing shot had struck one prisoner on the left side of the face. His skin and flesh hung in shreds and bathed his neck in blood, a frightful sight, but he talked perfectly cool. "Next time I'll give you hell for spoiling my beauty."

Late in the day Alvin struck up a conversation with a reb. "What is the war about?"

"Y'all came down here. I fight to defend my home."

"All right," Alvin asked, "why do you suppose we came?"

The reb's eyes flashed. "Yankees have a thousand religions but no piety. No honor neither—just hunger for wealth."

Alvin had no wealth to speak of—not even a dollar in his pocket.

"Our side will never give up as long as leaders can muster a brigade."

Alvin started to take exception, but it was time to move along.

Rebels abandoned six pieces of artillery, gun carriages, one caisson, a large number of small arms, knapsacks, blankets, everything that impeded flight. The stink of sulfur left the air, but their cannoneers still had soot-black faces, so their own mothers could not know them.

63

We felt fine over the captures. Will, Cyrus and their soldiers had not gotten into the fight but hoped for a better task next time. During the battle, shells bursting made a grand sight. Unused to such scenes, it seemed all the world reveled in ruin. Hours later not a sound disturbed us. The excitement, confusion and noise yielded to a feeling of profound stillness.

General McClernand pulled accolades onto himself and reported Captain Stewart of his company reached the enemy first. Certainly no Union company moved ahead of Sergeant Cook and Joe Carter of the 4th Illinois cavalry. Cook mustered into the 4th, as a private but soon afterwards received promotions to corporal and sergeant. He commanded 20 men, the extreme advance guard, rode into Fort Henry first, pulled down the garrison flag, and it remained in his possession and evidence of the damned lies in McClernand's report.

Charles H. Dickey, Journal
Volume Three, February through October, 1862
Capture of Fort Donelson; Carnage at Shiloh; Camp Fever, General Hospital; September and October of 1862, Absent with *and without* Leave

February 7, 1862: The 4th Cavalry rode in pursuit of the enemy. Everyone said rebs were fearless, but after Fort Henry I wondered if they got just as scared as we did. When our commanders gave up pursuit, we returned to Fort Henry. On the way back we met 3rd Michigan Battery boys going after abandoned guns. They asked for an escort, but after a hard day the major refused to order anyone to go. "But if any care to volunteer, they can." Twenty of us rode out, found the guns all disabled one way or another, so we left them behind. The official report gave the 3rd Michigan Battery credit for taking guns, no mention of a cavalry assist or the 41 prisoners we brought in.

Union soldiers, who had not yet been at the front, rushed to get a good look at "secesh" and began to joke at them. The rebs took taunts silently, until one fair, young fellow called out in a drawling tone, "Y'all will sing a different tune by summah."

Our men responded with derisive whoops.

But I cringe. Knowing southern men as I do, the glare in that Confederate's eyes and agreement from his fellow soldiers prophesied doom to come.

We remained a week at Fort Henry, sent out scouting parties and then marched toward Fort Donelson, some ten miles east on the Cumberland River. Well armed with Sharps carbines, we felt ready to give good account of ourselves.

Grant consolidated forces and sent the gunboats downstream to the Ohio with orders to come up the Cumberland River for an assault on Fort Donelson. Rain increased flooding, wiped out two roads and delayed General Grant's plan to attack February 8th. He wanted gunboats to engage from the east while the army attacked west and was very impatient to get to Fort Donelson. "If 15,000 men hit within days, they will be more effective than 50,000 a month later." Overall commander General Halleck "Old Brains" remained silent on the subject and never approved Grant's plan.

Just one day made a great deal of difference. Confederate General Pillow arrived at Donelson February 9th and found the river battery unfinished. Scouts said the 10-inch Columbiad and 32-pound rifled cannon remained unmounted. Pillow put things to rights, however, and readied armaments in three tiers on the bluff that rose above the river. Sixteen guns in all—the lowest battery 20 feet above the water, the second 50 feet above the water, and the summit 120 feet up with heavy siege guns where the waterway bends slightly to the east. Rebs had probably stolen the Columbiad from a Federal arsenal. Now taking it back would be the devil. A large caliber, muzzle-loader, it could fire high and low trajectories, sending solid shot or shell long ranges. An excellent coastal defense weapon.

Will received orders from General McClernand to march out four miles. At sunrise the next day the whole command marched toward Fort Donaldson, keeping frequent communications with Colonel Oglesby's brigade, which reconnoitered the country.

February 12th, men marched in unseasonably warm weather. A fair blue sky shone above, and they walked as if attending a banquet. "We march unopposed." An infantry soldier discarded his heavy coat, and others did the same.

"Fort" Donelson had no brick or stone walls, just earthworks, protecting 15 acres of encampment. We must have another victory. Failure was unthinkable. One triumph doubled determination. Gunboats hastened along the river to the point of attack. Nighttime rewarded us with a clear, cloudless sky and full moon. The old man in the moon illuminated the trail—but his blue-white face scowled.

The enemy camped on the opposite side of a creek, impassable through backwater or from the Cumberland River. We moved to the right with Colonel Oglesby's brigade in the lowlands west of Fort Donaldson. Commanders threw our cavalry forward to occupy the heights, scout and reconnoiter. The rest of Colonel Oglesby's force moved south, while artillery dragged up the steep, wooded hills. Skirmishes occurred on the south ridge and across the valley toward the left of the enemy's position.

The enemy shelled the middle redoubt. Under orders of General McClernand, Will marched three infantry regiments and Taylor's battery across the valley, leaving McAllister's battery and one infantry regiment on the western ridge. Our cavalry moved right to hold the enemy in check. It felt grand to advance with other horse soldiers in a well-aligned front, steady reins and dazzling sabers.

At dark Colonel Oglesby's right became engaged where dense underbrush had not been scouted. Orders came to go west. We bivouacked under a sapphire sky without tents on a wooded bluff, stroked by comfortable wind. Making rounds in the dark was a dangerous occupation, however. Men felt skittish and ready to shoot at shadows. A crib of corn and several hives of honey stood at the foot of a bluff, so the horses had plenty to eat and we enjoyed honey, sweet as home. Reassuring comforts until a man beside me mumbled the Twenty-third Psalm, not once, but three times over.

The hillsides surrounding Fort Donelson made me mindful of home. Its ravines stood higher, but early spring greenery brought the bouquets Ella had picked to mind. I pulled out the most recent letter from Belle and read it again by firelight. Belle had written news of a new colt, not Aurora's foal this time, but another mare. I wondered, did this horse need assistance? I should have been home to help. Belle failed to tell me how the birth went. "The new arrival is a filly. I've named her Biscuit, in honor of mother's biscuits and how we loved them." What a great name! I should be the one to train the colt. If a colt is improperly handled from the start, later corrections fail. If I were home to train the filly, she'd welcome my touch, enjoy my company. I could give her proper care. Apples from my pocket to treat her, but no spoiling. The first few weeks set a horse's behavior. No help for that, however, with me on a ridge 500 miles from Ottawa.

General Grant now rode a roan called, Fox, a powerful, spirited animal of great endurance, another superb mount. The disparity between slender commander and massive horse would look greater if not for the relaxed way Grant rode. He didn't seem to control Fox, but became part of the beast like a centaur. Grant saluted our escort with his saber, then slid it into the scabbard. As he headed out, he whispered in the horse's ear.

The Confederate commander of Fort Donelson was a former United States Secretary of War, now Brigadier General John Floyd, aided by another Brigadier General, Gideon Pillow—both political generals. General Floyd, in particular, had reason to fear capture. He had been United States Secretary of War before the South seceded. In his official capacity, he removed arms from northern arsenals, misappropriated public property and sent materiel South. The North branded him a traitor. The third Brigadier General, Simon Buckner, CSA, happened to be a former classmate and friend of Grant's. Made me wonder how I'd feel fighting a friend like Alvin, hard to puzzle that through, and I gladly set the question aside.

The fortifications at Donelson defended against ground attack, so

Grant decided to repeat the plan from Fort Henry. He sent gunboats to pummel fortifications from the river and infantry to catch fleeing rebels.

Admiral Foote is a patriotic, Christian gentleman, who preaches sermons to his crews and any of us in earshot. Fervently religious, but also a fearless warrior.

The night before battle, crowds of men clustered around the chaplain to shed their sins. Thoughts of meeting the Creator made heathens suddenly pious, so the chaplain asked them to sign a pledge: For the purpose of preserving my Christian integrity and growing in grace, the undersigned does hereby promise scrupulously to refrain from intoxicating liquors, from the use of profane and indecent language, Sabbath desecration, falsehood and licentiousness, and promise further to attend when practicable the preaching of the Word of God and faithfully caution and admonish others in regard to any departure from the terms of this agreement.

The promise to refrain from booze gave many men pause. For soldiers took to liquor, fondly called Old Red Eye, Spider Juice, Pop Skull, Bust Head or Rock Me to Sleep, Mother. The taste for libation afflicted soldiers and officers alike. Privates always claimed a right to imitate leaders to the extent they got dead drunk, weaved and spewed, even men who were church elders at home. However, the day before a pitched battle life everlasting weighed heavily, and many men put their marks on the chaplain's pledge.

Others relished the upcoming fight. "We must whip them or all go under the sod together."

A third cluster wrote letters home. I fell in with this last group, but didn't write much for myself. I took down messages for fellows who could not write. A boy named Dewitt asked me to write to his mother, so I took his message down word for word to let the woman know it was, indeed, from her boy. "If permitted to live, then I expect to return home and see the people and eat your fine mincemeat. We could get home this summer if fighting goes well. I reenlisted for three years, but I am not wanting to get home too bad yet a while. If rebs do not surrender, I hope to God that our government will exterminate the whole crew of secesh officers and leading men."

Before lights out, our company sang "The Star Spangled Banner," and the sound of brave men's voices made my spirits swell.

Success at Fort Henry built confidence in the navy. Boats assumed position February 12th, but the enemy hid and not a soul could be seen. A gunboat opened fire, hoping to draw return and unmask the enemy, but no response came. The fort appeared evacuated. After firing ten shells, the boat dropped down three miles and anchored, where the sailors became targets for Confederate sharpshooters.

The mild spring weather changed suddenly. The wind switched around, roared down the river and over the bluffs. Hands grew so cold and stiff I could barely finger the bugle. My lips quivered, and lungs hated to breathe in. Early blossoms froze, flew off the trees, and chill cut to the bone. Windblown sleet and snow attacked both sides. At eleven o'clock we heard heavy firing in the direction of the fort and got ordered out at once. We took everything, not knowing how far we were going, but before we got to the foot of the bluff, firing ceased and we were ordered back. Some of the boys tried to rest in a fast-falling snow. Most stood around fires shivering—at all times ready for action if called upon.

Valentine's Day held no love for mankind. Early that morning crews covered boat decks with chains, sacks of coal, lumber—anything to protect from punishing shot. Four ironclads formed a line across the Cumberland, closed within a mile and a half and opened fire, but the shots fell short.

Confederate gunners held higher ground, and this day they did the pummeling. When Union gunboats closed range, Confederates calculated well and rained shells down. Rifled shells have an outrageous screeching sound that pains human ears. To hear half a dozen screaming at once and smoke rising from boats is the most awful scene ever witnessed. Deafening cracks echoed through the ravine as solid shot crashed and whizzing fragments tore through plating, which reverberated like struck bells. Anxiety gripped me. My tongue and throat went dry and parched.

Confederates showed determination, valor and precise execution. When a ball got lodged in one cannon, a corporal leapt onto the parapet, used a log and rammed the missile home.

"Now, boys, see me take a chimney." The gunner tore up his coat in lieu of wadding.

The boat flag and chimney fell with the shot.

Watching from one side, I became numb—Charlie Dickey disappeared—in his place sat a bugler, confined to a saddle. Someone impotent, anxious, disheartened, not me.

Though Union missiles hit rebel gun placements, destroyed keyhole embrasures and cast heaps of earth over the platforms, they got worse than they gave. A solid shell glanced through the *Carondelet* and leapt after sailors like a beast pursuing prey. It knocked down a dozen men and burst through the side. Other officers and crew held their stations until a 128-pounder struck the anchor, smashed it into flying bolts, bounded over the vessel and took away part of the smoke stack. When returning fire, a port gun exploded, set the boat ablaze and left it to the mercy of the battery. More withering fire rendered the gunboats helpless, and the navy drifted back. The Admiral meant to repeat the Fort Henry victory, but this time Confederates cheered the sight of Union gunboats set adrift.

However, Union infantry still had Fort Donelson surrounded. Confederates had three choices: surrender, sit tight or cut their way out. Plunging temperatures froze the ground. Neither side lit fires. Men on both sides bedded down in the ditches and behind logs as shelter from cutting winds. Few of us closed our eyes. Even the horses, after their manner, brayed the suffering they endured.

Under cover of darkness rebel troops left rifle pits and maintained silence while they massed infantry, cavalry and artillery. Jolting gun carriages should have alerted the Union, but Federal pickets struggled to stay alive and did not keep good watch. Grant conferred with the navy and was not on the field, as Confederate General Pillow moved his whole division.

The next morning Union skirmishers and snipers deployed first. Snipers carried long-range rifles with sights delicately arranged. They did not maneuver as units—just filled canteens, took biscuits, found cover behind rocks or hollows and waited.

My lips kissed a frozen bugle. Along with other Union calls, reveille rang the woods. Numb infantrymen shook snow from frozen garments. The day barely dawned, and the men's eyes remained dim. Companies had yet to fall in when the woods became alive. Screaming an alarm, pickets rushed back on the camps. Regiments formed, officers mounted, commands rose loud and impatient.

A sharp sound broke the stillness. Every ear found it. Eyes followed. A light the size of a small star, darted through the air, higher and higher. I saw it before I heard the report; the star reached a summit and started to descend in a beautiful curved line. Now a rushing sound, a coming tempest and the noise became furious. Primitive instinct jolted alive. Space above filled with deadly missiles, senses bewildered, complicated and overpowering roar of musketry, cannon, shrieking shells, lurid artillery flames lit the scene. I was ignorant of the enemy's strength and unable to see movements. Except the day of final judgment described in the Bible, man cannot expect to hear anything more awful. The deafening roar overcame awareness—incessant crash of musketry, continual zip, zip of bullets, screams of wounded, death shrieks when men die. Bullets hummed within a few feet of me and cut nearby twigs. If I held out a hand, I could have caught a dozen.

Pillow's advance opened fire on Oglesby's right, and rapid volleys ensued. The noise said, 'this is your last day on earth.' The banging, screaming, even the smells of powder, souls sinking down, the sky itself falling, nothing ever so real. Nothing can ever be.

Rebels made a fierce attack on the right, and the brunt of the battle fell on infantrymen, especially against the 11th Illinois regiment. Colonel Ransom, normally in charge, was wounded in the battle, so Will took over the brigade. I don't know how many, but Confederates marched in a long column, got through the infantry line but halted when they saw our cavalry. When shots rang out, I reached toward a friend, John, to show him the enemy's position—but they shot him in the heart. The call came to charge. I could not help John, so I leaned forward, gave Rhoderic three kicks and charged.

The sudden thrust of hooves dulled men's voices and took me from anxiety to calm. An exuberant rush, made on impulse, caused others to follow and Rebs to turn back to Fort Donaldson. There our regiment came under artillery fire, an uproar of heavy guns, falling trees and flying splinters. Forest echoes multiplied the sounds. Shells cut sturdy pines in two. David Anderson fell to the ground, his leg literally in pieces. As a Christian, David prayed, and cannon thundered, Amen.

Trees surrendered with roars of anguish, as if they were beasts. Trunks became powerful weapons, deranging both sides. Advancing lines lagged in the forest; some men swung around insensibly, struggling to keep alignment. We came upon two men beside an abandoned cannon. The younger of the two held up his arms in surrender. The other, who turned out to be his father, lifted his gun and killed a trooper. Our men riddled the father with bullets and took the son prisoner.

Next we supported Taylor's and Dresser's batteries while they shelled the rebel works. Again under fire, one shell burst two yards away, stunned me badly and I could not hear in my left ear, but we suffered no casualties.

Shell and shrapnel met the Confederates, but they closed ranks as though nothing happened. On they came. A luckless horse and rider went down, but the balance of the men swept on. Some others fell or leapt wildly over the stack of bodies and horses. Still they came. Our cavalry drew up close, and received the order to charge. A trooper on my left cried, "God grant us victory over our enemies!" Which side prayed louder? Which side had God's favor today? Two sides closed, nearer, faster for a violent collision. The dead fell. Wounded men crawled to the rear. A long-range hum became the sharp whacks of close firing. When balls hit, the soft wallop of flesh mixed with cries of mangled men. The ground in front rattled and wailed with incessant fire, but the front remained unbroken, and our rear showed no stragglers.

The pace increased, and the full mass ran through whistling bullets. Smoke swallowed the blue line. Horses turned end over end and crushed riders beneath them. The air choked me; my chest heaved for the breath it craved. The clashing of sabers, firing of pistols, demand for surrender and cries of combatants filled the air. Gun smoke halted the Confederate advance. Their line tumbled back, pressed as if by demons.

The distance between the works and bivouac was short. Confederate brigades came up in a kind of echelon, left in front, and passed by regiments left into line, without halting. Oglesby's Illinoisans on the right held their ground and, returned fire, suffered in full measure. Rapid exchange, monstrous clangor of muskets and scores of men reddened the snow with blood.

Confederate Nathan Bedford Forrest rode around the rear, but we were told to hold position.

After an interval the Confederates struck Will's brigade. Soon Will was engaged along his whole front, infantry against infantry. His men repulsed the first charge and advanced to the top of rising ground. A fresh assault followed, Union artillery across the valley opened in support, and Will's men repulsed the second wave. Tremendous explosions took place overhead when wide-throated mortar opened up. In quick succession one blast followed and another. Steadfast, his men clung to the brow of the hill as if theirs by holy right. An hour passed and another hour without cessation of fire.

The "rebel yell" meant they gained ground against him. Infantry grew short on ammunition and had to take what they could find in boxes of dead and wounded. Far right companies gave way, holding up empty cartridge boxes, which encouraged rebels to sweep around the flank. Finally

Oglesby ordered the division to retire.

Near Will's position John A. Logan's 31st Illinois maintained position. Logan rode in a gallop behind his line screaming fiercely to his men. Will's men closed up, but then a shortage of ammunition silenced their rifles. Rather than keep men without cartridges under fire, Will ordered soldiers to retire and coolly changed his men from front to rear, as if on parade. Rebels charged and threw them into brief confusion, but the men clung to their colors and made good a retreat.

The road dipped into a hidden gorge, walled on the right and left in thicketed woods. Confederate infantry flung at Will, but General McClernand rushed Taylor's Battery forward and swung three, twenty-four-pounders into position. Now battle scenes of the morning replayed. The Confederates struggled. The woods rang with musketry and artillery. Bullets mowed down brush. Union regiments behaved with great gallantry, and rebels fell back to their entrenchments. Artillerymen never slackened. They singed their hair and beards, burned hands, faces and holes in their clothing yet kept up quick flares of cannon fire—smoke, immense roar, crashing, tramping, yelling.

When a shell burst within a few feet, even if it does not hit, it produces a peculiar feeling. Yet men held. Underbrush and treetops trapped clouds of smoke and screened the combatants from each other. Closer to the ground flames of musketry and cannon tinted the air red.

General Lew Wallace came up to the battlefield. Confederate chances worsened when these Union reinforcements arrived. When Lew Wallace approached, he met Will falling back. Will rode with his leg thrown over the pommel at a walking pace.

"What is your name?" asked Lew Wallace.

"Wallace," Will said.

"Wallace is my name, too." Confusion between Lew Wallace, 11th Indiana, and W.H.L. Wallace, 11th Illinois, had caused great profanity in the commissary and post office. "Are you retreating?" asked Lew Wallace.

"Yes," replied Will. "We are out of ammunition."

Lew Wallace asked, "How far back is the enemy?"

"You have time to form there."

Consequently Lew Wallace was ready for the Confederates when they appeared.

Will and Oglesby reformed their commands, resupplied ammunition. Then the cannonading ceased, and everybody wondered, what next? General Grant rode up, almost unattended. He carried papers, which looked like telegrams, and extended his fist. "That is where the Confederates have stripped their line." He instructed his commanders to retire to the heights and throw up works. "Reinforcements are near," he said, "and it is advisable to await their coming."

One officer spoke up. "An escape route has opened for the enemy."

Grant crushed the papers in his hand, but the sign of disappointment cleared quickly. Though another Confederate escape loomed, he said in a quiet tone, "Gentlemen, the position on the right must be retaken."

General Lew Wallace reconnoitered the hill and chose regiments to lead an attack. Dispositions took until two o'clock in the afternoon. The thrilling command then sounded, "Forward!"

Rebel batteries opened with all their fury. Our cavalry fought as sharpshooters alongside the 11th Illinois infantry. If an enemy soldier exposed himself along the breastworks, we picked him off. The infantry's colors got riddled with shot.

The enemy captured one flag. "I have the first prize," a Confederate shouted.

Private Wilson shot him dead and retrieved the colors. "And I the second."

We dismounted to go into action, but foot soldiers gained the objective without assistance. Some Union troops broke, but Confederates did not pursue.

In places the undergrowth was too thick for a rabbit to get through. What lay in wait beyond the next mound? No one knew. Generals McClernand and Lew Wallace moved to retake lost ground. During the advance, one colonel had a cigar shot from his lips. He took another and called for a match. A soldier handed one up, and the officer said "Thank you, now take your place. We are almost up." With steady nerve he ignored safety, spurred his horse to the crest of the heights and effected the maneuver to save his men. Flank companies cheered and deployed as skirmishers. The ones with Zouave practice showed their skill, crept along the ground when the fire was hottest, ran when it slackened, gained ground and maintained fire that sparkled. For the most part, bullets aimed at them passed over their heads and hit ranks behind.

Our fellows had no idea of giving way. The line moved forward and never stopped until the Confederates fell back. The 3rd Division halted within easy musket range of the rifle pits at three-thirty in the afternoon.

When night fell, guns grew silent, and Federals bivouacked without fire or supper. But Grant's commanders had placed men in the right positions, and Grant could order a general assault the next day.

Hearing returned in my left ear eight hours after that shell burst close—along with gratitude for coming out alive. Cavalry shut the road leading out, and the field belonged to the Union.

I picked out a clean-looking Confederate, who had been shot in the chest, and made a meal of cornbread and beef from his haversack. He wore a little pouch around his neck, a camphor bag, probably an old mammy hung it there to ward off fevers. In the dead man's shirt I found a pocket New Testament, opened it and read, "If thine enemy hunger, give him to eat." I thanked the deceased for obeying the letter of the Word.

Fatigue parties tended the wounded with no distinction between friend and foe. The labor extended through the night, and surgeons never rested. At daylight the Union could bring a superior force to bear. Would the Confederates subject their men to another battle? Did they see Grant's advantages?

The night was clear with a gorgeous half-moon, slightly golden with a blue tinge. The morning of the third day, cavalry got ordered to a spot half a mile south of the battle. In the distance I saw what appeared to be a brush fence, but when it moved, realized we faced a line of Confederates, who had broken through.

They saw us, too, and must have assumed our party was the advance guard of a large army. Without firing a shot, they turned back to the fort. If they got away, what would folks back home say? We remained in our saddles for hours to make sure no one escaped. But in another locale, Forrest plunged his cavalry into a slough, slipped past the right flank and crossed Lick Creek, which at the time was saddle-skirt deep. An icy crust covered its surface, wind chastised everyone, but they slipped away to Nashville without anyone firing a shot. Southern Generals Pillow and Floyd took to their heels, abandoning most of their men.

Confederate General Buckner was the only commander to stay and share the soldiers' fate. Perhaps he hoped to benefit from their friendship when he asked Grant for terms of surrender. Grant replied, "No terms except unconditional and immediate surrender can be accepted. I propose to move immediately upon your works." The two generals met at Dover Hotel, where Buckner surrendered troops and supplies. Grant had captured the most prisoners ever taken in an American war. Someone decided

U.S. in Grant's name stood for "unconditional surrender."

When General Lew Wallace reached the hotel for the surrender, he gave orders against gloating. "Move the line forward, take possession of persons and property, but not a word of taunt—no cheering."

After General Buckner surrendered, I served in the escort detail taking him to prison. He was a handsome, gallant-looking officer, a credit to his native state of Kentucky. When he first emerged from the Dover Hotel, outrage darkened his expression. The rebs raised their hands in weary salutes—for some men a monumental effort. The sight of Confederate soldiers loading onto transports didn't help his disposition.

Then one Union private gave a reb his blanket. "You're headed for prison camp in Illinois, Indiana, or Ohio, maybe as far away as Boston." Kindness eased Buckner's brow, but he did not smile until he saw the 2nd Kentucky Infantry. The prisoners marched along, and their mascot dog, called Frank, went along to prison. Frank had his own haversack around his neck, and Union guards stopped to provision Frank for the journey.

February 17, 1862, a day of sad offices, we cared for wounded men, buried the dead and did whatever possible to ease distress. I had no idea if the boy, named Dewitt, had survived. If he would again eat his mother's mincemeat or if the letter I helped him write became the last word she received. Squads of soldiers dug graves. Henry Johnson, assigned to headquarters, heard his brother Richard had been killed, got a furlough and rode out to find him. Henry kept going for miles, looking at every grave and corpse he saw. For two days he rode. Thoroughly disheartened, he kept on till dark. When he prepared to lie down the second night, he spotted graves under an oak tree. One last look showed a marker with his brother's name.

A black man sauntered over. "I heared the words at burial. They said he was a patriot, shot early in the action. Died wuthout a struggle."

"It will be hard to tell our mother he died so soon after leaving home," Henry said, "but knowing I found his grave will lessen her grief."

"Today I buried 68 men." The grave digger began to sway rhythmically. "And all, praise the Lord, shall have salvation on Judgment Day."

Henry came back to camp, more eager to fight than before. "I am ready to meet rebels, no matter how hard the battle or how far the march. I may be shot down like Richard. If I die, I have no fears as to what God intends for I know He wants to finish this war."

Midnight darkness wrapped the whole landscape, but I could not sleep. I sat at the foot of a tree—and saw a light flutter on the battlefield.

General Sherman also saw. "Private," he called, "go out and see what causes that light."

Soldiers had been cutting bits of clothing and locks of hair from dead Confederate officers as souvenirs. I imagined Sherman wanted vandalizing corpses to stop.

From a distance I watched the light move. Someone bent over the bodies, but not like a looter, instead touching gently as though assessing each man's pain. My gut wrenched, but I picked my way through the newly dead. As I went deeper into the truth of battle, the world started to spin. Eager to finish the gruesome errand, I tried to move fast, but corpses refused clear passage.

The figure of a woman emerged, bending over bodies, casting the glow of a lantern down. Two colored men stood by to help her. The circle of light revealed a jumble of gore.

"Madam," I called out. "You must not be out here."

"Who says?" Her voice rang clear as a trumpet.

"Why, General Sherman," I replied. "He sent me to bring you in."

She struggled to pull herself into an upright position "You go back and tell General Sherman I shall stay here as long as needed."

"I cannot make that report."

She tilted the lamp to light my face. "One of these men might be alive. Imagine, young fellow, lying out here in the cold and gloom among the slain."

"You must come with me."

"No. Epaulets, rank and even colors do not matter when good men become cannon fodder. I must save anyone I can."

I asked, "Who should I say is out here?"

"You tell General Sherman Mother Bickerdyke cannot leave, not if one man may be alive." She illuminated herself, a middle-aged lady, standing between the bodies of two soldiers, remarkable for their contrast. A full grown man had been in the act of biting a cartridge. His teeth still fastened on the paper, while his hand clasped the bullet. He had been shot in the forehead, and his transition from life to death immediate, the lust of battle still deformed his face. Next to him, a mere boy, strikingly handsome. A ball struck his right leg above the knee. He reclined on his back, stretched out arms fully extended, fists tightly clenched around the wound as he bled to death.

77

I reported Mother Bickerdyke's answer to General Sherman. He saluted her and sent me back with a detail to assist her search for survivors.

Telegraph lines spread the good news that Fort Donelson had surrendered, and the country went wild with excitement. Grant wanted to move quickly to Columbus and put it at the mercy of Federal bayonets. Admiral Foote repaired the river squadron, including three timberclads, seven ironclads, 38 mortar boats, tow boats, snag boats. Foote advised speed, too, no less aggressive than General Grant. However, General Halleck refused. Our camp moved back to Randolph Forges, two miles in the rear, and occupied deserted buildings. At least there we found good forage for our horses.

I received a letter from Cyrus. He slept in a tent belonging to Capt. R. Middleton, Benfield Sharp Shooters, 4th Mississippi, CSA. The area around Fort Donelson had a great many loyal Union people. Cyrus had 100 Tennesseans serving with him. Most towns and hamlets had strongly divided loyalties, slave versus free, national versus states' rights.

The fall of two river forts opened up middle Tennessee to Union control, including the capitol in Nashville. After the fall of Donelson, gunboats controlled the Tennessee River as far as northern Alabama.

We scouted the Confederates' trail, no tracking skill necessary, for guns, overcoats, blankets, haversacks, knapsacks—every paraphernalia of camp cluttered the roadway. They left behind a battery of six guns. Stragglers, completely fagged out, fell into our hands. A few rebs made a stand. A platoon under Sergeant Simison dismounted and captured twelve prisoners, including a major, captain and two sergeants.

Our advance, Bob Hume, Hiram Moulton and Myron Hare, overtook a lone rebel and supposed he'd surrender as the others had done, but instead he whirled and shot, hit Hume in the heart. The heavy, soggy strike a body makes falling to the ground is a sound I can never forget. The others went after the shooter, and I struggled to hold the mounts. *Gulliver's Travels* came to mind, when he visited a country where horses ruled, and men were foul beasts. How I wished to be home to reread the book—not here where it came eerily to life.

I then spotted a rebel close by, so I shoved the halters at another man and overtook the reb.

"You killed my father and for God sake don't kill me," he exclaimed.

I jerked the pistol into his face without any feeling of mercy. God's commandment 'thou shalt not kill' is easily overcome after the death of a friend, but grief in the rebel's eyes stayed my hand. "If you surrender," I said, "I promise not to shoot."

At that moment, we heard Moulton and Hare fire and kill the father, so the prisoner had not lied—just spoken prematurely. I took the boy down the road to Hume's body, had him lift it onto the horse, then tied the prisoner's hands. As we marched away, his head hung down. Twice he looked back at his father's body, left unburied.

Another prisoner spewed curses and called Lincoln "the Illinois baboon." The boys tore the filthy shirt off his back and stuffed it in his mouth to gag his taunts.

Bob Hume had enlisted just one week before he fell. He was a railroad station agent in Earlville and went down to Cairo just to visit, but patriotism got the better of him. He had not officially mustered into the United States service. Therefore, his widow could not collect a pension. The loss spurred me to write to her. I knew nothing about Pamela Hume, other than she was the widow of a brave man. 'Dear Lady,' my letter began. 'It is a painful duty to write of your husband's death.' I related Bob's eagerness in the chase, 'true to his brave and noble instincts, he was foremost in the charge.' Then told her how we attended the body and mourned the loss.

The newspapers called Donelson a "magnificent victory." It garnered 13,000 prisoners of war, 146 guns of the highest caliber and, more importantly, broke the line of defense. Prisoners got sent first to Cairo. I wondered if the stench in Cairo improved since it served as our camp. Rebel prisoners looked like a strange, motley crew, but they sure shot sharp.

We took possession of a Confederate colonel's tent, and a frightened negro appeared at the door. "M'name's George. I runned away from my master 50 miles distant then the colonel whose tent y'all appropriated took me as cook. The blastin' balls done scar't me," George said. "I passed the night in the hills." When we adopted him as our own cook, his wife and children came into camp, too. The couple worked hard, but authorities wanted to ship negroes away. George's wife and children, at least, should have gone. When it came time to part, however, George couldn't resist her pleading, so they stayed together and served us. Fidelity from coloreds surprised some soldiers, disgusted others.

Only a few white men thought slavery was a sin. "Take coloreds away from secesh," one man decided, "and turn them over to loyal southerners but don't send them to Illinois."

"Negroes don't have the skill of eight-year-olds when it comes to caring for themselves. They aren't fit for freedom."

"No exceptions?" I asked.

"Not a one."

In George's case I disagreed, so I borrowed a novel from Benjamin Whiting to teach George how to read. In return George danced for fun and made speeches, pontificating as well as anyone. He hoped to go to Illinois when the war ended. That was not a wise course, but I didn't tell George that Illinois had Black Codes to discourage colored people from moving in.

Losses from wounds weighed more heavily than the death toll. When casualties had first come in, we learned bad cases had yet to arrive. If that were true, it boggled imagination, for these men had wounds bad enough. Disaster was apparent on abashed faces, what scenes! The woods' perfume mated with pungent death, and high clouds draped a melancholy sky. Orderlies dropped men into open spaces, hundreds of fellows, screaming screams. One moment determined to survive, the next moment dead and gone.

Wherever battles tilled the earth hospitals sprouted. I quickly learned to avoid hospitals, as all soldiers did. Veterans said, 'if a man's sent to a hospital, he's done for.' Going there required courage, more than immediate death on the battlefield. A hospital is a lingering place. Some patients try to scorn death; many more court it. Attendants were few in number. Wounded or sick men, whatever their condition, got less than a quarter of the care we gave sick horses at home. When a man is lifted onto a surgeon's table, his scream is inhuman. Confusion all around. Not far away, gunfire revealed snipers still added to the casualty count.

The crack of a musket is most unnerving when it's the only one. A Federal soldier folded in on himself, a ragged hole in the back of his head, the contents of which stained his collar. He messed his pants as he died, an odor too common.

Surgeons dealt with horrid wounds. Bad food, insufficient medicine and male nurses, detailed directly out of the ranks, added to the death toll. The North, no doubt, has medicine and surgical equipment in abundance, but not where needed. Of all the harrowing sights in war, the worst come in the days following battle. The best men on earth lie helpless, mangled, alone, and they die.

I gazed at the sky for a sight of fresh blue, but eventually had to look back at deathbeds, plaguing the ground. The Medical Department had not prepared for a flood of wounded—and soldiers paid the price.

The newspapers printed directories of killed, missing and wounded, but the lists were woefully incomplete and never up-to-date because of the army's steady coming, going and dying. Mothers, brothers, even sisters showed up looking for wounded men, hunted for a time but often left without any news. Impossible to find a friend or relative, unless one knew where a specific man had been taken. Even in hospitals no one kept good records. If fortunate, when searchers returned home, they found letters giving the right addresses.

A minor commander issued orders to move when Grant and Sherman had not. Confusion, excitement and consternation over nothing. Federals had great military capability, a reliable and well-equipped rank-and-file. The problem was to organize and get the best service.

Cavalry got busy scouting and foraging. A trooper, named Stewart, was a small, beardless young man and splendid soldier. He lived in Batavia with his father, a frail man. When Stewart enlisted he took to army life, liked it, and I admired him, as all his comrades did. An officer called for volunteers to bring in wounded. Stewart responded first, and while carrying a wounded sergeant to our lines, a rebel sharpshooter shot him in the chest. He also kept a diary. Near death he wrote: 'The doctor says I must die—all is over with me.' On a blank page he penciled to his ailing father: 'I have been brave but wicked—pray for me.' I mailed the diary to his home in Batavia with my condolences.

In March guards brought in Union deserters, perhaps 300, marched them along, a motley collection, all sorts of hats and caps, a few fine looking fellows, some shamefaced, some sick, others dirty with filthy, long-worn shirts. They trudged along without quarter, one huddled mass, not in ranks. Some guards laughed, but all I saw was meanness.

An ambulance cavalcade evacuated wounded men, who might survive the journey to a general hospital. Lurching wheels caused men inside to cry out in pain. Their screams drew the attention of guerrillas. The ambulances held 60 wounded men, including officers. Civilian teamsters drove the two- or four-wheel ambulance wagons. Teamsters had skills as horsemen but no qualifications to move wounded or mount a defense. When marauders attacked, the teamsters ran. The wounded men surrendered, but rebels ran amok. The officers included a lieutenant and a captain. The rebels dragged these two out on their backs and pinned the captain's feet to the ground with bayonets. Then gave him 20 thrusts, even through the mouth and face. When a bayonet grates on human bone, the sound defies description. The remaining wounded got murdered, blood-stained bodies left on the ground. As they finished the grisly business, we charged upon the scene. Some fellows, not quite dead, moaned and groaned.

A few guerillas slipped away, but we grabbed two so-called officers and 17 men. The captured men went under guard, but then some Union troopers decided they should die. They took the two officers to separate places and shot them, then marched the others to open ground, shot and pinned inscriptions to their breasts, explaining why they had died. They hung the bodies from trees. All for revenge—one side as bad as the other, teaching the opponent how to hate.

We lifted the Union dead, but one fellow screamed. "God have mercy!"

We gently placed him down, but by the time someone brought a stretcher the fellow was truly dead. So his unidentified body went into a grave. This burial ceremony left me shaking.

Perimeter guards brought in a slave boy with his eyes clamped shut. His master had told him Yankees have horns.

"We are not going to harm you," I said.

One eye opened a slit.

To convince him his master had lied, I took off my hat and showed him my hornless head.

Alvin asked him, "Where's your mother?"

"She been sold."

No one asked the boy questions after that. Just gave him a large portion of beans and let him sleep atop a blanket.

Part of our regiment got ordered south to destroy a railroad crossing. We had strict orders not to disturb residents. General Grant said, "We are fighting the Confederate army, not women and children." We rode south for two days, burned the railway bridge, made fires and put the rails on them, bending the iron out of shape.

A few days later I received a furlough to go north. I reached home early in the morning. No one stirred outside, and I walked into Ann's house unannounced. She sat at the table, moving breakfast idly around a plate. When she saw me in a dust-covered uniform, her fork dropped. Her hands went to her heart. She made no sound but the light in her eyes welcomed me home. When she caught her breath, she said, "I hear you have done well."

Words failed. I just nestled in her arms.

While home, Ann and I visited two Tennessee cousins, Frank and Truman, in Union prison after they were captured at Donelson. Stories of hardship prompted us to go. Many captives arrived in Chicago shoeless and without coats. Guards and prisoners came through different depots then marched to the southern suburbs. We could smell Camp Douglas before we arrived. The stench of foul sinks and crowded barracks reached out to envelop us.

Union commander, Colonel Sweet, refused to admit us with the excuse he could not risk allowing Confederate sympathizers inside the prison. We professed our devotion to flag and country, but the Colonel made no exceptions. Apparently Sisters of Mercy from the local convent had already tried to go inside, view conditions and report back to Chicago's mayor. Did we look like southern sympathizers? Hardly. Seems the Colonel feared what might happen if news of abhorrent conditions got out. Ann and I had no choice but to leave.

Even this early in spring I expected to find Ella tramping the hillside and spotted her tiny figure on the ridge. When I called to her, she recognized me and ran forward. The basket in her hand tipped and the contents spilled out, she ran so fast downhill.

"Careful!" I caught her in my arms and embraced a more mature woman than I remembered, one eager to see me.

She hugged close but then pulled away.

I grabbed her back. Ella still fit nicely under my shoulder. Near the frontlines, life was at the mercy of blind chance. With Ella, I savored each moment. Lively thoughts and sensations rushed through me, and I didn't want them to stop.

Ella blushed crimson. "Are you well?"

"Now that I see you much better."

"Your color is not good."

I had fought against jaundice since we camped in Cairo but did not tell Ella that.

"If it were summer, I'd make juice of radish leaves."

"Just walk with me. That's the best tonic." So we spent the afternoon tramping the hillside. I told Ella the story of our cousins. Many families had divided loyalties, and it seemed natural to confide in her.

Jennie saw us coming off the ridge. "What's this scandal?" She wagged her finger. "The two of you are not suited for one another." We didn't ask what she meant, but Jennie didn't care. She lectured us. "Your physical traits don't balance. The two of you can never marry."

Ella looked down at her boots.

Jennie kept on. "You could be brother and sister, for God's sake. You both have straw hair, blue eyes. Although Ella's are much bluer than yours Charlie—sorry. You both are worryingly thin. A man and woman must marry opposites. How can two people so similar expect to have strong babies?"

I laughed out loud.

"Charlie, you are an undependable character while Ella is completely faithful." Jennie pulled her aside. "Ella, do not consider him."

Ella turned away, so Jennie did not see her impish smile. That was for my benefit.

***

When I returned to the army, I asked Father. "Can we help our cousins in prison?"

He shook his head in a way that made it clear we must leave them to their fate. I found it hard to accept but could not defy Father. Instead, when I got paid, I sent some money to the Sisters of Mercy convent in Chicago to use for relief of prisoners in Camp Douglas.

A former slave wandered in. Someone had beaten him and ripped his lip, yet he smiled. "The Confederacy is licked."

"What happened to your face?" I asked.

He smiled broader. "My good looks are a small price to pay."

Secessionists hated Union soldiers, but did not fear us yet. After Donelson, they no longer despised us, not as much as before, but we intended to earn respect.

It was up to cavalry to discover their hiding places. Were any north of Memphis, Tennessee, or Corinth, Mississippi? We moved to Iron Landing, four miles above Fort Henry on the Tennessee River and embarked. Our boats arrived March 15th at Pittsburg Landing, the place steamboats put in on the west bank, a few miles south of Savannah, Tennessee. My first impression—Pittsburg Landing also resembled Ottawa's bluffs and made me mindful of leaving Ella behind. Similar to our home on the hill. This high ground gave fine views. New-growth foliage brightened the vista. Thick woods covered the terrain up to the water's edge. Cyrus was off somewhere, God preserve him, with Will's infantry. No leisurely tramps to

84

gather flowers with Ella and Jennie, here we must fight. After Donelson, the prospect made my heart sink.

Three companies went ashore and scouted four miles until we came onto a force of 100 cavalry. We gave the rebels a volley, killed a major and a surgeon and sent the rest flying. We went out again just at nightfall and ran into the same force. This time the rebels stood in line and let us get within 30 steps of them before firing. When we returned fire, the rebels broke but wounded three of our men and six horses. Martin Crawford got hit in the leg between the knee and ankle, and the same ball killed his horse. We sent Crawford to the rear. This wound spared his life because it assured his discharge.

We scouted Clarksville, a beautiful village on the north side of the Cumberland, marched through the streets but met no one except negroes. White inhabitants had left. Some soldiers exaggerated the importance of this, thought we had given rebellion a death blow. If rapidly followed up, they felt secession had to end.

On March 21, 1862, the army commissioned Will a Brigadier, which meant Cyrus became adjutant to a rising star. Commanders divided up the cavalry and dispersed it to several divisions. Company A became Grant's escort, three companies were sent to General McClernand, ours among them, and the other eight companies stationed with General S.A. Hurlburt.

Soldiers strung rope through trees and bushes to fence off the Landing. Inside they parked artillery, caissons, wagons, ambulances and the mules to pull them. Danger quickly reared up when a horrible scream echoed from the perimeter. Heavy woods made it impossible to see, but a detail went out. Darkness was so complete I trusted the ride to my horse. We found the sentinel dead. Another man was put in his place. When the officer of the watch went around again, the second man had disappeared. Seven guards got hit in one night.

General Grant arrived at Pittsburg Landing physically ill with fever and chills and distressed because of a spat with the high command. After the victories at Henry and Donelson, General Grant went to Nashville to gather information. He allowed troops to relax until the next drive. In his absence, looters descended, took slaves and walked off with booty. Officers with less success in the field blew Grant's reputation sky high, saying Grant was drinking and engaging in dissipations. Rancor, distrust and censure swirled around. General Grant asked Halleck to relieve him. Fortunately for us, General Halleck backed down.

Early wildflowers bloomed at Pittsburg Landing. The air felt soft and warm. Cavalry camped on a gentle ridge. Wet weather turned a depression at the rear of camp into a stream, which held enough water for the men. Taylor's Battery camped to the left of headquarters. Nearby Colonel McCullough installed five companies of the 4th cavalry. On April 3, 1862, General Smith took sick, and Will assumed command of his division, a great responsibility.

A skirmish in front of General Sherman's division resulted in three men wounded, ten taken prisoner but no one killed. After the failed attempt to visit Camp Douglas, I mourned the loss of a man to prison as much as to the graveyard. At 11 p.m. a drum roll sounded, several divisions formed in line but did not move out. The night was dark and rainy, and Will rode into Sherman's headquarters with Colonel McPherson. They found everything quiet and General Sherman in fine spirits because the skirmish had driven the enemy back four miles.

General Grant headquartered in Savannah, Tennessee, but made nightly trips to Pittsburg Landing. Chills, fever and his damaged reputation were not enough. Two more calamities hit. April 5th, torrential rain poured down, and Grant rode through darkness lit by flashes of lightening. His horse lost footing, fell and trapped Grant, injuring his leg. And Halleck ordered Grant to wait for Buell's army before moving. On an evening of horrible weather and mishap, Grant waited for Buell.

Eight companies of the 4th cavalry went to General Sherman with Father in command. Taylor's Battery was also reassigned to Sherman. Men felt bad about leaving old brigades; it seemed like breaking up family, but it was ordered. General Sherman created a striking figure on horseback, but close up he looked fierce. His red hair poked out at odd angles from his head. Pale eyes darted and flashed, while facial muscles pulled taut. He was too thin. Not just his eyes, his whole body remained in a state of alarm as though poised to rescue children from a burning building. He wore good clothing but cared for it poorly, seldom buttoned his blouse. He talked incessantly, which made him seem strange to those of us, who talk little and judge a man by his actions. General Sherman rode a beautiful sorrel racing mare, fleet as a deer, yet easy to maneuver. Any cavalryman envied that horse.

After the storm cleared, vegetation sprouted. Golden dandelions sprawled in profusion. The weather felt warm in the daytime, but delicious nights cooled enough to sleep well. Grant left his boot on the injured leg for two days until aides had to cut it off and relieve the pain.

Alvin Chapin called my attention to an immense flock of migrating birds. He called the sound, "noise," but I thought the birds made rare music, a rush of wings, faded to velvet motion, long drawn out with a few calls as high notes, like an etude. After night fell, their music stopped, replaced with croaking frogs, men's snores and eruptive coughs.

The countryside was healthy, and sick boys got better. Nothing of interest went on except reviews. Officers made the battalion form up three times in three days. Will's entire battalion went through the same, tiresome exercise. A hint of movement broke the monotony. Buell's troops, I believe, came overland from Nashville, but commanders kept details to themselves and nothing was certain. Everyone expected a fight soon, near Corinth. The rail lines of the Memphis & Charleston Railroad, running east and west, and the Mobile & Ohio Railroad, running north and south, were vital connections for Confederates. Around campfires, men whispered of the great battle to come. I shuddered at the prospect, for battles now meant blood, wounds and death.

We had ample food, however, and ate until we could not eat more. Normal rations consisted of coffee, sowbelly, Yankee beans and hardtack. Not many enlisted men knew how to cook beans. Often we ate them nearly raw. In this camp we paid a colored man, named Fred, to cook. His beans were soft as butter, and his coffee palatable without milk. Mother had spoiled me with the extras, warm milk and sugar in the coffee cup, and I struggled to drink the witch's brew in camp. Until Fred. His coffee made me mindful of the smooth brew at home. He also cooked flaky biscuits, rice, onions, sweet potatoes and stewed apples greatly contributing to everyone's comfort. I felt recovered from yellow jaundice, but chronic diarrhea plagued Alvin. Still, he refused to take the medicine the surgeon prescribed, said the dang stuff made him "see stars all the time."

"These are fine biscuits," I said, "and real coffee to wash them down."

"Your skin still looks yellow as—"Alvin ran to the latrine.

***

Will expressed dismay over the prosecution of the war. He did not send for Ann, but she wanted to ease her husband's burden, so she surmounted the difficulties of passes, foul weather and arrived at Pittsburgh Landing. Captain Coates of the 11th Illinois met her there. Alarming sounds of gunfire also greeted her, but Coates dismissed it as the return of night pickets discharging their guns. Captain Coates suggested he find Will, and until then she should stay on the boat.

Half an hour later Captain Coates returned wounded in two places, vivid evidence of fierce fighting. Now Ann could only wait.

Our company camped near a log-meeting house, someone said it was Shiloh church, a small affair made out of hewn logs. Johnny-jump-ups carpeted the ground in purple and yellow profusion. The petulant song of a redbird echoed through the woods. A continual stream of army wagons went to and from the landing with clucking wheels, drivers yelling oaths and cracking whips, mules braying. They assigned me to Major Bowman's battalion as bugler with no one to relieve me, so I had to be on the look-out all the time or risk playing the wrong call at the wrong moment.

April 1862 Shiloh, "Blow Boots and Saddles"

The Corinth Road and nearby bluff are the same height but cut apart by deep ravines and water courses. Streams formed excellent protection against attack on either flank; the land nearby was low and marshy this time of year.

General Sherman knew fresh rebel troops had arrived and fired on McDowell, but Grant had ordered Sherman not to bring on general engagement before Buell arrived. "Have you heard from Buell?" Sherman asked. When the answer was no, Sherman said, "Strange." He took out his map and placed it on the ground, but found no answer there either.

We received orders to be ready to scout early the next morning. Soon after dark the infantry spread blankets under trees to sleep. Anticipating battle they left tents behind and bedded on the ground, guns ready at their sides.

Sunrise that Sunday morning in Tennessee—38 minutes past five o'clock. A woodpecker tapped a sharp roll call. While we saddled horses, startled birds fled the woods all in a rush, and squirrels scattered. The next moment sounds changed in a flash. Lieutenant Hitt's horse got shot. The scene became one of desperate haste, terrible uproar and confusion, boys buckled on belts, and a staff officer galloped through the line, checked and whirled his horse, iron horseshoes crashing on tin mess plates. The horse's mouth flecked with foam; its eyes and nostrils red as blood.

Rifle fire awakened infantry regiments. Prentiss's line got attacked first, followed by an assault on Sherman's division. His beautiful sorrel got shot, so Sherman took a horse from his aide, McCoy, but it also got shot. He mounted his doctor's horse, and it went down. His orderly, Holliday, stayed close to the General's side, carried his carbine ready to defend Sherman, but a shot meant for the General killed him, too. Because his camp was at the front, rebs quickly captured Sherman's tent and other horses.

Sherman shouted, "Blow boots and saddles," and I blew vigorously. Damned to hell if I didn't, but also damned for doing so. While the notes still sounded, a soldier ran past earnest in his determination to get in line. The way he ran impressed me—then he got shot and his blood spattered my face.

Other buglers along the line caught and repeated the sharp, clear notes, a general call and demand, which cut through gunfire. Notes from bugle after bugle, drum after drum, front to rear, farther and farther away, sounds throbbing and rolling to rouse the men. The sun just now blushed the eastern sky.

Bullets buzzed around my head, but I got to my horse. Two battalions got in line in an amazingly short time. I heard screaming but did not want to see where the voices came from. Amid shouts and echoes, came the rebel yell, coordinated, high-pitched screaming, one-syllable sounds, *yi, yi, who, yip,* no two notes exactly the same, a thousand distinctive intimidations, hurled in our direction.

Not just his eyes but Sherman's whole body concentrated on the battle. He yelled orders for us to mirror infantry lines, keep out of fire as much as possible just advance or pull back as they did. "You men must discourage the enemy from giving hot pursuit." When ground troops moved forward, I wanted to dismount as a sharpshooter, but stayed in reserve, ready to charge. We formed a line near Shiloh church but got pushed back to make room for more foot soldiers. Wherever rebs advanced bodies paved brambly ground. A fragment of a shell struck Norman Powers in the groin. He slunk down by a tree with his carbine and revolver in his hands. "My time has come, but I intend to sell life dearly."

Will heard the roar of musketry, raced his men to the front toward Shiloh Church where he found a gap between General Prentiss and McClernand's troops. General Sweeney's brigade broke in pieces on the right. To my horror General McClernand withdrew and left Will exposed. Rebs dashed up, shrieking like eagles, and Federals on the left broke. Prentiss and Wallace got flanked, both on the left and right, lead tossed in from both directions. Prentiss wheeled his division left while Will about-faced to the enemy's flank. This wedged him in a vulnerable position. A rise of ground, normally barely noticeable, became a powerful headland when stubborn regiments defended it. Victory and disaster became equal possibilities in a sunken road. Shot and shell from the enemy came thick and fast. Trees rained branches, and Union boys dropped.

Assaults blazed with sheets of flame. The violence renewed itself again and again—and became a close-quarter, death grapple. Will and his men held while Confederates led brigade after brigade along the farm road, running through a small cotton field. Will reduced each assault to fragments. His corps fought twelve waves, each time losing more and more men, but they held together and fought with stern desperation. Their resistance delayed the Confederate advance and borrowed time for the rest of the army. When it came to his own safety my brother-in-law was brave, calm, cool in any strife. Will's men now aimed through a cloud of smoke and fire where they figured the enemy should be.

The rebels seemed countless. A sergeant, who carried the United States flag, got shot through the arm. Unwilling to see the flag fall, he gave the colors to another and went 20 steps to the rear but started to go back, appearing ashamed. Shortly thereafter a second bullet hit him in the neck. He died trying to hum a hymn.

Lines of men showed no fear—unbelievable if I had not witnessed the courage. We stayed on the field shifting positions, often in range of the enemy's artillery. When McAllister's battery lumbered to the rear, we followed. Couriers dashed up, racing for life, then raced away with replies. Pity the horse, with thick lather covering his flanks. Three times a commander called on cavalry to charge the enemy, and we got into position only to be sent back amid the screams as many boys fell. Many familiar faces will be seen no more.

Ann spent a long day on a steamboat. Wounded men arrived by the hundreds. Some could sit or stand, others came in completely helpless. She held bandages for surgeons. More and more men with gruesome injuries came aboard. Finally the deck became too crowded, and she moved to the top deck. The steamer continually transported men across the river. Over and back, over and back. The floors full of wounded, laid close like bricks in a row. Though dazed and horrified, Ann became a soldier, too.

The horrible screeching of hundred-pound shells shook the earth, and men threw themselves on the ground or sought frail shelter. Boys could not stand the scorching fire. Union troops became perfectly stricken. With so many killed, the rest broke ranks. Diminished in numbers, broken up by obstacles and the different speeds of running men, a trickle of retreating soldiers became a confused swarm. Constant flashes drove them, as did the sharp clean whistle of bullets and buckshot, thick air, hoarse with wails of wounded men. Each angry shout said someone new had been hit. Officers endeavored to restore order, draw up stragglers and urge them back but men jumped, fell or floundered rather than face the enemy.

Steamers stayed off the shore. They had to, or the rush of soldiers threatened to swamp the boats. At one point an officer, threatened the pilot with a pistol and ordered him to touch shore and take his men on board. The pilot pretended to obey him, but did not, which gave the frenzied man time to come to his senses.

Ann could be safer if she went below, but a show of fear on Ann's part made it harder for the pilot to stand firm. The presence of a gentlewoman helped quell turmoil. Her husband, father, brothers, brothers-in-law and dozens of friends fought today. Until she learned our fates, she tended unknown soldiers.

Ravines cut the field and timber choked it, leaving scant room for mounted movement. An order for cavalry to charge never came, a boiling disappointment, for we had trained for weeks. We waited, mounted, tucked under some trees, couriers ready to deliver orders across the field and, in my case, ready to play bugle calls. Dangerous service for men and horses, but no glory. A soldier's duty is to obey orders, and so we held back.

The men in the thick of it went through a baptism of fire. Rebels shouted as if being delivered from hell. Cries and shouts and smoke came from one direction and then the other. The line shivered and meant to burst. Regiments ceased to exist. My eyes disbelieved the sights. May God have mercy. A rout. Men turned their backs and ran. What had been confusion grew worse; the retreat became a stampede. How infectious fear is. It grows when yielded to, and once men begin to run, it becomes impossible to run fast enough.

We found ourselves in range of an enemy battery, and if their aim had been a little lower—catastrophe. Cannons make fearful noise. Curious how much louder guns sound when pointed at you than when turned away. A shell's long-drawn screech made my hair stand on end. Before they repositioned the guns, however, we slipped out of range.

Someone said the name Shiloh means 'place of peace,' but two armies practiced wanton destruction. Dead bodies and slaughtered horses desecrated the ground. The loss is personal; the loss is national. Men plunged. Horses reared. If hit, both cried sharp and quick. Animals screamed doubly loud as though owners betrayed their loyalty.

Generals Hurlbut and Sherman pulled us back. Will and his men came under triple fire. The road boiled with men and guns described by shouts, groans, order and bedlam. Rebel troops continued to crash and scream. Shrieks and murderous volleys shook the morale of men not accustomed to such clamor, and Will gave an order to pull back, but rebels surrounded them. Half-past four in the afternoon, rebs took General Prentiss prisoner.

Then a ball struck, and Will fell. Cyrus and three soldiers tried to carry Will to the rear. Two of those soldiers got shot, and the third ran. Cyrus could not lift Will on his own but dragged him to an abandoned caisson. Cyrus protected the body near some ammunition boxes and sadly left, escaping to the rear with the remnant of the division. Cyrus said, "Our great and terrible battle was over. A musket ball entered behind Will's left ear, took a slanting course and passed through his left eye." While superintending a pullback, Father learned Will had fallen, mortally wounded. That contained unstated worry because Cyrus rode at Will's side.

Over 2,000 Union soldiers surrendered. What would people say at home? Would local boys be forever disgraced?

On the rebel side, another hero fell. Confederate General Albert Sidney Johnston rode too far ahead of his troops and got shot in the leg. Johnston had opened the battle and caught us by surprise. He led from the front. His high-top boots seemed to be everywhere, directing his men and pushing Sherman back. During an afternoon charge, Johnston got shot behind the right knee but kept going until suddenly he slumped. When he slipped from his horse, rebel yells went silent. His injury paused the fight. The highest ranking casualty on either side became Johnston; the equivalent for Federals would have been to lose General Grant.

Revenge for Johnston's death enraged rebels. By nighttime Confederates pushed Federals to a pocket next to the river. The sun set red against the cliffs. The moon's waning crescent dared not shine on dispirited men. God only knows what nightmares haunted the soldiers.

We had needed every man that day, but a principal division did not get into action. General Lew Wallace mistook his orders and marched away from the fight. If he had been where Grant intended, the outcome could have been different. What could Grant do? How could we recover? As fighting ended for the day, it felt as if Confederates had dealt the Union a death blow. The nation staggered.

John Benson was a friend of Father's and a veteran of the Mexican War. He had made his living chopping cordwood or as a common laborer. I heard he fell at Shiloh, too, but could not find out where or locate the body for his family.

Nervous, high-strung General Sherman now showed a calm side. He held a key position—but with wholly raw troops, never before in an engagement. The ground undulated, and woods offered protection to soldiers on both sides. Confederates had made a number of attempts to turn the right flank, but Sherman posted his men in the right positions. His command decisions made up for deficient training. This day, however, rebels showed complete disregard for losses.

Grant declared, "We're not beaten yet by a damned sight."

How could he say that? Infantry had reached the limits of exhaustion—body and spirit. Rebels control our camps. Hunger gnawed, sharper than I thought possible. Confederates ate our stores of cheese, bacon and hardtack. They drank our coffee and tea. In some places, the lure of food caused a number of rebels to quit the field. I shuddered at what might have happened if they had not stopped to eat. Then Confederates spent the night in northern camps.

Cavalry occupied a position to the rear with nothing for the horses to eat. Some firing on our right front caused an alarm about ten o'clock. We were ordered into line and left in the saddle until morning as far as orders went, but after a while we dismounted and sat against trees, holding our horses. I lay sleepless wondering about Will and Cyrus. General Sherman had Holliday's body brought to his camp and buried under a bullet-scarred tree.

Rebs scavenged the field overnight. Their lamps glowed eerily in a rain shower. "Look 'it here—Yankee whiskey."

"Oh, be joyful!"

"Gimme a mouthful of that booze."

"And what have we here?"

"A photograph of someone's sweetheart."

"My mule's prettier'n that gal."

The sounds of carousing grew louder, and we envisioned the liquor supply evaporating as the band of brothers drank their fill.

"Figure d'is here battle's won?"

"Sure 'nough."

"Well then, fellahs, let us retire from the field."

The revelers staggered away. Had the Confederates truly won?

Rain fell harder to the peril of the wounded. Buell's Army of the Ohio moved up from Savannah, Tennessee, through swamps and pathless land. They ran a terrible race. His soldiers arrived breathless, footsore and faint with hunger; some regiments lost a third of their men, who dropped from the ranks and were left to recover or die, giving full force of meaning to the Biblical questions: What shall we eat? When shall we drink?

The storm provided cover for boats to ferry Buell's troops across the river. Steamers came out of obscurity, took on passengers and then vanished behind blue blankets of low-hanging smoke that covered the river. Each boat rode low in the water, ready to capsize. Ferries deposited reinforcements on our side. The sights on the landing must have added to the reinforcements' disillusionment. Along the beach several thousand soldiers huddled, most unarmed, many wounded, some dead. A confused mass of shell-shocked men and a few officers. Whenever a steamboat landed, demented soldiers had to be kept off with bayonets. When the craft pulled away, they sprang toward her and got pulled into the water, where some drowned. Men left on the landing suffered heavy rain, peal after peal of thunder and shrieks of the wounded, a night of horror. The sky shook with each clap, and earth trembled. Fleeting streaks of light, the metallic ring of explosions, fragments of shrapnel pinging as they hit unknown targets.

One man cursed a comrade for lying atop him but then found he swore at a dead man. Human nature tortured on the rack. Some dead. Some dying. Heaven filled their resting place with ankle-deep water.

Buell's men moved off the landing. Messages got passed along in whispers. Foot soldiers pressed closely to each other. If the column halted, many fell asleep, buoyed up by their fellows. Their feet struck dead men and at times hit wounded men with enough breath left to resent it. Lightning strikes might have allowed the enemy's guns to find our men, but thick forest helped hide arriving troops.

Supply wagons did not arrive as scheduled, but Grant did not wait. He ordered a counterattack. Commanders again decided cavalry could not be used. They sent us to gather up stragglers and return them to the army, an onerous duty, for many of the stragglers were sick and unable to march. We also retrieved ammunition from the dead, picking through cold bodies with grisly wounds.

As we rode through defeated companies, men held up bloodied hands to show they were not cowards. A fellow called out, "As God is my witness, I stood for our cause and did not shirk."

"Sure 'nuff," his companion said. "we're ready to die." But the wince on his face said otherwise.

Those fit for duty got sent back to reinforce parts of the line. When they moved out, the wounded cried, "Wade in and give 'em hell."

A train of four-horse wagons served as ambulances. Rebs and Federals alike left the field, not in small numbers, but in long processions. Some got carried on litters. Shattered fellows gave loud hurrahs to encourage those still fighting. I stopped to give a fellow a drink of water.

He nodded but barely took a sip. A bloody wound of his head was the reason.

"Take a breath," I said, "and I'll give you more."

The soldier tried to breathe, but the experiment failed, and I capped the canteen.

The infantry moved to the right flank of Sherman's division, this time with the support of Lew Wallace's division.

The Union attacked on the same battlefield as the previous day. The sounds of fighting increased. Wagons rolled. Horses screamed, got crippled and floundered in harnesses. Explosion followed explosion. The voice of a reb carried to my location, "Run for your lives." The battle got fought a second time—every bit as fierce—but in reverse. My heart pounded against my coat at the sight of bayonets plodding up the hillside. Here were Buell's reinforcements. The army may yet survive danger's dark hour.

At 10 o'clock Confederates rallied, and the armies went at each other like two armed mobs. This time our line held despite the continuous roar of cannon, crash, crash, crash, and volleys of musketry in quick succession. One part of the line surged forward but then staggered back.

By noon the front extended three miles, shrouded in smoke. Surely men could not see the targets, but blazed away in the direction of the enemy. Farm boys liked to conserve ammunition, not throw shots away. They grew up hunting small game like squirrels and learned to hit the heads, no other parts of little bodies, or they ruined the meat. Now, however, they aimed low, fired in a general direction. Let fate do the rest. If they hit an enemy, praise heaven. If not, reload and fire again. Gunfire rattled. Deep, shaking explosions and smart shocks, stray bullets whistled and conical shells marked the death-line. Still, the men cheered here or there in personal triumph. Orders went unheard in the din, which made bugle calls imperative.

Chaos became hysteria. Rebel soldiers stormed into a void but were too numb to take advantage. They walked, fired, stopped, reloaded, and in doing so, killed their own men. The Confederate offense faltered. The heavy forest confused communication. A musket barrage exploded along the front in roaring pandemonium. How did the blue line hold? Yet they did. Hard to see how—unless they feared getting shot in the back if they ran.

Union reinforcements meant we now outnumbered the enemy. Slowly rebels yielded, a little at one point and a little more at another point. The rebel retreat spread, and by half past one our army regained Sherman's original camp beyond Shiloh church. The order to mount up came. Our left swept up Lick Creek near Prentiss's original camp. The enemy still presented a regular front in good order, but the cannonade ceased, so cavalry went forward to pursue.

Our regiment arrived first and in minutes had 2,000 comrades at our heels, but then we discovered cannon placements a quarter mile ahead in brush so thick cavalry could not charge. General Grant ordered us to halt, wait, while he rode away to our left. A bullet ricocheted off Grant's scabbard, but he failed to notice. The cavalry's mass made us a target, so we moved to a ravine. Seconds after the last trooper rode over the rise, a shell burst where we had been, followed by many more. Infantry slipped through the brush to the enemy's battery and drove them back.

General Grant did not send further orders and when General Sherman came up it was nearly dark. Still, we went in pursuit and had some sharp skirmishing. The infantry, too, followed the rebel retreat, half mad with a glorious intoxication of success. Exhausted soldiers charged a quarter mile, then threw themselves on the ground unable to go one step farther.

The cavalry massed at Snake Creek, where we expected a fierce struggle for right of way. We rode for miles, parched for water, but when we came close, forgot our thirst. Bullets flew like flies. Rebels covered their retreat. With only one single corduroy road for us to cross, cavalry got ordered back.

Finally two exhausted opponents drifted apart. The battle ended with our troops occupying the same camps Monday night we had the previous Saturday. Despite their defeat, respect for two Confederate cavalry commanders grew. John Hunt Morgan gained a reputation for daring when he led a mounted charge late the first day, much to his credit. Nathan Bedford Forrest also showed himself to be a wizard of the saddle. He had sent scouts, wearing Union overcoats to Pittsburg Landing, and discovered Union reinforcements arriving the second day. Forrest sent appropriate warnings up the chain of command, but his superiors did not share Forrest's grasp of battlefield conditions.

Rebel prisoners included cadets from the Louisiana Military Academy where Sherman had been superintendant before the war. One cadet told the General how many students now fought against him. Sherman gave the young man socks and a shirt to wear, generous considering Confederates had cleaned out the camp. Sherman had lost all his money, two horses, saddle, bridle, bed—at this moment he also relied on scavenged goods.

When it grew dark, officers looked for a place for us to spend the night. We happened to be near the tents Will's men had occupied in the morning and took possession of them. Cyrus came and told us Ann was still on a transport at the landing. "What about the rest of the 11th Illinois?" I asked.

"Not more than 120 men remain." Cyrus averted his gaze. "The slaughter on both sides is unimaginable, not short of 12,000 killed and wounded. The wounded fill cabins, tents, steamboats, every conceivable place."

"I passed a man," I said, "whose stomach spilled out, and he held it in his hands."

"Do you know him?" he asked.

"A cousin of Ella's."

Cyrus put a hand on my shoulder. "Do not take extra risks. Mounted units don't have heavy losses all at one time like infantry but lose men through continual attrition."

"I hate to think what happened to Ann."

"It breaks my heart, too. The first night she stood on the boat deck, the red blaze of battle in her face and held an ivory-handled pistol ready to do her duty like a man. Elder Button, a naval officer, went to Ann during the battle to warn her."

"My husband commands a division and is safe," she insisted.

"Button merely repeated, 'It is an awful fight.'" Later on Cyrus went to tell her. "Will fell in full view of the whole division, and from that moment confusion reigned. I tried but could not carry him off the field." Cyrus again choked on the words Will was dead, and the enemy possessed the ground.

Ann filled another night slaking the thirst of wounded men. When soldiers neared death, she wrote letters to mothers, sisters or wives. Penning a few precious, final words to let other women know their loved ones' fate.

When it rained that night, Cyrus consoled himself Will no longer felt the cold. Cyrus gathered a squad to recover Will's body, as soon as Union forces cleared that ground. Monday morning Cyrus went to retrieve Will. To his amazement, Will still lived. The bullet had passed through his brain.

At ten o'clock, while Ann fed a wounded man, Cyrus went to her again. "Will has been brought in," and hurried to add, "we found him still breathing."

She flew to that boat. Will lay on the floor atop a narrow mattress. His face was flushed, but he breathed naturally, so like himself, save for a fearful wound in his head, a miracle and great joy—Will recognized her voice and clasped Ann's hand. "He knows me."

The surgeon said, "That cannot be."

Will's lips uttered, "Yes."

Father also heard the news—Will was not dead. Monday night at 11 o'clock, Father walked to the steamboat landing but learned Ann had taken Will to Savannah. General Walter Gresham gave up his room at post headquarters. Cyrus, Martin Wallace and Hitt Wallace went along to do what they could for Will.

Will's time grew short, but he remained calm. Ann watched every breath and tremor, unwilling to commit him to the care of God.

Father asked for leave to go to Savannah, but General Sherman ordered him to report on Tuesday morning with his entire command. For two days he pursued the enemy in the saddle. No delay could be more painful. Ann at Will's bedside, and Father unable to go to her. Finally Father snatched time for us to go. Will passed his fingers over Ann's hand and assured himself from the ring it was her. His grasp fell for a moment but searched for the ring again. Will lingered until Thursday evening when his pulse began to fail. He pressed Ann's hand to his heart, then waved her away. "We meet in heaven."

Ann clasped his body. "God led me here to soothe Will's last hours."

Men who bore the horror of battle, when they heard of Will's death, let tears run down their faces. Will's stubborn defense kept the enemy from watering their horses in the Tennessee River. Ann shared her loss with others because people quickly dubbed Will the "hero of Shiloh."

So many soldiers had died. North and South widows wailed. Previous death tolls seemed small, compared to the blood spilt at Shiloh. We became united in grief—our ranks much thinner but on both sides the will to fight remained.

I need not close my eyes to picture men quaking in fear, distraught, loading rifled muskets many times over—without ever firing a shot. How any man faced such withering fire escapes me. Though I survived, heartbreak rattled me.

I am not an expert on tactics but from my vantage point, generals had less to say about the outcome than the first line of soldiers. When shooting started, instinct silenced orders. The passion became—kill, kill, kill or be killed. Even survival faded. Blood-fever kept men in the field—it's the only possible explanation. One young rebel jammed a fence rail into a cannon muzzle, so his comrades could dash against the Union line.

Talking to others gives no reassurance. I pull away from other men. Their accounts fix morbid recollection. As they speak, wretched phantoms parade through my mind. I pour words into my journal, hoping to exhaust the vision, but terror rules—any man who says otherwise is crazy or a liar. Generals from both sides will write reports. I may even be asked to make some copies, but official information misses the mark. Battle plans go awry. The rebel yell is a soul-harrowing sound to hear. It's a wonder human ears can stand it. Heavy losses did not force rebels to surrender and, in fact, they have yet to yield. In my position, suspended between the ranks and command, officers who fail at the expense of soldiers put me on edge.

Belle wrote a letter about reactions back home. First people heard of a terrible battle which resulted in grand victory. Tuesday, April 8, 1862, the whole city rejoiced, but they did not see the dead or wounded. The next dispatch brought the heartbreaking casualty count and told them Will was among those killed. This news spread like a brushfire. Within ten minutes every flag in Ottawa lowered to half-mast. Groups with tearful eyes covered the streets.

99

General Grant sent Ann home with Father and full honors for Will's remains. Will's brothers and staff, his horse and possessions made the journey together and arrived Sunday, April 13, 1862. I belonged at the funeral, but was denied. I longed to be there, also longed for a few days to see life as it should be. Men sitting at windows reading newspapers; mothers getting little ones ready for Sunday school; cats stretched out on front porches. I willingly forego every military glory past, present and future, to tramp along the ravine with Ella for a few hours. No words need be spoken, for she shared the loss.

Will's funeral procession wound through Ottawa at four in the morning. Throughout the day thousands of citizens filed through the courthouse past Will's body. Rain turned the streets muddy, yet people thronged the funeral.

Someone asked General Grant what he thought of Will Wallace. Grant replied, "Had he lived, I would not be in command."

The 48th Illinois Infantry composed a tribute, asked me to write it down in proper style and send it up the chain of command: "Resolved, In the death of W.H.L. Wallace, the country lost a valuable citizen and devoted patriot, the army an efficient officer and brave soldier, who sealed his devotion to country with his life's blood. Resolved, That in General Wallace officers and men found an upright man; as commander, he was loved by all under him; a disciplinarian, but one who commanded respect and goodwill. Men of the 48th Illinois, who survived the battle at Shiloh will ever hold in graceful remembrance the name of William H.L. Wallace, whom they mourn now dead."

At Shiloh duty never ceased. My regiment pursued the enemy with other cavalry, infantry and artillery. We found dead soldiers still unburied, their uniforms caked with blood. These men came a long distance and took great pains to meet this fate. Even when corpses remained out of sight, stench made death impossible to ignore. Bodies changed color as they rotted. White men's faces went black, the appearance of negroes, an ironic fate. Burial details attended our men, but threw the enemy into gullies. They stood on top the rebel mound, straightened legs and arms, cracked limbs and tamped bodies down to fit as many as possible in a small space—took no time to register graves, notify next of kin, provide decent burial or identify the dead. They simply heaved dirt on the top. I turned aside and cried, not that anyone noticed.

Our company rode at the head of the column. Just a mile and a half out, enemy cavalry fired at us, retired a short distance and made another stand. From one point to another we drove them five miles. Then they made a last stand. Thomas Bail, a fellow I knew before the war, clashed sabers with a rebel. The reb raised up in his stirrups to deliver a cut, but Thomas parried the blow. The third finger of his right hand got crushed as the rebel's blade slid down his own. Thomas kneed the opponent, knocked him off his horse then looked down, deciding whether to kill him where he lay. An indescribable look came over his face—and he fired. "I can look at the carcass of a man," he said, "with the same feeling as a hog."

The main body of rebels fled, and we rode in pursuit. A riderless mare with a blood-soaked saddle ran nearby. A canteen on the horn was Confederate issue. I came alongside, and Rhoderic knew what to do. He spoke to her in soft nickers, "nnnhehheh," and put his head down to show the mare gentle intentions. The mare slowed and calmed down. I wiped the blood away with a handkerchief and took her along as a spare mount to give Rhoderic a much needed rest. Then we came upon Union stragglers, themselves bleeding, and I turned the mare over to their corporal.

When we left the mare, she squealed.

Rhoderic halted. "Come on, boy," I told him. "We are both sorry to leave her." Rhoderic dropped his head in resignation. A humbling sight—to see a horse show more concern for the other side than human beings.

Soldiers found another abandoned Confederate horse, this one raw-boned, ugly and apparently good-for-nothing. As a joke, the officer sent it with compliments to Colonel Lagow, an aid-de-camp for General Grant. Lagow was a wealthy man and kept an excellent mount. Everyone expected Lagow to reject the crude gift. However, Grant saw it and declared the animal a thoroughbred. "If Lagow does not keep the horse, I will." That settled the matter. Grant named the mount Kangaroo. With rest and care, he turned out to be magnificent.

When Confederates overran our camp at Shiloh, all our goods disappeared. I had no clothing except what I wore. Fortunately, I had tucked the current journal in my blouse and sent the prior volume home. The tent remained standing with nothing inside. Stolen possessions should have been a trifle compared to losing one's life. Yet the loss mattered. My friend Alvin is a stoic fellow, broad set, dark complexion and coal colored hair, but never dark in spirit—until now. The loss of his Bible and picture of his fiancée caused Alvin to glare and mumble.

101

I said, "Say it clear."

He shouted, "I will teach my children to hate secesh."

"Have you set a date for the wedding? Surely it's too early to talk about children." A cynical smile flashed over Alvin's lips but quickly faded. He gestured toward a broken tree, two fragments shaped like hands, splintered fingers above interlaced with those below. Other trees had large branches lopped off, or tree tops bowed to the ground. Bullets and grapeshot peppered bark, from roots to a height of twenty feet. Air frothed Alvin's lips. "I don't care what anyone says. I will hate them till the day I die."

We fell asleep on bare ground, and I dreamt I got the drop on General Beauregard. My name heralded throughout the North. 'Charlie Dickey, a hero assures his legacy as the man who captures General P.G.T. Beauregard, CSA.'

Next morning General Sherman detailed me as his bugler and glory faded. The General rode another new mount. The loss of his best warhorse made him look as insane as people claimed. That horse had shown extreme anxiety. From the action of the horse alone, he should know the enemy approached, but Sherman disregarded the horse's warning and refused to take cover. The General required all his horses and all his men to stay calm, possess speed, strength, endurance and keep up. Instead of dreams of glory, I spent the whole day in the saddle. That night I dreamt of featherbeds, roast chicken and buttery biscuits, my sister Belle made especially for me—no more dreams of capturing Confederate high command.

We caught the rebel rearguard seven miles south. Father commanded the cavalry, came up and saluted Sherman. "General," he said, "I see we face the enemy's cavalry. Grant me the privilege of fighting cavalry with cavalry."

"Colonel Dickey," Sherman replied, "kindly attend to your own business."

Father saluted and retired. I felt heat rise in my chest at his take down. General Sherman frowned and ordered infantry to engage. They started out boldly, but rebels had stationed men in an old shack at the side of the road. When the infantry passed, the enemy opened up. Shiloh left our boys panicky. They tumbled backward among our horses, fired their guns and threw us into confusion. An order was given to fall back and form a new line, and we rode out of the infantry.

A tall, lithe, straight figure with the look of an Indian led a charge, his right arm extended. His high, harsh voice made his men jump to obedience. A bearing I will never forget—Nathan Bedford Forrest in person. A Union soldier shoved his musket in Forrest's side and fired. The force nearly lifted the General out of the saddle, but he grabbed another Union soldier, hauled him onto his horse as a shield and rode clear of danger. He dumped the man once he broke free and galloped back to his own troopers. He had to be gravely wounded, but Forrest escaped.

After firing ceased, most troopers got sent back to the old camp where feed was available. Only our company camped near the enemy with orders to report to General Sherman at daylight.

He sent us out to scout the enemy. Men, who had died trying to walk out, lay in the roads, the timber. Destruction spilled out of Shiloh. Men fell in heaps, woods caught fire, clothing burned off, corpses populated the pathway.

Screams from wounded horses are as horrible a sound as I ever want to hear. Animals voice their shock without reservation. Horses sputter in death, blaming their riders, thudding as they collapse. One horse still alive gnawed his wound, all a frenzy, still hitched to a team with the other five dead, one horse crushed under the gun they had been hauling. Sergeant Cook did the merciful thing and ended the wounded one's suffering with a well-aimed bullet.

Abandoned, wounded men had fallen in the road. One beardless youth gave looks of entreaty. Blood oozed from a chest wound, and red froth bubbled at the corner of his mouth. A staff officer rode past at full gallop, struck a puddle and splashed mud in the soldier's face, which now turned in despair, as though asking to die in peace.

Sergeant Cook went over, wiped the man's face with a handkerchief and said, "Let me help you." The only reply was a death rattle, and in a few minutes he breathed his last. So Cook announced, "This brave fellow is dead."

Afterward Cook did not speak for some time. We all had seen mangled, eviscerated, limbless bodies but to experience death close-up when all else is quiet does not compare. The moment of death struck harder. The young man's life came to an unreasonable conclusion, but he mastered the transition better than Cook and I did.

A cavalryman cannot ride over a dead horse; his own horse bolts and refuses to do it. However, a horse will run over a dead man. Ever-moving horses trample bodies. When it got dark, Rhoderic's hooves thudded into a corpse, and I could not look.

Details worked for days to bury the dead—hurrying to get them away from sulky daytime weather, swelling sun and leaden-air heaviness. Excitement rules on the day of battle. Horror reigns for days after. I heard 3,500 men died outright, and hundreds more followed. Devastation looked like the open gates of Hell. General Sherman disbelieved his eyes—anyone with human feelings had to be shaken. "This scene," Sherman said, "should cure anyone of war."

One rebel trooper busied himself with the task of cleaning his rifle. After a battle every soldier has to do it, but this fellow, while sound of body, had a blank look on his face. He filled the gun barrel with warm water, plugged the ends and shook to agitate the water. Then he should have attached a rag to a ramrod and run it through with an abrasive, such as ashes. This man, however, never finished shaking the barrel. He kept on shaking, never able to complete the agitation, and no one compelled him to stop.

I tied Rhoderic to a wagon loaded with oats, ripped open a sack and entered one of the tents. Inside, a dead soldier rested on some hay. The next tent had two dead men, so Alvin helped carry the first to rest with the pair. We gave most of the hay to our horses but reserved some as mattresses and fell into exhausted sleep.

Again at daylight we saddled up, Captain Wemple in command. We rode left along the front and found a large house used as a hospital. While Wemple talked to the surgeon, we stood in the midst of 50 rebel stragglers, not wounded. The rebs had no officers among them and talked with us like neighbors. We counted 280 wounded Confederates. One of them waved me close. He had been shot in the belly and grabbed my arm. "Find a priest."

I pulled back. "No clergy are at hand."

A frantic look widened his eyes. "I'm Catholic. I need a priest and absolution before I die."

"Surely—"

His grip became a spasm.

I said, "May the Lord free you from your sins." And though I didn't know the rite, I fingered the sign of a cross on his forehead before he died.

We did not have means of taking so many wounded men off the field, so Wemple accepted the hospital's surrender with pledges to care for Union soldiers until ambulances came.

I picked up an abandoned officer's saber. Two young men who belonged to a Louisiana regiment watched every move I made, as I did theirs. They looked too neat to have fought in a two-day battle and were probably stragglers. One wore cavalry insignia, so I asked him what happened to his horse.

A mournful look filled his eyes. "A brilliant saddle horse tripped and fell."

We had passed many riderless horses, which got on much better than troopers without mounts. Further on we came to a large one-room house with no surgeon but a dozen wounded men. A corporal from an Ohio regiment lay mortally wounded near a bed containing a dead rebel colonel. We took the corpse out and placed the Union man on the bed. A regiment of reb cavalry dashed along a ridge east of us, so we could not stay to help him further.

Infantry pickets fired on the rebs, showering a volley of bullets over us. Because they aimed high, we reached the place General Sherman had lined up the infantry. While our captain reported, a private fired his gun, and Sherman ordered the private shot.

The man's colonel interceded. "He fought both days and remains on edge."

Sherman said, "Excuse him then with a stern reprimand." The General sent cavalry out again. We passed a dead Confederate artillery captain, 17 of his men, 18 horses, their dismounted guns and one exploded caisson—a battery that had come all the way from New Orleans. The captain still wore his saber in its sheath, his uniform, sash, boots and spurs resplendent. He looked ready to make a good fight, but his troops were a wreck.

The day became a blur of sights, smells and terrible camps. The land could not sustain armies this size. Rain made roads useless, difficult on men and horses. Buell's army suffered greatly. They had rushed to Shiloh and left equipment, tents and cooking utensils at Savannah. Inclement weather, stench and deprivation weighed men's spirits down. Terrain troubled us. General Halleck intended to march to Corinth in only two days and show the rebs his mighty army, but flooding rains carried away bridges. Halleck could not funnel 100,000 men along a single route, and his army could not negotiate the alternative route through thick timber.

Late at night we reported to General Sherman. His tent had no comforts, just a saddle to sit on. He just returned from a lively skirmish, and his staff scrambled to find something for him to eat. He ordered us back out two miles to picket. We reached our post in impenetrable darkness and sat on our horses until daylight. As sentinels we knew countless lives depended on us remaining alert. A soldier dozed at his peril and jeopardized his comrades. If I fell asleep, I also risked court-martial, with a maximum penalty of death by firing squad. The lightest punishment was extra guard duty. Mindful of the consequences, we ate cloves, and slapped ourselves to stay awake. The duty meant boredom with an equal measure of danger. One of Forrest's scouts mistook us for his company. He reached a point a rod away, and Alvin called, "Surrender!"

Like General Forrest earlier, the scout wheeled his horse. He nearly collided with Rhoderic. Our eyes met in surprise, but by the time I raised my saber, he dashed off, dancing through shots from the whole platoon.

When the full extent of losses at Shiloh became known, Union Major General Henry Halleck suddenly took a cautious approach—as a way to yield better results with fewer casualties. Halleck came to the field, relieved Grant, and divided Grant's men between Generals Thomas and Pope. Halleck declared, "Richmond and Corinth are now the strategic points of the war." The way he equated a small town like Corinth, Mississippi, with Richmond sounded surprising, but two major railroads crossed there, a vital place for the Confederacy. Halleck, as commander of the western theater, felt the outcome of secession rested in Corinth.

Citizens in Corinth must have heard the cannonade at Shiloh. The roar began for them, as it had for us, with Sunday breakfast—no semblance of religion in that. Every mouth spewed rumors as to the numbers, whereabouts and whatabouts of the Confederate army. One old gentleman, who worshipped Nathan Bedford Forrest, claimed, "It's impossible for Yankees to ride into Corinth. Rebels have made the town a staging point."

Two major railroads—the Memphis and Charleston ran east and west; and the Mobile and Ohio went north and south. Scouting revealed it as home to the county seat, Corona Female College, a brick courthouse, five churches, three large hotels and assorted small businesses. Homes were built southern style with a door in every room, facing the street to catch breezes and welcome winds inside. Immense porticos encouraged siestas. Rich people decorated their yards with shrubbery and neatly trimmed trees.

Its climate, however, left much to be desired. Corinth sat on low land between two creeks, a depression of earth filled with miasmal fumes and disease. Alvin and I called it a swamp. The town had muddy streets, the worst water and far too much sickness, but because its railroads led to the heartland of the Confederacy both armies longed to possess it—and we followed Confederates toward town.

Capture of the river forts had dealt secession a heavy blow. In Corinth, we expected revenge to stiffen rebel ranks and hoped we arrived before they entrenched.

Four gray sentries rode along the crest of a hill, but the first crack of our rifles sent them galloping out of sight. How many comrades did they ride to warn? Clanging Union infantry moved up river, Buell's we believed, but everything was kept secret, and nothing was certain. We anticipated another fight soon.

General Sherman marched two brigades toward Corinth and found the passage strewn with abandoned wagons, ambulances and limber carts for towing caissons. Abandoned limber carts showed rebels' desperation. Guns were driven into position on limber carts. In action, cannoneers detached the gun from the cart. The gunner mounted the sight and aimed. Another man consulted the firing table in the limber box to choose fuse time and prepare the round. Rebels had carted off cannons but abandoned limber carts and boxes, thereby crippling 20 batteries. Flags hung limp with no wind to buoy them up. Banners marked field hospitals, overflowing with wounded men. Southern surgeons wore blood-smutched aprons. Southern women showed up to help. One might expect southern women to turn deaf ears to the groans of wounded Union prisoners, but they helped all the boys equally and shared what comforts they had. One kind-hearted woman showed up with her seventeen-year-old son, bringing grits for wounded men to eat. When I thanked her for this mercy, she said, "My husband is in the southern army, and I cannot care for him, so we do unto others." After dark, she and the boy slipped through the lines to join fleeing friends. Wherever she goes, I hope God blesses her.

Alvin Chapin squirmed in the saddle.

"We will be called on soon enough," I said.

"I feel the worst being idle." Alvin grimaced. "I long to get back in."

I said, "Let's pray for the infantry's success."

Civilians in Corinth fled like deer as we approached. Planters, women and children scurried away; only a few stout-hearted folks remained. Most locals supported the South, spied for them or cared for the sick even though residents suffered at the hands of Confederates as much as Federals. Both armies cut timber and burned fence rails. Rebel camps ruined farmland with skill equal to "barbarian" Yankees.

Headquarters learned of another Union victory when troops from Missouri and Illinois defeated Confederates under Major General Earl Van Dorn at Pea Ridge. However, that meant Van Dorn hurriedly sent the survivors to reinforce Corinth. Regiment after rebel regiment rode the Memphis and Charleston Railroad into town.

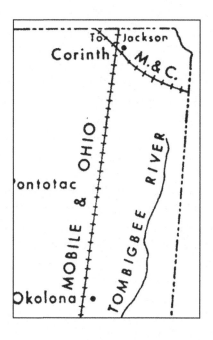

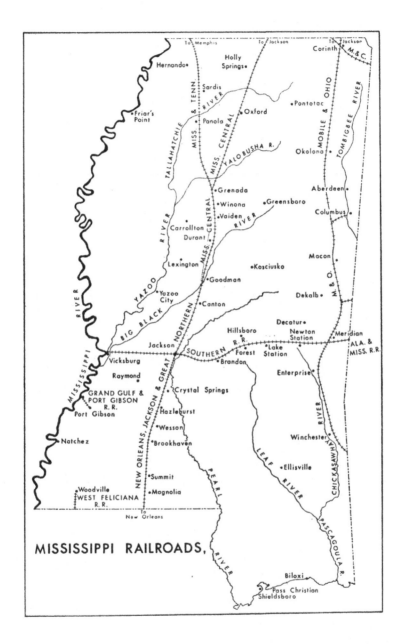

MISSISSIPPI RAILROADS,

On April 14, 1862, General Sherman ordered Major Samuel M. Bowman and the 4th Illinois Cavalry to destroy the railroad bridge across Bear Creek. Major Bowman picked 100 of us to drive enemy pickets across the Creek. Rebs set fire to bridges to impede our progress, but we dashed up the Creek at full speed. Bowman also placed a mounted platoon on the eastbound track to stop trains from that direction. The rest of us marched into a swamp within a quarter mile of the target. Men dismounted, some to fight on foot and others went to work with axes. The bridge had two spans 240 feet long with stone piers and abutments. Bowman positioned two platoons as sharpshooters with orders to fire at the enemy wherever seen. To me he said, "Bugle an advance on the bridge."

One private failed to respond and straggled behind. Rebs demanded he surrender, but he cried, "Never."

Again told, "Surrender," he yelled for us to fight on—so they shot him. As good a soldier as any who wore a Union uniform, but unable to say the words, 'I give up.'

The party with axes reached the trestle and began to cut away. Others set the bridge ablaze. In one hour the span tumbled into the swamp. Five hundred feet of trestle gone, but we had no means to destroy stone piers. In the process we killed four enemy guards, took two prisoners and returned to camp before sundown.

By April 24th all the southern reinforcements had pulled into Corinth. Estimates said rebels now had 70,000 men. Van Dorn arrived April 30th to supervise the building of earthworks and abatis. We watched seven miles of fortification go up along ridgelines fronted by marshy, meandering creeks. Five crescent-shaped works with siege guns guarded the roads leading in, the so-called "Beauregard line." Confederates felt no need to construct works south of town because the Tuscumbia River shielded them from rapid advance. By May 1st the South had created a great rally point in Corinth.

The slow Federal advance gave them time to complete preparations. Every Federal soldier expected a battle worse than Shiloh. Undoubtedly Beauregard and Van Dorn prepared to turn prior defeats into victory.

While the army kept moving, our health improved. Spirits rose, and we became confident of ending the war. Cavalry scouted and picketed. Much of the time pickets served in sight of rebels. The sides skirmished almost daily, and yet on May mornings, when rifles ceased firing, birds sang sweetly, the morning breeze brought the perfume of flowers, and it became hard to imagine why we had to fight a war.

I wrote to my sister Belle and asked hard questions. 'How does Mrs. Campbell seem to bear the loss of Daniel? We all lost a fine friend when

Daniel was taken, and no one feels his loss more than I do. I think the army lost many of its best men. Yes, I know it did. I pity Sergeant Lish's family. Fellow soldiers respected him. Clark Winchester's mother will mourn his loss, too, as we all will.' Clark had written a final letter, and I forwarded it for Belle to put into his mother's hand. A banner at the top of Clark's letterhead showed an eagle in flight, streamers flowing from its beak, bearing an inscription, 'One people.' The motto below said: 'From Canada to the Gulf of Mexico, from the Atlantic to the Gulf of Mexico.' One people—Clark had died to unite us again as one people. I wrote another letter to Ella but not about war. Writing to her was a diversion. I described terrain and pressed several wildflowers in the page, hoping they arrived somewhat intact to show her the Creator's handiwork.

Union pickets served within speaking distance of rebels, agreed not to shoot each other, put down our arms, walked between the lines and saluted each other. 'How are you Yank?' and 'how are you reb?' Then proceeded to have friendly chats; shared meals of hardtack, and bade each other farewell. 'Perhaps the next time we meet in battle.' 'I'll give you the best licks I can if we do.' They asked if we were the 4th Illinois Cavalry, and we proudly said so. 'We know you from several brushes.' 'That a fact?' 'You worsted us at Shiloh, but we're not afraid of Illinois sodbusters.' 'We can give you reasons to be.' 'You pose no threat to us, for we're proud to be the 1st Mississippi Cavalry.'

After his victories, General Grant sent for his wife and their young son, Jess. The day they arrived I served as part of the General's escort. Grant rode out to meet Mrs. Grant's train. When the train pulled in, General Grant could not wait for his wife but jumped on, greeted everyone kindly and worked his way through the train. "Is Mrs. Grant aboard?"

When he emerged with Mrs. Grant on his arm, a broad smile brightened his face. He escorted her and Jess to an ambulance, serving as her carriage. Before she stepped in, however, Mrs. Grant turned back to look at General William Farrar Smith, whose face turned red with chagrin.

"Whose ambulance is this?" she asked.

"It belongs to headquarters," said Grant, "I use it at my pleasure."

Mrs. Grant leaned closer to him. "On the train, Baldy said *his* ambulance would be at the train, and he would drive me and Jess wherever we needed to go."

"You didn't know I would come to meet you?"

"Oh, I assured the general you would. However, he insisted military matters weighed you down, and I must depend upon his hospitality."

General Grant left Baldy standing at the depot.

I think Mrs. Grant a model lady; medium size; healthy complexion; brown hair; blue eyes, which are crossed. She dresses well and busies herself knitting every idle moment. All-in-all worthy of a general. Their close family bonds made me ache with loneliness.

Three classes of women inhabit camp, but they stay strictly aloof from one another. Wives and daughters of colonels, captains and higher officers constitute the first class. Rough cooks and washers who have husbands along are a second class. The first two groups never concern themselves with the third and smallest group. Some females in the third tier have elegant manners but live in seclusion without the respectability of wedding rings. They strut around in hoops and crinolines, tempting us to catch them, but seeing the Grants together reminds me of John's advice to wait for marriage and I find ways to stay busy.

The distinction between classes of women is not lost on General Grant either. He exploded in anger when guards brought him a straggler, who had assaulted a respectable woman. The victim told a tearful story. "He took out a revolver and said, 'God damn you. I will blow you to pieces if you don't let me do it.' I was sitting with a child on my lap and got up to leave. He pushed me on the bed and entered my person with his member as well as he could." The General sprang up, seized a musket from a guard's hand, struck the offender over the head and knocked him to the ground. Grant had an extreme horror of such crimes and ordered the offender arrested. I shuddered for the violated woman, but even more for that soldier. Grant showed no mercy. A man is a fool to commit rape when willing women can be found.

A provost marshal shaved the rapist's head in front of his company. His captain made a promise. "I'll have you sentenced to hard labor and drummed out of the service."

Grant also issued orders against taking civilian property. This, however, men ignored with impunity. Enoch Hunter got caught gutting a pig. His lieutenant berated Hunter for violating orders, until Hunter explained how it happened. "I was sitting down by a tree with my saber across my lap, and the pig ran against it and killed itself."

The lieutenant relented, thinking this a satisfactory explanation, and we dined on roast pig, including the lieutenant.

In her next letter Ann wrote a strange warning. "Guard against unfeeling recklessness."

The word 'unfeeling' made me blanch. After Shiloh, I put feelings aside. 'Unfeeling' is precisely what I wanted to be, but couldn't write that to Ann. Instead I replied, "I am safe. Providence preserved me in battle and enabled me to do my duty." The words looked stiff on the paper, but I sent them off unchanged.

At the end of April we raided near Purdy, tore up a lot of track rail, burned ties and trestlework and captured an engine because the train crew stopped to hunt for a break we had cut in the telegraph wire. We rode at night, but our guide got lost in the dark, forcing us to halt until daylight. Night overtook us a second day, and the command got scattered in the dark. The main body arrived in camp at midnight, but quite a good many straggled in the next day.

It rained a good portion of the time, soaked us and turned roads to muck. My clothes did not dry for days. Most soldiers had only one pair of pants, and these became caked in mud. Quite a sight—men standing bare-footed in the rain in their drawers, washing trousers. Some, however, did not take them off, just stepped into a convenient mud hole and washed out the worst.

Commanders scheduled the campaign against Corinth for April 29, but different branches had trouble coordinating movement. Pope moved out first. Buell had to negotiate several major creeks, still rain swollen. Thomas marched on better ground along the high ridge. In addition to staggered starts, each army met different resistance. Cannoneers moved their own guns, an unenviable job in hilly terrain. The driver rode one pack animal while controlling others. Artillerymen must work in harmony. Other regiments can be reduced in strength and still remain effective, not so artillery, which must remain complete in all its parts—men, horses and materiel–all serve or falter together.

On May 4th cold rains came. Operations stopped. Water flowed in the tent like a river and threatened to wash me away. The whole army stuck in mud. Advance became impossible, except by building a corduroy road. The drinking water filled with tadpoles and wiggletales. Infantry had to work in the rain late at night when wagon trains arrived. When the rain diminished, the army continued its offensive.

Engineers continually repaired roads or constructed new ones. Considering weather and terrain, the armies moved at good speed. Perhaps too easily. The lack of Confederate resistance lulled us into a sense of security.

Rebel deserters indicated their men were dying from illness, muddy water to drink and reduced food rations.

"Then came the final insult," a deserter said. "The Confederate Congress conscripted us. We signed up for a year but got told we must serve two more."

"So's we're goin' home to care for our families."

How many remained to defend the town? We celebrated the growing number of deserters.

Union General Pope asked for trouble, however. He advanced his troops to Farmington, a park-like plateau covered in blue grass with copses of woods—where the Confederate right wing stood firm. May 6th, Beauregard responded to Pope's deployment. Pope had played into rebel hands by isolating one brigade. The men exhausted their rations and expected to be relieved, but no replacements appeared, only column after column of Confederates, flying battle flags. Some Federals ran. Others opened fire. Rebels gave an unearthly yell, a high-pitched howl that rose from deep inside as though demons gave it strength. Their advance came double-quick. The roar of artillery mingled with musketry rattles. Confederate artillery shells hit the Union line, and bodies flew in the air. A new Federal line formed but gave up and skeedaddled back to the main army.

A Confederate battle flag flapped in the breeze. The flag looked hateful and defiant. I wanted it down, so I held on it, let my gun fall until the sights reached waist-high. Then smoke obscured the bearer. I fired anyway, and the damned thing still flew.

The 8th Wisconsin got caught in the thick of fighting, including their mascot, an eagle called "Old Abe." When rebel cannons found correct range, soldiers hit the ground. Old Abe flew off his perch, too, and prostrated himself on the dirt, flattened, spread eagle next to his Wisconsin handler. The soldier picked up the bird and gave him a stern order, "Hold your perch," but Old Abe refused, not once but six times. The handler finally threw the pole down. The eagle crept close and stayed at the soldier's side until the regiment rose to retreat, then the bird leapt up and resumed its perch.

Old Abe's renown spread, and the 8th Wisconsin became known as the Eagle Regiment. The good news passed down the line. "Old Abe eagle came through the fight. He lost a few feathers is all." The 8th Wisconsin saved nothing except themselves and the eagle. They left behind weapons, blankets, overcoats, knapsacks and diaries, which provided information to

114

the enemy.

Other units coveted Abe because the bird dined on insects and vermin. Lizards crawled thick on the ground like grasshoppers back home. Loads of snakes like cottonmouths and copperheads also around. Old Abe knew how to handle the biggest serpent, but I felt sorry for him. His handlers clipped his wings and tethered him to a perch with a strong cord. When the army marched, Abe's handlers walked with the color guard, a place of honor, but the name Abe was a dishonor. That nickname did not please Mr. Lincoln. He hated the name Abe. Nobody who knew him called him that. Even his wife called him "Mr. Lincoln" or more familiarly "Father."

An eagle made an enviable companion, however, for the way it handled vermin. When a lizard ran inside Alvin's shirt, and he danced a jig to dislodge it and then had to go wash his pants before he appeared in public again. When I asked if he fed the lizard to Abe, Alvin swore under his breath.

Sherman's Division covered the extreme right of the Union line at Corinth. Cavalry did picket duty and scouted nearly every day. We stationed along a road where everyone expected rebel troops to pass. "You will be relieved soon." But, replacements did not arrive, and we sat on our horses all night in a drizzling rain, two in each place, a few rods apart with orders to remain vigilant. My partner, John Cleveland, leaned on his horse and slept until morning. I did not sleep because gnawing hunger kept me awake. However, I did not see or hear anyone.

Two cavalry companies under command of Captain L. D. Townsend got the honor of pushing reconnaissance forward. They met the enemy's picket and drove Confederates some distance, gaining a vital position at the crossroads and protecting the right flank from attack.

Rebel deserters, who came in now, claimed large numbers of reinforcements had arrived from New Orleans, South Carolina and Georgia, inflating the enemy by tens of thousands of men. Had reinforcements truly come? The Union moved barely a mile, stopped and sat for days. Soldiers wanted to move quickly to secure Corinth, even if it meant a major battle. Complaints became contagious. "Is it beginning to look like something will be done?"

"If Halleck turns us loose, this rebellion will soon be put down."

"No question of doubt we can drive them to the Gulf States."

What Halleck waited for we couldn't guess. He ordered men to dig rifle pits and throw up earthworks on a much-exposed outpost. Then put the 20th Illinois and a section of artillery under command of Lieutenant Colonel Richards to hold it. But no advance.

Two contending armies faced off four miles from each other. Neither ready to give ground or advance on the other. Our reconnaissance trips repeatedly met enemy pickets or reconnoitering parties.

Newspaper correspondents wrote scathing articles about Halleck's hesitation, so he banned reporters from camps and stopped soldiers' mail. The loss of newspapermen meant nothing, but losing letters hit hard. We all longed for letters. Each new one more precious than the last. Ann filled hers with encouragement. Belle provided fun and gossip. Ella posed questions in her letters, concerned about my safety. In the last one she gave me a blanket pardon, "Never mind others so much. Take care of yourself and come home as soon as you can." Her words boosted my spirits. Ella cared more about me than my conduct as a soldier, something no one else said, or even suggested. Everyone else in my circle expected me to prove my bravery and never flinch.

Letters meant the world to Sid Smith and Frank Warren. Frank had a new wife, and Sid an old girlfriend. Each received five letters a week. Sometimes the ladies' news made them turn pale, but to cut off letters completely amputated their loved ones, as if without anesthetic. They made up their minds to desert, but Sergeant Cook found out. "You boys gonna quit, just when we get ready to fight?"

"There's limits to the things a man can stand."

"And your women?" Sergeant asked. "How do they feel about shirkers?"

This made Sid and Frank pause. The choice to stay or go became a hard one to make. After some hemming and hawing and private discussion, they stayed loyal, if indignant over the limits of army life.

We scouted and came in touch with a considerable force. After a short skirmish, Sherman ordered me to blow retreat. My jaw quaked. I didn't like to do it, as the enemy might hear and catch us as we returned through a narrow passage only two men could use at one time. Fortunately, rebs did not follow.

Building entrenchments at the end of every advance meant hard duty. Every man became an engineer. Murmured criticism of our snail's pace buzzed like an insect swarm. During heavy rains the quartermasters failed to bring up sufficient food and forage, so General Sherman ordered every ounce of provisions "regarded as precious as diamonds." Continual alarms meant we slept armed, just spread blankets and bedded down with gun and accoutrements. On many occasions we jumped up and formed at short notice. Foreboding grew. An all-out fight against a strong Confederate position had to come soon.

One night gunshots got up a scare. Pickets ran in, "We were fired on." So all rolled out in minutes, guns in hand, fanned out but found no enemy. When we learned the source of fire, everyone had a good laugh. Two privates had gone foraging and encountered a squad of pigs. The two got placed under arrest and scheduled for court-martial. No word issued on the fate of the pigs.

Sharpshooters, hiding in the trees, practiced their skills. Rifle balls whizzed by our heads as we stood guard. Worse yet, friendly fire. A soldier from the 6th Iowa shot a man from the next regiment crossing beyond the line, even near friendly units a soldier had no assurance of safety.

Halleck delayed so long men grew complacent. Boredom overrode fear. We learned a new game called baseball. I showed no skill swinging the stick to hit a yarn-covered walnut, but enjoyed the game nonetheless. Even when cannons fired, soldiers refused to stop a game.

Enemy cavalry ran around in bodies as large as 1,000 men, threatening supplies, so we patrolled every day. Red Sulphur Springs is a picturesque place, the best I ever saw, with double cottages, horse stables, kennels, quarters for the servants, all in good repair. White Sulphur Springs, four miles farther, looked nearly as good. In one house a dozen finely dressed ladies gathered, and the major sent me to make inquiries. Up close the ladies looked pretty, quite a treat to observe.

My approach caused a flurry.

"You are the first Union soldier we ever saw. None of us have ever been North."

They delayed me asking questions about geography and society.

"On Sunday we indulge and come together."

"And the men?" I asked.

"Not at home."

Then one belle asked, "Where is the main body of your army?"

"You are all wearing finery," I said, "so I will not trouble you with details."

Our captain figured the ladies expected Confederate officers. He found their tracks within a mile of ours, but they had veered into a swamp on the run. A dozen Union boys returned to the house and ate the Sunday dinner, but without the company of the ladies who had flown.

Cannons from both sides played several times a day. The Union line stretched ten miles long and besieged rebels. Hundreds of rebels deserted, saying they received less than half rations for ten days. One Confederate battalion mustered 500 local citizens into service, but even the commander ran off. Five deserters came within our lines, and one carried a dozen eggs, which we considered more valuable than prisoners.

If deserters lived nearby, they went home. They had none of the qualities of army men anyway. Their dress was dirty, their arms rusty or uncared for, their general appearance like vagabonds.

On our side, divisions got in each other's way. Union officers had trouble directing an army this large. Strict orders forbid fires and noise. Commanders went to great lengths to keep their positions secret, only to find they faced other Federals, not the enemy.

Meanwhile the army inched closer. A whippoorwill serenaded camp for over an hour. Corinth was a fine place for wildlife. Nights were deliciously cool after sunset. General Halleck had relegated General Grant to oblivion. Grant moped around various headquarters and spent time with Sherman. Hard for Grant to remain quiet, however, and he produced a plan of attack, suggesting we go in from the northwest where Confederate defenses appeared weakest. Halleck scolded Grant in writing. Grant threatened to resign until Sherman talked him out of it.

Danger of skirmishes receded, and siege developed. Talk went back and forth across enemy lines. "How far is Corinth?" one Union soldier shouted.

"So damned far, you'll never get thar!"

The longer we waited the more soldiers complained about "Grandma Halleck." I was anxious, not for another fight, but to end the suspense.

Citizens must be praying for the ground to open up and swallow both sides. Armies created havoc for local people. Buildings got destroyed and crops ruined. Their fields stood fallow. Abandoned farms made Midwest boys homesick. Made me want to plant a crop of potatoes like I had done at home. At the rate we advanced, the harvest could come in before we moved.

Cotton fields were bare—no one planted this year. When coloreds ran toward Union lines, tragedy followed. Union soldiers opened fire just to keep negroes from giving away their positions. If rebels caught runaway slaves, they lynched them.

Locals all chewed tobacco, except the very youngest. The extensive habit was even taken up by women who appeared to be ladies. Chewing left streaks of dark hue around the circles of mouths. Some, referred to as 'public women,' offered favors. Several nights two sisters visited our post to offer themselves. Soldiers favored the young one. Though only fifteen-years-old, she received many pokes. The same age as my sister Ann when she and Will fell in love. I stammered an excuse, "I haven't enough money," so she offered to accommodate me without pay. When she spat tobacco juice, I walked away.

General Sherman moved forward May 16th. His men dislodged Confederates from cover, but their officers demanded, "Hold your ground. Don't give way to damned Yanks." We pushed forward enough to provide room for artillery to move up. To keep going, I kept eyes front, did not look at the suffering all around. Otherwise I might stop. We rode after the enemy and held the ground they abandoned. The men erected an excellent parapet and held the location several days. Sherman praised the effort as "the prettiest little fight of the war."

Confederates continually harassed. If someone stood up, the first glimpse of a cap prompted a sharp rifle crack from one of the most hated opponents, a sniper. Sharpshooters climbed trees and used us for target practice. But they needed no practice. If rebs had the same standard we did, to become a sharpshooter a man put 10 consecutive shots in a ten-inch circle from 200 yards. Boys learned never to call out a warning or raise their heads. When we located a sharpshooter's nest, we spared no effort until the butternut uniform fell heavily to the ground.

The army made another move on the 21st. Earlier in May the heavens had provided fresh rain water, but by the third week weather turned fiendishly hot and dry. We captured a Confederate captain, who said, "Nearly the whole army attends sick call each morning."

"Bad water?" Sergeant Cook asked.

"The water courses are dry."

"And food?"

"The commissary fails us. We've nuthin' but rye coffee and horsebeef."

Time hung heavy for us, but delay meant disaster for General Beauregard, so on May 21st Confederates marched out of Corinth and assumed attack positions. The vanguard caused a lively skirmish, but problems quickly developed. Troops, wagons and artillery filled and then blocked the route. General Van Dorn sent out scouts, who found Federals already occupied the position he wanted, so his men filed back to the entrenchments.

We held position, brought up reserves and prepared for any eventuality. May 24th we cleared out a nest of rebels. May 27th another skirmish started along the line. The next day General Halleck regained his nerve and ordered a general advance. Units sent men clambering up tall trees with spyglasses. Infantry chased rebel skirmishers. For a while the enemy held, then trembled backward in confusion. Some Confederates contested but failed to drive Federals off. Yells and cheers showed where we captured companies. General Sherman led cavalry south to secure the right flank and provide reconnaissance. Reserve troops filled in each position vacated, and in this way Sherman worked the army to the teeth of the rebel works.

The day grew quiet. We sat so close we could hear the rebel drums in camp and railroad whistles. The chaplain led us all in prayer. How did Halleck plan to attack? Maneuver around the south and west? Bombard the town into submission? Ten-horse teams pulled in siege guns. The biggest ordnance took 10 yoke of oxen or 20 horses to pull. When they fired together, the earth shook.

We marched into Corinth the morning of May 30th—only to discover the enemy had gone. Dummies fitted into uniforms wore broad smiles and manned logs painted to look like cannons. To keep Halleck from suspecting withdrawal, southern commanders had maintained camp fires and kept drums beating. Coloreds loaded stores onto railcars and burned whatever the South couldn't carry—blankets, beds, tin plates and pans, cups, knives, clothing—flames overtook great mounds of supplies. Castoffs marked their trail—men and ammunition went, the rest stayed behind.

One jubilant black man, in a high state of excitement ran forward, waving a white flag. "Dey's all gone!"

More and more Federals leapt over the breastworks, cheered and pranced about. Even the eagle, Old Abe, whirled on its perch.

Rebs left a sign. "Halleck outwitted. What will Abe say?"

Cavalry raced in the direction rebels escaped, but their final units had felled trees, blocked the route, destroyed bridges and made it impossible to get through. Once everyone understood the Confederate army slipped away clean, profound disappointment set in. We cursed an enemy, who lived to fight another day, and grumbled Grandma Halleck's name.

After the failed pursuit, our horses huddled near a stream and drank. How different the regiment looked from the day we marched out of Ottawa. Back then troopers sat tall, wore new uniforms. The bugle and drum played rousing music. Now we were the dustiest group ever seen. Jaded faces looked as if we were the ones whipped.

General Sherman consoled us. "The guts of the Confederacy are now exposed. From a military stand, we have opened a door to the cotton states."

General Halleck saw cause for jubilation and declared the rebellion nearly ended. "Let the army enjoy the rest they have earned." Then he divided and subdivided armies until few detachments remained strong.

Soldiers asked me to help write letters home, saying they expected to muster out within three months.

***

A man with the intriguing name S. S. Grant wrote General Grant to say he had an important offer, but illness confined him to a bed. "I beg you to call."

When Grant went, he found an inert gentleman reclined on a chaise. "I own the finest horse in the world, one seventeen hands high. I want you to have it because I never can ride again."

General Grant took the closest chair. "You are too generous."

"Not at all, sir, knowing your passion, you can give the horse a good home." General Grant promised the horse never would suffer mistreatment and shook the gentleman's hand. "I will use him as a battle charger." Cincinnati has to be one of the world's finest horses.

Grant had a peculiar way of mounting, put his left foot in the stirrup, grasped the horse's mane near the withers, rose without a spring, simply straightened the left leg till his body rose high enough to throw the right over the saddle. He never climbed the animal's side, made no jerky movements, always up in an instant without effort.

June 30, 1862, General Sherman ordered our company to fall in with his division. Enoch Hunter and I rode as advance vedettes. We ran into a few rebel cavalrymen at Hutsonville, but they gave way without a fight. Two miles from Holly Springs our advance guard passed unmolested, but then the road filled with rebels. Cavalry from Hutsonville had set an ambush. We wheeled into line, dismounted and gave rebels a volley. Alt-

121

hough we opened sharply, the rebels ran out of reach. In the stampede a young rebel trooper lost control of his horse, which broke and plunged backward. The horse fixed her mouth firmly down against her breast. The rider cried, "Whoa. Whoa. Whoa!" but to no purpose. He pulled his saber to menace her but decided against killing her. He raised a leg as though to jump off, but the horse closed the distance so quickly he did not jump either. The rider kept crying, "Whoa," and hauled on the bit, but the whirlwind, countercharge of a frenzied, lone Confederate continued.

Fellows raised carbines but had no need to bring him down. Heels-over-head both horse and rider tumbled. The reb leapt to his feet. A trooper shot the crazy horse, but the butternut uniform scurried into the thicket and, appreciative of his daring, we just watched him scramble. Seconds later we became too busy to worry about one boy.

A column of rebel cavalry came over the hill 300 yards ahead. The shots previously exchanged were merely against their vedette. General William Hicks "Red" Jackson and his force charged down the road as if to cut us to pieces. But pulled up and sought shelter in the woods beyond Holly Springs. If they had carried through, how many of us might have died?

When the danger passed, I picked up a carpetbag containing a boiled ham. Some rebel had lost his dinner, so we put it to use.

A Mr. Cox, who lived nearby, witnessed the commotion. When asked, he claimed, "Positively there ain't no rebels nearer than Holly Springs." He made no attempt to hide the rancor in his voice.

Then rebs came at us again. Cox must have known they waited within hearing. Without orders every man in our ranks fired at once. Half the opposition tumbled down; the rest scurried back to cover. In the melee Corporal Tuesburg fell dead, and three others got wounded, so we positioned sharpshooters to cover the rear and moved out.

We stayed near Holly Springs a week until part of the army went west to Grand Junction to repair the railroad. We acted as guards. It was an uncertain time for cavalry. Grant had not decided how to organize horsemen. Western cavalry had no clear mission. Instead mounted troops performed many, varied services, recovered locomotives, built roads and got scattered into mere squads, subject to infantry officers.

In contrast, Union General Pope concentrated his cavalry into a division. That prompted General Grant to establish a cavalry division, commanded by Father, but nine days later Grant revoked the order and divided mounted troops between Colonel Lee of 7th Kansas, Edward Hatch

2nd Iowa, and Benjamin H. Grierson 6th Illinois.

A boy, fourteen-years-old, got picked up with a load of prisoners. First Sergeant Brooks discovered his name was Elisha Caldwell but was undecided what to do with a fire-breathing reb so young. "Where are you from?"

Elisha gave a curt reply. "Johnson City."

Brooks chucked Elisha's chin. "That's close enough to send you home to your father."

The boy slapped his hand away.

Just then another prisoner yelled, "Hurrah for Jeff Davis!"

This enraged a Union trooper, who raised his carbine and shot the fellow pointblank.

Elisha flinched but quickly recovered. "I want to be exchanged, so I kin go back to the Confederate army."

"At your age," Brooks said, "you belong at home."

The boy coiled as if to strike. "I hate my parents as much as the Union."

Further questioning revealed his father staunchly supported slavery and had sent money to Kansas to bring them in as a slave state, so the bad feeling between son and father did not involve politics. We handed the hellion over to a provost marshal, who could deal with Elisha however he saw fit. Regulations allowed leeway dealing with children. Elisha wanted in the worst way to be free of his father's control, so they sent him to Small-pox Island near Alton, Illinois. Hopefully he survived the sickness raging in camp.

General McPherson ordered us to break camp. Stores moved by steamboat. The effective force went overland. The army reorganized again—to undo the mistake Halleck made breaking up and dispersing forces. The Army of the Tennessee went back to Grant. President Lincoln called Halleck back to Washington and left Grant in charge. The longer the distance between us and Old Brains the better.

Countless officers, politicians and even citizens claimed President Lincoln as a friend—and traded on the President's name. Everyone claimed "Honest" Abe for himself. All expected favors because of the way the President received people cordially, spoke to them without derision even though many deserved to be tossed out on their ears. I, too, counted Mr. Lincoln as a friend but kept the connection secret. Superiors didn't need to know Mr. Lincoln used to bounce me on his knee.

123

Grant faced a formidable task—defend 150 miles of territory and protect supply lines, including 85 miles of the Mobile & Ohio Railroad, subject to harassment from Confederate cavalry, vigilantes, lone bushwhackers, partisan rangers and guerrillas, all active in the region. General Grant added three cavalry companies to his bodyguard, including ours.

After we arrived, General Grant appointed me adjutant because I was the only man he knew. The more I saw of General Grant as a commander, the more I appreciated Halleck for leaving. While adjutant of the escort, I served at headquarters, though not on Grant's staff.

Worry lines creased Grant's brow, yet his methods did not change. Stroking his beard seemed to help Grant think. His penetrating voice had a clear sound and carried considerable distances without yelling. The tone quality made it possible to hear him over camp commotion. He had no music in his feet, however, and never tried to keep step with drumbeats. One of his aides whispered the reason. "The General is tone deaf. Military music in particular annoys him."

The plantation taken over for Grant's headquarters had fragrant plantain, mimosa and magnolia trees. The scene loosened up conversation, but Grant had no fondness for small talk. A mostly silent man, he walked away from meaningless flattery, but soldiers believed in him. On the occasions Grant talked to enlisted men, he spoke of horses, hogs, cattle, farming, things familiar to Illinois, Iowa, Indiana and Ohio boys.

Mrs. Grant visited again and this time brought two of their children. She enjoyed old Scotch songs, the kind I knew well. A young lady, named Anna Held, came along as the children's governess, and Miss Held taught me a comic duet called the "Dog and Cat." Miss Held had many charms, but General Rawlins saw her virtues, too, and soon outranked me in Miss Held's affection.

We took over civilian homes for army use, also churches and theaters. Some nights I filled a table to play euchre. Places with pianos felt like safe havens. Any time I had a few spare moments I played. Even though I had been away from the keyboard for months, the piano drew me back. When growing up, playing was a joy if the instrument had good sound. In war, however, whether well-tuned or a screeching tin-tin, an opportunity to play became a gift I shared with anyone who cared to listen.

When General Grant left to command at Chattanooga, General McPherson added me to his escort. A civilian named Theodore Davis trailed McPherson's units. Davis was two-years older than me, tallow-faced, wore enormous high-topped boots, a jaunty cap and did not seem up to the rigors of army life. He sketched scenes for *Harper's Weekly* and proved stronger than he looked.

At times half the men reported to sick call as unfit for duty. Instead of Davis, I was the one who took sick. A hospital was the last place a soldier wanted to go, but they sent me to one in Northern Tennessee. A line of dead bodies near each other, covered with brown woolen blankets, led to the facility. Men dug fresh graves nearby. In my ward one doctor cared for 100 men. They put me on a hard cot. Only a few men had mattresses filled with straw. Stale air inside the building made me struggle to breathe.

I fell into a stupor. Occasionally noises filtered in, wind rustling trees, men coughing. I opened my eyes briefly, closed them again, dared not look. I longed for Ottawa—like a child sent away to a horrid school I was desperate to go home to the warm, familiar place where sisters made life clean and safe. What was Ann doing today? How about Belle; did she play piano? Or Jennie and Ella, had Ella found another young man to keep her company? Thoughts of Ella made me girl-sick. Peter Reynolds lived not far away in Peru. He favored Ella. Did he ride over to take her for long walks? I tried to lift myself up but fell back down. The next time I saw Father I'd make him swear—never to punish a soldier for deserting a hospital.

After I regained coherence, I wished for oblivion. Stench filled the air, vomit and diarrhea, no better school of suffering existed anywhere. One Irish man wriggled fitfully. I believed he was Irish, for he clutched a Celtic cross. He rested naked to the waist except where bandages encircled him, a fine built man with sun-bronzed face, neck and hands, elsewhere lily-white. The bandages covered the bullet hole in his lung When the steward gave him stimulants, he mumbled. For a while he breathed with even cadence, then suddenly opened his eyes and gave me an urgent look of surprise. When he turned away—he rested silent in death.

The ward nurse was sick, too, yet his commander detailed him to come to the hospital and work over the rest of us. He had an old, sallow face. A gaunt widower so he said, but with children. He expressed a desire to have strong green tea, abandoned his patients and went toward the kitchen. After a few steps, he fell down, rolled into a ball and coughed till an orderly took him away.

A boy called J.T. had gangrene of the foot, bad enough to cost his toes. A regular specimen, rough and hearty. Sweat trickled down his temples onto the linen. Then alternately he shook and shivered.

The boy at the end of the ward had an unquenchable appetite for something pungent like pickles. "Brother," he called to anyone who came near. "Brother, can I have pickles to eat?" After the orderly consulted with a doctor, they gave him the only thing they had, horseradish and an apple.

One fellow with typhoid fever thought surely he must die. Male nurses refused to talk to him because they had orders to keep him quiet. But he grabbed at one viciously, and the nurse cried out in pain. "Here now. Let go." The patient refused, so an assistant surgeon ran over. "If you recover enough to travel, I'll get you a furlough." No reward was coveted more than a furlough, and the patient became an obedient child.

On the opposite aisle a lady sat by her son, an artillery man, shot in the head but still rational. Surgeons had no skill to operate on the fellow. From the chest down he was paralyzed. At least he had the consolation of his mother's tender care.

I stared so long, she asked me, "Do you know my son?"

"No, my brother-in-law had a head wound but I was on duty and not able to go see him."

"Did he survive?"

I could not say the words.

"Bless you."

A youngster closest to the door suffered from pleurisy. He took no interest in anything. Though only age sixteen, fortitude failed. The ability to recover varied from man to man, cot to cot, but everywhere groans. Everything impromptu, no system. Except men moaning.

One morning my eyes opened to a soldier, coughing over me. I tried to get up, but he pushed me back down. "Still alive?" he asked.

My gut jumped, but it had no food left to vomit.

"You're not looking too good this a.m." Fortunately, he moved off to assess others.

The artilleryman had died of his head wound, for mother and son were gone. They put another man in the bed. I was glad I asked his name when I did because by the time breakfast came George was not in a mood for talk. After supper George's nose bled. I called for someone to come and help, but no one answered, and blood soaked his shirt.

"Thank you, friend. I don't expect them to help a Confederate."

I said, "General Grant told the Medical Department to give men every attention possible, making no distinction between Federals and Confederates."

"Ha, how do you know?"

"I served on his escort. Besides, when a man's sick, he deserves help." I yelled for a nurse repeatedly, but no one came. None were on duty at night.

George muttered all night—at no one in particular—his illness talking. Luckily the flow of blood staunched on its own.

In the morning the steward dosed him with some sort of tincture.

"What are you giving George?" I asked.

"Nux vomica," the steward replied. "It will either kill or cure him."

After that, George picked at his clothes. His passing delivered a severe blow. The steward showed me a picture of a wife and two boys George left behind.

My father heard of my illness, came and took me away to Grant's headquarters. I fell in and out of delirium and, at times, didn't know Father. Strange dreams plagued me. In one my mother handed me the most delicious cherry pie. In another I rode Cincinnati into battle, but not to charge the enemy. I used the world's greatest horse to superintend a withdrawal.

The surgeon put me in a room over Grant's office and treated me for miasmatic disease of jaundice. First he gave cathartic and then tincture of strychnine to sweat infernal toxins out. I heard them talk as if I were not there.

"I'll do what I can," the surgeon said.

"What about Charlie's chills?" Father asked.

"Think nothing of that," the doctor replied. "Bodily temperature is unimportant."

Father came to my bedside. "Charlie, I'll see what else can be done."

In my addled state I took offense at negro servants and told my nurse, Henry Newcomer, to keep them out. When a negro came in, I became violent, and Henry told the negro to restrain me. I jumped from my cot and ran to the window, which had a large sash open to the floor. As I lunged forward, the negro got hold of my shirt. I left it in his hands and threw myself out headlong. Fortunately I landed in a holly instead of a wood crate of rifles below.

General Grant saw me fall past his window, ran out with an orderly and picked me up. I got knocked senseless, but came to in a short time. The medical director gave his opinion I would die if kept in the South, but

Grant had restricted sick leaves. To skirt his own orders, Grant assigned Father and me to recruiting service, and Father took me north. God pity any soldiers in army hospitals.

Sister Ann met us in Cairo and took good care of me from that moment on. Back home, I became a burden. Many nights Ann sat at my bedside. I spent my twentieth birthday in bed, barely able to lift my arms.

A man from town, named William Knapp, appeared at Ann's doorstep. "I hear Charlie is home. I need to see him."

"He is too ill—"

"Stand aside."

Mr. Knapp bounded up the stairs as if Ann's home were a public house. He banged doors until he found me. "Charlie." He shook me. "What can you tell me about my boy?"

Ann ran into the room. "Stop!"

Mr. Knapp raged. "I need to find my son."

"Charlie cannot help you."

"He must."

Ann stepped between me and the distraught father. They stared at each other until he backed away. "Is it too much to ask if a child is dead or alive?"

She put a hand on his shoulder. "I will ask Father to see what he can find out."

Mr. Knapp's footfalls pounded the floorboards. His son reportedly died near Memphis, but records were poorly kept. Even in hospitals, the flood of sick and wounded meant half the bodies got buried as unknowns.

Because of Ann's care I began to heal. Alvin sent a troubling letter. Our company guarded regiments out on forage. Four boys: First Sergeant Joel Carter, Lycurgus Hyde, Jim Ferguson and Jake Stevens went voluntarily. When returning, they rode into an ambush. A bullet hit Hyde in the chest, and he died before they got him into camp. Buckshot wounded Carter and Stevens, but Ferguson escaped unhurt. No rebels were found, so it had to be citizens who opened fire.

On August 23, 1862, Colonel Ransom telegraphed, "You must not tell anyone where you have been as it is not known and better not be. Come up as soon as you return. We will have to get your papers right." On August 26th, Ransom sent a second telegram. "Hurry."

Ann wanted me to stay. "You are not strong enough yet."

The doctor disagreed. "Charlie is fit for duty."

When Ella heard I was leaving, she ran over and found me buttoning my shell jacket "You can't do this."

"I have no choice."

She gave me a wild look, as if I were a robber. I reached for Ella's hand. She pulled away. Just as well. Touching her would have made leaving harder.

***

I returned as far as Lexington. Major Gibson took charge of men who had been on sick leave, so I joined him. The rest of the 4th cavalry marched to Bolivar. Rumors claimed 2,000 rebel cavalry camped 12 miles west of there, threatening a small post at Chewalla and the railroad to Bethel. I was not well enough to go with them, however. I found it impossible to ride. I wrote to Ann just to let her know I had arrived. Instead of going to the surgeon and subjecting myself to purgatives, a colored orderly treated me. He made a quart of strong tea out of hickory bark. "Drink it hot, all at once," he said. It had an offensive green color, and the taste was intensely bitter, but I downed it before turning in. The next morning I felt better. Throughout my illness, all the doctors had limited my intake of fluids, made me sweat and administered tinctures to increase urine output. The colored man proved the doctors wrong; his slave remedy provided a better cure.

Charles H. Dickey, Journal
Volume Four, 1862 War Intensifies
Terrors of the lame and infirm, Return to Duty, Quartermaster Corp

Rather than let me rejoin my company or Grant's escort, the command ordered me to Illinois to enlist replacements. Before I reached the transport boat, however, I came upon a lynching, this time a white man. A black man helped me cut down the corpse. "Leave one of da dead man's eyes open to watch for treachery." Together we carried the body to the man's home.

When the widow opened the door, she staggered backwards. Her face looked bone tired, as if the poor creature didn't have the strength for tears. To see a woman suffer made my throat feel queer. Mayhem was not her fault.

The slave shook his head. "The massah refused to take Confederate script for da meat in da smokehouse."

"Your own people lynched him?"

"Not my peoples. No sirrah—"

The widow pointed to their bed, where she could clean and prepare the body, so the slave and I placed her husband there.

***

The government had ceased recruiting last April, a grave mistake considering the death toll. Now Secretary of State Seward urged state governors to "follow up recent successes and crush the rebellion." Illinois Governor Yates called on men to fight for "flag, country and liberty," but this year's parades and rallies paled compared to those in 1861. Although the North had used only a small portion of its manpower, a booming war economy and busy farms left few men willing to enlist—especially now that the term was three years. Long casualty lists had taught everyone war was not a ninety-day game. The solution: bounties. The War Department authorized a $25 advance of the $100 normally paid at a man's honorable discharge. Some cities added their own incentives to entice young men to enlist. Recruits thought they could save enough to buy their own farms. I enlisted fellows from Iroquois and Ford counties, boys I did not know, families I had never met.

***

September, 1862, I returned to General Grant's headquarters near Corinth. I wrote to Ann to let her know my strength was returning and to thank her for saving my life. Ella had also rendered gentle care and spent hours watching over me. I wanted to write to her as well but failed. I wrote a draft thanking her but tore it up. The way Ella had cried over my sickbed was hard to mention. The way I left her even harder to broach. Better for both of us to wait. Heal the rift in person.

Night after night the regimental band played; high-spirited tunes did more to calm eruptive fevers than any dose of cathartic. Music became a healing influence, so when a local planter invited us to a dance, I was eager to go. Officers feared a plot to take us prisoner and decided against it. As the time neared, however, the thought of dancing was too good to pass, and they took a chance. We went armed, in case someone tried to get a drop on us. We knew precisely where rebels posted pickets, went close, dropped down and crawled past.

At the house, four men wore butternut uniforms, a troubling sight until the host assured us. "These good ol' boys just wanted to dance. Besides, I have scoured the countryside for females, enlisted laundresses and officers' wives alike, ransacked the entire district to scare up 20 women for the affair. You have to stay. Recruiting women is not a safe occupation." He pointed to one matron. "That gal yonder attacked me with a hoe, 'Dance during this horrid war?' she cried, 'Clear out of my yard.' But I quieted the lady and convinced her to feed me supper. By the time she served pie, she had softened, and I invited her to come and give me a dance or two."

A handful of Union supporters lived in the area, but many more people opposed us. Putting the two sides together at a dance meant anything could happen. One rebel's steely gaze put me on edge.

Then the music started. What a disappointment, especially the fellow playing piano. George Figley pushed me forward. "Help him out, Charlie."

I made a polite suggestion. "I can give piano renditions of Virginia reels, waltzes, quadrilles and polkas."

The piano player jumped down and headed for the whiskey jug. "I gladly let y'all take over."

A violin, flute, fife and flageolet completed the ensemble. Locals warmed to the music. One lady was the homeliest woman God ever made, thin as a scarecrow with a bird's beak, yet she danced every dance, lively on her feet. Soldiers starved for female companionship eagerly held any warm body. The dresses of most ladies were relics, visible evidence of shortages. Only one young lady wore a current style, low neck and short puffed sleeves, glistening green taffeta. Her painted fan of copper and roy-al blue matched the trim on her gown, a captivating sight. Finery suited her. This young woman elevated her chin and pursed her lips. Blue uniforms followed irresistibly in her wake, but she shooed "damned Yankees" away.

"I am the officer of the day," a captain said.

"As if I care—" Her speech sounded lazy. The pronoun 'I' reclined in her throat, almost a sigh. Her hairstyle put other women to shame, luxurious, wavy and blond lighted with flashes of amber. She was tall and slender with fine form and moved with grace. Watching her stroll across the room, it became hard to breathe. A shadow of hysteria hovered over the piano. Six rivals clamored for her attention. Should I approach or wait for some of the competitors to knock each other out? The taut line of her jaw, the gentle sway of her skirt, everything about her was seduction.

She glared at northern men who asked for her dance card.

George Figley stammered, "M-m-may I have a dance?"

"Y'all m-m-may certainly not." Her disdain looked instinctive. Her malice effortless.

My heart beat waiting for someone to ask her name.

George asked, "Do you live in the area?"

When the foragers came, did she beg to save chickens and hogs? Did she howl? Curse?

"Just visiting. Father sent me behind the lines for safety, but I don't like it here. Cain't wait to go South again and avoid Yankees." She prattled, sure in coquetry.

"Where is home?"

"Natchez."

George swallowed hard and did not say how many Union troops now occupied her home.

When someone asked her name, her breast filled with air. Another sigh. "Miss Leah Robbins."

"Miss Robbins," the captain said, "When I call at your home tomorrow, will you join me in a carriage ride?"

"I belong to the South. My heart is with Her."

"I will not remove you from Dixie, just share its pleasures."

Miss Robbins shuddered. "Even if I had no other way of amusing myself, I must refuse. To be seen with you would cause me to die of shame."

She looked over her eyelashes at him, but I envisioned her looking at me. I courted. I called. I had her on my arm—and boldly locked her in my embrace.

The captain laughed. "You can wear a veil to protect your identity."

"My conscience would be behind that veil with me." She turned away, stunning in condescension. "If southern soldiers hear of women keeping company with Yankees, why it's enough to weaken the strongest man in battle. Sicken the stoutest heart."

Private Charles Creed swept her away for the opening waltz. Her back stiffened like a board, but she allowed herself to dance. Creed had a handsome face, clean-shaven, with bright green eyes. As the energy of the tune engulfed them, Creed's courage grew, and his smile brightened to match his eyes.

Girls at home danced well, but not like Miss Robbins. Her trim figure looked too delicate for Creed to touch. Her uniqueness wooed. Petticoats peeked out of the hoopskirt as she danced. "Nightingale Waltz" was no challenge to play but the piano had the tone quality of a tin can. Yet, I played fervently as if music could reach out and touch her. The waltz melody soared on the violin, so much so I wished the violinist played less admirably. The couple was the only one moving across the floor because other men fell under Leah's spell.

At the end of the waltz, suitors surrounded her. Her temper turned sunny, her smile ready, her manner flattering, but something hid behind her expression. A glint of cunning?

Daniel Hughes asked her, "Do you have a beau?"

Every soldier leaned in. The scent of her pomade—Lilly of the Valley—drifted near. Her mouth glistened like sweet syrup.

"Listen to you!" she protested. "Have you a sweetheart at home?"

Daniel ran a finger inside his collar.

She stared at him. "If a Confederate invader went north and asked your fiancée impertinent questions, how would you feel? Would y'all rush home to defend her honor?"

Rivals laughed at Daniel's expense. My heart thumped. She fluttered her fan and turned somber. "I had a beau, but he's gone. Dead and buried. Replaced by sap-eyed Yankees."

Daniel did not let this pass. "Men who take up arms know the risk."

Another soldier reassured her. "You need not fear us, Miss."

"Need not? Need not!"

I thought she would slap him.

"Food is scarce. Our means to make a living gone. Cotton burned by both sides to keep it out of the others' hands."

Those of us, who longed to dance with her, were destroying her way of life.

"We have nothing." Her voice rose. "Know nothing except that armies fight around us. Casualties are heavy, our friends and loved ones are surely in the ranks, but whether at Corinth, Lexington or Frankfort we have no means to discover. The days wear on. We sit at windows until we can endure the suspense no longer. When night falls, how cruel and preposterous to go to bed unaware of our fate."

I cut the song short and left the piano. "Gentlewomen have many trials to endure."

Moisture brimmed her eyes. "Southern women are equal to any test Yankees care to devise." Her expression softened. "Here now, let's turn to suitable conversation."

I inched closer, but then Creed heard an alarm. Men jumped onto the porch railing to look. "Rebel cavalry!"

Her admirers scattered, and she called after them. "Y'all are in for it!"

I took her gloved hand and brushed it with my lips, respectful of feelings yet intimate.

A quivering lip betrayed her.

Just one touch lit a fuse.

The commotion grew outside, so I followed in pursuit of our enemy, her neighbors. The chase produced no result, just one more run into the dark.

Rebels remained thick on the roads. I wanted to risk going back, but surely she had left the dance by now—where was she staying? I did not know where to find her. I pictured her reading in a drawing room while a slave puts her bedroom to rights. She rested in a graceful, impressive way, her beautiful eyes eloquent with sadness. Does she rail against Mr. Davis's prosecution of the war? No, she is a woman of society in the best sense. A lady, such as Leah, loved companionship, had native wit, an acute mind, knowledge of books and men's motives. If I talked to her privately, she might reveal a woman's tender feelings. Did her eyes now betray loneliness? Leah. It's improper to use her first name, but I already feel something between us. The correct way to refer to her is "Miss," but here in my journal I pull her close. Use her Christian name. Intimacy is "proper" between us. For me, the longing is physical.

I turned to my journal to keep a record after my fashion with big and little stories of war, the ones I find important. So many pleasures have fled. My breath taken away to think what earthquakes and shocks soldiers suffer. I write, not because I might forget her name, her demeanor or manners but to register a delightful meeting. One bright spot in a somber picture, she is a concern, as no southerner before. Her ordeal. Her fate. She was so pretty when she danced. The mind's eye cannot look away.

***

Miss Robbins, my Leah, rode with me in the next skirmish—made strict performance of duty harder. I conducted myself in ways she condemns, burning railroads, taking prisoners, crippling the South.

In the upcoming weeks our company protected forage details. The North cannot persuade rebels to be loyal. For fighting to end, we have to make citizens remove their support. Troopers struck country estates and emptied larders as a way to bring war to the populace. One sergeant, named Salsberger, enjoyed this greatly. Salsberger trounced into fine houses as though each one harbored rebel fugitives.

In one mansion Leah ran down the stairs, all heat and lightning like a summer storm. "Surely those who invade women's homes must feel God's wrath."

My heart shook.

Salsberger wiped muddy boots on the carpet. To quiet her, he wrote a receipt for goods taken.

She slapped it out of his hand.

"Are you sure?" he asked.

She kicked the receipt further away. "Y'all going to shell this house?"

Salsberger grinned. "That can be arranged."

"Do it soon." She displayed like a peacock. "I shall stand on the porch. Aim for it, create a huge hole and bury me."

"You could take cover in the cellar."

"No, sir, I refuse to retreat—though shells fall thick. And, Sergeant, you can count on all southern women doing the same. Y'all cannot bomb or starve us into submission."

"This home would make an excellent hospital," Salsberger said. "Instead of shelling we can bring 100 patients for you to care for."

"Much better places exist for the sick."

"How is that?" he asked.

"I know how to put arsenic in food and will do it."

"Well, your father has offered his service as taster." Salsberger walked away.

"Yankees are the meanest, most dastardly people on earth," she shouted. "Southern generals soon will take Grant prisoner and shut him in a cage, and none too soon." She arched her back in angry cat fashion. Then she saw me watching from the front hall.

She blanched, a momentary flutter of embarrassment. Then shook her skirts to hasten the sergeant's exit.

I picked up the receipt. "Please take this."

Her sable brown eyes blinked. "No." But she did not remove her hand. Instead she looked down as if to appraise my touch.

"You may not need reimbursement now, but some day—"

Her demeanor changed to sadness, expressed with the same completeness as anger seconds before. "Do not worry about me."

"I cannot help myself."

She jerked her hand away. "Then I am truly sorry for you." At the dance she had been gay. Now despondent she looked even more beguiling. "I wish I were a child again," she said.

"For the innocence?"

"For the ignorance." She tore the receipt in half and brushed past me. I had lustful thoughts and grave misgivings. The only life she knew had slipped out of her hands. I took the pieces of the receipt, thinking one day I'd give them back, willing to wait until she could accept them. Glad to think I might be able to help her.

Than night sleep eluded me. 'Where are you now? Do you toss like me? Do you calculate your loss?' Minutes dragged. I longed for her more than anything in life. As my custom had always been to put feelings into writing, I began a letter. "Dear Miss Robbins, Tonight I am on a scout, several miles from camp with little prospect of returning, I pull up my saddle close to the fire and write you a letter. The smoke tries to drive me away from the light but I cannot go until I tell you what is in my heart. An outdoor blaze inspires a poetic letter, but war drains a man, and I find it hard to narrate my feelings. Circumstances offer no opportunity to become your friend or confidant. I expect at any hour to be in another skirmish. I am not in good spirits. Not ready for a dash against your side. If an order is given to charge, of course I will, but I have no eagerness for it, no desire to go out. Politics and a nation's inability to compromise has

136

brought us to this."

At this point, I stopped to read what I had written, found it lacking, tucked the paper into my journal and started over. I wanted to write, 'Pray for me, for I feel I am the one in bondage.' Of course, I could not put that in a letter to a southern lady. The second, third and fourth attempts I tossed into the fire. I watched them glow red and turn to ash. She slept miles away, and I must leave her behind as fighting moved on. I called myself a fool. She called me Yankee monster.

I struggled to sleep that night and many more. Fantasies of meeting her filled my head, fabulous and arousing. Burning intensity suggested I resign and replace duty with fealty to a wife. To ease the urgency, I took a bottle of whiskey and drank until the night blurred. But sleep did not come. Half a bottle strengthened the intoxication of Leah's voice.

Next morning with my head pounding and mouth full of cotton, my passion refused to cool. Denied companionship, any young lady became a temptation—Leah more dear. I pressed tobacco in a pipe with shaking fingers. Pipe smoke had sickened me at school, but now had a calming effect. Hezekiah, Sam, Frank, all the men talked about women. Many had sex with loose women or found relief in self-abuse. But my mind dwelt on the treasure of embracing Leah. Lying with her on a sofa. Made it happen in my thoughts. Conjured her. Made her mine. The good feelings— heavenly torture. No camp woman could satisfy the longing for Leah.

***

Cone-shaped Sibley tents arrived, not as large as the old ones, but holding 10 men instead of 16. At night my friend Alvin fancied himself at home and dreamed out loud, argued with relations who apparently gave advice. Alvin tossed, vehemently rejected interference and filled sleepless nights with constant muttering.

We scouted in every direction, posted pickets every day but did no fighting. This duty was drudgery. When men received pay, they took every opportunity to get drunk. One adjutant, who I will not name for his sake, got so full of booze he removed his sword and threatened his colonel. "Fight me without weapons, you damned son of a bitch. Fight or go to hell."

A court-martial sentenced the adjutant to removal from service, but a review board reversed the verdict because witnesses testified the colonel and adjutant had been gambling and drinking together. Martin Wallace did his best to keep strict discipline and forbid the sale of liquors in the regiment. Impossible to keep all booze out, but cutting supplies kept fights and misconduct down. I supported Martin because drink ruined regiments and didn't help me, either. He tied three of the worst boozers to a post to sober up and let temperate men run after small bands of bushwhackers as a reward.

A detachment made an extended trip northeast, tracing those bushwhackers. Gone nine days, we lived off the countryside, stopping at a planter's house to see what they had to eat. The lady of the house had only corn dodgers and sassafras tea, not coffee or real tea. "The more sassafras is steeped the better it is. This batch," she said, "has been steeped three times."

Charlie McKennell sipped and passed it back to her. With utmost politeness, he said, "I wish, madam, you would steep mine again."

Boys laughed heartily, but the woman turned her back in a way that made me sorry for the little she had.

A horse threw Joel Carter and broke Joel's leg, a bad injury, but also good. The break meant discharge, and he could go home.

Union General Rosecrans felt he had secured Union defenses at Corinth, so Grant moved his headquarters to Jackson to superintend all the forces in the field. Then scouts informed Grant Confederate Van Dorn was moving to recapture Corinth.

This time Union artillerymen used long-range guns as they should and sent terrific volleys of shell, grape and canister. About ten o'clock rebels stormed out of timber. All firing ceased. One column of about 2,000 men formed in plain view, then another and crowding out of the woods another, firm paced, a fearful front. Rebels looked as if they intended to walk over the Union line.

Nothing is so hard as to stand firm and face a steady tramp. One soldier examined his gun to see if it was clean. Another to see if his was primed correctly. A third shifted from one foot to another. Others pulled at their blouses, felt cartridge boxes, and so on, inspecting themselves or equipment rather than face the steady advance. To just wait and remain still becomes oppressive.

When Confederates advanced one-third the way, the infantry got ordered to lie flat. Uneven ground screened them, and a second line to the rear looked like the first ones rebels had to fight. When rebs came over the banks, Federals opened up with dreadful effect. In a few seconds the entire line fired and cut down the column. The line reeled like a rope but held. Determined Confederates gained the outer works, but Federals counterattacked. Confederates had massive numbers. Fighting grew vicious. Heatstroke prostrated victims, who fell down, looking as if they had been boiled. As smoke cleared, a mass of bodies in butternut clothes writhed.

The Union fell back to the inner defense, and rebels must have gratefully watched night fall. Everyone expected fighting to rage again the next day. Each side needed to prepare, but infantrymen desperately needed rest. Blacks now cast lots with the Union. All night long hundreds of slaves threw up breastworks and barriers to protect Union men.

When the sun rose, Confederates saw new batteries atop the ridge. One Confederate commander did not get his men in position and delayed Van Dorn's plan. Finally rebels came. When lines of gleaming bayonets cleared the woods, the rebel yell echoed across the field in an uphill charge.

"Ready. Take aim. Fire—shoot away! Damn you!"

Not a single bush screened rebs from the terrible storm of shot, but they pushed on like demons. Confederates gained the town and assaulted the fort. Blood ran down in streams.

When Confederates stampeded across town, Rosencrans cursed his troops, "Stand firm for the nation!" Rebels drove to the yard of Rosecrans's headquarters, but that spread their forces too thin, and the thrust came to a halt. Those who had battled their way in received no support. To avoid further disaster Van Dorn withdrew.

Confederate prisoners were half-starved, their haversacks empty. One contained a few roasted acorns. Their men had gone into battle without rations. When he heard, the commissar said, "The war won't end until the acorn crop fails."

Other battles got more newspaper coverage. However, none required more courage or left more gore on the field than the second fight for Corinth.

**

Corinth became a hornet's nest of freedom when President Lincoln issued a preliminary Emancipation Proclamation. As the death toll mounted, the War Department decided to use slaves to turn the tide, but the new policy caused a great stir in northern society and the army. Prior to Preliminary Emancipation, negroes feared coming forward. Masters said Yankees put slaves in irons, sold them in Cuba, shackled and whipped them—

139

worse than in slavery. But the promise of emancipation overcame fear. Coloreds did not wait until next January when the law went into effect. They flocked to the Corinth garrison, and a crisis developed. Army regulations required commanders to aid blacks but did nothing to relieve hatred. Most soldiers abused Mr. Lincoln for his 'abhorrent' policy. "I hear Halleck's puttin' regiments of darkies in the army."

"Yup, Old Brains, wants blacks to show themselves in battle."

"I hope ta God they do, for none will escape."

"I don' know. Coloreds run fast, I hear even outrun bullets."

"Arm a jackass, I say, if he can fire a musket."

"I'm for anything that saves whites."

The army dealt with soldiers, unsympathetic to coloreds, by housing them in prison until they revised their opinions. This lessened rebellious conversations, but not men's loathing.

Once blacks heard freedom waited in Corinth, they came with nothing—just escaped alive. Grenville Dodge, who commanded the garrison, quartered them in old tents, sheds, huts and hovels. People walked many miles and arrived half-clad, half-starved, enduring weeks in swamps and wastelands. Dodge clothed them in dead soldiers' uniforms. One three-foot child had nothing to wear but a grown man's clothes.

Alvin carved a wooden musket and gave it to the boy, and the child learned the manual of arms as well as any soldier, just from watching soldiers drill. The child had deep wine-colored skin, handsome in its way. His father had the same rich color with fine, smooth skin, finer grained than mine, not hairy or sunburned. Labor made his arms hard-muscled, a fine physique except where marked by the lash.

Black military units took men like him, and we all waited to see if former slaves could follow the discipline of army life.

The hospital employed several hundred negroes, some bright and useful. One army surgeon took exception to their presence and ordered all colored removed. However, the surgeon did not count on Mother Bickerdyke. Rain poured outside and filled the streets with mud, but Mother Bickerdyke ordered a wagon to take her to General Hurlburt's headquarters. Though late at night, the General gave her written authorization to hire negroes—and directed surgeons to carry out her wishes.

November 3, 1862, I received a promotion to Second Lieutenant. I was glad of a promotion, but wary of the reason behind it. Big red letters across the face of the paperwork read, "Promoted for meritorious conduct at the battle of Shiloh." My face flushed hot to read that. So many men deserved recognition. If Governor Yates knew how diligently I sat on my horse during the battle, surely he'd promote someone else.

That evening we went west in the direction of Chestnut Bluffs. We bivouacked at 10 p.m., the next morning ferried the river and stopped at Lee's plantation, which struck me as a place Yankees had never tread. We put a pack of hounds to flight, frightened the darkies and discovered a garden full of vegetables. Our corporal had the honor of liberating the smokehouse. A private fell over a barrel of dried figs. Others captured fat hens, twisted their necks and amputated their limbs with skill.

Inside the master's bureau drawers buried treasure—a dozen pairs of cotton socks. The ones I wore passed their natural lifetime long ago.

We convinced a slave he was free, and the grateful fellow slaughtered a calf for supper. We loitered overnight because Lieutenant Colonel McCullough, commanding, was too drunk to proceed. While soused, he ordered Sergeant Toothill to bring a rope and hang a local rebel. The Sergeant walked off to find a rope, dillydallied until the Colonel fell asleep, so Toothill could ignore the order and put an end to hanging.

We marched 20 miles toward Brownsville but stopped to take prisoners and confiscate supplies. These prisoners showed distinctions of rank on their collars, but the uniforms had no consistency, just a predominance of gray over butternut. Faces looked unacquainted with water, hair shaggy, not the best picture of southern chivalry. We even captured some of General Jackson's men, so we asked about old-lemon squeezer.

"The General is fine, thank ya. Teaching us to kill Yanks."

We also seized horses, mules, 20 bales of cotton and a horde of the colored race. One colored man, named Randall Johnson, knew the area west. "A large number of Forrest's Confederate Cavalry went home on furlough in that neighborhood." He pointed the location on the map. "Near the home of McCaleb."

Lieutenant Colonel J. B. Cook and Lieutenant John Wallace, another of Ann's brother-in-laws, conducted a long interview, became satisfied of Randall's veracity and decided to go after the Confederates.

"McCaleb's nephews, Jim and Charlie, have fine horses in the barn," Randall said.

Nine o'clock at night our detail reached a rope ferry at Chestnut Bluffs. The ferry could only carry six men and horses, so Cook took Randall and 15 soldiers around the outer circle to McCaleb's two-story log

141

house.

McCaleb had taken the first watch but sat dozing in a chair. No sound could be heard inside the house until Cook's footsteps stood beside him. Then Cook whispered, "How are you Mack? I want to see the boys."

McCaleb jumped. "What boys?"

Cook answered, "Jim and Charlie."

McCaleb's voice rose. "They ain't here."

The Lieutenant took a lamp, went up the stairs and brought the cavalrymen down. Lieutenant Cook shook hands with the host. "Good night, Mack, if you ride over to Trenton come and see me."

McCaleb did not utter a word.

Cook reached the rendezvous at three p.m. with his prisoners. It took another hour for John Wallace to arrive with 10 more prisoners.

Next we rode to arrest Steve Jorden and his two sons, but Randall took us through heavy timber and got lost. We wandered around until midnight, gave it up as a bad job and got some rest. Toward morning rain soaked us. When we arrived at Jorden's, another detachment had made the arrests while we wandered the woods. However, Jorden's slaves cooked breakfast, and we ate well for the first time in four days.

Though he had led us in the wrong direction, Randall became a valuable recruit, not as a scout, but tailor and seamstress. His ability with needle and thread surpassed most women. He fixed countless coats and trousers, charged ten cents to fix pantaloons or a dollar to make them over. Some days he made four dollars.

Using deceptive maneuvers, Confederates slipped away to Tupelo. Attention now shifted to Fort Pillow, Memphis and the Mississippi River. Fort Pillow stood north of Memphis on bluffs overlooking the Mississippi. Taking Fort Pillow meant Union dominance.

We nearly reached the Fort, but because of rain and intense darkness we bivouacked near a house. Roaring fires were needed to dry off. Because the house had the best chance to burn, we set it ablaze and bedded down. Reveille comes earlier for cavalry than other units. Before we eat, we feed and groom our horses. After breakfast we walk our mounts to the nearest stream or pond to drink. That done, we report for duty. We have 15 minutes to fall in. Men answered roll call with every expression a man can give—cat calls, rooster crows, wolf howls, yells and whooping. Anyone missing gets recorded for extra work or punishment.

On December 13, 1862, Father received orders to strike the Mobile and Ohio railroad and destroy as much track as possible. Colonel Hatch from the 2nd Brigade reported with 80 handpicked men, well mounted, with 40 rounds of ammunition, rations of hardtack, ready for a six-day scout. Father marched 800 men to Pontotoc 45 miles away. The sky turned thick and gray, smelled of rain. On the way we captured a small party, who claimed rebel infantry from Bragg's army camped five miles east. The prisoners placed another strong rebel force at Okolona, where only three houses remained, the rest destroyed.

Father sent men dashing east. In the beginning we rode through a gentle rain, but this changed to a violent storm that turned the roads heavy. We never found the large forces, only stragglers and remnants. Father detailed 100 men to take prisoners and two wagons loaded with harnesses, Confederate surveys and maps behind the lines to safety.

One artilleryman did not regret capture. "Rebels," he said, "will soon give up. The Confederacy is played out."

Major Coon took 100 men forward to strike the railroad, telegraph lines and bridge north of Okolona. They stampeded a party of rebel cavalry, took a few prisoners and attacked a train coming south. At full gallop his men fired on the engine. One trooper leapt from his horse onto a car but jumped off to avoid a post on the track ahead. Major Coon burned the depot, commissary's stores, destroyed a bridge and trestlework, but failed to stop the train.

Father led us through a terrific rainstorm. He turned 51 on his last birthday. I felt the rigors of the ride. How much harder was it on him? Rain poured like what is known in tropical lands. Through a curtain of water, I saw his shoulders slump, as if too weary to go on. I kept close, but Father disliked the attention and sent me to the rearguard, out of his wake. He did this for me, knowing my concern for him might make me reckless of my own welfare. When he sent me away, however, anxiety grew. My body felt too small for my skin. In this war anything might happen. I had no illusions I could protect Father but wanted to be at his side.

By nightfall we got within six miles of Tupelo. The approach road zigzagged through low, muddy ground, much of it heavy timber intersected by streams, passable on frail bridges. One such bridge had two planks laid lengthwise for a floor without any side supports. One trooper crossed as a test, leading his horse. After that, the rest of us took our chances swimming the horses. The stream ran swiftly, and some horses floundered in the current, plunging fearfully, but they withstood the ordeal while we

143

came out looking like drowned rats.

A broad light appeared north—rebel campfires. We pushed to within three miles of Tupelo. Locals mistook our scouts for rebels. One planter mistakenly confided in us. "Be careful. We spotted Federal troops north of Tupelo, so the Confederates here fled south."

Hearing this, Father sent us in the direction of Major Coon's advance. When the enemy saw us, they fled. In two days we destroyed all the trestles and bridges within 34 miles. Also burned—large quantities of timber along the track to prevent repairs. We began to march before daylight and closed after dark, stopping once a day to feed, usually from ten a.m. to one p.m. Our horses and men lived off the countryside, dining on fresh meat, sweet potatoes and roasted carrots, a diet that kept men cheerful.

What we had thought were rebel campfires turned out to be the blazing depot and fires of Union troops. Lieutenant Colonel Prince destroyed trestlework and captured eight wagon loads of equipment, including new wall tents, barrels of sugar, small arms and ammunition. After they loaded as many spoils as they could, they destroyed the rest. A bridge gave way under the strain, so they had to burn another wagon.

Wednesday night, December 17th, the whole party camped at Harrisburg, a deserted town. When we broke camp, Father took the lead, a dangerous place. Anyone who rides the advance takes great risks. Officers do it to gain general confidence and hold onto men's respect. Westerners can be led—but not ordered around. Whenever Father commanded in front, my heart raced. The death rate soared for officers in the lead. Father's reputation had brought men into the cavalry. They depended on his command experience. What if he fell? A sharpshooter's bullet might hit any moment.

Scouts reported a rebel force, six or seven thousand strong ahead. Father worried that rebs could cut off his small command, so he closed up the column, threw us off the road and passed four miles north of the enemy. Our vedette tangled with rebel flankers, captured three, wounded one. Smoke of their campfires showed how close we were. Rhoderic was worn out, as were all the horses, while theirs were rested. If possible, Father hoped to avoid superior numbers on fresh horses. If not, he wanted to fight at their rear. He sent guards to the right flank. They located the main body three-fourths of a mile west. Father dispatched couriers to advise General Grant of the rebel position. At sundown we made a demonstration. When night fell, we crossed the Yocona River. Father then learned the couriers misunderstood their orders and had not left the column, so he dispatched others at once.

We returned to camp without one man killed, wounded or captured. Military prison now meant long, hard time. Exchanges had broken down, and both Union and Confederates struggled to feed huge numbers of prisoners. Did our cousins remain in prison? I hoped they got out before exchanges stopped. The rumors were bad, scurvy, lung disease, small pox. Captives fell down and died in prison pens. Captive men became livid mummies with horrible looks in their eyes. Some tactics can be forgiven but not that.

Around campfires men sang, "Home Sweet Home," which I find hard to bear, much preferring "John Brown's Body," which changed each time we sang. Even men who opposed abolition raised their voices. "John Brown's body lies a-moldering in the grave. His soul's marching on." The song created general satisfaction. The idea a soul marched made us sing with great gusto, and the Glory hallelujah chorus reached crescendo. "John Brown's knapsack is strapped upon his back! His soul's marching on! Glory, glory hallelujah. His pet lambs will meet him on the way. They go marching on! Glory hallelujah! They will hang Jeff Davis to a sour apple tree. Now, three rousing cheers for the Union. As we are marching on!" The rhymes made no sense if pulled apart, but the harmony among men made a great deal of sense.

General Sherman provided one more point of satisfaction. When Sherman rode in, boys revived. "Let me see old Pap." Sherman's coat was unbuttoned, a black hat slouched over his brow. He was in the prime of life and perfection of health, a tall, gaunt frame, restless eyes, bronze face and a crisp beard completed the grim visage of war.

"Where's Pap?"

Sherman called out, "Take care of yourselves on the march. You have more work tomorrow."

With General Grant now in overall command, we advanced toward Memphis. Grant put Father on his staff as chief of cavalry and Colonel Martin Wallace took command in the field. I rejoiced at the changes. Too many times, I watched Father collapse at night. His age worked against him, especially when no house was available and he must sleep on hard ground. To have Martin take Father's place—a relief. Besides, no one better existed. Men respected Will's brother Martin, not only because of their admiration for Will, but also because Martin showed the same concern for privates' safety.

I returned to Grant's escort. On the trail I used a split rail for my pillow. The next morning I awoke with Rhoderic over me, his forefeet touching my side. Rhoderic nuzzled my head. I rolled delicately out, while he had the good sense to stand still. "Good boy." I stuck my palm under his mouth and let Rhoderic sniff. "You stood guard while I slept and stepped carefully while I woke."

Father accompanied General Grant on a trip to Memphis, a welcome diversion. I enjoyed it, too, because we did not have to be always on alert. During one lull I fancied Will rode along. Will had been a knowledgeable rider, knew how to talk to a horse, when to give a mount the reins, never used a harsh touch. I missed him every day.

When we first entered Memphis, the place seemed dead, no business doing. As more soldiers arrived and passed through, ladies of the night appeared to provide services. They walked streets, solicited, wore showy dress, even flashed immodest views in public. Father turned away from the diversions of such ill-famed women, and his glare warned me to do the same.

At headquarters we had a colored laundress. Ruth's hips spanned as wide as the Mississippi River, and she held her head high and chin level, using her head as carrier for a bushel basket of clothes. The clean handkerchief tied around her head kept her hair in check. Her skin was the color of cinnamon, and she was the mother of six, but none were with her.

Alvin asked her, "Where are your children?"

"The three oldest," she said, "two girls and one boy done been sold to a cotton planter over'n Alabama." The white master had fathered her children. "The three little ones, massah keeps till they's older. My youngest babe is nearly as white as y'all."

I shuddered to hear a man sold his own children.

"Do you care?" Alvin asked.

"Shua, honey, I loves my chilen just like you mammy loves you." Anguish covered her face. "The lord gave! The lord gave—!" She could not finish. Her bereavement went beyond consolation.

When we broke camp, she shook every hand, bid us goodbye and said, "I axe God's blessing every day for you soldier boys and your mothers."

For a time we stayed in the home of a Union man named Cossett. I had good times singing with his daughter, Corinne, and playing her piano.

When not singing, silence separated Corinne and I like a locked gate. War made it impossible to be friends. Society outside the parlor was broken. Southern women flounced to the opposite side of the street if Federals appeared. Negroes, poor foreigners and rowdies grudgingly tolerated our presence. Long-established residents hated the sight of us. Inside the parlor, however, music broke down barriers. Corinne enjoyed stanzas of "Amazing Grace" but frowned if I played popular ditties.

Headquarters then moved to Holly Springs, Mississippi, and I stayed in a home where the owners also called Yankees the "scum of the earth." Their parlor had a curious musical instrument, composed of glass bowls, which I struck with a pencil. To my delight each bowl gave out a clear, musical tone. Using a cork on the end of the pencil I managed to play "Old Hundred." *All people that on earth do dwell. Sing to the Lord with cheerful voice. Him serve with fear, His praise forth tell, come ye before Him and rejoice.* One of the best loved hymns on earth, even without choir or pipe organ, its smooth melody rang through the house.

Then the door sprung open, and a lady floated in. She combed her hair smooth and tight over her ears then swept it up into braids on the crown. Ribbons hung down both sides to complete her coiffure. Her wide white-work collar looked a decade old. A mound of petticoats fluffed her skirt, and she wore a bust-crushing long corset. Such fancy "at home" clothes had to be the ones she wore receiving callers. "I heard you playing a good church tune."

"I love sacred songs." The whole truth was I love church music more than any other part of Sunday services.

She scowled. "If you strike the bowls, you'll break them. Let me show you how to play. We fill them part full of water to create different tones, tune them carefully, then dip a finger in the water and pass around the edge like this." Her finger produced a mellow G-note.

When I played the proper way, the softness in her eyes suggested we were no longer enemies.

***

One noon we stopped at the plantation of a Union man, and General Grant went in for lunch, while we guarded the road. An hour later General Grant came out. "The gentleman reports a Confederate force in the neighborhood. Mount and get underway." Scouts later reported Confederate cavalry arrived at the plantation moments after we left. If General Grant had been captured that day, who could have taken his place? None I can name.

They gave me a few days' leave at Jackson, Tennessee, where Cyrus served as replacement for General John Logan, an impossible man to replace, even temporarily. John Logan had made a name for himself at the Battle of Belmont. Conspicuous throughout the fight, Logan rallied his troops even when their position became untenable. Men held him in high esteem because he spurred his black horse into the midst of a wavering line, shrieking to rally his men. Fellows called him "Black Jack" for his dark complexion, hair, drooping mustache and reckless disregard of danger. Cyrus felt no one could replace General Logan.

Jackson sits on rolling ground, and when it rained, muddy hillsides became treacherous. Residents owned costly homes surrounded with tasteful gardens. One gentleman had planted 10,000 pines and hollies, but Yankees destroyed several thousand trees and burned his fences. Residents, dedicated to the southern way of life, received us as cruel invaders, while slaves became jubilant, "Glad to see y'all, yah!"

Our detail went to Corinth to escort Mrs. Grant and little Nellie. The trains did not connect according to schedule, and Mrs. Grant had to wait several hours. Another order came, so Father rode off, leaving me to care for Mrs. Grant. Nellie Grant was the only daughter in the family. General Grant doted on her, and I kept nervous watch over this fair young girl, who attracted too much attention from baggage handlers and travelers. I took Mrs. Grant and Nellie to a mansion for lunch where Nellie told the story of the battle for Memphis on July 4, 1862. The fourth was also Nellie's birthday, and she had been present near the battle. "My brother, Fred, said rebels exploded bombs to celebrate my day, but I did not understand who told them it was my birthday. Later I asked Father why he fought rebels when they were making such a fine display for my birthday."

After lunch Nellie invited me to play mumble peg. She produced a pocket knife and stood opposite me with her feet shoulder-width apart. "Ready to play?" She threw the knife and struck the ground a hair's breadth from her foot. Her eyes flashed. "Now you."

The second player is supposed to toss the knife at his foot, too. Whichever player sticks a knife closest to his foot wins the game. "Impossible to come closer than you did."

She grinned. "To win, you have to put the knife in your foot—then you win by default."

"I want to win," I said, "but my comrades might think I stuck my foot to shirk my duty."

"Then you are excused—from mumble peg. Do you play marbles?"

At the end of Mrs. Grant's visit, I installed them in the train's cleanest car. As I left, however, I heard Nellie's voice call, "Lieutenant Dickey, you forgot something."

I turned back eager to correct an oversight.

"You forgot to kiss me goodbye," she said.

Though grounds for court-martial, I kissed her cheek.

***

A new song for the bugle reached us in 1862. The first time Leonard practiced it everyone stopped to listen.

"What is that tune?"

"Taps." Leonard polished his horn with a handkerchief. "We play it at dusk and for funerals."

"Give us the tune again." Its plaintive notes pulled more men close. This time Leonard faltered and slid uneasily into the high note.

Such a memorable tune, easy to learn by ear. "Let me try."

The solemn look on his face revealed Leonard could not hand over his bugle, not at that moment. "Soldiers also request it by the lyric first line, 'Day is Done.'"

Its melody was worthy of countless repetitions. I borrowed another bugle and practiced until I could perform it reasonably well. The melody touched my soul, an easy tune and yet hard to play without faltering. Even virtuoso buglers like Leonard dropped notes.

I accompanied Father on inspections, pleasant duty as a commissioned officer. One sweltering day in July, however, Father fainted. Later I went to check on him at his hotel and found him in a back room sweat-soaked with fever. I got better quarters with windows and a breeze blowing through and stayed with him all night. The next morning he felt better and went back to duty, despite my misgivings.

General Grant planned to move to Holly Springs, Mississippi, establish a base, move further south to Grenada, from there to menace Vicksburg. Confederate President Jefferson Davis picked a commander for Vicksburg unpopular among rebels. General John C. Pemberton came from Philadelphia but defected to the South because his wife was from Virginia.

Grant knew Pemberton. They fought together in Mexico in the same division. People said Pemberton had curt manners but, to our disquiet,

149

extensive artillery experience. To block our advance Confederates established a line, straddling the Mississippi Central Railroad at Grenada and tore up the rails leading north.

They assigned me to the Quartermaster Department under Colonel Fort, work I did not fancy except when it took me to Cincinnati. After requisitioning all the supplies, I had two days left and used them to visit relatives in Kentucky. I found Aunt Ann at home alone. She met me with open arms and drew me into the massive brick building, suitable for a large family, a homestead like olden times, where comforts and blessings clustered for birthdays, wedding days, Christmases, departures for school and happy returns. Her joy at seeing one of her nephews bubbled over. Much of the furniture had been covered to keep it from becoming worn. Books and embroidery flanked her old armchair. "Your uncle is out on plantation business." She swallowed hard, did not say when he might be back, had her slave kill a chicken for dinner and then she drank too much wine. "How fares your father?" I did not allude to any war news or our changed relationship. After a polite but strained visit, I returned to Memphis and performed quartermaster duties no one else wanted to do, such as take a boatload of disabled mules to St. Louis. Animals like these are crucial to warfare. Without them the army cannot move supplies, and the disagreeable job served the Union well. Experienced veterinary surgeons and ferriers staffed the animal infirmary and saved disabled stock from being turned out to perish. They even cured glanders thought hopeless.

Father took command of a three-brigade Cavalry Division. However, under this arrangement the First Brigade went to Hamilton's wing; the Second to Hatch; and the Third assigned to General Sherman. So the "Cavalry Division" existed in name only. An officer who outranked Father commanded each wing, and those officers made it clear who controlled mounted troops. So when army and gunboats moved down river, General Grant left Father in command in Memphis.

Vicksburg perched on steep bluffs and overlooked a sharp bend in the Mississippi River. As long as the city remained in Confederate hands, rebels threatened commerce from the Great Plains and Ohio Valley, cutting off access down the Mississippi. Southerners also brought provisions from Texas through Vicksburg for the rest of the Confederacy. If Grant took Vicksburg, he cut the South in two.

Fred, General Grant's eldest son, came down and spent many nights sleeping in the General's travelling tent. When it came to meals, however,

Fred ate with enlisted men because the food they foraged tasted better than the charred meat his father insisted cooks serve at headquarters.

Soldiers didn't take Fred foraging, however. It was dangerous, unbecoming and not fitting for the commander's son. Too much mischief happened. It's a marvel the ways men get themselves killed. John Brush drank from a bottle he found in a deserted house and poisoned himself. He had orders not to steal, but men like John felt free to do what they please.

The terrain near Vicksburg has all conceivable shapes, full of ravines, hardly passable. Oaks, basswood, sycamore, cottonwood, magnolia, palmetto and underbrush full of briars, nettles and poisonous weeds blocked the path. Long gray moss hung from the trees in sheets, swung loose in the wind and gave the country a somber appearance as if nature had fallen into decline. Heavy air campfires created smoke that blinded us. Pine knots and pitch in the wood darkened faces until we all looked like soldiers of African Descent. Despite these hardships the men became healthier. Veteran soldiers had learned how to care for themselves under southern conditions.

I got away from the quartermaster and returned to my old company for an expedition. Venting our feelings became a habit of troops as we moved through swamps or across uplands. Each man's song differed from others, but the mix echoed through the woods and floated up to the sky to proclaim our strength. Engineers had repaired the railroad to the Tallahatchie, but secesh were treacherous. From the Tallahatchie to the Yockney River we followed the enemy closely. At a distance we passed a large force under Rebel Commander Earl Van Dorn on a raid. High streams made movement through unfamiliar territory risky, but we needed to protect the railroad and telegraph. General Grant needed the Mobile road. He tried to get Helena troops placed under his command, so he could send Sherman south toward Vicksburg. This was denied.

Pursuit took us toward Coffeeville, where we rode into a trap. Confederates placed a four-gun battery in a spot hidden with brush. Three hundred yards farther sat two long-range Parrott guns. They held fire until we closed. The point-blank range mowed down dozens, and the colonel ordered a retreat. The enemy pressed hard on the flanks, but the larger line repulsed them, not without loss—nine killed, 56 wounded and 56 missing.

Cavalry pitched into anything we came across—whip or get whipped. Lieutenant Matt Wallace took a detail toward Trenton. That evening Captain Shepardson and 45 men joined us at the ferry at Chestnut Bluff. Two miles out we spotted fresh cavalry tracks and charged. What a sight, the perfect discipline and alignment of well-trained soldiers, pushing forward. Two rebels rode in the timber to our right. They made no effort to escape, in fact did not seem to see us till we ran up to them. One swore he was not a soldier, the other gave Captain Shepardson his revolver, the only weapon he had.

Lieutenant J. B. Cook took a company off in one direction; the Captain and rest dashed after the column, which left me with the prisoners. "What will they find?" I asked.

"A group two hundred-strong, expecting them and in position."

The Captain had only 60 men. I let the prisoners go and caught up just as our men dismounted.

Rebels had deployed in thick woods. We returned a few rounds, but Captain Shepardson ordered us to mount and fall back. Ed Powers did not hear the order and got taken prisoner. Shepardson was wounded and fell into the enemy's hands. J. B. Cook took command. The rebels had a larger force and an advantage of position, so he decided to get back to camp. Dissenters wanted to charge and rescue our captain, but we circled back to camp.

Shortly after we returned, Captain Shepardson and Ed Powers drove up in a carriage.

"Where'd you get the horse?"

"Took it from civilians."

"How did you escape?"

I helped Shepardson slide down. A tourniquet on his arm had staunched the flow of blood. "I told them what fierce fighters our men are. Helped them think you'd make another attack. So they let us go."

The rest of us joined the army at LaGrange. Below Holly Springs we skirmished with the enemy, cavalry and a Michigan battery doing the work. The rebels made brave stands at the Tallahatchie and again at Oxford, but we dislodged them and took several hundred prisoners.

December 4th we pursued the rear of the rebel army. General Pemberton had 10,000 men for us to bother. Timber provided cover, but underbrush made it hard to keep together or know what a day held in store. When we rode unfamiliar ground, dark feelings and fearful apprehension came, not for personal danger, but general calamity. We harassed the rebel army and, by extension, citizens trapped in the middle of fighting. War came to their orchards and homes. During one heated skirmish, a well-dressed lady picked her way across the road, parasol in hand, no haste in her movements. She accosted Sergeant Cook but remained calm. "Be so kind as to tell me your commander's general order."

"No order that I know of. General disorder prevails right now."

"Then why are soldiers flying and yelling so noisily?"

"They expect a shell to burst over their heads any moment. You must take cover, Madam."

"Ah." She curtsied and turned to go, but stopped to arrange the parasol at the right angle to protect her face from the sun. She slipped away as calmly as she came.

Lieutenants Hyde and Matt Wallace rode together on the left and suddenly came out of the woods near some men wearing blue and some in gray. They looked like Federals with prisoners, and the lieutenants approached, finding they were rebels with Union prisoners. Matt put on a bold front, rushed up and reached. "Give me that gun."

The rebel drew back. "I don't know about ten of us surrendering to two of you. Give us *your* weapons."

Matt had a Colt revolver and gave it up.

Lieutenant Hyde had an old rusty saber he couldn't remove from the scabbard because a horse had fallen down and bent it. "You may have my saber, if you can remove it from the saddle." Disarming him took time, and another of our men, Bill Movern, appeared at the edge of the clearing.

One rebel rode out. "Surrender."

Bill drew his carbine, near enough for the rebel to hear the lock click. "I'm not in a humor to surrender just now. Damn you—you surrender."

Strangest thing—the rebel obeyed.

More of us came in sight, so Hyde grabbed Matt's Colt. "You are surrounded." Reunited with our lieutenants, and with prisoners in tow, we kept intervals of 30 yards. When we spotted three cavalrymen, wearing blue, they dismounted and got behind the fence. We went forward at a slow walk until bullets zipped at our heads. A bullet stung the soldier in front of me in his face. He arched his back. Then dropped.

We dashed, squadron front, drawn sabers, yelling like demons. The blue-coated rebels jumped on their horses, and we gave parting shots.

Custom was for one company to ride the advance one day and in the rear the next. Colonel Hatch's Brigade joined us, which made our force 2,000 cavalry and two pieces of artillery. The day I rode the rear rebels possessed a fighting humor. Bullets zipped at a lively rate of speed but too high to hurt anyone. We rode in fours and swung right-about. Two companies went to secure the road. Then rebels came for us double quick.

The first line and artillery paid our respects to the rebs. Another group dismounted, formed three lines and added their fire. Mounted troopers guarded the flanks. Three-fourths of the men fought; one-fourth held horses. The enemy's infantry charged across. At 70 yards Federals rose and fired carbines and artillery, a murderous volley. Their column reeled and tottered. A quarter of the rebels fell and checked the progress of the others, who had to step over fallen comrades. Moments like these break me free of my past and future. Something larger possessed me. I had no destiny, only to play out this moment. My group fell in by a fence. Officers went to the rear with the lead horses, and we fought with no one in command. At first we held together, then drifted. Twice we formed new lines. At a bend in the road, boys squeezed into the line. I took cover behind a bush. When the enemy advanced, I heard no order to fall back and did not realize the line retreated.

Elliott Hyde cried out, "We better get out, the rebels are flanking us."

I turned around and saw Elliott but not another blue coat in sight. The instant I looked back Elliott threw up his hands and fell over backwards. A ball entered the left eye—shot through the brain—he didn't utter a word.

I matched the great horse Flora Temple's race time riding out, passed through a shower of lead from the whole rebel line. How did I not catch a bullet? An angel protected me, and I escaped. My friends rushed up, grateful I had made it. Then one asked, "Where is Elliott?" and I had to confess he had fallen.

It was now getting dark. Commanders called for volunteers to go back and form another front line. I had to go, find Elliott's body and bring it back for decent burial. Fifty of us went, but the rebels advanced no further, so they called us in.

***

Lieutenant Colonel McCullough commanded the rear and ran into enemy infantry. McCullough was a long-time friend of Mr. Lincoln and served with special permission of the President. They had met when Lincoln was a lawyer on the Eighth Judicial Circuit. McCullough had lost one arm in a threshing accident many years before the war. He was also blind in one eye, but he joined the 4th Illinois Cavalry, commissioned as Lieutenant Colonel. Cavalry duty suited him because he was a superb horse-

154

man. McCullough had served at Fort Henry, Fort Donelson and Shiloh. However, at Coffeeville a bullet struck McCullough in the right leg. He dismounted but got shot twice more, killing him. Rebels captured McCullough's escort, marched the prisoners toward Coffeeville and left McCullough's body on the field.

The balance of the Union army was near Oxford, so we had no support nearer than 18 miles. That day all we could do was get out. When we fell back, Father asked for permission to send a flag-of-truce-party to recover McCullough's body. It took days, but they brought the body in, and Lieutenant Hyde accompanied it north to Bloomington. Another of Mr. Lincoln's friends had fallen. Proof sorrow struck Mr. Lincoln as hard as anyone.

Lieutenant Colonel Herrick, Seventh Kansas, became provost marshal of Coffeeville with six companies at his disposal. He meant to take all horses, mules and equipment he could find then destroy munitions he could not seize. A force scouted all roads leading from the town, bringing in any animals fit for service.

Herrick also arrested citizens suspected of collaborating with the enemy, but after Colonel Lee interrogated them, they got released. In fact, townsfolk treated the soldiers well, offering wines and liquors of all kinds. One rosy-faced girl welcomed us with open arms, but one look at her blackened, missing teeth spoiled my desire for companionship. Coffeeville held a trove of intoxicating liquors. Fourteen barrels of whiskey, belonging to the Confederate army, in just one warehouse. Most soldiers had no supper or breakfast after a long fight. Even teetotalers began to drink.

At the south end of town one company served picket duty. Captain Sawyer stationed a guard at the entrance of the warehouse then found a place for breakfast. He, too, drank an exhilarating amount.

While he ate, a couple soldiers stormed the storehouse, but the guard held them back. When Captain Sawyer came back, he bellowed, "Arrest the offenders."

One man attempted to explain, but Sawyer drew his pistol, "I'll shoot if you say another word."

The man again spoke, and Sawyer fired. From that range even a drunk could not miss.

Anger broke loose. Someone fired at Sawyer but missed. Sawyer rode for the shooter, who spurred his horse. Sawyer pulled the trigger again and shot his rival in the head. The company erupted in jeers, taunts and fired more shots at Captain Sawyer, who rode to town, mortally wounded.

At a courthouse one-half mile distant Colonel Lee heard the disturbance. He dispatched Martin with a company to quell mutiny.

When cavalry surrounded the drunkards, Martin offered the death penalty to anyone who hesitated to surrender. His lack of fear disarmed the men, and they gave up. Martin ordered a humane punishment—the disgrace of giving up their regimental flag. His restraint prevented rebellion from spreading.

Colonel Lee withdrew the main command from town but left Martin behind with a detachment until all the scouting parties returned. It was nearly impossible to collect drunken soldiers. One company after another staggered in. A few men formed a line; others came along and collapsed to the ground.

Jerry Hough felt good, threw himself back to shout "hurrah," overdid it and went kerplunk in a mud hole. As he was unable to say more, we finished the hurrah for him. When Jerry picked himself out of the mud, it was hard to tell who he was.

Officers did their best to enforce order, but could not stop all the robberies and outrages. Martin risked his life gathering the troops. In this and so many ways army life required good luck and cleverness to survive.

A regimental court-martial convened. The sentence of the court deprived 200 men of one-month's pay. A general court-martial was also called. Trying the gravest offences took officers away when they were needed in the field.

Confederate General Van Dorn continued to disrupt Federal progress. Nathan Bedford Forrest operated around Jackson. Union forces stationed across the region went to intervene. The enemy's force was all cavalry and Grant's nearly all infantry, which allowed secesh to evade our troops and strike railroads. A Union force assembled at Pontotoc while Father was east on the Mobile road. Grant ordered more cavalry and two brigades of infantry to go in that direction. Before these troops moved, however, rebel cavalry passed safely north. Grant sent an ominous warning to all commanders to hold their posts "at all hazards."

Although he received Grant's order, Colonel R. C. Murphy at Holly Springs took no precautions. He failed to notify his command about the danger. Instead Colonel Murphy put Grant's telegram in his pocket and went to dinner.

Van Dorn divided his force, sent half by a side road to Holly Springs,

156

and the rest by the Ripley road. At daybreak rebel brigades swept in. Horsemen attacked from the east, northeast and north. On the road south, enemy patrols prevented Union reinforcements from going to the rescue. Surprised out of sleep, confused Union men did not form a defense. Rebels captured the supply depot with tons of medical, quartermaster, ordnance and commissary supplies. They plundered warehouses, cut telegraph lines, tore up track, burned the supplies they could not carry, remounted and withdrew. Rebs also captured paymasters with large amounts of greenbacks. A few paroled Union soldiers turned around and attacked, but it was too late.

A humiliating day—Confederates also took Mrs. Grant's carriage and horses. Most devastating—rebs destroyed a two-thousand-bed hospital. What crazed fools were they? Didn't they see the hardship of wounded men on both sides?

The rebs blew up buildings in the center of Holly Springs. Long trains of cars got burned and private property destroyed. Explosions killed civilians. If Confederates treated their own like this, what might they do if they invaded the North?

When we arrived, women scurried in all directions. Union soldiers went into every house, nook and corner. All sorts of paper turned the streets white. The east side of the square formerly held large brick buildings, which had become one shapeless mass. In the Roman Catholic church soldiers pulled pipes out of the organ, scattered the library, and one reckless soldier climbed the steeple and stole a silver statue of Jesus.

One civilian woman raised an upper-floor window and screamed. "Soldiers are breaking into my room, and they will kill me!" She was a good-looking woman with four children at her side.

I assured her, "Do not fear. No soldier will disturb you."

Later on a provost guard arrested the same woman for shooting one of our men, assigned to guard her house.

We came to a man sitting against a stump, wearing Confederate homespun clothes and coonskin cap. The coon's tail hung over his face, and he wore a broad grin.

Father spoke to an orderly, "Find out what that fellow means grinning that way."

The orderly dismounted and shook the fellow. "Why, he's dead."

"Where is he hit?"

Removing the cap showed a small bullet hole, revolver probably, through the corner of his eye, but large enough to blow a hole in the back of his head. The dead man clutched a handsomely mounted, muzzle-load squirrel rifle. "Look at what he brought to kill us with." The orderly took the gun as a souvenir.

Another Union General, Morgan, had heeded Grant's warning. Morgan's small detachment occupied a mill. When Van Dorn dashed up at the head of his column and demanded Morgan's surrender, he replied, "Come and take me." In search of easier conquests, Van Dorn rode away.

To retaliate for losses at Holly Springs Union soldiers took or burned everything man or beast could subsist on for a distance of 15 miles.

Just before Christmas 1862, Confederate President Jefferson Davis issued his own proclamation, calling for retribution of Union crimes. He proclaimed the South would treat black Union soldiers and their officers as perpetrators of slave revolts and turn them over to the respective Confederate States for punishment. He promised the death penalty for Union General Benjamin Butler and his officers, if they ever fell into Confederate hands. Davis gave Confederate states the responsibility for carrying out the sentences, however, thereby washing his hands of the executions. What did he hope to accomplish? He could not intimidate Butler or regular army officers. Perhaps President Davis wanted to intimidate black men, but the opposite happened. Slaves grew more eager to enlist. Coloreds wanted to show Jefferson Davis he committed a great blunder.

In the field, Confederate officers had differing notions on the treatment of black prisoners. Some, with a thirst for vengeance, massacred blacks even if they surrendered. Others treated negroes like soldiers and shipped them off to prison. Sometimes black prisoners got siphoned off to work on rebel farms as forced laborers. Would I enlist under those circumstances? The risks for slaves rose, and their rewards drew further away.

Christmas Day nobody felt like celebrating. I reflected on the army's progress. At the outset people said it would end in 90 days. Then speculated war must end by the beginning of 1863. As 1862 closed, I could no longer envision an end. More horrendous fighting was the only certainty.

General Sherman disembarked from Memphis with 30,000 men, boarding transports for a landing site on the Yazoo. Some of the boats looked pretty well used up, and soldiers who boarded such rickety vessels mouthed prayers. While on transports, we drew half-rations. Officers had to pay boat operators for their meals at a cost of a quarter each. I only ate once each day, not three times, for I hadn't been paid for months. Starvation became a regular occurrence. The government blundered, and we came up short. Degraded by hunger men grabbed anything to eat, cornmeal mush or uncooked pork. I ate raw sow belly and, in justice to that hog, she tasted good.

On the Yazoo we did not see a man, woman or child until we moved 15 miles from its mouth. There guerrillas shot from the banks with muskets and squirrel rifles, managed to kill one sailor and wound several others. When troops landed, we moved to Johnson's plantation. The road led through numerous bayous and swamps to Vicksburg. We camped on soaked ground, a dismal place for an army. Water backed up, and levees could not restrain it.

Aide de Camp until February, 1863

Some veterans from the Armies of Potomac and Cumberland also joined the thrust down the Mississippi. Hearing stories from the eastern front made me count my blessings and realize other soldiers fared worse than we did. Reinforcements got lost or stationed too far away. Privates found themselves under sudden attack with explicit orders not to fire. Eastern generals hesitated, hesitated some more, failed to get an advantage of position and privates bore the cost.

Distant train whistles sounded in Vicksburg, one indication heavy reinforcements pulled in. Bridges through waterlogged areas had been destroyed. Yet Sherman prepared to attack.

Cavalry stayed busy patrolling and scouting. One matron fainted at the sight of us. When revived, she cried, "For the last month, I have quivered with anxiety, watching for Yankees every minute, straining my eyes in the direction you might come, going to bed late, up early, so you did not find me asleep."

I wanted to reassure her but couldn't because more soldiers headed her way.

Our regiment became hardened—brown, thin, mud-spattered—but looked superb as we dashed along. Our picket station covered five miles, took 20 men to cover and required extra vigilance because it was far from camp. Distance put us on edge. One moonlit night Jim Carter served the witching hour. Suddenly he saw a man come down the path—and shot away. The report of Jim's carbine brought us toward him in a jiffy. When we arrived, Jim looked sheepish. "It looked like a man before I fired." It looked like a tree stump now, and that is what it was.

The third week of January we moved to Colliersville, 25 miles east of Memphis. Lieutenant J. B. Cook commanded the company because Captain Shepardson and Lieutenant Hyde still passed out punishment in military court. On January 27th, scouting parties went different directions. Our group of 26 men found a rebel trail. Further on we met three Union infantrymen on two old horses, who had been taken prisoners but then paroled. "Rebel cavalry," one private warned, "wear Union uniforms."

Lieutenant Cook asked, "How many of them?"

"Sixty-four."

Cook decided to overtake them. We galloped for two miles and surprised them at a house. A mounted picket in the gateway let us approach without raising an alarm. We did not expect to have the advantage of surprise but dismounted and crept forward on foot. Bushes provided good cover. When we fired the first volley, rebels broke, as if the devil pursued them. We chased until we depleted the horses, and the enemy got away.

Lieutenant Cook took a scouting force to Mount Pleasant on February 9, and we met 40 rebel cavalry. He again deployed us dismounted. We gave them a few rounds, but the rebels disappeared pell-mell.

By February 25th Martin Wallace's company had 50 men sick or absent, nine detailed and only 36 on duty. The saddest comment was—he had more able-bodied men than other cavalry units. Continual work and poor food wore away good health. We fared better than most because our shelter was better. We put stoves in our tents, which no other company had. We had bought sheet iron at a cost of eight dollars each. An entire regiment had only 176 men and 100 non-commissioned officers for duty. When the commissary failed, we broke up hardtack crackers with a rifle butt, soaked them or fried in grease to soften. These "sheet-iron crackers, teeth-dullers" and "worm castles," in honor of the weevils and maggots found in the boxes, became a staple. If we soaked hardtack in coffee, we could skim off the vermin. We beat coffee beans with rifle butts until the powder got fine enough to go in a pot and boil for ten minutes.

When an expedition to forage for beef came along, we rejoiced. If the army could live off the land, no one wanted to depend on supply lines. Army commissary meat was tough, old or rotten, so bad Alvin Chapin declared, "I can throw a piece up against a tree, and it will stick for all the world like a blue-bellied lizard." Army beef came pickled. We called it "salt horse," briny and rank when cooked. A bunch of privates paraded a piece

160

through camp on a bier, gave it a funeral, complete with military salute and shot a volley over the grave. We needed files to sharpen our teeth in order to eat it and joked we never had to carry meat. Maggots made it travel, and we put on extra guards to keep them from taking it clean away. We ate whatever came, at times downing the meat raw, for it was less tough that way. If we added water and fresh vegetables to make stew, it helped disguise the taste. Worst of all was rancid grease for frying—that strangled the gut. Army vegetables warranted derision, too. Commissaries sent dehydrated shredded vegetables packed into tight cakes. Instead of "desiccated," men called them "desecrated." Tasted like baled hay. Cooks were supposed to put the cakes in boiling water. If a man ate a cake dry, he began to writhe in agony as the cake expanded within.

Men relished fresh meat and produce wherever they found it. No farm in our path saved its root cellar or granary. We went out to collect sheep, cattle, fruits or vegetables. Though we gave vouchers, citizens called it stealing.

On one forage trip I galloped along a secluded portion of road, far ahead of the others. Under the meandering rails of what southerners call a crooked fence, I saw green calico. After a few more yards, the figures of a man and woman in a horizontal position come into view, the man uppermost. Within four rods they heard me, jumped up, the most sheepish looking soldier ever seen. The private asked about his regiment—said that he and his *wife* got left behind, so they sat down to rest. I felt sorry for any woman led astray and now slave to sexual appetite. Still, seeing her enjoy carnal desire made it hard to ride on.

***

We caught up with the brigade at daylight. I toppled into rank-smelling weeds and fell asleep in half a minute. Half an hour later someone raised an alarm. We rode to investigate, but we didn't find any rebels. We stopped in a grove, and I slept again this time as deeply as Rip Van Winkle. A few hours rest did me a world of good.

When I woke, Martin sent Ohio Cavalry around the rear of the enemy. After waiting for them to get in position, we charged. The Johnnies made no resistance, broke and fled in great disorder. If the Ohio boys had gone promptly around, we could have filled a small prison, but they arrived late and the rebels escaped.

March 7th, we found sugar-cured hams stored away and enjoyed the rebels' loss as our gain. On March 12, 1863, Martin led us toward Jackson's Mill. A local man saw our flankers coming through his field, fled to his house and armed himself. Troopers ordered him to come out, but he refused and fired. Soldiers battered down the door, fired upstairs and he fired down. Joseph Young fell in the house badly wounded, and Thomas Roberson fell mortally wounded. So soldiers set the house on fire, forcing the man out.

Martin confronted the prisoner. "What do you have to say for yourself, Mr. Forbes?"

"Oh, I was mistaken."

"From the look of my men, you aimed well."

"I am a Union man," Forbes protested.

Because he had been wounded in the right arm, Martin left Forbes at his house, and we later confirmed he was a genuine Union man.

After burying Thomas and sending the wounded one out, Martin proceeded 25 miles to Galway station on the Mobile & Ohio Railroad to communicate with Colonel Grierson. Up until now, Confederate Cavalry had garnered glory at the expense of Union troopers. We wanted to make a reputation, too. Martin sent detachments to make feints and confuse Confederates while the rest of us tore up railroads, burned crossties, freed slaves, burned storehouses, destroyed locomotives and commissary stores, ripped up bridges and trestles, burned buildings and inflicted more casualties than received.

An unintended tragedy occurred during a warehouse fire. As flames collapsed the building, we turned to go, but a father ran up, frantic, looking for his son. The next day we heard the father wailing. He sat among the ashes, holding the blackened skull of his son. My thoughts whirled at the scene and tumbled back many years when Father and Mr. Lincoln had a vehement argument over Mr. Lincoln's House Divided speech. Now, I understood why Father advised against that speech. This calamity, a father wailing for a lost son, was why my father feared war—why we all should fear war. Father had told Lincoln it was a mistake to say plainly that a house divided cannot stand. Lincoln stoked sectional fires with that speech. Southerners took it as a declaration of war. People somehow forgot war tortures fathers and sons.

In March we received partial pay. The paymaster let us draw two month's salary, which paid us through the previous November. Men with families to support became demented to get in line for the paymaster. "That is all?" They swore. "The government can go to the devil." Privates needed the $13 a month to feed their children. They enlisted for that reason. Without it, loyalty got severely tested.

When men got paid, they also visited a village east of where the railroad bent. Cabins had been built using army supplies. Negroes worked there cooking and keeping the village supplied. Some women reserved themselves for officers. Others served enlisted. No prostitute did double duty. No one crossed the line. At pay time, lines grew long, and men fought each other for a place. The average fee for a poke was three dollars. Between pay periods the whores did special services and charged accordingly. During a woman's indisposed period, she wrote letters for men to send home. I viewed the proceedings, satisfied my curiosity, watched long enough to see lustful creatures carry on a lucrative trade, but the letter writing made the whole proceeding hard to accept. One soldier had trouble expressing his feelings, so the wench made suggestions. "How about: My heart struggles with mighty waves of tenderness. I wish I had you for my bed.'"

"My ramrod is stiff," the soldier said. "Finish the letter while I get some relief." He paid her for writing and then paid another whore for a poke, so his wife received a whore's letter and then probably a husband who came home with the clap.

On March 28th the bugler blew "boots and saddles." His strong tone got us in line in only a few minutes. Rebel cavalry had attacked a nearby railroad, and we went to cut them off, but they moved a different direction. Two days later a force of 60 men, under Lieutenant Taylor, made nearly the same, unsuccessful circuit we did on Saturday, another erratic skirmish. Official accounts treat skirmishes as small bits of a greater war. However, they were more important than that. When we punished southerners on their soil, men dropped out of the rebel ranks and headed home to defend their families. Federals tore up floorboards in family homes to find hidden flour or a bag of rice, leaving mothers begging for food. Soldiers took clothes and money. Mothers didn't know what in the world they could do. What if the enemy went on a rampage through Ottawa? Would I fight miles away to prevent southerners from sacking Indiana or Missouri? No, I'd rush home to defend Belle, Ann, Ella and Jennie.

Couriers informed us Colonel Benjamin Grierson began an expedition. I felt sorry for men who served an officer like Grierson because he feared horses. One had kicked Grierson as a child, temporarily blinding him and scarring his face for life. He avoided horses. Unfortunately, when

163

he volunteered for service in 1861, they put the horse-hater in the cavalry. He requested a transfer to infantry, but General Henry Halleck refused because Grierson looked "wiry enough to make a good cavalryman." His full beard disguised the scar the horse left on his face, but any other duty suited Grierson much better than riding. He loved music and had taught himself how to play seven instruments.

However, they gave Colonel Grierson orders to create a cavalry diversion. He and three regiments of cavalry, 1,700 men, plunged south through a gap in rebel lines, rampaging the heart of Mississippi, ripping up rails and tearing down telegraph lines. Their purpose—make Confederates wrestle with all sorts of dire possibilities. How well they disguised Grant's intentions could make or break the Vicksburg offensive.

They made a forced march for seven hours over roads bogged down by heavy rains, caught the rebels on Big Creek, routed them and destroyed the Confederate camp, stores, trains, ammunition and records. The papers included the names of citizens engaged in smuggling and valuable maps of the countryside. Grierson then scoured the country southeast, losing none killed or wounded while leaving rebels well scared.

Daylight on the morning of the 10th, we learned Captain Grierson and the 6th Illinois Cavalry surprised Confederate Brigadier Robert Richardson's camp, but the secesh fled. Martin sent a courier to Grierson to see if he wanted help, but Grierson answered Martin should go and do what he thought proper, so he took us west and tracked down a squad of Richardson's men. Lieutenant Smith drove them along the road. Martin ordered another company forward to support Smith. The main rebel body turned south to Beaver Dam Bottom where the enemy evaporated. Rain came down in torrents, which made bottoms hard to pass, but a quick advance caught Colonel R. F. Looney, Major R. A. Sanford and Captain D. Bright. After securing the prisoners, Martin camped on the plantation. Colonel Looney had commanded a Confederate regiment at Shiloh where we lost Will. Did Martin have special plans for Looney? Engage in revenge? Such thoughts were beneath Martin; he put distance between himself and the prisoners. Strict discipline kept Martin going—he did not dwell on Will's loss or seek vengeance.

Grierson reentered Union lines at Baton Rouge, raising the reputation of western cavalry, as the first large incursion to succeed. His troopers seized 1,600 horses and mules with 200 able-bodied slaves. Slaves drove the stock back to Union lines. Few mules had ever worn a halter, which became apparent when slaves harnessed six together on one wagon. Before they went five yards, the team piled up and tangled. Black men wrapped their arms around unruly animals' necks, spoke gentle words in mules' ears, unhitched and untangled the team, bringing them into astonishing submission.

The cache of new livestock meant used-up animals could go to the rear. I received another horse, which I also named Rhoderic. Horses fit for duty needed shoeing. Still, we congratulated Grierson for bedeviling secesh and supplying new mounts.

We returned to camp in high spirits. What greeted us, however, turned feelings sour. Weeks' of slop and offal from tables and stable made flies congregate. Arriving pests begat hundreds of offspring. Mosquito nets became the fashion, thanks to a major who tried one. Camp smoke usually kept mosquitoes away, but I got a net, too, for protection against flies. Fleas and rats constituted the third and fourth plagues. Someone needed to design a net to keep all vermin out.

Bright, intense sunlight made days burn hot. Men fainted, worried and lost patience. If excused from duty, I went to my tent to rest but napped too long. The sun moved and poured rays into tent, which gathered and retained heat. Unbearable for someone who remembered ice creams, lemonades and cool garden bowers—such as I enjoyed with Jennie, Ella and John at home. I forced those memories shut and took up my copy of *Hardee's Tactics,* the study of which made sleep come back.

On June 7th other regiments left, and we held the place alone. For the first week it was constant duty, our horses hardly unsaddled. The next week Martin combined us with other detachments. I rode in the advance guard when rebel cavalry ambushed. Rhoderic got hit, staggered and slunk down. Even though wounded, he twisted away—did not crush me. Three men and one more horse also screamed and collapsed. I rolled away. Rhoderic's nostrils did not move. He had died while falling.

I grabbed a mule as a replacement. Lieutenant Baker accidentally shot his own horse in the charge but caught a rebel horse and leapt up. The chase took us through water belly-deep on the horses. Baker fared better than I. The mule was a brave animal but one with its own pace. No amount of encouragement from me altered his gait. Hatless troopers rushed by me, hair flying, whooping, cursing, horses frantic as the riders. Their scabbards and canteens swung and clanged. Hoofs thundered in a scene of rage. I passed two shotguns, which rebels had dropped, but the mule decided we must keep going. When he finally reached the fighting, rebels scattered into the brush. Undoubtedly scared off by the fearless mule—and rider.

Afterward we went east. Colonels Hatch and Meisner joined us with their cavalry. Then south to the Tallahatchie River. We constructed a raft to get ambulances and two-pound cannons across. Then swam the horses. The mule enjoyed swimming more than he ought and refused to get out the other side. I grabbed his ear to tell him in plain language to get out. He apparently hated anyone touching his ears because he swung his head, nipped at me then lurched onto dry land.

The column caught three rebels in the road.

Colonel Hatch interrogated them. "Where you boys going?"

"Headed to Texas on a furlough."

We had our jackets off. Grey shirts made them think we were Confederate, and we took them prisoner. I guarded a wiry little Texan, who made fun of my plucky mule.

"I'll do much better with your horse." And approached his quarter horse.

His shoulders drooped. "I was a cowboy before the war."

"Going back to it afterward?"

He did not answer, and I did not question him further. I did not want to know. I felt sorry for him but not sorry enough to let him keep his sturdy horse.

A Union soldier set fire to the courthouse at Fathernola, and flames spread through town. We picked up 50 rifled muskets found in the jail, a caisson and two battery wagons. The printing press had a partial typeset: "The Yankee's have come, look out for your hen roosts." The editor did not stay around to finish it, so the boys struck a different message and posted notices on buildings not burned down: "The Yankee's have come and rebels have run."

After we crossed the Tallahatchie, the command broke up. We had orders to burn everything except dwellings. A blaze of fences created suffocating smoke. Rebels fired on us, then broke. I could not see through the smoke, but I fired in their direction. The thud of a fallen body echoed along the ridge. Allen Andrew and I rode up to the rebel in his last agony.

Allen dismounted and did a war dance. "You kilt him, Charlie. Kilt him!"

The Johnnie's eyes followed every move, and I gave him a drink of water. I had ridden over too many battlefields, passed too many dead, decapitated, disemboweled men and did not celebrate.

"It does my heart good." Allen continued to dance.

A too-tight hitch compressed my chest.

"Would that the whole Confederate army were thus."

Death did not sicken Allen. Loss did not oppress him. I closed the reb's eyes with my hand.

Grant pushed soldiers south from Tennessee toward Vicksburg, Mississippi. He also added General McClernand's troops to Sherman's command with orders to transport them north of Vicksburg on the Yazoo River. Confederate General John C. Pemberton commanded the rebels and shifted troops to counter Sherman at Chickasaw Bayou. Sherman pushed the attack but met rifle pits and batteries he could not pass—a disastrous defeat. He withdrew in the nick of time, just before heavy rain set in, which could have swamped his forces and made it impossible to move artillery and stores.

Grant then based troops at Milliken's Bend, Louisiana, several miles upriver from Vicksburg. General Grant's body servant became a fixture in camp. Bill was as dark as charcoal. He had escaped from his master in Missouri early in the war and appeared in the Union camp at Cairo. There he attached himself to Colonel Boomer and resisted all efforts to send him away. Bill wormed his way into the officers' mess tent. When Colonel Boomer died in an assault, Bill promoted himself to headquarters but knew how to be useful. He studied Grant's habits and anticipated the General's needs, gradually taking charge of Grant's personal care as valet, waiter and all other personal requirements. Grant ate sparse meals, abhorred red meat. The sight of blood made him ill, and Bill protected him from any meats not charred. Bill made pork and beans or found fruit and buckwheat cakes, Grant's favorite foods. A useful sort of man, and Grant hired him.

The geography of Vicksburg became a formidable foe, one continual pile of hills and a fort on nearly every one. Their engineers had turned every ridge into a high-ground stronghold. Between Memphis and Vicksburg on the east side of the Mississippi River we found a vast swampy plain with little dry land. The approach covered immense distances, which meant mud and misery. Despite the lack of reliable maps, Grant moved. Approaching from the north also stretched supply lines. Stay-at-home civilians demanded action, but swampy ground trumped popular opinion, and we struggled against wondrous, thorny surroundings.

Grant needed to get men on the dry ground behind Vicksburg. He tried to bring a gunboat through the Yazoo delta—blocked. Twice he attempted to dig a canal, requisitioned local negro men from plantations, put them to work digging in an attempt to alter the river, so gunboats could pass Confederate batteries. Officers went onto plantations, took the books and called off the names of men they wanted. They offered slave owners no payment. No promise to send the slaves back. Negroes went eagerly, expecting freedom. But the Mississippi River had its own notions about a canal. Dysentery, diarrhea, malaria and fevers took a heavy toll on workers. Men also fell victim to heat exhaustion and sunstroke. The labor of making the cut was far greater than the manpower applied, so cavalry scouted for passages through the swamps. We found no clear navigation.

How could he get men downriver? Grant moved his army in his mind, blocked it out and reduced military strategy to geometry. He balanced present barriers against remote ones. He had none of a commander's bearing, no distinctive feature, no sentiment. The way he handled the business of warfare without friction or noise set him apart. People had to look carefully to see what he did.

After Grant set a plan in motion, he spent all day, dawn until past midnight in the saddle. "Close up fast," he said to men, talking around an unlit cigar. Soldiers nodded and doffed hats. Grant never inspired cheers—just dedication.

A march put troops below Vicksburg, but on the wrong side of the river. Army transports and the navy gunboats now had to run past the batteries of Vicksburg, so the army could cross the mighty current. Narrow strips of land behind levees made normal operations impossible. Yet this had to work. We had one advantage. Though turtle-slow, Union ironclads and gunboats caused great fear among rebels.

To distract Confederates, Sherman's men demonstrated north of Vicksburg. Two divisions boarded transport steamers, regimental bands blaring on the decks, boat whistles screaming to ensure the enemy did not miss the movement. His troops skirmished for two days then returned—in a much quieter way.

Cavalry provided reconnaissance along the Louisiana shore of the Mississippi, questioned residents and slept little. One master, who could no longer ride, trusted his slave, Jacob, to go out and do errands. Jacob knew the roads and conditions. "A fine road," Jacob said, "jus' fine, leads from Port Gibson to Bruinsburg." Here was information useful for Grant's plan.

Rebels had a huge advantage of position along the heights of Vicksburg. Sherman and McPherson opposed Grant's plan as too risky. April 16th on a moonless night, Union sailors piled cotton bales, hay and sandbags around vulnerable parts of the boats and set off. The low-slung boats drifted downstream like phantoms, steered to hug the Louisiana shore and approached the gauntlet. This time Admiral David Dixon Porter led the fleet. Every man in Grant's army relied on Porter's skill and cooperation. Every sailor knew the risks.

When an alert rebel sentry raised the alarm, Confederates set fire to abandoned buildings and tar barrels, which brightly lit the river and uncovered the fleet. A rebel cry went up, "Open fire!"

Porter steered the boats toward the Mississippi side to make it harder to shoot close-in targets—but barges lashed to the sides made it hard to maneuver. Seven gunboats and three transports lumbered across. I held my breath.

The rebel battery had a remarkable gun called "Whistling Dick" for its screeching, tortured sound. Dick filled every heart with dread. The enemy opened up from all sides. As Union boats rounded the S-curve several hits found their marks. General Sherman had foreseen danger and placed spotters in yawl sailboats. Their orders—if boats get blown to bits, rescue the survivors. The Mississippi dwarfed these small, single-sailed yawls, and the men braved unremitting rebel artillery. The pilot of one ruined vessel clung to a plank, but rescuers plucked him from the water.

Protected by water-soaked cotton bales—and heaven above—all the other transports got through. Eyes, not tear-free, greeted their arrival on shore.

Federal troops loaded onto transports April 30th. Admiral Porter's flagship and gunboats performed guard duty, and the armada shoved off.

We searched the banks for Confederates. Sailors stood at battle stations. The contest began. Thousands of eyes watched the fleet. We passed a spyglass around to see the deadly game. The boats lurched. The breeze swept smoke from the transport vessels, all packed with blue clad soldiers. When they landed at Bruinsburg, thanks to the advice of the slave, no enemy was in sight. They found one man at the landing, but sailors took him onboard and detained him to prevent news from spreading. A messenger boat brought General Grant across.

When two other corps got ashore, Sherman brought his men down. The uproar when Federals ran past Vicksburg was phenomenal. Now the entire force was in position south of Vicksburg.

May of 1863 tens of thousands of men moved. In seven days' time men fought at Port Gibson, Raymond, Jackson, Champion's Hill and Big Black River Bridge. The enemy put up spirited fights, but every Union soldier knew we had to keep Pemberton and Johnston from bringing their armies together. Champion Hill's became another mound of death. McPherson's troops pitched into the Confederates and fought there for many bloody hours while McClernand, who should have brought his men in as well, hesitated.

Rebel defenders fell back to Big Black River, 10 miles east of Vicksburg. One of McClernand's brigades were disappointed they missed action at Champion's Hill, so when rebels crossed the Big Black River, they went after them without orders and swept them away. The way they rampaged led us to believe if these men had acted earlier, they could have smashed Pemberton's troops. Exhausted faces of rebel soldiers said we had squandered one more opportunity.

India-rubber boats brought prisoners across the Big Black. Navy sailors inflated vulcanized rubber boats with hand bellows then bobbed across the twenty-mile wide Big Black in these tiny rafts. How glad I was to serve the cavalry. Federals also used India-rubber inflatables to construct floating bridges. In one night engineers completed four bridges. Inflatables have to be much sturdier than they look.

Sherman's soldiers set fires in Jackson, Mississippi, the state capitol. In their enthusiasm, soldiers exceeded orders to destroy materiel and punish civilians.

News arrived that Confederate General Van Dorn had been killed, but not in combat. He took another man's wife to bed, and the husband discovered them. Whoever the jealous husband was, he supported the Union cause when he killed Van Dorn. The Confederates had lost Albert Sidney Johnston and now Van Dorn, who had bedeviled us at Holly Springs.

Did another great Confederate wait in the wings to take command? A beautiful woman had made Van Dorn reckless. He courted danger and took advantage of a fragile woman. Once awakened, apparently the lady had sexual appetites. Did all women? Were they bombs waiting to be set off? How could I learn such things? Was Leah innocent? No husband or betrothed stood between us. I decided to write a letter. "I have pleasant memories of meeting you." I filled a page with tender lies. In truth, the memories tortured me.

The letter found her, and when her reply came back, the May weather suddenly seemed blistering hot, but it was my body heat rising, not the thermometer. She gave no indication of her health or status. No acknowledgment of my correspondence. She wrote treason, defying President Lincoln's Proclamation of Amnesty and Reconstruction. "I, Leah Robbins, do solemnly swear, in the presence of Almighty God, that I faithfully support the Confederacy, protect and defend the Constitution of the Confederate States, and renounce the Union of northern states and all Yankee aggressors. That I will never abide by or support the proclamations of President Lincoln." The toll on southern families grew steeper with each battle. War came to their homes. Bloody wounded died in their parlors. Husbands and sons went out and tried to do something about it. Women waited in anguish and endured battles alone. War hardened everyone, and women like Leah saw themselves as comrades in arms. Was this a test to see what I might do? If so, I hope I passed. I tossed the evidence of her treason on the fire.

In the push to Vicksburg the Union army cut its supply line and lived off the land. We commandeered provisions locals could not afford to buy. This forced food prices even higher, so poor women and children went hungry. Corn was out in tassel, but none close to the city. We had to forage further away but also found blackberries, apples and figs.

Then in May, Grant decided to assault the stronghold. Union guns unleashed an awesome cannonade and set the air on fire. The ground shook. Long tongues of fire darted out of the mouths of guns. Rebel guns returned the favor and assured the infantry they had warm work ahead. Infantry came out of the woods and formed. Colors clearly marked three battle lines. My heart sank to see our boys carry ladders. At the top of the hills, defenders waited in silence until bluecoats got close, then their yell sliced brutally like a Bowie knife. Their volley melted down attackers. Shiloh again? Up high flickers of movement. I envisioned hundreds of men yanking triggers. Muskets punched their shoulders. Smoke. Fumble in the cartridge box. Shiver and reload. All over the ravine men fell. Others rushed to earthen walls, dropped low. Rebels kept firing, no longer massed volleys but a steady, deadly hum. Heaps of bodies became obstacles for the men in a second wave. Never had I seen braver men. Very personal

171

killing, for rebs heard each man holler when struck. My arm jerked and covered my face.

General Sherman watched, too. Grim determination kept his eyes focused on the sacrifice. Commanders had reasons to be optimistic, the incredible Mississippi campaign had resulted in one victory after another. Men, too, had every confidence in each other. These capable veterans could whip rebels with one mighty assault—or so we thought—but they were repulsed with heavy losses.

Undaunted by failure, Grant made us do a more complete reconnaissance. Had we known this meant he'd send infantry in again we should have made stronger statements about the enemy's strength. Three days after the first disaster, infantry formed again. When cannons fired at them, veteran troops threw themselves to the ground. Once the weapons discharged, troops rose up and rushed forward before the crew reloaded. A deadly earnest game because proficient crews fired two rounds per minute. General McClernand reported a breakthrough on the left. His report of success prompted General Grant to send Sherman and McPherson to renew attacks. Their penetration was short-lived and descended into disaster. Southerners repulsed us at every point. Thank heaven, Pemberton was not an aggressive commander like Van Dorn or Stonewall. Those commanders would have counterattacked that day, run right over the hill while we were down. Instead, Pemberton hunkered down. He had the best ground. And asked his soldiers to hold it.

The aftermath drove horror into every man's heart. Wounded men called out, screamed, cried, pleaded. But sharpshooters waited to pick off anyone who tried to rescue them.

"I can't stand this," I said.

Alvin held me back. "If a wounded man cannot crawl out himself, even if evacuated, chances are he will die."

"But listen—"

"Water," a voice shrieked.

"How can we stay here?" I asked.

"You listen." Alvin grabbed my collar. "If you get killed, I won't forgive you."

I started out anyway—but blacked out.

When I came back to consciousness, a plum-sized lump stuck out on my forehead where Alvin had knocked me senseless. A wave of nausea struck as I tried to sit up. Through this haze, I realized the wounded men's cries had eased off. One weak moan filtered in.

After dark, I walked behind the lines. Wounded men filled hospital tents, rundown shanties and barns. Dusty floors got covered with straw. Exhausted surgeons bent over makeshift surgery tables. A few men came, detailed as nurses, but they knew nothing about wounds beyond a cut finger or a boil. Doctors separated victims into three groups. The ones mortally wounded, meaning shot in the head, neck or gut, they gave morphine and set aside to die. Ones slightly wounded got set aside to wait. Surgical cases lined up in a queue for a turn on the table. No one sheltered them from the sights or sounds. By and by, a man took his turn at rough surgery.

Infantry regrouped behind hillsides as protection from rebel shells, still within a mile of the enemy, in some places not more than a few yards. The Union line ran along behind logs and stumps, so they could pop a bullet at shadowy movement. Confederates fought to defend their homes and families and never were more effective. They dug holes in the ground, so we could not see them, only spot the smoke if a gun discharged. Such men defied conquerors, had too much hatred to wish for peace, joyful almost when they faced death. I imagined thousands of prayers, going up to God to give them victory. Vicksburg's school children, as part of their daily lessons, undoubtedly learned to curse the Union.

No one declared a truce to bury the dead. Vultures floated overhead. Days went by, and bodies grew rank. In May's heat the stench grew. Some men had died six days before. Finally General Pemberton sent a message to Grant, asking him in the name of humanity to recover and bury corpses. Flags of truce finally came out. Details buried hundreds, if not thousands, of dead soldiers while the rest of us aimed at the rebel lines. Piles of twelve-pound shells sat near cannons, but no one violated the white flags.

On a scout we came to a small, hewn-log house with a well. Soldiers, rabid with thirst, pleaded to leave the ranks for water, a privilege not always allowed in enemy country. This time permission was granted. General Sherman rode in to drink as well, and he noticed a book on the ground. "Private," he called to the nearest man, "hand me that volume." It turned out to be the Constitution of the United States and the title page bore the name 'Jefferson Davis.' Sherman sent the soldier to find a resident.

A negro confirmed the house belonged to the Confederate President Davis, and another Davis brother owned a plantation nearby. Sherman found elderly Mr. Davis at home, tended by a niece, both overwhelmed with grief to see "damned" Yankees overrun the area.

Shortly afterward, David Call rode directly in front of me. A bullet struck his face, so loud the "thwack" made me shudder. He stopped a bullet in my place. I was too shaken to write to his family and asked Alvin to do it for me.

Heavy losses and the terrain forced Grant into siege operations. The City of Vicksburg had nine-mile long redoubts, log-reinforced trenches and 30,000 defenders, but General Grant had 70,000 men, and a cat could not sneak out of Vicksburg undetected. Both sides watched each other's movements. Siege guns fired and made residents run for cover. Cavalry patrolled areas to the Federal rear and carried messages from one end of the long line to another—the heavy toll on horses caused a rapid decline in our effective strength.

With a siege underway, a backlog of mail and newspapers arrived. Ella wrote about Ann. "Your sister's brow knits with worry. For whom, she does not say. What she leaves unsaid is more potent than any declaration she makes. She and I hang on every word, every scrap of news from the front—about you, other kin and friends."

I sent a response off to Ella immediately to let her know I was yet alive, asked her to visit Ann often and treat her as a sister in my absence.

Desperate heat plagued us. Both defenders and assault troops sizzled in the sun. Union artillery created a semicircle around the northern, eastern, and southern flanks, and David Porter's Union gunboats lobbed shells from the river. Black gun smoke filled the air. Brimstone burned our nostrils. Guns gave hell to Confederate effectives and citizens alike. Shells burdened the air going in and out of Vicksburg, ascending and crossing paths with spectacular clouds of smoke. Bombardment reached the city and its cliffs in a constant rain of debris. Confederate gunners returned their compliments. The sun set like a huge ball of fire, the moon rose over Vicksburg, truly a scene never to be blotted from memory. Even in pitch dark, shells targeted the city.

Slaves dug caves for terrified residents to escape cannonades. Bombproofs honeycombed the hillside. Military men viewed cannon duels as tests of skill, but they fired so often every breath reeked of powder. Loud peals of artillery reverberated. Rebel batteries placed together in line formed deadly defensive positions. Guns belched forth case shot and shrapnel. My heart ached for children, who must live in constant dread, startled by every sound, their mothers not knowing what form danger might take, longing for news from the outside world, yet shuddering to think of those reports.

If Grant feared the challenge, he didn't show it. How did he stay calm? If we got whipped, it meant our cause was lost. The odds twisted my stomach. Rumors abounded. We heard Joe Johnston headed in our direction again. If so, we must drive him off, as commanders said, 'at all hazards.'

Lead whispered, 'This one's for you.' Across the great Confederate redoubt terrific musketry made Federals run herky-jerky. The city was all confusion. Soldiers felt tolerable safe in pits though they always had to remain vigilant. The most dangerous part was going in or coming out of trenches. Men went pale, muttered courage to themselves and ran.

Other times Blue and Gray declared informal truces and traded tobacco for food. If firing eased for a while, the contenders got acquainted.

Johnny Reb asked, "Who you gonna elect as the next president?"

"Certainly Old Abe," the answer went back. "Anything new on your side?

"A new general."

"Who might that be?"

"General Starvation."

"Well then, Reb, come on over and have some coffee with us."

"Havta decline, for this very night we'ze comin' over to take you in."

"No, sir, we cannot see things in that light."

Men fired bits of hardtack across the line at the enemy, and the Confederates were glad to have it. Bad as our stores were, Confederates fared worse. One reb called out, "Hey, Yank, we want cornbread, not hardtack."

"Sorry, Reb, fresh out."

We intercepted their food shipments and found mold and cobwebs in Confederate cracker boxes. Didn't seem possible to eat any of it. Secesh deserters confirmed horrid conditions. "It's only a matter of time before they feed us hooves and horns."

One midnight shots rang. Turned out to be a feint, but it tricked a couple of our boys. Gunshots at midnight are a dangerous business with a particular talent for jumbling a man's head. The next letter I wrote home went to our neighbors down the road. "Tell Henry, not to feel desperate about killing a reb before the supply runs out. And tell him not to enlist."

Rebs tossed hand grenades the size of goose eggs at our lines, but these exploded only when they hit in just the right way. Impact on a hard surface exploded them, not fuses, so soldiers on both sides made a game of catching grenades in blankets and tossing them back.

One Copperhead newspaper, *The Chicago Times*, outdid all others agitating for the North to give concessions and stop fighting. So an order came down: "The sale or introduction of the *Chicago Times* is hereby forbidden until further orders." General Sherman called the editors traitors, railed against appeasement. "Stay-at-home citizens are convinced the South can fight indefinitely, but if it lasts 30 years we must fight it out. The moment the North relaxes, the South will assume the offensive." Sherman wanted the army to suppress all newspapers like the *Times*. The number of Union deserters was growing, and newspapers encouraged soldiers to shirk. In his capacity as Colonel, Father got called to serve in military courts to deal with deserters. When General Grant heard about the newspaper ban, he countermanded the order and let papers flow freely, even those printing disagreeable content. Thankfully southern newspapers remained ferocious and declared reconstruction impossible. With a few insincere professions about peace, Confederates could have secured an armistice. Send everyone home. But chivalry demanded the South continue, and Sherman's prediction of a thirty-year war looked likely.

I watched two soldiers slip out, headed north, but did nothing. I did not want men ready to desert next to me in a fight, so I let them go. I longed for home, too, especially when prospects for peace looked dim.

A few men deserted because they didn't want to serve with blacks. Prejudice outweighed reason. Different ideas about nigger soldiers divided the ranks. Some men hated them for no reason other than race. Others didn't trust their will to fight. Whatever the reasons, coloreds received scant training and got sent into battle against Confederate veterans, slaves one day, soldiers fighting their masters the next.

When Grant decided to blockade Vicksburg, he drew troops away from previous outposts and filled the gaps with black soldiers. Six months ago, Milliken's Bend had served as Grant's headquarters. Now that the main thrust moved south, the army left a few soldiers at Milliken's Bend for garrison duty. The detachment included a few white men but mostly freed slaves from Louisiana and Mississippi. Milliken's Bend was one way for Confederates to get in and out of Vicksburg and relieve the city. Captain Miller described the fight. "Four Texas regiments marched at night and attacked Milliken's Bend at 2:30 a.m. on a Sunday morning. Texans drove Union pickets hedge by hedge, across ground overrun with briars and tie-vines. When rebels gained open space, they screamed. 'We give niggers and white cohorts no quarter.' Fearful excitement heated the blood of advancing soldiers as well as defenders. They exchanged deadly fire, and Union soldiers, not killed, fell back.

"Even a black boy who served as a cook begged for a gun." As soon as I heard that, I had hope for the outcome. One man often turns the tide of battle, in this case one boy acting bravely. Under fire, fear is a wildfire, but so is bravery. Feelings spread from one man to the next. One boy stands firm, and his fellows fight. One man turns to run; others follow. To fend off the Confederate assault, commanders told Union troops to hold their fire. If soldiers maintained the discipline to wait until word is given, patience makes them formidable. This time, however, faulty weapons caused trouble. Union cavalry should have been there to guard the flank. Without any mounted troops to stop them, rebels flanked the fort and rushed over entrenchments. Inside men fought hand-to-hand with bayonet or the butt of a musket. Bayonet fights rarely happen. Firearms mow men down before the lines come close enough for bayonets. This time, however, opposing lines crossed. Casualties showed point-blank powder burns on clothing. Two corpses lay together, each with the other's bayonet in his body and claret streaks of blood across the faces. The brave, young cook sustained a gunshot, the kind he may have survived, but Confederates answered his plea for water with bayonets.

Admiral Porter moved the Union ship *Choctaw* within range of Milliken's Bend and lobbed shells at rebels. As Texans pulled back, Union reinforcements came across the open field. One negro captured his former master and brought the prisoner into camp.

"Why didn't you shoot him?" others asked.

"Mo' fun to watch him squirm."

The coloreds had not yet completed musket training before they fought. Many men didn't receive rifles until the day before. Now mangled bodies lay strewn along the breastworks. Even though raw and untested, coloreds' tenacious defense proved they could fight. Six hundred black soldiers met death, not rashly but steady and obedient to orders.

Captain Miller wavered on his feet. "I never felt more sick at heart than when I saw how brave soldiers had been slaughtered, one man had six wounds, all the rest with two or three. I never more wish to hear the expression, 'The niggers won't fight.' Come with me and I can show you the wounds that cover the bodies of brave, loyal soldiers." Every southern fire-eater called arming blacks a great calamity.

Here was a lasting way to hurt those who supported slavery. If negroes made good soldiers, southerners knew they had lost their slaves and could never reclaim them. At Milliken's Bend blacks prevented rebels from cutting through Union lines. Their defense with an assist from Admiral Porter enabled Grant to tighten a noose around Vicksburg.

The way we lost these brave men put other soldiers in ugly tempers. Why the hell did we come? To endure swamp mosquitoes and die in impossible assaults?

Mississippi's heat oppressed us. My friend, Henry, who could not spare it, lost 20 pounds. "God be thanked for His mercies," he said.

"Which mercies?"

He pointed toward the 17th Illinois. "The infantry creeps into rifle pits every fourth day and stays for 24 hours. A generous God made us cavalry."

Infantry boys fixed up awnings of wild cane to have some relief from the sun. They crouched on ground full of insects, bugs a plenty.

Continual cannon fire shattered nerves. Vicksburg wasn't like an open battlefield where cannoneers tested their bravery. Out in the open, several batteries got placed in line to defend positions. Every soldier sees the truth of it—the only way to safety is to push forward and overrun artillery—not so in Vicksburg. Gun batteries belched. Shot all day at anything, nothing or phantoms. Both North and South had ample powder and shot. Skilled cannoneers let loose at leisure.

At night bombs put on shows. Union mortar boats anchored on the other side of the river. Charges got loaded with a keg of powder. Cannoneers needed long strings to pull such locks. A flash came first, and 15 seconds later I heard the sound. Bombs rose high in the sky, fuses bright all the way like falling stars. Shells had casings three inches thick and powder enough for a dozen big guns. The mass reached an apex of 1,500 feet, descended in a great arch and made a hellish blast. Not hard to imagine the damage to homes and churches. After the Union tightened the noose around Vicksburg, commanders placed siege guns. Then mortars rained down from the east as well as from the river.

At this point I returned to Grant's escort. To protect against Johnston's forces, Grant set up an additional defense line behind his first, positioned inland toward Jackson, Mississippi.

178

The 8th Wisconsin was typical of regiments who sealed off the city. They held a position opposite the city, served as sharpshooters and prevented the enemy from escaping. Occasionally units like these received shelling from the rebels, but they were not driven from their post. Of course, their mascot eagle, Old Abe, held his perch, too. Tall tales reached us—the eagle made aerial reconnaissance and passed vital information along the Union line. Just how an eagle with clipped wings did these amazing feats was never explained. But we had the entertainment of hearing the rebels jeer at Abe, "Wild Goose" and "Yankee Crow," as if somehow insults could demoralize the bird.

Expressions hardened; faces blackened from sunburn or grew sallow from malaria. No more Union attackers rushed forward. The siege ordeal lasted more than 40 days and 40 nights. Then it became clear General Pemberton had no hope—for reinforcements or that starving rebels could force a breakout.

The third day of July firing ceased, and negotiations began. By this time Grant's beard was turning gray, the color of iron. He wore it close-cropped. Grant sat impassively, while General Pemberton pulled his whiskers continually. Hopes had been raised and then dashed many times. Firing was heard to the northeast, which we could not account for, so we hesitated to believe this was the end. The fire turned out to be jubilee in a Union camp, soldiers giving vent to their joy, firing off several hundred rounds.

Dawn broke in spectacular fashion on the 4th of July. We still wondered. Were the rebs truly done? Must we watch for an escape? Quiet hovered over the lines. Finally loud huzzas broke, and we heard Vicksburg aimed to surrender at 10 a.m. It did not end with glory in battle, but taking Vicksburg—hard to put the feelings into words. Men fell to their knees, talked over one another in babbling voices, threw hats into the air. Alvin grabbed his head with both hands, as if his mind could not believe the news. Even General Grant's eyes gleamed.

Then rebels began to walk out. Rather they stumbled. The contrast struck me. Our robust men looked well-fed and in fine form compared to skeletons in butternut. Strange to see men who a few hours before shot at each other, chatting, mingling, even shaking hands. It surprised secesh when we did not cheer. Guns fired a national salute—this time with blanks. Union soldiers fell in. Secesh soldiers hated to surrender on the day the Founding Fathers declared independence. Brave men wept. What bitterness. How could they give up? It was against their nature and tradition to surrender. Starved men staggered as if drunk. They were greasy with dirt and sweat. In their place, how would I act? Grateful to live one more day—or too despondent to take the next breath?

The band played "Hail Columbia" and more rebels came out, some delirious, others maniacal. When we marched into the city, we found munitions unbounded but children too weak to stand. If the siege had gone on, it must have ended in mutiny or madness. Military quarters were filthy; the hospital the same. If Grant had lost patience with the siege or political pressure forced him to charge the works again, many more men would have died. Rebels fared much worse than we did. How long before we wore out the Confederacy?

It took time to issue provisions to so many prisoners, so individuals traded food for tobacco. Tobacco rebs had in supply, food none. Hunger made army bread fried in pork fat a delicacy.

To borrow from coloreds—a day of jubilee. Vicksburg was ours.

News also came regarding General Robert E. Lee raiding in the east and striking Union territory—what kind of brave soul attempted that? Did Lee succeed? Or did the eastern army finally whip rebs? Dare we hope the Army of Northern Virginia got trounced?

Where was Nellie Grant on July 4th? I asked Grant's aide how Nellie celebrated her eighth birthday. "Did she know Vicksburg surrendered on her birthday?"

"Not sure if she knows. She is raising money at a Sanitary Fair in St. Louis for the soldiers' benefit," he said. "She dresses up as the character of the Old Woman who lived in a shoe." Just the thing. Nellie as the center of attention, making people pay for the privilege of meeting General Grant's beloved daughter. Surely news reached her. The Union captured a great city in honor of her birthday.

Then I received a sobering letter from John. "Corruption makes me tremble for success in the field. Officials enjoy wealth and put it above the misfortunes of the country. God forbid money misobtained. May they see the blood of brave men and the tears of loved ones on every corrupt dollar." Agitation kept me awake several nights. Armies buried the country under countless casualties while profiteers raked in money. What hope did the nation have? The country struggled, down on its side like a mare giving birth. A vulnerable time, when death hovers near for mother and colt. Could the nation survive? Was our republic being reborn? What did President Lincoln say when he heard of our victory in the field? Did it lift his spirits? He always gave soldiers sincere thanks for their patriotism and suffering, warmly praised their courage and recognized their service. Whatever he said, I imagined the Kentucky modulations in his voice rose with intense feelings. In 1861, Mr. Lincoln had said, "Soldiers who bear their country's cause are the only real thing."

The city of Vicksburg certainly did not feel real. Union soldiers searched everywhere, under porches, even outhouses to make sure no secesh escaped capture. What an insult—for Yankees to raid privies. A regiment of black soldiers then marched in. Black men well-dressed and toting guns challenged local authority, a fine show for coloreds, a dark day for the South. Secesh women wailed and tore their hair. Children hid behind their mothers' skirts.

Destruction marred every street. Dirt covered everything. Some residents, the fortunate ones, had left months ago. A mortar struck one house, straight down, roof to cellar. Another house lost half its rooms. The greatest curiosity was the hillside, where homeowners tacked carpet to cave floors and walls to keep dust down. Tunnels filled the ravine.

Union soldiers ransacked houses. After what the troops had been through, they saw plunder as a right—an expression of newfound power. It took strong hands to control them. Some commanders did the right thing; others ignored the looters.

One southern citizen defended his household. "Get off my porch."

A woman appeared behind him, a waifish figure who reminded me of Leah, although her hair was darker and her eyes not nearly so bright.

A sergeant raised his pistol. "You have no say." He cocked the hammer with an eager thumb and pointed the gun in the homeowner's face. The woman ran forward, but the owner pushed her back.

I put my hand on the barrel. "Easy."

The sergeant's eyes glared and strangely remained unfocused as if he peered through cataracts of hatred.

"Are we victors or vandals?" I asked.

His lips curled into a snarl, but he lowered the gun then pulled negroes off the street. "This is your new home." He installed the couple in the house, displaced the owner and gave the family's clothing away. He could not bully the whole South, so he made this hapless man stand in. The sergeant's anger could not be undone.

181

Charles H. Dickey, Journal
Volume Five, Summer of 1863 to February 1864
March out of Vicksburg, Wounded in the Shoulder, Field Surgeon's Care

By the time Vicksburg fell, only 300 out of 800 cavalry troopers had horses healthy enough to mount for duty. Out of those, some horses no longer trusted their riders. When cannons shot, skittish horses turned hell-bent for the rear. Horses had learned, like men, to lack dash. They suffered more than we did for want of decent food. Grain was not to be had in Vicksburg, and the government did not bring forage downriver. The Army of the Cumberland, besieged at Chattanooga, swallowed up available supplies. The lack of feed rendered livestock useless.

President Lincoln declared August 6, 1863, a day of national prayer and thanksgiving for recent victories. Throughout Union-held territory commanders suspended drills; chaplains held church services; soldiers received passes to attend. After chapel I went for a walk. Rather I drifted unaware. Suddenly I found myself on the Vicksburg hillside where 250 men had died in a space of about twelve feet. Without a bugle, I hummed "Taps." *Day is done... To thy hands we these souls, Lord, commend.*

General Grant left Sherman in command at Vicksburg. What will history record about Grant? It should say he balanced the nearby fight with the remote. He took a natural course. As a person, they won't call him a great hero. Perhaps call him a sensible man.

News of Federal victories from other areas followed Pemberton's surrender. Good news from many points—Banks took Port Hudson, Meade whipped Lee in Gettysburg, Price repulsed at Helena with heavy loss, Bragg driven back in Tennessee. Our whole camp rejoiced. Sherman now wanted to cut the Confederacy in two. He had proposed the idea when he commanded at Cincinnati and, for his pains, people called him "Crazy Sherman." Those of us who served with him knew better. He broke up railroads and bridges to make it nearly impossible for southern armies to threaten the Mississippi River again.

Before leaving town, I took a block of wood from the Pemberton-Grant oak, where they agreed on the terms of surrender. When time permitted, I planned to whittle a star as a keepsake.

Two columns rode out, one under General McPherson, the other with Sherman. As part of McPherson's bodyguard, our five companies led the advance. The second day everything seemed in order until rebels charged down a hill. Their cavalry used frequent dashes to torment Union soldiers. A single rifle flashed, but many more followed. Panicked troopers in front turned and dashed backwards. I called out, "Rally!" and a few did, but the enemy overrode them. Horses piled up in a writhing mass. We fought with sabers, cut rebels out of their saddles and then charged other Confederates wearing Union clothes. The scuffle knocked Rhoderic over. Fortunately, Rhoderic fell without crushing me and rolled back up, or we would have been ridden over.

I reined in, tightened my knees and leaned forward. Rhoderic outstripped the enemy. When I got ahead, I turned in my saddle and fired my revolver into the pursuing force. Pretending I had support, I shouted, "Rally. Rally!"

The Confederates stopped and—for a wonder—did not fire a shot. I went around a bend in the road, rode half a mile and found our men, now under the command of Captain Collins.

Part of our force had left to perform guard duty. The remaining four companies turned and found the enemy where I left them. When we rode in, I was at the left of the line and aligned our force, partly protected in some woods. Suddenly I felt a jolt at my left shoulder. I turned to see who had hit me with a club but found no one.

A blood stain grew along my sleeve, so I moved to a sheltered spot. There I found a man face down with thick brush twisted over top. He groaned, unable to speak. "Let me get you to a more comfortable position." I turned him and put my canteen to his lips. He murmured an inarticulate request. The shoulder straps indicated a Confederate major. I made an assumption. "I don't have any brandy." A look of disappointment spread over his face, but he died a moment later.

Another wounded soldier repeatedly called for help some distance off, but I could not go to him. Whether he received attention, was Union or Confederate, died or recovered, I never found out. The boys fought for every foot of ground, drove the enemy step-by-step and once more became the advance guard for the column.

A half hour later a doctor rode up and saw blood dripping from my cuff. "Let me see how badly you are injured."

"A flesh wound," I said, "not serious."

He made me stop, so he could look. "A ball went through. You will not fight more today."

"I must," I said. "I am adjutant of the battalion."

183

He probed the wound. "The bullet came out without touching bone." He bound up my shoulder, and when I tried to get on my horse, I faltered and fell.

"You've lost too much blood. If I had not come along, you could have bled to death."

He dosed me with opium and put me in an ambulance with other wounded men headed to the rear. One man complained of being cold and asked me to lie beside him. "What's your name?" I asked.

"Sam Campbell."

"Now that we're on friendly terms," I said, "I will try to warm you." The opium made me drowsy, and I fell asleep. When the ambulance hit a rut and jarred me awake, my new friend Sam was dead. I did not move away, not right away, but straightened his coat and combed his hair with my good hand.

Noise came from the left—or was it the right—the din of cannon rattled fog-filled air. Another wagon carried dead men. A still arm pointed straight up and shook as the wagon rolled down the road, appealing to heaven for vengeance. We lost too many handsome men, fighting over plots of ground. I begged God for fortitude but could not lift my head up. The ambulance jerked along for two days and finally deposited us in a hospital at Canton. From there a surgeon sent me to Vicksburg, another tedious, jarring journey. Pain radiated with every bump. I longed for Rhoderic. He knew how to carry a man, while the ambulance driver did not. My arm swelled amazingly, a wonder I did not die of blood poisoning. By the time I arrived at the main hospital, fever set in. My constitution became unbalanced. Soldiering had exhausted me.

The orderlies left me alone on a mattress filled with leaves. Memories came and attended me. Ann and Belle, Ella and Jennie flittered in and out. Leah, too, appeared in a beautiful gown, royal blue my favorite color. Her eyes brimmed, but she remained silent. I reached out, took her hand in mine. She shivered. What was it I felt through her skin? Fear? Loathing? She remained wordless like a stone-faced judge waiting to hear evidence in my trial.

The hospital surgeon applied cerate to keep the wound open. General Sherman's adjutant granted me a month's furlough, but the doctor refused to let me go anywhere until the "secondary suppuration" took place. He said it could take up to five days, and waiting became the hardest trial of all—lying in bed with nothing to think about except the tardy progress of my wound.

I dreamed of Leah Robbins at night, but when awake Ella came to mind. Where was she? How was she? Did she feed soup to other wounded soldiers? How lonely I felt—and yet not alone. A soft Indian summer and harvest moon replaced the roar of cannon and coughing men at camp. Such silence! I desired Leah and longed for Ella—wanted both. Either. Just to gaze in a woman's eyes, touch my fingertips gently to a soft, pretty cheek, draw comfort from nearness, even steal a kiss of love. Hold a rush of passion back for love's sake, love as I breathe, unable to stop for more than a moment. Pressure inside grew. I must inhale. Exhale. Gasp for breath. Eagerly attend the gentle sex, womankind is the one, true source of relief.

My wound did not cooperate. Five days, six, seven unproductive. I grew tired of war and everything connected with it. My mind tumbled down a trap door—I was growing up, got sent away to school where I starved. Another school and another, no cure for being homesick at any of them.

Finally pus erupted the wound which, according to the doctor was a sign of healing, and he released me. I boarded a steamer with hundreds of other invalids. Stevedores also loaded coffins, some occupied, some empty. "Why load empty coffins?" I asked. The answer—for men who died along the way. Did they load sufficient empty coffins? Hard to travel in pain, even more painful to understand the possibilities.

As the steamer approached Ottawa, the smell of the prairie revived me. Rich, black earth deeper than a plow can furrow has its own mellow fragrance. Soon followed by the scents of my father's house, where Belle made biscuits and Ann roasted hens, where folks laughed, Belle's piano echoed through the halls and Mr. Lincoln was a familiar friend.

Over the next weeks shreds of fabric worked their way out of my wound, gray threads from the shirt, blue from the overcoat, if white the threads came from the undershirt, if dark blue part of the blouse. When the field surgeon had bandaged the wound, he failed to draw out the dirty clothing.

Many months of sleeping outdoors made the house close in, so I went to the porch and made a bed on the floorboards. I carried a patchwork quilt along and wrapped up in the scent of washing soda.

Ella appeared one afternoon with a bouquet. "Not summer flowers, but heartfelt nonetheless." She had gathered dried pods and stems and tied them into a spray of fall color. "This is lobelia." Her hand brushed mine with mesmerizing effect. "The little pods hold seeds."

"Let's go plant them."

Her face lit up.

"How long will it take for them to grow?"

"Next spring they should sprout." She rushed to the yard. "How about your old potato plot?"

I traipsed behind her. The plot faced southeast. Ella pulled out weeds, scuffed and leveled soil with her hand, eager to get dirty. With my arm in a sling, I had a good excuse to shirk and just watch her bend to the task, a tender sight whether flowers grew or not. Together we stripped the seed heads from the dry stems and planted the next generation. She sowed without much preparation. "Nature can take over from here. You must come home to see them take root and grow."

"I will do my best."

Her brow furrowed. "Come home to stay."

***

On my return to duty, I held onto the image of Ella happy and carefree as she scattered seed. I went ashore at Vicksburg. A mansion previously used as regimental headquarters had been razed and breastworks put in its place. A negro woman who had worked for the Grants recognized me. "When da house was destroyed, I hid the music in my cabin."

She brought sheets that the Grant's governess and I sang as duets. "Thank you," I said. "This is thoughtful of you."

A smile teased her lips. "Glad to give it to you. It ain't my kinda music. No dancing, hand clapping nor no foot tapping."

The regiment now encamped near Natchez with Martin Wallace in command of horsemen. His orders were to disperse rebels, raid surrounding countryside and help drive the enemy into smaller areas. Frequent fights kept everyone on alert. When rebels cut off a forage train, white and colored cavalry boarded transports in Natchez, went down river ten miles and disembarked on the other side. When we found the enemy, we charged for a quarter mile, and our company got ahead of the main body. Rebs decided at that moment to rally, so we formed across the road.

They shot Cy Simmons in the chest. "Somebody retrieve my pistol."

I retrieved it for him, but Cy waved it back to me. So I emptied it in their direction while Cy slunk down. He smiled at me and bled to death. I felt a sharp pain in my left leg as if a knife had cut me. I looked down and discovered a ball had cut a hole in my trousers and grazed my leg. By then the command reached us, and the enemy fell back.

One soldier near the side of the road cried out for water. He had been shot in the shoulder like me. Also like me, the ball had passed through him. I bound up the wound, mimicking what the surgeon had done for me—but not soon enough for him. Two men had died in a matter of moments. My temper raged. After a brief intermission, rebs came in a column, heads down, no yelling, no churning, just a sullen, heavy tread and hep-hep-hep of boots at the double quick. We kept fighting until three a.m. Scrimmage in darkness created strange and fearful pictures, some skedaddling on our part, but I refuse to name men who turned, not even here in a private journal, lest someone pick the book off my dead body and find out which fellows lost courage. Another regiment came to support us but made a poor cut, and the enemy got an opening to concentrate against us. The moon shone full and clear. Nature calm and resistant to change, grass rich, black walnuts on the trees and yet a battle raging, many good fellows lying helpless amid the rattle of muskets. The god-awful rebel yell came across the field, but our men screamed back. Martin Wallace stood solid and showed his men how to be determined fighters. When the enemy finally pulled back, four of them were dead and several more boys prisoners. They indicated we had fought 250 of the best men in the Confederacy, the 7th Texas.

Martin took us back to the transports and Natchez. When I arrived in camp, I found a report indicating I had been killed. Thankfully, I headed it off before the news got dispatched home to Ann, Belle or Ella.

The next expedition, under the command of Colonel Embury Osband and Major Chapin, combined ex-slaves with 75 white men. Our detail headed into Arkansas, hoping to arrest some rebel cavalry who had decided to hang negroes and drive off livestock. I commanded 15 men. After ferrying down, we came to the "old river," as people called it. Long ago the river changed course and left a lake. The first glimpse was a wonder. Thousands of wild ducks, geese and swans covered the surface. Never have I seen such a display of fowl. From bank to bank the whole stretch of water, black, white and brown with birds. A concert of wildlife—coons purred, whimpered and growled low tones while thrushes sang sweet melodies.

We marched 25 miles and camped near some negro cabins. The scout proceeded to Meriwether's Ferry on Boeuf River. Colored soldiers camped near the house and the whites camped in a cotton gin, both surrounded with waterlogged swamp. Although no rebels were known to be nearby, we posted 10 men on each road, 10 more to guard the camp. Still, I felt uneasy about the perimeter. In unfamiliar country a force could come from any direction. What would General Grant do? I needed his knack for seeing the whole landscape. The enemy might appear any moment. I could not shake the feeling, so I added vedettes between the roads.

Even so, I got the men up and saddled before daybreak just as a volley reverberated behind the cotton gin. During the night rebels had slipped between pickets. They shot volley after volley, which stampeded the horses.

A negro company got all mixed up with my men behind a rail fence. No time to disentangle them. So I passed along and told each soldier to fire low. Steely eyes watched and waited until I gave the order. "Fire at will!" One negro fell, and I took his carbine. The enemy matched us shot for shot. All we could do was keep firing.

Darkness gave the rebels an advantage, and they charged the 1st Mississippi Cavalry. Other officers got the balance of the negro regiment into line, and they held, at one point fighting hand-to-hand, but rebels could not dislodge them. All these coloreds were raw troops. Though they had cause, no one showed any sign of panic, even when comrades got killed or wounded. If the coloreds deserted, panicked or suffered simple defeat, the whole notion of arming blacks might fall apart—along with prospects for ending the war. There never were such men—not slaves—men. How different from the first day at Shiloh when whites straggled back in confusion. This was a much smaller battle but just as fierce. I claimed victory. "Confederates are dispersing into the woods."

"Hurrah!" a trooper shouted. "Each reb running a different way."

I found I had soaked my shirt with sweat, but never felt so proud of anything as our black Billy Yanks.

At daylight, rebels carried off their dead and wounded, except one man within ten feet of the fence. How close they had come! If I hadn't gotten the boys in shape before daybreak, what might have happened? What if colored troops succumbed to panic? Many white men did the first time under fire. Even these wounded men refused to go to the rear. Any man who stood unbreakable should count among veterans.

We pursued the enemy but did not find the main body, just 10 enemy dead. More of their wounded must have been thrown on horses and led away. We left two men too severely hurt to travel behind with an assistant surgeon. He staunched the bleeding and decided to stay with them until the boys could be moved. We took other injured men to camp. I remembered what it was like to feel every bump and jar radiate through a wound and proceeded slowly. Along the way we captured horses and mules to cover our losses, although the quality was not as good as the ones lost.

Major Cook boasted about the colored troops. "I could have held the enemy off till the last man was shot."

As we headed toward Natchez, we repulsed a number of rear attacks, but finally the rebs gave up. Audacity made up for what we lacked in numbers. Because the enemy force outnumbered ours many times over, we ferried back.

When the paymaster arrived, the money he issued was, once more, less than what the men had coming. The government remained three months in arrears. Henry Johnson lost his temper. "No amount of money is enough for what we endure."

Alvin looked him up and down. "Seems fair—for the likes of you."

Everyone laughed heartily—especially the paymaster. But their amusement died down quickly and an uneasy silence replaced it.

Our colonel eyed blacks, waiting at the end of the line for their money. Waiting to receive a disparity in pay. The government paid blacks less than whites.

Not aware of how closely coloreds watched, Alvin kept after Henry on the subject of money. "Just be thankful you are not paid what you're worth."

Henry opened his mouth to take exception, but the colonel's expression turned harsh, and Henry accepted his wages, not with grace, but in silence.

The colored filed in last, their heads high, regardless of the inequality of pay. Expressions carved in stone. They deserved more pay than whites for facing rebs who gave no quarter.

White troopers presented grievances to Father. "Where is our back pay? The War Department is a pack of good-for-nothing thieves, getting rich on supplies meant for the troops, and would die of fear if they ever heard a cannon blast." Father rode into a mutinous group without escort. Fear for his safety clutched my heart. A few men held back and kept their opinions quiet until they saw which way things turned. Others surged as a mob, but Father refused to say anything until they formed up decently.

189

The sergeant cried, "Fall in! As recognition of the Colonel's rank."

One old veteran, who had served from the beginning, cried out, "Do not curse him. Never will we have a better commander."

When they stood in military formation, a sense of discipline crept in. Father held up a hand for silence.

But the men shouted for their back pay. "And stop the unnecessary labor put on us—just to keep us busy while waiting for the next battle."

"I swear on my life," Father said, "to use my energy to get what is owed." Men made menacing sounds in their throats. Some tilted chins to the ground. But the mutiny withered. Later, when we called the roll, dozens had to be marked absent without leave. At the war's outset men came for excitement—but disappointment wiped those reasons away. The quest, for soldiers who stayed, became just hold on long enough to undo rebellion.

During the summer I got a short furlough to go north and act as the groomsman for another colonel, who married Miss Emma Gilson from Kankakee. Thomas Ransom, now Brigadier General, was supposed to go but could not be spared from the front, so I had the honor of taking his place. Any trip back to Illinois, no matter how short, was a blessing. Miles and miles of prairie passed by the train window. Such rich soil, just waiting for a plow. If I shirked, who would turn me in? Not war-weary locals. I could resign my commission and get paperwork through. Then the train passed Charleston, where Lincoln's family had settled. Mr. Lincoln's relatives still lived in the area. He was a product of this land. The next time Mr. Lincoln came to Ottawa how would his visit go? Would he look at me—or through me? When we next met, I wanted Mr. Lincoln to smile with the warmth I had known as a child. Mr. Lincoln's approval became a reason to return to duty.

Back in camp, I had to make quick work of packing because a steamer arrived to take the regiment north. Before eleven o'clock the next morning we boarded, bound to Memphis, where I served at headquarters. Secesh filled neighborhood verandahs to capacity. To close the day I sang with Charlie Hardin and Billy McLarsen. Before we started singing, locals took the night air, but a few measures of "Rally Round the Flag" sent southerners scurrying. Only Union sympathizers remained to hear "The Battle Cry of Freedom" or "Cheer Boys Cheer" or "Red White & Blue." They gave long and loud applause, and from the choice of songs we learned which neighbors were fire-breathing rebels and which were loyal.

Sunday morning church services made an impression. A good many local parishioners welcomed me. Their ceremony of Holy Communion awed me, and I hoped to benefit by taking the sacrament. The woman next to me didn't need the hymnal. She knew all the songs by heart and sang in a sweet voice, but one muffled by the deep mourning veil shrouding her face.

Serving in town I began to regain weight lost in the field. I had fallen from 143 to 132 pounds, and the flesh between my ribs still looked whittled away. I worked confirming and copying rolls with Captain Chandler and Mr. Mitchell, tedious but important work. Captain Champion of the 63rd Illinois from Bloomington moved into the boarding house with us. He sang bass well and filled out our quartet. Champion stood six-feet tall and strong, and his deep bass voice rolled like distant thunder, an all around good fellow. Lida sang soprano, Lou alto, the Captain bass and I sang tenor. When we got going we made some noise. Our rebel neighbors gave me a secesh song, titled "There's Life in the old Land Yet," but I had no enthusiasm for learning it.

Guerillas became thick in the area. They had kept quiet for some time but came back stronger than before. Their attacks made it impossible to wage "soft" war against civilians who protected ruffians. Blistering assaults hit supply trains then guerillas scattered and blended with locals. Rather than meeting us in battle, raiders slipped under cover of darkness and captured soldiers and supplies. A few thousand marauders, sheltered by the community, could immobilize an entire army. The Union had to return terror in equal measure to what was received, and civilians paid the price.

Belle wrote a letter about our Ottawa neighbors and her own accomplishments on the piano. Though she reported nothing earth-shattering, her letter energized me, as if I went home for Sunday dinner. Before the war I lived every day surrounded by family, never separated from relatives or friends. When my enlistment ended, should I sign again? Service in headquarters set easier. Army life tamped down my high-strung nature. The decision was harder than I expected. Father had returned to Ottawa to rebuild his health, so I wrote for his advice as a colonel *and* my father. If he was not home when the letter arrived, I asked Ann to get it to him as soon as possible for I needed an answer.

Brother John wrote back from Ottawa. Father was traveling but gave John advice to forward. "Charlie better enlist—if he thinks other men in the company and regiment feel agreeable toward him." John expanded on

Father's advice. "Father expressed no doubt it was best for you to go back to your former company and leave headquarters." What was wrong with staying at headquarters? Too close to an ample supply of whiskey and fallen women? More glory in the field? If I were home, Father would allow me to question his reasons, make sure I understood what was best for me, but to do that I needed to see his face. Watch eye movements. Consider how tightly he held his posture. Without personal guidance, I wavered. Most of all I wanted to slip back to Natchez and find Leah. Serving in the field meant more opportunity for that.

Besides, a chance for promotion to captain seemed like a good possibility; seven-eighths of the company wanted me. I only knew of one man I needed to watch, and no one liked him. After one grueling scout, my antagonist, Thomas Mead, came to headquarters to find me. Before this he always showed meanness of spirit. Today he said, "We want you back."

"In the past you worked against me."

"Every company has its clique." He tapped a hand over his heart. "Even with coloreds, you show pride of conduct."

"We can all hold our heads high."

Thomas pledged friendship, and others followed to express support. So I reenlisted. However, it took a week to get my papers straight, move out and follow my company. When the paperwork came, I embarked on a worn out steamer. The soft sighs of water against the hull brought ladies to mind, but this was a closed boat, no courtesans on board. One cabin had a piano, a miserable punishment to play. The G key below middle C was broken, and the rest sounded tinny. Even classic songs came out sounding low-down, so I left the keyboard and borrowed a book called *Lady Audley's Secret*. The story opened in a unique way: "A noble place ... a house that could never have been planned by any mortal architect, but must have been the handiwork of that good old builder, Time." My fascination with such a house kept me reading, and then the story turned personal. The baronet's daughter, Alicia, was an excellent horsewoman and a clever artist, spent most of her time out of doors, riding about the green lanes or sketching cottage children, plowboys and cattle, all manner of animal life that came in her way. The character made me think of both Leah and Ella. The horsewoman being Ella, who spent time outdoors, and the artist was Leah, with tapered fingers ideal for sketching. I began reading to fill the empty hours. As the story developed, however, it delved into the female character. "She set her face with a sulky determi-

192

nation against any intimacy…" This caused commotion inside. Like Leah, the woman was so often admired she lost her need for suitors. Perhaps I could understand Leah through reading. I read more, and my reaction became visceral. "There was something almost touching in the manner and tone in which he spoke to her—half in deprecation, knowing that he could hardly expect to be the choice of a beautiful young girl, and praying rather that she would reject him, even though she broke his heart by doing so, than that she should accept his offer if she did not love him."

What did I hope to see in Leah? The author knew the ways of the world more than I did. Some southern women used talents and bewitching smiles to secure favors from Union officials. The suitor in the novel was a baron. Would Leah look at a lowly lieutenant with soft eyes? If I rose in rank, might she consider me? Or continue to reject me regardless of accomplishments?

The boat docked at Helena sometime during the night and laid idly at the wharf till ten in the morning. A picturesque place, set in a spot between high bluffs, but like so many places, filled with soldiers and showing effects of war, missing fences, buildings infested with bullet holes and deeply rutted roads.

Men, too, showed the ravages of war. I could tell which men were veterans from the looks of them—stale, unseeing and lounging gaits. Battle-hardened men without airs who moved by rank, and yet somehow indistinguishable from one another. In an atmosphere of scalding heat and stifling dust, perspiration drenched uniforms. Dust clung to hair, beard, eyebrows and eyelashes and became muddy plaster, disguising men's faces out of semblance to humans. I spent my twenty-first birthday covered in pulverized soil—and glanced at my reflection in the water. My face had become that of my discipline wielding grandfather.

I returned to the living conditions in the field and soon regretted the choice. I wanted a fire and built a good one, but wind drove the smoke, filled my tent and blinded me. One officer drank every day. Little love was lost between us. I guessed he disliked me as heartily as I did him. I welcomed the rancor. I could not get favors from him and did not ask for any. I could command better than he.

The regiment scouted until we learned the towns, streams and fords as well as men who grew up in Mississippi. Then we moved to Messenger's Ford, on the West Side of the Big Black River, twelve miles northeast of Vicksburg. This camp was the best I ever had, populated with magnolias, white Beech, half a dozen hollies, ornamented with Spanish moss in long rolls. Squirrels skipped around the trees. Coons and owls made music for the night. God's glorious trees provided shade, shelter, lovely to look at, but like every camp, the place had its share of pests. The biggest nuisance—chiggers determined to bury themselves under my skin.

I cheered the promotion of Martin Wallace to Colonel in a Brigade under Colonel Edward S. Winslow. On the 25th of September, Winslow commanded as we forded Big Black River. The next morning before dawn we moved toward Canton. Wary men marched by twos and filled the road for nearly a mile. Colonel Winslow gave instructions for the advance guard not to get more than half a mile from the head of the column, but troopers smiled at this order, as we had formed the advance many times. At every hilltop we dismounted and scanned the road ahead without showing ourselves to the enemy. All was quiet and no sight of any troops anywhere.

The city of Canton elicited emotions, hard to suppress. Sherman had perfected a policy of making war hard on civilians. Few men remained, so women scampered to save their property, some militant, others crying, one laughing hysterically. Their fine city, a seat of fashion, wealth and southern refinement—ruined—a fearful reward for treason. We confiscated anything we could use on the road: corn, wagons, carriages and horses.

The countryside teemed with rebel scouts. Ten miles out we discovered Confederate cavalry, equal in strength to ours. The enemy formed two detachments, half stayed 300 yards behind the others. Their commander should have deployed them on higher ground. With their first squad so distant, Lieutenant Cook wanted to break their rear. We charged down the long slope, screaming like devils. Shot poured into our flank. Fear flickered; my nerves rattled more than usual. Rebels fired while still mounted at 200 yards, fled and then dashed past their own rear squad. My nerves settled because we operated as an organized body of cavalry, not just scouts or escorts. We supported and received support. A long overdue use of cavalry. Finally in the third summer of the war, we proved our worth as horsemen. Sergeant Cook said, "Now the War Department may see what western cavalry can do—and allow us to do it."

A steamer brought some friends of mine, Frank, Jim and Bill from LaSalle county. At first, they recoiled at what they saw—bare-faced boys; sallow men; threadbare officers and seedy generals; the prevalence of diarrhea, bilious fever, yellow eyes and malarious faces; the mud, mist and the rain. I felt it best to say it straight. "The sights destroy all ideas of gallant-

194

ry," I told them. "Conditions are hard, but through it all men do their duty."

Though I must make them into soldiers, I disposed of formalities. I drew full uniforms, got my friends into saddles and sent them to the river to wash. Soldiers were supposed to bathe once a week, but many men ignored the order. My friends had arrived notable in their dirt. "I bathe every day I can," I said. Frank and Jim accepted my suggestion; Bill less favorably, so they dragged him to the creek. When they came back, I complimented them on their transformation, remembering the disruption new recruits felt. I kept them away from a group of veterans who had served two years and were demented to go home. My friends acted stoic but emotion showed in the song they chose that night. "Many are the hearts that are weary tonight, waiting for the war to cease," and "Many are the hearts that are looking for the right, to see the dawn of peace." I quickly had my fill of that and said, "Let's have an old story."

"Such as?"

"Alvin, tell the boys about the day a lizard crawled inside your clothes." Frank and Jim pestered him until Alvin told the story. Bill merely stared at the fire's embers. Hopefully after a few days, he can see how games and pranks help.

Everyone's spirits rose when the company left for a ten-day scout. Soon after we went out, First Lieutenant Ed Main sprained his right hand and could not fire a weapon. He thanked heaven we returned without an engagement.

At night I fell into my tent, but sleep did not follow. I went back to the fire and "talked" to my sisters and Ella by reading their letters. The pages had begun to tatter from repeated reading.

War took another turn when the army organized the 1st Mississippi Cavalry (African Descent.) General Grant promoted Embury D. Osband from captain to colonel of Mississippi USCC. Other officers, the lieutenant colonel, two majors, three first lieutenants, regimental surgeon and two assistant surgeons also came from the 4th Illinois Cavalry. If a white man served in a black regiments, it meant opportunities to advance unavailable in the regular army. Since the early days of fighting, former slaves had worked as servants, cooks, grooms and teamsters. Later Grant used black soldiers for garrison duty and occupations that freed up white men. He professed no faith blacks could bring fighting to a close, anymore than Germans or Irishmen. To him, blacks were soldiers, no more, no less—

but they deserved to be treated as such.

The notion slaves might make good soldiers went down hard with the rank and file. The question of how to employ negroes troubled bigots. Yes, their presence withdrew labor from the South. Yes, every slave taken weakened the enemy and made it harder for Confederates to continue to fight. But that did little to soften resistance when Grant ordered blacks to the front lines. This raised another worry. How would rebels treat captured blacks? The best chance for African troops to stay alive was under officers, qualified to lead them in a fight.

Deep dissatisfaction grew. The air thickened with rumors of revolution. Some whites advocated installing a military dictator. I overheard a conversation among officers in "favor of a change in Washington." I shivered. Men, who swore to protect the Union, now declared against the government for emancipating slaves. "We fight the battles, risk life and limb. We don't free slaves."

"By God, we have a right to dictate government policy."

Everyone knew slavery was abolished as a practical matter, but serving side-by-side with slaves was different.

Arming blacks roused bitter feelings in the South. War-weary people renewed their will to fight against us. Southerners again united in action— and rededicated themselves to our destruction. Confederates hanged some captured Union soldiers of African Descent and proclaimed their intention to murder more. In response, General Grant made no threats or pompous declarations. He merely announced it was his duty, "to hang captured Confederates if the practice continued." Military hangings stopped; private lynching did not. Rich planters drove niggers away from battle lines to keep blacks out of Federal hands.

To fill colored regiments, Grant sent expeditions into Louisiana to bring back able-bodied blacks. I anticipated giving them a long training period, but none followed. Blacks got mounted on captured horses and thrust into active duty while they learned. Just the opposite of the weeks we had drilled in Ottawa, Springfield and Cairo. White recruits had floundered, needed six weeks of daily drill and still felt unprepared. Coloreds learned under fire, guarded picket lines never exempt from attack. More than once, they left a drill to repel attack—but they wanted to serve even under these conditions and especially wanted to become horse soldiers. The cavalry seemed a good place for them. Some have unmatched skills as horse-doctors and showed themselves as fine riders.

In turn whites grumbled. "To hell with niggers."

"I will shoot one quick if he gives me sass."

Veterans puffed up. "While we performed day and night, rain and shine, blacks did as they pleased."

"We are the slaves now." And so forth, white boys ranted. The ambition for many men became separation from niggers. Emancipation created a rush of sympathy in a few soldiers, but great rancor in others.

Martin Wallace rose to the new challenge. He enforced strict discipline in his base of operation at Brownsville Landing. I washed off the grime of three days' march, dropped into a childlike sleep, unmindful of the babble of voices around, only to hear "fall in!" and jumped to my feet. Reports said 300 rebels with cavalry had moved near Jackson. To go after them we cooperated with Colonel Lindorf Ozburn. Martin must follow Ozburn's orders, impossible as they were. "You will endeavor to cultivate a conservative friendly feeling with the people where you will be." Had Ozburn ever commanded in the field? Our men looked haggard; white faces had turned dark red with sunburn; gaunt with fasting and severe duty. Wiry, not heartier, but hungry for battle like wolves. Disheveled from sleeping on the ground, dirty from riding through clouds of dust, soaked over and over again with rain or perspiration, and plastered with fine-grained soil, until trousers became stiff enough to stand alone. Always in the open air, never penned in four walls or roof. Joined by blacks, we flew after rebels. But feeling 'conservative and friendly?' Not these men. Soldiers set aside sociable manners—in each engagement they became Huns, first and foremost consumed with winning.

Captain Hudson of General Grant's staff accompanied us toward Big Black River. We camped in drizzling rain at nine o'clock. The lack of feed for our horses forced them to browse on brush. We hardly drank our coffee and rolled onto blankets when Lt. Brand, the scout on whose word we had gone out, came to report rebels between us and Vicksburg. Everyone dashed back onto the road we just left. Brand took two companies down a side road to get to their rear, while the Colonel and remainder proceeded slowly to allow Brand to get in position. Then we dashed and surrounded the house they were said to be, but the rebels had left.

Colored troops came in with two prisoners. The rest got away. A prisoner said, "We thought you was guerrillas and did our best to escape." We sent the prisoners to Vicksburg, returned to camp and did not get to sleep until half past twelve, my saddle as a pillow.

I was awakened twice to make changes in the guard. At three-thirty I got the troop up. The scout led us this way and that, got lost three times, so the Colonel stopped on a deserted farm, killed a cow, fed us and decided reports of rebels were untrue. He turned around and went back to Vicksburg, arriving at four p.m. Pursuit of the enemy was a farce, but it showed how well colored recruits rode.

The next action—Lieutenant Cook led a four-mile chase after three rebel companies. We saw only dust, heard shots and had no way to know whether we chased 14 or 14,000 men. I gasped for breath as the hooves beat the dirt. Then we ran into Texas Rangers, covering the rear. When Lieutenant Cook's horse fell in the road, we abandoned pursuit. However, the spirit of the chase pleased the Colonel. We picked up 17 abandoned carbines and camp supplies. Soon afterward Lieutenant Cook became Major of the 3rd United States Colored Cavalry. The coloreds showed no hesitation, even against Texas Rangers. Few expected them to be so bold.

Major Harry E. Eastman, 2nd Wisconsin Cavalry, searched for the enemy and at a plantation owned by Mr. McKay heard which road the enemy had taken. We marched toward Port Gibson and discovered their trail going west, followed it instead and our advance guard stumbled onto rebels posted behind a narrow, steep redoubt. Enemy cavalry had taken possession of Alfred Ingraham's plantation, not far from Port Gibson. We entered a gate at right angles to the road without seeing the enemy because they sheltered behind a hedge and high picket fence. Eastman dismounted 50 men and sent them to flank the Confederates' left, but before they completed the move, the main rebel column flew through a rear gate. We rushed the enemy, and they scattered like spray. Again we pursued. At every available cover the rebels wheeled to block us. They chose positions well, but Eastman refused to stop. Then they took position behind an embankment, which commanded the only approach. Shots flew over our heads. If not, they could have decimated our troop.

Two-thirds of our force dismounted, sent horses to the rear, took cover and scattered rebs again. The time it took to remount gave them a mile lead. Catching up brought us unpleasantly close to Port Gibson. Our horses were exhausted and men low on ammunition. Therefore, Eastman finally broke off, and Martin Wallace and 4th Illinois Cavalry took the front. We returned over the same six miles of road just fought for and found nine dead and two mortally wounded rebels, dead and disabled horses, cartridge boxes, arms of every description, everything that could be cast off or kicked away. Eastman's face beamed because we had come through well.

Of the six prisoners, we sent four forward and left the two mortally wounded at a plantation. The prisoners had no firearms. A rebel boy, too young to shave, blurted out. "We cast away our arms if not able to hold them." Thanks to his innocence, we found 45 more guns.

We also left David Kingsbury at the plantation for care of a thigh wound. He was a strange fellow who disliked women, always shuffling away with downcast eyes when one approached him. No one knew what caused David's strange reaction. The matron of the house received all three with humanity. David's eyes went wide, but this time he could not shuffle away. I rinsed a rebel's shirt in well water, no soap being at hand, and tore the shirt as a tourniquet, which the matron used to staunch the blood. Despite her effort, David succumbed. Now his eccentricity is gone forever. I wish I had gotten to know him better, tried to understand his discomfort.

A black trooper had been wounded in the wrist but begged to continue. Since David no longer needed a tourniquet, we used the same rebel shirt as a bandage and let him return to the ranks.

Three horses also got wounded, so we took replacement mounts from the prisoners, and left the disabled horses in the care of plantation darkies.

While I applauded Martin Wallace's success, I feared for his life. Like his brother Will had been, Martin led from the front, a deadly place. He seemed to be in a contest with Eastman to see who was more visible in battle. Major Eastman slapped Martin on the back. "At Ingraham plantation didn't we have a lively fight?"

Martin clenched his teeth but kept silent.

I shuddered at the word 'lively,' but a colored trooper, named Daniel, nodded his head in agreement.

I studied him. "You stayed calm when pursuit got hot."

"I just stand my ground."

"I find that harder and harder to do," I mumbled.

He lifted his chin up. "Us colored see further."

"To the end of fighting?"

"To history moving—the country changing."

"I wonder if you are right, or if the nation has stepped into quicksand."

When Captain Ramsey was ordered up river to redeem Rosecrans, Ramsey looked considerably thinner than when I saw him last but said his general health was good. He sent best regards to my sister Ann.

We learned Mrs. Grant was coming down and expected to remain with her husband, so we thoroughly cleaned camp and prepared for inspection. Mrs. Osband also came. Soldiers from miles around rode over to catch a glimpse of the ladies. No one has an idea the pleasure of seeing a gentlewoman in camp. It rained every day, but spirits improved because of the wives. Some rain to settle the dust was desirable, but instead we got a deluge that saturated everything. Officers tightened discipline—hats off to the ladies, they bring out the best in otherwise despondent men. The company had been running loose. One of the officers now showed up at roll call. The boys all turned out when commanders showed enough interest to come out, too. The inspection we prepared for, however, did not happen. Apparently Colonel Wilson did not like to be out in the bad weather.

John Wallace, now Colonel Wallace, stopped at the door of my tent. "Charlie, I'm on my way over to the depot. I have to leave and want you to see Emma safely onto the train tomorrow." His hands trembled, I knew, at the thought of leaving his wife.

Taking care of her was the least I could do, said so, and did not dwell on the subject of their parting. Around Emma, John became a patient man, as thoughtful and indulgent as she was with him. The two of them together made me ache for a loving wife. Not that the couple ever made a display of affection. The softness in his voice and the gentle looks they exchanged showed the tenderness they shared. I walked with John, but when we got up the hill, his train rushed past.

A mischievous gleam lit his eyes. "I have been misinformed as to the departure time."

"Now you can escort Emma yourself."

He smiled and wasted no more time talking to me.

On the way back I stopped at headquarters to secure sick leave for one of our men but instead received an order. "Go out and collect loose niggers." Our company started out at eight a.m., traveled 40 miles, collected 30 negroes with many pack animals, muskets and shotguns. After riding all night we returned at five the next morning.

Newspapers reported thousands of freedmen under arms, doing good service. "They have more reason to fight than we do. They fight to get wives and children out of bondage, while whites fight for an idea." What if slaves had been declared free at the start? If they had been in the ranks at Shiloh? Could the war be over? Of course, many northerners still felt sour about freeing slaves. The public wanted to save the Union but not welcome slaves into their towns. I wished President Lincoln talked more about freedom. His high-pitched voice had the carrying power of a steam whistle, and his mind found what was right. He could make the course clear.

On October 15th Colonel Winslow's Cavalry Brigade started out at the head of General McPherson's corps with eight days' rations. General Logan, former Illinois Congressman and Mr. Lincoln's friend, came along. We went by way of Messenger's Ferry to Brownville, where we charged, skirmished and displaced a force of rebels. General Logan flung himself into the melee, rallied Federals and stemmed a rout. We fought until dark before falling back a short distance to bivouac.

The next day two columns separated, one toward Clinton and the other toward Canton. Each branch looked splendid, bright arms glistening in the morning sun. Our regiment and 5th Illinois Cavalry led the Canton march. I rode in the advance but soon got called to the side where infantry engaged the enemy. We guarded the flanks until two p.m. when the enemy finally gave way.

We then escorted General McPherson and staff to the other column and took the advance again. Until we came to a cornfield with rebel artillery occupying a prominent, defensive position. We advanced a skirmish line, but their artillery opened up with the correct range, so we shifted back and dismounted farther out of range. We took cover behind a bank. Again shells rained. When we saw cannon smoke, we hunkered down. Shells burst close but did not hit us, so we jumped up, swung our hats and yelled, all in fun.

October 18th our regiment took the lead. We ran into a strong picket force but drove them for half a mile. After making a deep cut, down and up a rise, a long line of infantry suddenly appeared with cavalry to protect their flanks. Artillery massed behind them. Three hundred yards separated us. Their artillery could reach five times farther. Without orders we halted, and the column closed up. The rebel battery fired four rounds of grape and shell. One shell scooped along and took two legs off a horse then buried itself in the ground without exploding. It could have blown us to atoms, so Lieutenant Hyde yelled, "Four right about," which we executed with the precision of a drill.

Another shell came through our column, angling through three sets of four men, killing Grandy's horse and wounding Charlie Munnikhuizen's horse, so he had to leave it. The same shell burst and killed one of Colonel Winslow's orderlies as he came to order us back. Rhoderic plunged forward unmanageable, bursting the harness breast strap and girth. I tumbled off with the saddle between my legs. An orderly caught Rhoderic, threw the blanket and saddle on and gave me a leg lift. I mounted without girth, held on with my knees and scrambled to rejoin the troop.

Rebel cavalry followed us but halted when we did and waited until we moved again. We guarded the rear until three p.m. when the 4th Iowa Cavalry relieved us. The infantry went in another direction and left cavalry on our own. Three men in our regiment received grievous wounds, two men killed. We guarded the rear all the way back to camp.

The third week of October, cavalry reported to Lt. Col. Cox, Chief Commissary. Twenty of us provided protection for drivers headed out to scrounge cattle. I had been invited to a dance at a local home that night, but the beef scout kept us out. My choice would have been songs over food. Fortunately one of the ladies noted my absence and invited me to a candy pull the next evening.

On Sundays I inspected knapsacks, which meant a review of every man's belongings. Soldiers who carried too much fell behind. If a man kept his knapsack light, he fared much better. Properly packed gear made all the difference. After inspection I fed and watered Rhoderic then went to services at a Presbyterian Church. Services had full attendance—of widows and orphans. Mr. Morgan of the Christian Association preached from the Book of Daniel. His thick brogue made him hard to follow, and he repeated himself many times over but his subject piqued my interest. Biblical Daniel prayed and continued to pray daily even as he walked in the lions' den. Bullets whistling past my ears and cannons shaking the ground had to equal Daniel's danger.

"A Christian soldier is effective," Preacher Morgan cried. "He is firm in conviction of an afterlife, a strong belief that makes him, conscientious and willing to die. A refuge waits for him in heaven, where God tells us there are no more wars or rumors of wars.

"Though he dies by the sword, he fears no evil for his soul will be released from the vale of mortality to walk with God in heaven." That made me fidget and wish he finished. A soldier has many reasons to be faithful—faith in his ability to aim a weapon, faith in military discipline, faith in watchfulness, faith in the ultimate success of a cause, but faith that overcomes fear? At Shiloh I mouthed prayers. Vicksburg, too, but fear never left. Preacher Morgan said that had to be my fault. "A man must take it upon himself to be instrumental in the answer to prayer." Did rebs trust God to make them fearless, too? Mr. Morgan left me with more questions than answers.

On the next forage trip we came upon a procession of rebel deserters, but the usual meaning of the word did not apply to them. They shuffled along in a slow, worn way, at the limit of endurance. Their costumes did not deserve to be called uniforms. Some had bare feet; others one shoe; one man naked except for a shirt on his back. A tale of misery and collapse. Two trudged along like a couple with arms around each other, afraid of getting separated. Some wore lice-infested blankets; others had sacks on their shoulders. We administered an oath of allegiance to these clay-colored escapees and sent them North. One horse blanket found new use. A rebel fell down, and I placed it over the corpse.

Society improved at headquarters. Officers' wives and daughters improved all facets of military life. The possibility Ann or Belle could come made my heart flutter. Emma Wallace returned, and she wanted Ann to come down, too. Then we learned Ann's home had caught fire. Fortunately she discovered the blaze while small, and neighbors managed to put it out. I trembled to think of her narrow escape.

Down here, houses like Ann's had no one to rescue them. Engineers destroyed one to make room for fortifications, a pity to destroy such an excellent home. Even with the structure down, the grounds remained beautiful with gravel walkways through gardens—except at one place where a rebel colonel lay shot five times.

When a courier saw me, he reined up. "I have news about your brother." During reconnaissance toward Canton, Martin Wallace skirmished with rebel cavalry. Cyrus now served with Martin. Cyrus and others had halted to feed the horses. At a fork in the road, the enemy attacked, but Martin and his men repulsed them, and then they camped for the night a mile from town. Closer to Clinton they again ran into an enemy force—this time with artillery. Mountain howitzers opened up with shell and shrapnel. The ideal weapons here, howitzers are highly mobile even in rugged terrain. These cannoneers got Martin and Cyrus in the line of fire. Cyrus shouted, "Every fellow find hiding," but the forest offered insufficient protection. The howitzer spoke again, and the missile was shell instead of solid shot, exploding mid-air, sending fragments every direction, many falling among the men. In the field soldiers have no way of knowing how experienced a gun crew is. Sometimes cannoneers fail to adjust the elevation, and shots pass overhead. Sometimes deadly accurate. "The whole time," the courier said, "I never saw a better officer than your brother Cyrus—cool, deliberate, obeying orders in dignity even when musket balls flew thick as hail. The enemy must have lost one hundred men killed, wounded and prisoners. The cannonade lasted two hours."

Martin and Cyrus moved near the Clinton and Vernon crossroads—again against enemy cannon securely posted. The boys ached to fly at them, but darkness prevented an attack. The rebs made a ruckus on the right, and rebel yells rolled ferocious, as insistent as an eagle's scream. But the rebs did not come. The command camped for the night with cavalry on picket duty. All did their duty, and the courier praised Lieutenant Colonel Martin Wallace, "an efficient and gallant officer."

***

General Sherman continually conjured up some new dealing. We didn't know what he might do next. At times troopers worried about his fits, but Sherman had a mission. He knew it was impossible to protect all the railroads. Confederate Generals Hood, Wheeler and Forrest had lighter commands, and Sherman's large force could not match their fast movements, so Sherman detached himself from supply lines. Other commanders called this a cardinal sin, but he abandoned the old character of warfare. Sherman fought a war of geography, not just against the opposing army. Further criticism came when he ignored guerilla bands, bushwhackers and deserters. He said, "Ruffians deplete southern lands as effectively as our army, so we will let them pursue insidious ways." When Union men raided, people called it "jayhawking," not a bird known to nature, but men feared for predatory deeds. "Bushwhackers" were Confederates—no distinction in criminal behavior, just the same sort of chaos. Countless homes got ransacked and smokehouses emptied. How was Leah now? Did she deal with the jayhawks? Concern welled up like blood from a stab wound.

Our company joined Major Funk's command, along the way passing a residence with a gray-haired matron at the gate. Her face provided a window into a harried mind.

A trooper called out. "Take heart, mother, the war has to end soon."

She pointed to a camellia in resplendent bloom. "To cut the flowers," she said, "means certain death."

The trooper gave a cheery response. "The South will be back in the Union soon."

"If it always had been so, my heart would not be broken."

"I wish I could ease your sorrow," I said.

"No amount of water," she said, "can save severed stems."

When we moved on, Major Funk brought us to a ridge where we met 20 rebel cavalry. Their carbines and rifles flashed fire at us, and the path grew hot, but we ran them two miles before they escaped.

We kept on scouting, picketing or guarding forage trains. To honor President Lincoln's proclamation for the first Thanksgiving, I arranged to go to Vicksburg for supplies, but a boat arrived with a paymaster on board. His visit came like a thunderclap. The government was months behind, and no one had written the company roll calls. I forgot about preparing for Thanksgiving and helped with the work. Soldiers' families back home might be destitute. Before dark we finished the rolls.

The paymaster gave several months pay, and I expressed $150 I didn't need to my brother John with instructions to invest it. My trip for Thanksgiving delicacies never happened, but spare cash made it easier for men to stomach beans.

During winter, combat slowed because of cold, rain and snow, and the men built permanent sleeping quarters. Several joined together and erected log cabins with thatch roofs. They plastered mud between the logs to stop icy winds. If the ground had been a camp before, they moved into huts from the prior winter, complete with previous occupants' lice, fleas, fouled water and waste dump. Lettered signs over the cabin doors described, not the shelter, but the owner's state of mind: Walker's Happy Family or First Avenue Hotel. A few showed patriotic fervor: Old Abe's Parlor. Others depicted a grim fact of life: Chateau de Hardtack.

Fear of shelling, night attack and picket lines took a toll on troopers—add exhaustion, bone-chilling cold, sticky mud, poor food, too little of it, bad water, rats, stink and no end in sight. Some men managed to bear it. Others reached their limits. One fellow shot off his toe, knowing the wound did not get him out of the war—just this campaign.

In December we boarded steamers, landed at Natchez and camped on the Pryor plantation east of town. Two days later we moved inside fortifications just north of town. We scouted or guarded forage trains every three days—in addition, every day posted pickets on seven roads, each consisting of 10 men and non-commissioned officer. This arduous duty exhausted horses and men. Troopers with no horses stood nightly guard duty around camp, especially to protect the few horses held in reserve.

Before Christmas, I secured a pass that allowed me to visit Leah. When I arrived, however, her father barred the door. "I pray you and she are safe," I said.

A hard look warped his face, and he slammed the door.

The windows rattled with the force of his anger. I withdrew to the public sidewalk yet lingered, intent on any sound. I heard nothing. No music, no movement. The eaves whispered my hopes for Leah, 'peace, prosperity and safety.' I scanned the windows hoping for a glimpse. My mind shaped her face—there behind a curtain in the upper window.

Now I fully understood men who deserted, so they could return to wives and lovers. Emptiness made my mind malfunction. I could not leave. Could not go forward. Darkness fell over the house. No one lit lamps. If I remained, how long would they sit in darkness? Rather than harass Leah's family, I marched away.

***

Lieutenant Knox, a mustering officer enlisted enough blacks to fill four companies. Some white soldiers, who abhorred recruiting niggers, spoke treason. "Currently no rebels come within forty miles of this camp, and we see no earthy reason to stay—except as escort for colored cavalry."

"What a fall—from escorting Major General U.S. Grant to stealing niggers." Some boys acted crazy around colored troops. I wrote Father to ask what he thought of arming blacks, but then tore the letter up. I knew his stance. He was not what any minister called a pious man. Nonetheless he felt blacks had souls and god-given rights—on that point he and Mr. Lincoln agreed.

Two captains and one lieutenant left to serve on a military commission, so Lieutenant Smith and I became the only field officers for the whites when we got orders to scout northern Louisiana. Coloreds served under Major Chapin, who commanded the expedition, but I wished Martin Wallace had the column. He inspired more confidence than Chapin.

A colored orderly improved my lot. Dick took care of my horse, kept my arms in good order and rode along on the scout. He could cook anything, even turned possum into a tasty meal.

When 11 black women and children stumbled into camp, they looked as if they had gotten the worst of war. They had nothing I call clothing to wear. One woman had three children clinging to her side, said she had been on the road for some time; a more forlorn, worn-out creature I never saw. Her master used her like breeding stock to increase his holdings. Her four oldest children were still in slavery. Her husband dead. Desperation had pushed her into hiding. Still, the plantation held the rest of her family. Losing kinfolk and children made her stay as long as she had. Most slaves felt the same, tethered to a plantation because of family.

While they waited to get quarters, the fugitives questioned us. "The curious expressions we heared—a forecast of liberty. Do it include us?"

"Yes, you can leave your masters for good."

Some of them bore marks of injury and abuse. "But we heared slaves are to be sold to pay the expenses of the war."

Was that true? No official word to that effect.

Major Chapin said, "That cannot be true."

Was he sure? Or just expressing a belief?

True or not, the slaves rejoiced. "Spread the news of freedom! Oh, happy, jubilee day."

The prospect of blacks pouring into camp gave me pause. The blacks we had did well as soldiers, but the prospect of training scores more made me consider a transfer east or even west to Texas, some corner where no one knew me as Colonel Dickey's son. For Father's sake, I studied patience, forgot wrong-thinking. Still—a hollow feeling filled me.

The next scout dampened resolve further. We marched 150 miles through cane brakes and bad roads. A large enemy force never materialized. We found just one rebel private, who scurried into the sugar cane. He fired twice with a splendid, breech loading Maynard rifle, but running spoiled his aim. Three shots chased him. His foot caught in a vine, and the boys got him. He made no resistance. That became the total shooting done on our trip. On the way back we captured a chaplain of the Texas Cavalry, one more private on furlough trying to get home and one Mississippi gent, bearing dispatches. The rebels we pursued had left and crossed into Arkansas.

While we were out, robbers hit our camp. The 8th Illinois Infantry camped close by, and it is not known whether they pilfered our goods, or bushwackers did.

Thank heaven for Dick. The last night of the year he made me a cup of coffee, which tasted better than it had a right to. As I finished the last drop of my New Year's "celebration," they brought in the body of Hank

Ellsworth. Hank had packed his gear for home, eager to leave and get married. Only he did not count on a sharpshooter's bullet. Hank was a year older than me.

In January of 1864 I moved back to Skipwiths Landing, and Ann finally came down, but I was ordered out on a trip that lasted late into the night. While I was away, her boat left. When I returned from a mud ride of 30 miles and found I had missed her, I walked away, so others didn't see my distress. I consoled myself that she went on to Natchez, much better for her. Skipwiths Landing was a nasty, muddy place, which did not improve until summer. War devastated the area. Soldiers pulled the boards off houses if the owner was a rebel. Dry wood burned better than green timber; it made no difference whether it was some nicely painted ornamental piece around a rich man's door yard, fence or pig pen—soldiers took it just the same.

A northern man named George Bristol came down to get a plantation back into production. He had big plans, talked of getting a chaplain, starting a colored Sunday school, contraband camp and returning acres of fallow ground, covered with wild mustard, back to cotton production. A cash crop looked attractive to him, but what guarantee did he have rebels wouldn't burn the cotton as soon as he raised it?

Information garnered from civilians raised an alarm. About noon "boots and saddles" blew, and we got in line. A detachment of 26 men, under Lieutenant John Champion, headed six miles east, to meet a force of rebel cavalry. The balance of the regiment stayed in reserve at camp. At a gallop we reached the target in an hour.

A negro perched on a fence waved us down. Lieutenant Champion asked if he had seen any rebels. "Why yes." His head jerked toward town. "A whole heap of them."

"Well, how many?"

"A thousand."

"Are you sure? That many?"

"Oh yes, and more, dare had ta be 10,000."

The Lieutenant expressed doubt about the count and asked, "Can we whip them?"

"Oh yes," he said, "you'ze can whip 'em easy." As we pulled out, the colored man cried, "The time of deliverance has come."

No fight occurred this day, however. We found a rearguard of 20 men, protecting a rebel force of 300, so we returned on Pine Ridge Road rather than fighting ten times our number.

Scouts then found the trail of Confederate brigades under General Wirt Adams and Colonel P. B. Stroke. That evening we built fires to warm ourselves and make coffee, but an order came to douse fires. After a couple hours passed, the command let us have a few small fires, so we could eat supper.

Valentine's Day, 1864, we rode in a torrential rain. I had not sent Ella a valentine card and preferred to forget what day it was, but Alvin boasted about the girls back home. "I sent five Valentine cards," he said.

I pushed on.

"Aren't you going to ask which girls?"

"Do you know five eligible girls?"

"Think I'm bluffing?" He straightened his legs and stood tall in the saddle. "What if one of them was Ella?"

I spurred Rhoderic from a walk, to a trot, to a canter and a gallop, surprising a rebel guard at breakfast. Because Alvin and the others had followed, we drove them across the creek, burned seven full army wagons, two railroad abutments, destroyed several hundred rods of track and two trestles, bent rails and burned a warehouse with 100 bales of cotton. So much for Valentine's Day. Our gunfire confused the rebels. We left wounded on both sides of the Creek. They reformed inside a stockade, which commanded the bridge. Each Union trooper carried 40 rounds of ammunition, not enough to continue this skirmish. A few Confederates passed on the far side of the creek, so we expected them to annoy us later. That same day the balance of Sherman's force rode into Meridian, Mississippi, and captured the city. Then 10,000 men worked at willful destruction. Depots, storehouses, arsenals, hospitals, offices and hotels ceased to exist.

February 18th men from our regiment and two companies of the 2nd Mississippi Colored Cavalry started out with three days' rations of coffee, sugar and hardtack. Everything else we must draw from the countryside. We went 16 miles to Morgan's plantation to guard parties hauling cotton to Natchez. While part of our force kept watch, others foraged or scouted. James Bronson became a foraging legend. He could hear hogs squeal and chickens squawk at long distances, swore he heard animals breathe. When he brought in a hog, we singed the bristles off over a fence rail fire. Not as neat as the job done at home where the method is scalding, but it worked well in the field. We moved another six miles, stayed until the 23rd and when we returned brought in five prisoners, 100 horses and mules, a trove of cotton and forage.

March 12th the provost guards shot Menzo Wagner, nephew to Captain Hapeman. He had deserted at Trenton, Tennessee, but returned under President Lincoln's amnesty proclamation. They placed him under arrest awaiting trial but gave him the liberty of camp. Inactivity weighed him down, or perhaps he anticipated a sentence he could not abide. Menzo convinced two other boys to leave with him. They ran past the guards, started for town but met a citizen in a lonely place. Wagner robbed the civilian. However, provost guards had followed and emerged from behind a clump of trees. Menzo and the boys ran, and the guards commanded, "Halt." Two boys stopped, but Wagner kept running, so the guards fired.

Such goings on happen. Provost guards are here to stop bushwhacking and lawlessness. They did their duty. Menzo was a good soldier, when he faced the enemy, brave but reckless. A woman caused his downfall. While stationed at Trenton, the commander detailed him as a private scout—or spy. He moved around in citizen's clothes, met and fell in love with a girl named Beth. When his regiment left the area, he was ordered back but did not report. Instead he took Beth to Canada and married her.

Boys in camp sympathized. Frank Davis pulled out a picture of the girl waiting for his return. "You have a girl back home, Charlie?"

A tingling feeling crept down my spine. "Not spoken for."

"Just as well. Yesterday I received a letter from Stella. She married a neighbor. Says she waited two years, but childbearing had to start soon."

Thomas Williams spat. "I got worse. My wife sold my property, left me and moved our children to California with another man."

Frank let Stella's picture fall from his hand. No great beauty. She had a broad, flat nose and square face, but her eyes sparkled—with what—mischief or eagerness? The war had gone on too long for Stella. I tapped the picture of Ella I carried in my pocket. What if Ella married? She had every reason to take a husband. I packed Menzo's belongings, so Sergeant Toothill could send them back to Illinois with Menzo's remains.

Charles H. Dickey, Journal
Volume Six, March and April, 1864
Mississippi warfare

Soldiers did awful stealing. When drunk, they became devils. Of course, no one knew from one day to the next if he would survive. Getting drunk eased the nerves for a while. But full of booze, men run rampant, steal, pillage. To stop it, inspectors pounced down on trains and columns. Searchers found every imaginable contraband, even a communion challis. An inspector gave it to a local church to find its owners. Other stolen items went to citizens or got destroyed.

April 3rd we crossed the Mississippi River for beef cattle, but this time not foraging. The government had taken over Surrett's plantation on the Louisiana side. Young blacks worked the plantation and treated us to a fine dinner. We did ample justice to the feast. Plantations for ten miles had been confiscated and leased to discharged Union soldiers, who helped supply the army with food.

The Postal Service did a good deed when they began free delivery for mail marked "Soldier's Letter." I took it as an open invitation to write as many letters as possible to Leah. So many men took advantage that sutlers ran out of paper and envelopes.

Sunday, April 7th, John Calvert guided an advance vedette along Meadville Road. John was a Union supporter, who used to live in the local neighborhood. A rebel gang had driven him off, turned his wife and child out and burned the plantation. John's wife made her way to Natchez in a carriage, but rebs followed whooping, yelling and shouting, which frightened her so badly she became deranged and, even now, remained in a broken state. John looked away from the charred remains. "My home used to be a grand place to raise a family."

We came out of a clearing near the ruins of John Calvert's house, put spurs to our horses, ran in a slave cabin and caught a guerilla just as he bounded off his bedroll. John shook a revolver under the man's nose. "You no-account, white trash! Where shall I shoot you?"

The man even looked like a weasel, thin, brown face.

John brought the gun to the man's groin. "Need your penis? If I shoot you there, I do the world a service. No future scalawags born to you."

The outlaw transformed his face, turned it benign, innocent almost.

John shook with fury. "Only a mongrel cur chases down a woman and children."

The guerilla laughed aloud. "Does your wife miss me?"

John cocked the pistol.

I waited for him to shoot, but then John pulled up. I pushed the rebel toward a private, who quickly led him away. When I placed my hand in the middle of his back, I could feel John tremble.

He took several deep breaths. "I have already killed several of the gang but am now under bonds to keep the peace."

Next we stopped at a house where John's cousin, Miss Calvert, lived. While we fed the horses, she made breakfast. The boys rested near the stable while John invited the officers, including myself, into the house. After she served us warm cornbread, so delicate it crumbled on the fork, Miss Calvert played the piano. Hard to decide which appealed more—her skill as a musician or a cook. Then gunshots rang out. We rushed out of the house with Miss Calvert screaming, "Don't shoot them, don't shoot them, take them prisoners!" She waved frantic hands as if that might save her neighbors.

We ran to the road where troopers were firing at 20 rebels. For some reason, I had perfect aim even though running. I shot, and one rebel fell from his horse. The man looked mortally wounded. The balance scattered in the woods. We carried the wounded man to the house. Miss Calvert sent a colored boy running to roust a local doctor. She railed at John, "I told y'all not to shoot."

Lieutenant Hyde stepped forward to comfort her. The ball entered just below the victim's ribs on the right side and went clear through to the left side. John and I tried to staunch the flow of blood. The doctor did what he could but called it hopeless.

The sucking sound of the reb's breath became echoey. Other noise quieted. Birds outside still sang, Miss Calvert still wept, but these sounds receded. The world escaped notice. More and more, I found myself in a fog. One or more senses shut down. At moments I should be fully engaged, life became abstract. I forgot I stood or sat. The man approached death and loss registered in my mind, but I didn't care to watch him suffer. I recorded it, yes, but somehow pushed it away. For later entry in the journal. Write it. Don't think about it, just let words flow, somehow let the story find its way onto the page. Real thinking and feeling had to be denied. An unknown man died. Might made right. Yes? No? Killing a man has consequences—for the war, for the victim, for the shooter, but none I was able to understand. I tried to find the words, but failed.

After that incident, Lieutenant Hyde resigned, married Miss Calvert and stayed South, although he had a wife and two children in Illinois.

***

I received a surprising letter from Frank W. Tuppen, dated March 21, 1864. He had joined the navy and served on one of the transports. "Dear Charlie, I received a letter from Ottawa that said you had been wounded. It said severely, and I wrote to Ann, expecting to find you at home recovering. It did me good to hear you are all right and back in the army." How dangerous was his duty? Hopefully on board a transport Frank was safe. I wrote back to inquire, wish him well, but stopped short of assuring him I was all right.

***

Martin gave us chilling news about a garrison of black artillery men and a cavalry detachment of white men, largely new recruits, protecting Fort Pillow. "Nearly 600 men died in its defense," Martin said. "Confederates occupied surrounding steep ravines and then Nathan Bedford Forrest drove the defenders inside the fort. A sharpshooter killed the Union commander, Major Lionel Booth. General Forrest sent in a message, calling for unconditional surrender. Major Bradford, now in charge, asked for time to consult with his officers. Forrest agreed but then saw smoke from three boats, which could be bringing reinforcements. Two rebel detachments went to the landings where reinforcement might come ashore.

Alvin cried, "No surrender!"

Martin said, "That's what Bradford answered, no surrender, but marksmen on the ravines forced Union defenders to stay down while troopers swarmed the walls. Wave after wave came over, leapt inside to quick, dreadful slaughter. Bradford did not lower the flag but sent men to escape on the river." Martin had to stand and compose himself before continuing. "Rebels posted on the landings slaughtered them. Half the garrison died, most of them black."

Nathan Bedford Forrest cemented his reputation as the "wizard of the saddle" and at the same time earned one for butchery. A strong Federal force had to remain in Memphis, with the unenviable task of trying to check Forrest, or he could plague Sherman's spring campaign.

Then news came of another, more personal tragedy. Brother John sent word of fighting at Grand Encore, Louisiana. "The report stated

General Ransom suffered a wound in the leg, and his adjutant had been shot through the head and killed instantly." That adjutant was Cyrus. A yawing sensation filled my head.

John had a letter from Sergeant Treadway, who rode at Cyrus's side when he fell. Treadway sprang from his horse and found Cyrus lying on his face, raised his head and found a ball had pierced his brain. He attempted to carry the body off the field but failed. Rebels sent down a storm of shot and shell. I knew such scenes—shouts of those engaged in the struggle, smoke all around, flames leaping. Federals abandoned the field—and our brother. "In his great grief," John wrote, "Treadway did not secure Cyrus's sword or personal possessions. Much worse, he did not remove the body."

I read that, sat down and wept.

Alvin moaned, "Lord, God Almighty, Charlie. Don't do that."

"Cyrus has fallen." I didn't care who saw me sob. Did Treadway go back? Could Cyrus be lying on the field mortally wounded? Where was Mother Bickerdyke? Did anyone run to his side to help?

"Tears are no use to you and worse for me." Alvin shook me. "I can't stand it. Please—"

Charles H. Dickey, Journal

Volume Seven: 1864 - Mustered Out

Brothers' war and Brother Cyrus dead, Service as Provost Guard, Inspection, Serving alongside troops of African descent, Resignation

On April 29th John wrote confirmation Cyrus had fallen. "He was kind and gentle and brave, but he is with the angels." My legs collapsed. Cyrus was so good. The army, completely unworthy. *Oh, gracious God.* Cyrus enlisted as a private; immediately elected to sergeant; became sergeant major, May 2, 1861; promoted to first lieutenant, August 3, 1861; adjutant general U.S. Volunteers on May 1, 1863, with the rank of captain, not yet thirty, eldest son of T. Lyle Dickey and Juliet Evans Dickey. *How will the nation remember him? Good, gracious God.* What of Ann? How much more can the nation require of her? Many hearts bleed. Ann's had been crushed, and I sat miles away, unable to go to her.

Cyrus fell five miles from Mansfield, Louisiana, the exact location unknown. He served nobly, but that gave scant comfort. My protector, Cyrus, gone. Agitation charged in and out, left me inert.

The first week of May, Father got a message from General Ransom. An officer on the Red River said Cyrus was still alive. Father started at once for New Orleans but met Ransom along the way. The outcome could no longer be doubted. Cyrus was dead. No one represented manhood as well. Father returned to Chicago.

Still numb, I joined a scout on May 19th, commanding Companies A and B. The first order I gave my companies: "If I fall, don't leave me behind."

Their eyes shone bright against grimy faces—but as to my request, seemed deaf and dumb. Unable to tell them why. I barked, "Mount up." And prayed God *save me from an unmarked grave.*

At daybreak we rode 26 miles into Fayette then turned around and rode back. The path contained dead bodies, not in cemeteries but exposed. We saw rotted, maggot infested corpses along the byways and ditches, in farm fields and forest, and one particular body, beautiful in life, now lay naked and blackened. The corpse spoke loudly. 'I was conscripted for a purpose of state. Who mourns my passing? Who even knows I am here?' No one. The corpse had no knapsack, identification, not even a pocket Bible or letter near his person. Though it was not our duty, I took time to bury him and place a marker, "Here lies an unknown soldier."

While we attended the dead, Aleck Mead went into the woods to relieve himself. Did someone bury Cyrus? I dared not think about it.

Daniel Hughes said, "Since the dead are unable to speak, someone should say a few words over the grave."

Truman Garratt sneered. "The dead are loathe to speak. What needs to be said is reserved for loved ones. We have no ability to make up suitable words."

Daniel's face froze. "Someone needs to say a few words."

My voice failed.

Truman removed his cap. "Let us pray. Almighty God, we ask you to look with favor on the man's life and character. For today we bury a noble man and testament to our suffering nation. Amen."

Daniel patted him on the back.

"Where's Aleck?" I asked.

Three of us loaded rifles and followed his path. Not far in, we found Aleck bent over a thicket of abundant fruit, stuffing his mouth with raspberries. "Did you ever see more beautiful berries?" he garbled.

"Are you going to share?" Fortunately nature was generous, much more generous than Aleck.

I had no appetite. Countless wounded men got abandoned in open places, left to die, to be gnawed by animals, run over by wagons. Or scraped off the ground by horse teams and pulled into shallow graves. My friend Alvin refused to talk about it, so I pulled Henry Johnson aside. "Let's take sacred oaths to care for each other if we fall."

Henry knew about my journals. "I've written a final testament." To prove it, Henry pulled the paper out of his cap.

Inspired by his forethought, I took a separate sheet of paper and wrote a dying declaration. *My dear family, I think of you continually even on my deathbed. I trust I die in victory. Of course, I wanted to see you once more before I died. I hope it is consolation to know I died in the full discharge of my duty.* I rousted Henry. "Swear again, if the worst happens, you will bury me, mark the grave and tell my family where I'm buried."

He had been trying to fall asleep. "Huh?"

"Don't abandon me on the wayside."

"Let me sleep, or I'll bury you here." Henry rolled over.

***

The next time out, we guarded a cotton train. The Treasury Department issued permits, required to purchase cotton in the Confederate

216

states. In Mississippi a merchant could purchase cotton for as little as 12 cents a pound, transport it to New York for 4 cents a pound then sell it for $1.89 a pound. The lure of cotton wealth enticed many dealers—and an equal number of robbers. Hence the need for military escort. Nice work. Men fought, bled and died for country, but commerce must have cotton—and cotton remained king.

May 19th, 1864, a dispatch said General Grant had whipped General Lee three successive days in Virginia, removing any doubt about the ultimate outcome of war. However, southern newspapers painted a different scene. One Missouri rag carped at Grant for being a butcher, no gentleman, belittled him against General Lee, claiming if Robert E. Lee had Grant's resources he'd send all the Yankees back to Massachusetts. All the newspaper men and all the armchair generals miss the mark. One side is not braver than the other. Bullets fly, and men get swept away. They rush into the thick of fighting, and 'kill' is written on every face. Soldiers mix in indistinguishable heaps. In any battle the commander who has more men—not afraid to die–drives his opponent off the field and declares victory. We are all butchers in this war. All. Not one of us can avoid the label or say we have no guilt.

While public attention shifted east, we struggled. Not half of our regiment had mounts. Horses suffered from ticks as much as men did. For the horses, certain bug bites cause dramatic weight loss, muscle tremors, bloody urine and high fevers. These ticks turned horses into traveling skeletons.

Cavalry used up horses as fast as we found new ones. We took every horse and mule we found. In three years each trooper ruined between six and eight horses. I rode my fifth horse, named Rhoderic. Although she was a filly, she responded to good care, tolerated the name and did what I asked. In return I gave Lady Rhoderic the respect a faithful mount deserves. When she wasted away, too, I sent her to the rear to regain strength, prayed for her recovery and moved on to a new Rhoderic, captured from the enemy.

Patrols of two or three men from each post went out four miles every day, dangerous work. Men got cut off, captured or ambushed. I decided the best way to escape was to charge like a demon and make rebels regret getting in my way. Any time a scare came up, we forced their hand. Each encounter differed, shaped by experience, condition of the horses and boldness. But we never hesitated, halted or commenced aimless fire and, in doing so, kept casualties to a minimum.

William Warren and Captain Shepardson brought recruits to camp in May, 1864. I split up the new men and relied on veterans to show them the subtleties of a cavalry charge. The hardest thing for a cavalryman to learn is when to fire a revolver or carbine and when to rely on a saber. Confederates wore swords but rarely used them. When cavalries dashed close, sabers work better. Recruits already possessed an appreciation for the power of horses, but no one could teach them about erratic behavior and nerves when shelling began. Horses may sidestep, bolt, fall; take control away from riders. The first test in combat was the hardest, but riding into battle never got easy.

We could treat new men to good meals, however. A black cook, named Jim Johnson, made miraculous food and managed to buy potatoes or beans for half what white men paid, which made it impossible to understand why soldiers still menaced him. One of the new troopers produced a horsewhip. "We fight against secession, not to free slaves." The campground grew quiet. "I would rather shoot blacks," he said, "than rebels."

The taunts burned my ears. The recruit had his blood up. Whiskey-stoked hatred twisted his face into a scowl. "I scorn the idea we need a darkie for anything."

I had to do something, grabbed a fiddle and played a rousing rendition of "Camptown races." I strode to the heart of the melee, bent at the waist and directed the fiddle at Jim's feet. His eyes grew bright as stars, but he understood and began to tamp out the tune.

Angry men softened, but the horsewhip cracked.

I feigned insult, "My playing doesn't suit you?" I didn't know the antagonist, only that murder lit his eyes. So I changed to a sentimental ballad, "Home Sweet Home." A tenor started to sing, "Be it ever so humble, there's no place—" His clear, strong voice inspired goodwill.

The angry recruit looked undecided. While he wavered, a squad came in with a rebel deserter. Attention now shifted. The horsewhip became a tool for questioning the prisoner. One application of the lash made the rebel proclaim, "Confederates have organized at Tupelo, mustered five-year regulars. England and France came in to support the southern states. Within 60 days those governments mean to sustain us!"

Sounded like a huge boast. Even if partly true, northern armies were in for a rough go. While soldiers examined the prisoner's sincerity, Jim

Johnson slipped out of camp. Our next meal suffered accordingly. I hoped Jim fared better.

Before we could confirm the enemy's strength at Tupelo, a soldier named Wade ran afoul of the regulations. He had reenlisted as a veteran, and his name went through, but when the others mustered in, he grew sullen and remained in quarters. As a result, he drew no bounty. Wade was held for service, but they stopped his pay. I worked with officials to clear the matter but without success. Wade didn't take the news of my failure well. The following roll call they marked him as absent.

On June 6th "boots and saddles" sounded, but I was ordered to fall out and serve as officer of the provost. When the 4th Illinois Cavalry served provost, citizens did not set a single fire. This day one local named Mrs. Pye extended extra hospitality. Rebels had told her Federals burned houses, so she took all her valuables and hid them in the woods. Our foragers found them and brought them safely back to her, so she invited me inside her home. By the kindness of Mrs. Pye, I took an afternoon nap on a feather bed, the first house I'd been inside for weeks. Serving as provost officer often meant staying up all night making arrests, so I welcomed the special luxury. However, after one stop in Mrs. Pye's house, I never went back. After so many months outdoors, I enjoyed a good campfire. I came to it, thirsty, hungry, exhausted, but in its blaze found comfort. A bed of fir branches lined with a blanket, near a crackling fire left nothing to be desired. Men drank coffee, shared what had happened that day—hairbreath escapes; bullet holes through hats and clothes, exhibited for all to see; hot pursuit discussed. Heads nodded. Men became one mind, one body—consoled one another and directed rage at the enemy. Everyone happy at being alive. One more day safely closed—a subject for congratulations. A calm night fire lent beauty to eventide.

When serving as provost, we also corralled any Union soldiers running about without passes. We ran steeplechases after drunks. If they tried to run on foot, we snatched them without dismounting. If they came along quietly, they spent a night in the guardhouse and got released the next morning without further punishment. If they resisted, we favored them with cold water dunking, followed by a period of hard labor, how long depended upon how far they skedaddled. Many curses assaulted us, but we have orders.

A fine looking negro girl pointed down a hidden lane. Her skin was golden, more yellow than brown, and she was the property of Millie Ellsworth. Her gesture showed us where Mrs. Ellsworth hid her horses and mules. When Mrs. Ellsworth lost her stock, she had no proof of the yellow girl's involvement, yet she beat the slave with a rail, broke her arm and bruised her shamefully, so the girl ran into our camp. Alvin found a place for her in a teamster's wagon headed north.

Only six lieutenants remained in the regiment for duty. Two of us were detailed each day as officers of the guard. My post was the Pine Ridge Road. I took one day's rations, a blanket and forage for Rhoderic and was not allowed to quit the post for 24 hours. Rain or shine I must stick, wear my saber and pistol the whole time, use the ground as a place to rest. As I hobbled to my feet one morning, I heard the distant crack of a rifle and felt a thud against my breast. I crouched down out of the sniper's sight. The other men heard the shot, too, and pursued the enemy. Fortunately I had tucked my journal inside my shirt. The rebel shot me squarely in the journal. I had to write that night's entry and many subsequent ones around the hole.

One June 15th a force of 75 men and 100 coloreds, under Captain Merriman, crossed the Mississippi River with two days' rations. We traveled all night and next day scoured the country for cattle. The weather drenched me in sweat. The mosquitoes bit ferociously and refused to let me sleep. It was ever hot. When Captain Dashill and Lieutenant B. F. Hyde went out with 100 men, they had better forage, returning with 40 head of cattle while we found none.

July 4th passed without firecrackers, gingerbread, ice cream or soda water, none of the pleasures of home. Then we heard about soldiers placing a monument in Vicksburg where Pemberton surrendered to Grant a year ago. Unable to ride over and join the festivities, half the camp spent the evening drinking whiskey. Far-off cannon boomed, and to deter troopers from loading a 24-pounder, the chaplain raised his voice in patriotic prayers and oration. Slurring drunks took up his fervent song, "Glory, Glory Gl-ll-oooory," amazing in their dissonant tones and faulty tempos. I silently prayed we could all spend the next Fourth at home.

The subject in camp turned to the fall presidential election. We spent long hours worrying about the outcome and wondering if soldiers could cast votes. If Mr. Lincoln were reelected, it blighted rebels' hope for a ceasefire. Illinois boys wanted desperately to go home and cast ballots. When approached for furloughs, General Sherman's face looked set in stone. He accepted some coffee. A trail of steam rose from the tin cup. He stared eastward without blinking. "I have no doubt Mr. Lincoln can carry his home state—furloughs denied."

So Illinois cavalry chopped up the countryside. Sherman smashed railroad tracks to the rear with a goal of isolating Atlanta. July 9th under cover of darkness, we crossed the river with a regiment of colored cavalry and three pieces of light artillery, arrived at Cross Bayou by daylight and confronted rebels. Artillerymen threw shells at them, then we charged and chased for three miles. Two times the rebs rallied to check us, but undulations in the terrain afforded cover and we advanced within a short distance. We crowded them into close quarters, but they refused to stand and instead took flight.

Rhoderic and the other horses had reached their effective limits. We had no feed to give them and scant forage in a countryside gripped by war. The return trip to camp was 40 miles, one long, hungry trek.

July 15th, Major General Dana came from Washington to inspect the troops. We thought of him as Secretary of War Stanton's minion and treated him coldly until we learned General Grant had taken Dana into his confidence. When Dana tallied the numbers, he found the regiment had 510 horses but only 220 serviceable. Major C. T. Christensen did a similar inspection at Natchez, Mississippi. That effective force of 806 men had 220 serviceable horses and 290 unserviceable. Dana also detailed the lack of equipment and arms: Clothing tolerably good. Discipline and general condition good. No suitable drill ground and, therefore, units not well drilled. Many recruits had never yet mounted. We had 11 four-horse teams, one two-horse team, eight four-mule teams and one six-mule team. Even the officers: Captain Wallace, Captain Smith, Lieutenant Allshouse, Captain Hitt and Captain Wardlaw lacked mounts. These five men possessed eight horses between them. I rode Rhoderic Number Seven, a Morgan, small and compact, sable brown color with a white diamond on his face. A horse of good endurance. More than previous mounts, the Morgan adapted to my style. I never rode a more agreeable horse, a worrisome trait because one of the captains might take him away from me. Rhoderic came from a long line of horses bred to please and acted like my close companion. The officers must have understood because they let us remain partners.

July 18th ten companies went toward Natchez to find horses. We moved in silence, so citizens did not hide their stock. Didn't even tell our men the purpose until we divided into squads. I found a horse hidden in a cellar. Secesh covered their tracks, but we still found what we wanted.

Alvin took three fine horses from a planter's stable. "What compensation do I receive?" he asked.

I wrote a receipt. "You can collect after the war."

"Ha!" he cried. "I won't live that long."

"Convince your neighbors to end the bloodshed, and you might."

"My property is gone or ruined. We all have nothing left to lose."

I stuck the receipt in his hand and turned away. He kept it, unlike Leah. Her father's receipt was tucked away in my journal. One day I could place it in her hand, a day I no longer wore a spattered uniform, when fighting ended and the government made reparations for southern losses, one day. God Almighty, make it one day soon. For now, I am the enemy, their goods forfeit. And she haunted me perfectly.

July 22nd our effective force ferried across the Mississippi to hunt down rebels who were raiding plantations, run by Federals. The secesh were celebrating their successes with drink, enough to become inattentive. We slipped in and opened fire. Thick air held the smoke close. Their return volley pulsed orange, as if the air itself caught fire. Three men dropped, two dead and one wounded, but after that rebels showed no desire to fight. Scant resistance became the pattern. We had not gotten a real fight out of any rebel cavalry for weeks. Instead they played a game of strike and run.

Joe Carter's horse, Old Sled, became excited in the pursuit, took the bit and ran into the rear of the rebel column despite all Joe did to hold him. Seeing he could not stop he steered for the center of the road and split their column. Plunder flew as he ran against them. Some yelled, "shoot him." Others cried, "take him prisoner." However, they did not shoot for fear of hitting their own men.

The rebels crossed in a muddy place, scattered some, and Joe tore after. Unfortunately, Old Sled fell down, got up without Joe and raced off with the rebels. Joe scrambled out of the mud and ran behind a tree. Just as he came around one side of the tree, a rebel came around the other.

Neither of them looked particularly interested in securing that tree and ran in opposite directions.

When we picked up Joe, Alvin berated him. "Why didn't you shoot them all?"

"I only had one load left in my revolver and might get into a pinch where I needed the last bullet to save myself." We followed Old Sled's trail, hoping to pick up the horse, but Joe hasn't seen Old Sled since.

August began another line of duty when we manned pickets on the Up River Road. I used three of our boys and 14 negro infantrymen. The coloreds stood picket every other day, and we furnished noncommissioned officers. Former slaves made excellent pickets. They obeyed orders to the letter without comment. On one occasion, however, a black's strict attention to duty nearly cost his life. A mounted squad needed to pass through a breastworks a negro sentinel guarded. The squad had a perfect right to pass, but a corporal had instructed him to 'let no one pass' and then went away for breakfast.

"Ride over the nigger and go ahead," a soldier cried.

The sentinel did not flinch. "If you undertake it, someone gets hurt for sure."

Fortunately the corporal returned and rescinded his command.

On August 5th, 1864, our entire effective force picked up three days' rations and 80 rounds of ammunition and joined infantry and artillery. This meant a fight was certain. While I lifted the saddle, John Hitt ran over. "Swap duty with me," he begged.

"I cannot shirk—

"But I'm ordered to picket duty," he said, "and never have been in a fight since I joined."

"It's my duty," I said.

"You were in a skirmish a few days ago."

"If something happens to you, what then?"

"The fortunes of war." He looked desperate for a fight, so we switched places. If anything happened to him, could I forgive myself? Fortunately, John's trip became a success, the kind that encouraged men to fly banners, polish arms till they glitter and forget, for a while, how enemy rifles pour shot into the ranks.

The next excursion John and I both rode out. We crossed the Mississippi River on the ferry and started out in a southwestern course. Another force, under Lieutenant Colonel McCaleb, went out on the Concordia Lake road. Colonel Farrar commanded the expedition, accompanied by the 28th and 29th Illinois, two regiments of colored troops and one mountain howitzer. All night we slogged through a swamp. At daybreak we came onto 75 rebel cavalry, skirmished, fell back, and the rebels rode to join a larger force.

Captain Wardlaw heard that a friend of his, a Captain Montgomery, commanded the rebels, so Wardlaw took a white flag and walked alone toward the rebel line.

Wardlaw stayed all night but the next morning shared what passed between them. "Montgomery warned me, 'We have better troops than before, and you Federals cannot run about as you have been doing.'"

"What troops are those?"

"Texas Rangers," Wardlaw said, "the ones famous for mischief. They intend to clean us out."

"How did you reply?" Alvin asked.

"I said, 'We are not deterred.'"

"What did Montgomery say to that?"

"Montgomery stood firm. Claimed the Texans had charged a Union gunboat and captured it. I told him none of what he said deters us from coming out as often as we want. 'Prepare to get whipped,' was his reply." Wardlaw's voice rose. "War is God's greatest game. I assured him our men were veterans, no longer doubtful. With that I shook my friend's hand, and we parted company."

Wardlaw spoke with conviction, but his arms hung heavy like made of lead and pulled his shoulders low, a much less daring figure than when he went across. Wardlaw struggled to keep his expression blank. One slip and he risked uncontrollable feelings. None of us could choose who we faced. Wardlaw pretended war was a great game, but his bravado in matching rebels boast-for-boast made me uneasy. Someone had to lose. One boast does not whip another; men must do the job.

Montgomery's cavalry had menaced us all too well. They tore up railroads to interrupt our supply line. Fortunately engineers repaired lines almost as fast as secesh destroyed them. Locals feared Montgomery as much as Yankees because Montgomery's cavalry did equal harm to citizens. One lady said she preferred we came instead of Montgomery. "I see no difference in the conduct, but it is easier to hate Yankees than boys from Alabama or Mississippi."

A nearby report of a howitzer woke us, and we galloped toward the sound without waiting to fall in. Captain Wardlaw took the lead, and the rest of us organized into a column of fours. A short distance from our pickets we charged. The rebels broke, made several attempts to rally and form a line, but we gave them no chance. They scattered into ground thick with timber, levies and ditches. We knew nothing about the lay of the land, while they knew everything, but we killed five of them and took seven

224

prisoners.

Captain Montgomery was among the rebel dead. When Captain Wardlaw saw the body of his friend, who advised us not to come out and get whipped, his face went white.

John Blair shot one of the prisoners and stood over the twisted body—he shot again and again until Wardlaw pulled John away. Both men muttered in anger. Their faces looked fierce beyond any ability to control.

One rebel prisoner recognized Wardlaw as the nighttime visitor. "Our handpicked men can whip all the Yankees from here to Natchez."

Another prisoner with a red, inflamed face sunk to his knees and then to the ground. "Do you always fight that way?"

I assured him, "This is our style."

"You got an advantage this time because you had other troops at your back." The red-faced reb regained his feet.

John Blair heard this exchange. "But we walloped you single-handed." And he knocked the man back down.

We marched eastward, gathering forage for the horses, now Captain Osborne in command. Men took what was necessary, and I gave vouchers. I commanded Company C along with Lieutenant Main. If Osborne took negro recruits, their women and children also joined the column. To accommodate them, we confiscated buckboards, stylish carriages, hay wagons, surreys, sleds, coaches and became a ludicrous procession contrary to any rules of order.

Huge southern gardens, abandoned by owners, became ours. Fish caught for the masters' dinners, circled conveniently in pools near kitchen walls, and filled our fry pans. If we needed a bridge, we tore down a house to build it.

My company started as rearguard, an assignment of honor, and continued in that capacity for three days. Guarding the rear generally rotated between companies, but we kept the privileged assignment until the fourth day. When the column turned back by a different route, we led the advance, but this assignment was also an honor. Being in the lead through new territory allowed us to capture any Confederate soldiers, home on furlough. I sent a sergeant and one trooper ahead to scout around. When they reached the edge of a bluff, carbine fire greeted them.

The trooper galloped back. "The whole rebel army is on that hillside." I sent him to tell Captain Osborn, detailed another man to hold the horses and joined the sergeant, who busily emptied his gun. The rest of our men took position behind trees. If rebels came up the hillside, they could swamp us, so I hoped to trick them into thinking they faced a large force. "Fire as rapidly as possible!" I ordered.

The enemy did not retreat. Neither did they advance. Lieutenant Main came up with his squad and, because he outranked me, took command. He liked my tactics, however, and also sent men down a side ravine to open fire on the enemy's flank. Rebels retreated pell-mell. Colored soldiers followed the Confederates down to the bottom.

Their charge stopped on a bluff that opened into Yazoo Valley. We let rebels hold it, and the whole command, negro recruits and all, turned toward Vicksburg. Osborne sent me to command the rear and make sure none of the Confederate force followed. We held them off till the outfit got well ahead. After an exuberant farewell volley, we galloped and caught up.

The column did not halt until sundown. I fed my horse and dropped down on the spot and slept. When I woke next morning, I found myself in several inches of water, Rhoderic at my side. I still clutched the halter in my hand. We had now moved behind Union lines and a short march brought us into camp.

***

One-hundred-ninety men and nine officers crossed the Mississippi headed for Galespy's plantation. Some cavalry reported to Lieutenant Colonel McCaleb; others rode down river to Captain Wardlaw. Colonel Farrar took infantry aboard transports. When we arrived at Concordia Bayou, Martin Wallace took charge of the cavalry. At daybreak we pushed on and came out at Mud Bayou. While we watered the horses, seven men brought up a gun. This severe march in extreme, dry heat taxed the horses. A continued march promised to break the mounts down. Yet our advance skirmished and drove the enemy to a plantation. Martin's men assaulted the road along Mud Bayou, and the enemy fell back toward Trinity Road.

At Mud Bayou we expected to find a rebel camp, but they had vacated. Lieutenant Colonel McCaleb's force arrived, and Martin assumed command of all cavalry. While the command saddled up, vedettes found a large cavalry force along a levee. Infantry and artillery took up position behind the levee, and cavalry dashed. One mile distant we came to their battle line, several hundred-strong. Their left found cover behind plantation buildings, but their right remained in an open cotton field.

Martin formed a battle line and advanced. Within 100 yards of them, heavy fire hit, coming from both the cotton field and house. The men pressed into close quarters, and rebels scattered in all directions. We pursued for four miles, then heard the bugle call to end pursuit.

Infantry and artillery wrestled for Galespy plantation. Rebels gave way, made another attempt to stand, but when we charged, they fled. Our second chase lasted five miles then Martin collected scattered cavalry, reunited us with infantry and detailed troopers to escort ambulances. I didn't want to know how many men had fallen, such numbers befuddled my thinking. I had learned it was better not to know. The rest of the force moved to Lake Concordia. Captain Wardlaw had sustained a severe leg wound, so we installed him in one of the ambulances.

Cavalry made a circuit around Lake Concordia and swam Concordia Bayou. We marched steadily all night and at daybreak met another column. We charged the rebels in a column of fours, but they increased their pace. It surprised us to see them deploy in Illinois Cavalry style. As we clashed, we recognized each other and pulled up. In the dim twilight we had mistaken Union men for rebels.

We all went together and met Colonel Farrar, leading a regiment of colored infantry. They had stacked their guns in the road for the night, but word came rebels lurked not far away. For two hours we charged everything in our path, while I struggled against irresistible drowsiness. When we finally found the secesh, Colonel Farrar positioned himself on a levee and swung his hat as we passed. "Give them hell, 4th Cavalry!" He kept shouting until we moved out of hearing range.

A number of us deployed on the left as flankers. Two rebels fell behind the rest. Joe Carter said, "Their horses must be crippled," and asked permission to dash ahead and take them. When the request was granted, Joe cried, "Come, on Charlie."

I reined beside him.

"Charlie," he said, "let's see who has the better horse." He rode a large, dapple stallion and continually bantered how good his horse was. Joe spurred his horse, and Rhoderic kept neck-and-neck without urging from me.

The two rebels, we meant to catch, had great mounts, too, and easily kept out of the way.

We raced far ahead of our comrades, so I cried, "We need to slow up and watch for ambush."

He agreed, "Let's let the command catch up." We halted in grasses growing as high as our heads, tall enough to conceal men and horses. Timber grew to our left along the lake, where the rebels had gone.

When the command caught up. I took the middle of the road, and put one man on each side. I emerged from the weeds first—and faced three rebel cavalrymen, poised and ready to shoot. Rhoderic skidded to a halt. They fired too high. My companions fired, too, but the Johnnies scampered away unharmed.

Back at camp, colored workers danced and shouted. "Atlanta is surrendered. Oh, Day of Jubilee." If General Sherman had truly succeeded, it was also a Jubilee day for Mr. Lincoln, for he stood a better chance of reelection.

September 22, 1864, Major Mindret Wemple commanded detachments of cavalry, infantry, colored artillery and colored infantry, taking us to the plantation of Mr. Williams where we seized 51 wagons of corn and cotton and 140 head of cattle. The enemy hit our rearguard, however, and kept up a running skirmish for six miles. William Knapp shot one rebel off his horse, but no one on our side got hurt. Sergeant Moulton found two mules and a horse saddled and tied in the woods. Moulton decided the animals belonged to some rebel cavalrymen and decided to give them a good home. He also left a note thanking the rebs for their contribution to the Union war effort.

The next morning J. W. Phelps, the captain's clerk, volunteered for patrol. He didn't have to go—just wanted a diversion from paperwork. He wore an officer's blouse and, when rebels ambushed, got targeted as one. Buckshot struck Phelps in the face, killing him instantly. His parents live in Ottawa, and I wrote to them to say we were with J.W. when he died, brought him back and gave him a proper burial. I neglected to say the ambush retaliated for the capture of two mules and a horse the day before, merely stated that he died a heroic death, serving his country.

The first of October we consolidated able-bodied veterans and raw recruits into five companies. Part of the brigade, including white and colored cavalry, artillery and signal corps went to Woodville, Louisiana. Ten miles out, we heard heavy firing, coming from Bayou Lava, but firing receded faster than we advanced, so we resumed our trek to Woodville. There we surprised rebels, captured 12 prisoners, one caisson and 12 army wagons with teams, destroyed telegraph wires, captured the mail and forwarded prisoners to Fort Adams.

Rebels on the flank prompted Colonel Osband to send half the colored cavalry to the left; the balance of us went right. Those sent left came under severe fire. Sharp explosions swelled into a crackling roar. Major J. B. Cook and the 3rd United States Colored Cavalry charged through the woods, stampeded rebels, cut down the ones who deserted and drove off the gunners. With the battery now undefended they secured the guns.

Our part of the column met stubborn resistance. A bullet struck my gun, glanced off and passed between thumb and forefinger, a trifle, but even this small wound stung like hell. Another bullet tore a hole through my jacket. A half-hour later we captured a twelve-pound howitzer, two six-pound smoothbore guns, 150 rounds of fixed ammunition, horses with complete harness, three battle flags and 41 prisoners. Our loss—no one. Those numbers I can tolerate. *God, give me as many close calls as You want, as long as no one falls.*

This fight occurred near the residence of one Judge McGhee, who had provided breakfast for the rebels. However, we enjoyed the feast and gave the Judge a half-hour to move out before we burned his residence and the quarters he built for Confederates. His larder contained sweet potatoes the size of acorn squash in Illinois, so we liberated those before setting the blaze.

At Woodville we found a large commissary store, containing salt, sugar, tobacco and cotton. Osband estimated the worth at a million dollars. He sent captured property to the boats, burned what we couldn't take. We expected to find rebel forces at Woodville, too, but missed the enemy. Instead we captured their subsistence stores, a telegraph station and Confederate dispatches. Any other time Woodville could lure me to stay; the town sat among rolling hills and pastures, just north of the Louisiana State line, as good a place as any to settle, but the army needed us elsewhere.

Picket duty became my main occupation. The war moved off with Sherman, and fierce fighting went southeast. We served like a garrison while his bummers made "Sherman neckties" out of southern railroads. As he marched through Georgia, northern newspapers that had bedeviled Sherman in the past calling him insane, now praised him as the greatest general since Napoleon. His success in the field made it possible to think about resigning my commission. A promotion to captain didn't seem likely, serving in the backwater. All the excitement went east. I could indeed go home. Ann and Belle prompted these thoughts, as did Ella. Ella's letter said, "enough has been given. Time to come home."

Yes, the time felt right—to visit Leah Robbins. What I hoped to gain by this I cannot say. Primarily to let her know my service was ending. I hoped to see a change in her. War feeling was played out in me. Had she changed, too? Hardship as a teacher, either softened or entrenched politics. Which one happened to her? Regardless of what I found, I had to try.

The house was boarded up. The fence gone. I asked a man on the street, "Do you know where the residents are?"

He eyed my blue uniform.

"I am a friend of Miss Robbins."

"Ha! She has no love for Yankees. Not now, or ever." He harrumphed and turned away.

Soldiers rode rough through the city. Idleness and drink created devilment in them. Veterans became some of the worst toughs. Captain George Gamil became a notorious drunk. He had been wounded in the face, permanently closing his left eye and collapsing that cheekbone. The Captain drank only when in pain, also a permanent condition. He chased a colored woman down and carried her into a ruined home. They found his body and declared the cause of death "drunken debauch."

I spent a tense period waiting for a discharge, worried a stray bullet would find me during these last days, but I finally embarked aboard the *Hannibal*. As the boat left the dock, I pulled a letter out of my breast pocket. Though I had read it countless times, I succumbed once more.

October 29, 1864

Dear Lieutenant Dickey,

Certain friends tell me a Union lieutenant requested information about my whereabouts. These concerned citizens gave a physical description matching you, a tall, lean, fair-complexioned man now sunburned. Therefore, you are the primary suspect. Why you made inquiries I cannot imagine. It upsets me to have any Yankee speak my name or suggest he has reason for concern.

I write only to tell you, desist! Do not trouble yourself about my situation. I have moved to Natchez at the invitation of friends, although their circumstances are reduced compared to how they lived before the war, they are generous hosts. We all must make do. It is impossible to recreate society as it once existed. Citizens return home. Stable their horses and mules (the animals, I know, are of

230

great interest to any cavalryman.) Gardens of vegetables remain untouched by bummers or bushwackers. It restores some faith in mankind to see a man pass an onion bed without stealing. I pray I never again witness men's depravity. Soldiers stole onions more than any other vegetable. Imagine—onions declared as contraband of war, not humble vegetables existing through the hard work of the grower, who has a god-given right to the fruit of his labors. Why even the Baboon Mr. Lincoln said a person has right to eat that which her own hand earns without the leave of anyone else.

Some local citizens celebrate news of the war's end—to me an abhorrent sentiment. Weary southerners welcome peace at any cost, while I cannot accept submission. Defeat means disgrace. Desolation reigns in the South, and yet when Federal troops pass, young, well-bred ladies wave handkerchiefs, wish them well and tell them to return after they muster out. Anger wells up in my bosom. To think southern women bow to Yankees, who kill our men. These same hussies coaxed their beaux off to war. Yanks parade, smile and shout, "Hurrah." The devil take them, and he'll be sure to do it.

I write to tell you I am alive in body, but not spirit. Above all, do not make further inquiries I implore you. I remain a loyal daughter of the South.

Sincerely,
Miss Leah Robbins

I returned the letter to my breast pocket. Despite her protest, I read cause for hope. Why did she tell me she had moved to Natchez? She could easily remain silent on that point. She had the qualities that make men change sides. Famous men, like General Pemberton, left family and the North behind to support the South. Perhaps she hoped I could do that, too. If she refuses to change, can I? Could we be happy somewhere in the middle—perhaps live among the Kentucky branch of my family? Can she and I both become less high-strung? Offer humane terms of surrender?

I resigned my commission to find out. Now I headed to Natchez. This time I did not consult Father or John. I didn't want their counsel. I had to see for myself. On the way to Natchez I rehearsed what to say. Im-

231

agined the scene and how it should go. Rehearsed until chivalry became second nature. I had to try.

Here ends the record of my military service. Now I leave the page. Go back to living. This is the last journal I plan to write until I find a happy ending.

Chapter Five
Charlie Dickey
Natchez, Mississippi, October, 1864

In Natchez, Charlie rode past a rebel burial ground, large and thickly plotted. Some graves had stone markers, many more had wooden ones. How many graves belonged to leaders who advocated war? Those officials had sacrificed a generation of young men.

Rebel veterans walked the streets. Charlie could identify them, even without uniforms, from the wan faces and skeletal frames. His uniform marked Charlie as well. One reb stopped him. "What regiment do you belong to?"

"Recently mustered out of the 4th Illinois Cavalry."

The rebel mouthed words too faint to hear—but held out a hand in greeting.

"Which unit did you fight for?" Charlie asked.

Another reb gave the answer. "He was with Pickett's Division."

Charlie shook the outstretched, sharp-boned hand.

The veteran's grip tightened. "When we surrendered, we stacked 45 muskets, out of a division 10,000 strong."

Charlie nodded. Any man who held his place in line deserved admiration.

The rebels wanted to talk about the war, and Charlie listened to a couple stories, then excused himself. Would Leah extend a greeting? The last act between North and South had yet to play out. Harmony or dissonance, which would result? Personal happiness hinged upon the nation's.

Natchez escaped the devastation suffered elsewhere. Confederates had fired few shots, if any, to defend it. Instead Confederates concentrated forces at ill-fated Vicksburg, 80 miles upriver, and Port Hudson downriver. Charlie saw buildings that needed extensive repairs to wipe away neglect, but structures remained standing. Yankees spared smaller homes but targeted large manor houses, owned by well-known Confederate supporters. Those estates they plundered, used as barracks, barns, jails, hospitals or officer quarters.

When Charlie made inquiries at a bank, an employee showed him the door. Farther down the street a barber had painted over an old sign and declared himself to be a "Unionist Barber." Charlie decided to test the barber's goodwill.

Once the hot towel came off, Charlie inquired about Mr. Robbins, a well-to-do merchant.

"Ha!" the barber cried. "No one's well-to-do these days."

"He had a thriving—"

"I know exactly who you mean." The barber snipped close. "But it's poor, old man Robbins now." The barber cut at reckless speed. "Mr. Robbins has $58,000 owed to him. He'll be lucky to collect ten percent of what's owed—with slaves runnin' free and planters gettin' no compensation. Credit done been destroyed. Life savings gone."

"Surely land is still collateral."

"Banks don't take land as security from southerners. All Robbins's customers are ruined. Interest rates are usury. If Robbins ain't bankrupt yet, he soon will be."

With a razor at his throat, Charlie kept quiet.

The barber splashed astringent. "Look for poor, old Robbins where steamboats dock."

"How will I find him?"

"The white-haired gent driving a cart."

***

Mr. Robbins drove a wagon half full of firewood. The purser on the steamboat was not impressed. "That's all?"

Charlie waited until they completed a transaction and approached with a discreet voice. "Mr. Robbins, sir, I am glad to find you."

The man's hand jerked up, as if out of habit, but then he refused to bring it forward and take Charlie's. Charlie invited Robbins to dine at the hotel. Initial hesitation gave way to hunger. Over soup, Robbins talked of plantations leased to northerners or given away to negroes. With the oysters he spoke of levees neglected. Over roast beef, how southern merchants had no choice but to stand aside and let northern capitalists conduct business. With pie, Charlie learned negro labor was available but unreliable. Southerners expected the worst following surrender, and so far the worst had come true. Over coffee, Mr. Robbins lamented, "I was forced to send my daughter away to Vicksburg to live with my sister-in-law."

Charlie pulled papers out of his pocket.

"What is this?" Mr. Robbins asked.

"Your receipt for goods confiscated during the war."

"How—?"

234

Charlie continued to hold the documents out until the importance sank in. "This verifies the validity of your claim. You need both documents to file for compensation."

"Where did you get these?"

"From Miss Robbins."

Her father's eyes went wide.

"You are entitled to fair value of the goods."

He swiped up the papers but pushed back from the table.

Charlie didn't want him to tell Leah how he came by the receipt. "I prefer—"

Mr. Robbins stomped away.

"Wait," Charlie called, but Robbins rushed out the door. *Wait. I hope to see Leah.* Robbins did not wait. Now what? Should Charlie be the one to wait? Come back after war ended? When peace was assured? How long could that take? In the meantime would she stay in Vicksburg? He couldn't risk missing her again.

***

As Charlie neared Vicksburg, reminders reached out to snag him—splintered trees, patches of burnt brush, blackened ground, canteens, other debris, graves. A rented horse, one he also called Rhoderic, walked over ground where countless soldiers had suffered. This Rhoderic walked with its head bent down. He had no stamina, just tentative steps.

Charlie didn't press Rhoderic, just closed his eyes to the surroundings and let the horse plod the trail. Charlie pictured Leah in the flicker of candlelight. Blocked out thoughts of any other beaux. How did a man fight a battle for affection? *Please God, heal the rift.*

Rhoderic lurched toward the Big Black River Bridge, approaching Vicksburg. Charlie didn't know what he expected to see, but not this. At the end of the battle, the Union buried the dead but must have done the work in great haste. Feet stuck out of the ground, exposed by wind and rain. A skull lay abandoned. A half-buried photograph showed a wife and blond-haired girl child without names or identities. The dead soldier who loved them could not say.

Federals had placed the district under military rule. Former slaves roamed the area. On the outskirts of the city they built a refugee camp. Lived in filthy hovels. No white folks came to help. Where were all those staunch abolitionists, who for years had lamented the fate of slaves? How about the government? Why weren't officials here to ease suffering—and

235

help blacks pay the price of freedom?

Prior to war, Vicksburg's house slaves had more freedom than field hands. They knew where to get alcoholic drink and buy a gun. Now whites took away former privileges. Fashionable Vicksburg buildings had become piles of brick and mortar. Someone must be blamed. Someone's hands bound. Someone arrested. In front of every drinking saloon, groups of tall, fierce men carried heavy chains, glared at strangers and uttered words of retribution.

"Nuthin' will be gained by reconstruction," one white man cried, "but degradation."

"We are not yet whipped and don't intend to be."

General agreement. "A little more sacrifice will make us safe."

The neighborhood between Main and Jackson Streets prompted Charlie to load his pistol. Negroes had no way to support themselves, except the women who had no sense of decency in language or action. Men fought over them. Encouraged by the women, they pulled pistols and claimed mating rights. What kind of place was this for Leah? Angry expressions greeted Charlie everywhere, coiled his insides. He made inquiries with merchants, hoping they could 'connect me with an old friend.' No one offered clues. They acted deaf and dumb—except the one shopkeeper who threatened to send him to the bottom of the river.

Then Charlie heard a whisper, "Masser?" He turned toward a coal black face. "Jim Johnson?"

"Yes, sirrah."

Here was the camp cook Charlie had saved from a whipping. "Are you in trouble?" Jim wore clean clothes but looked thin and drawn.

"I works for a lady on Oak Street, who might know 'da girl you want."

Charlie nodded and followed the black man's wake.

**

Mrs. Annabelle Humphrey said, "I play both sides. In the presence of Unionists, I profess loyalty. With southern neighbors, I become a rabid secessionist. One view does not impinge the other. I merely become sociable to any party. Be forewarned, however. In mixed company I never admit to having northern friends."

"Understandable in these times."

She agreed without hesitation. "Life demands latitude. Before the war, defeat was not in the southern vocabulary. Now we accept it as a price for an end to fighting." Her smile was brilliant, inappropriate and corrupt without self-reproach. "I understand General Sherman feels it will be easier to replace the entire southern population than reconstruct us subordinate to the Union." She fingered her bodice. "Sherman is right, you know. We are the devil to subdue. But let's talk of you. Jim tells me you are searching for someone. You came to the right woman, for I know everyone."

"I hope to find Miss Leah Robbins."

Mrs. Humphrey looked through her eyelashes.

Her flirtation came as a surprise. The widow had to be 15 years Charlie's senior, yet she moistened her lips. "Friendship between you and Miss Robbins cannot be. It is a black disgrace for her to entertain a Yankee."

"Surely society must be reconciled."

"Talk of unification makes her ill. Miss Robbins prides herself in making fools of Yankees." She took Charlie's hand, and he managed to tolerate her touch.

"I understand completely." Her expression became severe, as if raising substantial doubt. "You hope romance can overcome politics."

"It is wonderful that you understand," he said.

"But Lieutenant Dickey, you must not call on Miss Robbins. One of her admirers will shoot you."

"I have faced greater danger."

Her eyes flashed. "Dozens of dangerous fellows will rush to defend her honor. I cannot dissuade you?"

He patted her hand. "I am grateful for your help."

"I see. Well, then come tomorrow afternoon. Jim can drive, and we shall call on Miss Robbins."

When Charlie left the widow, shouts and heavy boots echoed down the street. Gun shots followed. He felt a jolt of fear. Should he trust the woman? In the current climate of hatred, he must be careful. The only recommendation for Mrs. Humphrey was that she had hired Jim. But it seemed unlikely she did that, or anything, without an incentive.

***

No hint of welcome warmed Leah's voice. "What duty brings you to Vicksburg?"

"I came to see if I could be of service to you," Charlie said.

"I wrote and told you to stay away. Did you receive my letter?"

"No," he lied.

237

"Testimony such as that," Leah said, "demands a Bible. Shall I make him swear, Mrs. Humphrey?"

Mrs. Humphrey chewed on the question before answering. "He pretends concern, but he really demands acceptance."

The air in the room closed in. "I have resigned my commission."

Leah questioned Widow Humphrey. "Did he ask about me?"

"Just whether your loyalty to the southern cause is exhausted."

Leah left her chair and strolled to the window. Finally she turned. "I will hate the South's rivals until the day I die."

"Soon," Charlie said, "South and North will no longer be rivals."

Her voice grew sharp. "This from a Yankee, poor in dignity, honor and manliness." Her eyes narrowed. "I don't see how you can hold your head up while engaged in Yankee barbarism."

The venom in her voice took Charlie's breath away.

Mrs. Humphrey fanned herself in a leisurely manner. "At least she tells you these things in person."

Leah's eyes traveled over his clothing, as though pricing the goods. "He is in better shape than when we last met. Last time, he wore a filthy uniform, too large for the man inside." She frowned. "Now he is well fed and clean. Why should invaders live better than people who own the land?"

"I had hoped—" Charlie said.

She faced him squarely. "Here is what I hope—" But she left off explanation. Instead ripped the collar of her blouse and ran out the front door, screaming, "Outrage!"

Passersby halted. Neighbors came running.

Her hand fluttered toward the place Jim stood. "The nigger! He overtook me, choked me down." Leah collapsed into the arms of a convenient gentleman.

Mrs. Humphrey did not defend her servant.

Ruffians grabbed Jim. Someone produced a rope, which they tied around his neck. Charlie ran to Leah. "Surely," he said in a soft tone, "this is not the man."

She covered her eyes with a handkerchief and asked for water. A man guided her to sit down on the porch while another ran for water.

The mob tousled Jim.

A grin lifted the corners of Leah's mouth.

If she screamed at Charlie, he could understand. She had reason to lash out. She had lost so much, but a malicious grin? Her expression shocked him. "Don't let this get out of hand," he said.

Though she kept her voice low, her tone sounded rough as gravel underfoot. "Some southerners hope war will resume—and if our men have any chivalry left—it will."

Charlie had no way to distract the crowd, no fiddle or bugle. His pistol was insufficient defense against so many. "Why hurt an innocent man?"

She clenched her fist. "Love has made you stupid."

"This is beneath you."

"I may have liked you once but only in a platonic way."

Shouts rolled through a growing crowd. "Lynch the nigger!"

"Can you live with blood on your hands?" Charlie asked.

She blanched. "You swear to prevent further entanglement?"

"If that will stop you."

She lifted her chin. "Let me see that boy."

They jerked Jim forward and pitched him to the ground at her feet.

"His hands," Leah said, "show me his hands."

Two men pulled his arms, and the joints cracked audibly.

She sneered. "No, those are not the hands I saw around my throat."

"Are you sure?" A ruffian demanded.

Rancorous, ferocious, frenzied men crowded closer.

"It is not this boy, I say." With that Leah escaped into the house.

Men hemmed in, looked Charlie over, released the rope around Jim and waved it in Charlie's face.

A lanky citizen poked through. "I remember you. Wasn't you at Shiloh?"

"Yes."

"Do you remember shooting at one of Forrest's men who came up to your force by mistake?"

"Yes." Charlie did his best not to let anyone see him tremble.

"Well, glory, I know you," he said, "I was that man."

"Did you get hurt?"

"Not a scratch, but my horse got filled with bullets. I stripped the saddle and carried it over two miles to get back. General Forrest got shot, too, and you Federals nearly caught him when the surgeon dressed it." A bullet had struck General Forrest above the hip and penetrated almost to his spine.

Charlie remembered the day and the rebel, whose horse nearly collided with Rhoderic. "I am glad you weren't hurt."

The veteran shook his head. "If I had known what followed, I'd'a surrendered." He held out a hand to Charlie, who held it until the crowd dispersed.

***

Mrs. Humphrey had predicted disaster, and Charlie should have listened. Still, Leah's hatred, fevered eyes and vile words came as a shock.

Charlie put Jim on a boat headed north. When it came time to say goodbye, Jim swallowed hard. He made a steeple with his hands and pressed them against his lips.

A flutter ran through Charlie. He knew some of the obstacles Jim faced. "Your ticket takes you as far as Alton, Illinois. Be sure you don't cross over the Mississippi and enter Missouri. Many people in Missouri hold—" Charlie's voice broke. "Missouri was a slave state."

"Yessuh, I understand."

"Alton is not a welcoming place either. If I were you," Charlie said, "I'd keep going north, maybe all the way to Canada. The further north the better."

They didn't shake hands but shared a warm farewell nonetheless. When the boat pulled away, Charlie turned toward Rhoderic. He had fed him well while they were together, but the horse suffered from months of neglect. Charlie bought an apple and offered it to Rhoderic. The horse sighed in gratitude. "I wish I could take you home, but I only have enough money for my own passage." When he returned Rhoderic to the stable, the horse refused to walk to his stall. The groom yanked on the bridle, so Charlie stepped in. When he led Rhoderic, the horse hung his head but moved inside.

Chapter Six

Ella Linsley, The Wallace Dickey Family Cemetery
Ottawa, Illinois, October, 1864

Ella strolled to the cemetery near the Oaks. She had sewn a miniature flag to place on General Wallace's grave. She, Charlie, Jennie and John had tramped this same ravine many times, but years ago.

The flag looked insignificant next to the Wallace tribute obelisk, but General Wallace had been a kind, thoughtful gentleman, worthy of all tributes. Her prayer wandered. 'Please, Heavenly Father, keep Charlie mindful of his health. Spare him a relapse of bilious fever. We almost lost Charlie, too, but Your Hand reached out to spare him. Thank You, Lord, for Your mercy.'

Ella knew how much Charlie suffered. Colonel Ransom had written to Charlie to hurry back to duty even before Charlie's delirium eased. Ann kept the telegram hidden, fearing what might happen if he returned. To relieve Belle and Ann's constant vigil, Ella took several turns at Charlie's bedside. His breath often became short and shallow; his body bathed in sweat. "Can you try some soup?" Ella whispered.

He did not respond.

She spoke louder. Insistence brought him around.

His voice rasped. "How goes the war?"

"No major news." She brushed her lips to his forehead—to comfort herself as much as him. "Can you try some soup?" He threw up what she fed him and was in worse shape than before. She cursed, "Damned army."

"How easy to die," he whispered.

She added logs to the fire, hoping to sweat away his fever. What else could she do? Perhaps if she spoke about duty, it might bring him around. "The war is not won."

Later that night his fever burned out. Ann returned to his side, and Ella watched from the corner. Ann washed his face. "The worst is over."

"The worst is yet to come," he croaked.

Ella slipped closer. "How long can you stay home?"

Charlie studied her head to toe and then smiled. "You look well."

When he went back to the army, Ella waited to hear that he missed her. Then she waited to hear anything. His response? Neglect and unanswered letters. Charlie sent notes to Ann letting her know he remained alive. His failure to write to her worried Ella. At the start of fighting he had filled page after page with correspondence. The early letters described comrades and camps, horses, weather, birds, vegetation and even included flowers he pressed. Charlie knew how she felt about flowers and sent the kinds she loved. Then he took a downward slide. Later letters withered. Even the description of his duty dwindled down. 'Filled my time with pickets.' The words lacked feeling. The high-strung, eager Charlie she knew crawled into a cocoon. He pared life down, didn't see pleasant sights or hear any music. As fighting dragged on, his letters shortened. Then stopped. Do not get killed, she silently prayed. Charlie, do not leave me.

Chapter Seven
Charlie Dickey
Mustering Out, November, 1864

A familiar disappointment, the government did not pay soldiers in Vicksburg, Memphis or in Cairo. They loaded men like cattle onto boxcars without straw or bedding. Even a livestock dealer had more sense than to ship animals like that. After a miserable ride, Charlie arrived at Camp Butler in Decatur. The barracks stank, so he went outside and slept on the cold ground. After almost three years of service, he expected better treatment than filth. Government neglect had become impossible to bear. He told a stranger, "The government can go to the devil."

He arrived in Springfield on the eve of a presidential election, held on the 8th of November. The candidates, Mr. Lincoln and General George B. McClellan, generated great interest. Charlie took a straw vote among soldiers: Mr. Lincoln 337, McClellan 29. But would stay-at-home citizens vote like soldiers? Newspapers indicated Mr. Lincoln might lose Indiana, so commanders granted furloughs to men who lived in that State, and a number of men from Michigan and Illinois went along to the Hoosier State—to help sway the count for Mr. Lincoln.

After headquarters finished the muster rolls, companies got paid and mustered out. Among the last to go home, Charlie began the final journey. At every railroad station one or two men dropped off. Some hesitated to step off and separate. One teary-eyed fellow across the aisle twitched restlessly. When Charlie offered him a drink from his canteen, the man's dilated pupils proved he shouldn't be going home, not without care. He stumbled off the train in Metamora. No one met him on the platform. Was the life he left still there?

At first, Charlie hurried home, but as he rode away from the Ottawa depot feelings shifted. Snow had fallen the night before. A dusting covered branches and grass. Temperature danced around the freezing mark and dressed nature in a cloak of silver. Eagles screamed and overwhelmed prey. Ice formed on the Illinois River. Thoughts also creaked. Family and friends waited—but ghosts of good men who could not go home held Charlie back. Separation from Cyrus and Will grew stronger. Sadness now had a place at the family table. Their circle was broken. They buried the dearest, brightest and best their family had produced. While busy scouting unfamiliar terrain, separation felt poignant, at times overwhelming, but

243

now Charlie had to face his sisters. See empty chairs at the hearth. Husband, beloved head of the household, gone. Brother, who gave guidance and direction, gone. Ann and Belle always gave goodnight kisses to both men, now gone. When Will and Cyrus first donned uniforms, how bright and cheerful they had looked. God, help the nation. Sorrow like this afflicted the whole country.

Sunlight on snow made twigs and blades sparkle. Even on a splendid morning Charlie felt mindful of death. And careful of life, knowing it might end at any time, half expecting today to be his last.

He turned onto the lane, leading to his father's house, and Ella ran out. "Charlie!" She ran out so quickly she left her cloak behind. Her eyes sparkled like sunlight on the frosty landscape.

He slid out of the saddle, and she rushed forward. Her hair smelled of lavender. Charlie threw his overcoat around her. It was large enough to go around her half again. She wrapped up and nuzzled his collar.

Charlie nearly forgot the proper way to greet a lady. Holding Ella feelings of emptiness eased.

***

Every man eligible turned out to vote on election day. When the telegraph announced Mr. Lincoln's victory, veterans fired salutes, the municipal band played, choirs sang songs of praise and men drank countless toasts. "The election was no ordinary political contest," declared Mayor Rice, "but a struggle of the existence of America as a free nation."

Charlie drank to Mr. Lincoln's victory, too, and joined the crowd that filled the town square.

"It all began here!" a man shouted.

Charlie did not correct him. Mr. Lincoln had declared his candidacy for national office in Springfield, proclaiming a house divided cannot stand. Now that he had been reelected for four years people found reason to hope. Was four years enough to secure peace? If anyone could reconcile North and South, Mr. Lincoln could. Troops still in the field strengthened the President's hand. Those who stayed in the cavalry got consolidated into five companies and placed under the command of Major A. T. Search. His battalion combined with the 3rd United States Colored Cavalry under the command of Colonel E. D. Osband and Lieutenant Colonel J. B. Cook. Their successes made Charlie proud. Truth was, Charlie found it hard to lead a quiet life while war still waged. His mind kept going back. Fights invaded his sleep.

That night at dinner Charlie voiced his concern. "I should be there at the end."

Ann froze. "Study that well."

"Army life followed me home."

She glared at him.

"It's hard to explain."

She answered with a whisper. "If you spend a few quiet weeks, it will not hurt the war effort."

"You came to Shiloh. You saw."

Tears came to her eyes. "All the more reason I want you here."

How could he tell her? She had been near the battle but not in the middle of carnage. The demands, sights, sounds, percussion, emotion, overwhelmed a man. To survive, Charlie entered a higher state of alert. Now that he was home, he felt half alive.

"What if the war does not end for years?" she asked.

"It feels like something is missing from my life."

Complete black, mourning dress did not suit Ann. She clenched her jaw, and Charlie promised to think more about it. Next Charlie asked his father, "When Sherman backs rebs against the sea, what then?"

"Four years ago reflection and patience could have given the South years of continued prosperity. Last year, they might have saved their slaves, but now it's too late. They know it. All the powers on earth cannot restore their slaves." Father slumped in his chair. "The nation pursued war beyond all reason. No one knows the consequences."

Under Colonel Osband the 3rd United States Colored Cavalry pulled glory to themselves. From Tupelo to Verona, Franklin Pike to Benton, former slaves made their presence known. Christmas night of 1864 colored units destroyed railroad bridges and trestlework, burned railroad cars and warehouses, captured quartermaster stores and arms. They skirmished warm. When rebels ambushed from a railroad embankment, negro troops held together, used revolver and saber freely, fought dismounted. Exposed to heavy fire, they performed left wheel movements and managed to escape. Before coloreds showed this level of bravery, many northerners favored allowing southerners to keep slavery where they had it—but no longer.

On the morning of January 2, 1865, Confederates charged the advance guard of the 3rd United States Colored Cavalry. The blacks repulsed the charge and drove the rebels, serving under General Wirt Adams. Some rebs covered in timber, skirting the road. Others hid in church shrubbery. Two squadrons of colored cavalry fell on their flank, dismounted and drove the rebels from tree to tree. The combined cavalry force lost two officers and six enlisted men killed, wounded or missing—a tragedy for the families, but a moral victory for men recently held in bondage. Aleck reported it as the hardest cavalry fight the brigade ever had. He wrote that the men fought well, but he gave no death toll for the horses. How did the horses fare? Charlie sent off a letter the same day asking Aleck to explain. Weeks without battles, fatigues and terror left Charlie more anxious rather than less. Newspapers and letters kindled nerves. News from the eastern front occupied everyone. Worry increased when General Butler failed to entrench at Fort Fisher, withdrew and produced yet another Union failure.

Charlie also wrote to Aunt Ann in Kentucky to inquire about his cousins, who had been imprisoned at Camp Douglas. Her curt answer marked a severe change in attitude toward the northern branch of the family. "Frank died the first winter of captivity. Truman was exchanged but killed at Cold Harbor. To die at any time is the hardest service a soldier renders to his people, but to die in a prison hospital far from family and friends and lie buried beneath soil away from home and in an adverse section, must awaken sympathy even among the *hardest hearts*." Though Charlie had inquired about her health, she made no mention of her physical or mental wellbeing. It was like her to think of others—unlike her to ignore a direct question.

Charlie returned to Camp Douglas to visit his cousin Frank's grave. The government's lease for the prison had expired. Most of the 6,000 Confederate dead had been buried in Chicago's City Cemetery along the shores of Lake Michigan. Only 4,300 names, companies, regiments and states had been identified and recorded. The rest of the men were interred as unknowns. Charlie brought along the piece of wood he had taken from the Pemberton-Grant oak tree, where the generals discussed the surrender of Vicksburg. He still had the virgin wood, had not carved a keepsake yet. Now he decided to leave it on his cousin's grave as a gesture of peace. The wind lashed off the south end of the Lake and cut Charlie to the bone. The register showed Frank's name. However, Charlie could not visit graveside because of flooding. He asked the caretaker, "What time of year does the water recede?"

"It's a continual problem."

Charlie handed him the wood scrap. "This is from the Grant-

Pemberton surrender oak at Vicksburg."

"What am I supposed to do with this?"

"Can you whittle?"

"Sure."

"Then make of it what you will."

***

To distract himself from war news, Charlie took a job as night telegraph operator, a time of day when work was light. The telegraph was a "paper" instrument. Some nights he took train orders, which required careful handling, but otherwise had little to do. However, he listened to all messages passing over the line as practice to become a "sound" operator. Gradually his skill improved, and he translated messages by sound. If he got part of a message then floundered, he interrupted the sender and had him repeat words he missed. When he took one such message from Dave Smith, an operator some fifty miles north, Charlie broke in twice.

The second time Dave got angry. *You plug,* he keyed.

Charlie 'talked back' with the key. *You dare not insult me to my face.*

The following Sunday morning at the end of Charlie's shift, a giant walked in. Dave stood six-feet-three and bulky.

Charlie winced. "I changed my mind. Speak to me however you want."

Dave laughed from the belly.

Charlie explained his ambition to become a sound operator.

They became friends, and Dave helped him practice.

After weeks of improving news from the front, Charlie gave up thoughts of returning to war. Women's perfumes and polite conversation seduced him. To be closer to home, Charlie applied at the Caton Lines but walked in the day the message arrived about Mr. Lincoln's assassination.

The country lost its first citizen. Gloom deformed every face. Charlie had lost another friend. The first time Mr. Lincoln entered the house he seemingly came for Charlie. Later Mr. Lincoln called countless men to fight, but how many had Mr. Lincoln bounced on his knee?

Chapter Eight
Ella Linsley, Civilian Danger
May, 1865

Ella closed the cover on Charlie's last journal. Her bedroom was warm, and yet she shivered. The day Charlie had come home from the army Ella ran out to meet him, so eager she didn't take time to put on a cloak. Charlie threw his coat over her, and it went around her half again. Ella wanted to cover his face with kisses. "Welcome home—" Proper behavior did not restrain her. Something in Charlie's face did.

His expression turned even darker when she failed to accept his marriage proposal. Then she pushed for an explanation. Charlie stalked off, fetched the journals and thrust them into her hands. When she tried to repent, Charlie's face turned to stone. She took his hand, but he refused her touch. Heartrending to see him suffer.

When he stomped away, it was clear she had made a fatal error. Worse yet, the journals didn't solve the problem. In fact, her worries grew. Ella fingered journal number seven. The bullet hole made the danger real. The book had saved his life but, in one sense, did not spare him. What demons still haunted him?

A Bay-breasted Warbler outside the window taunted with a high-pitched, hissing call, "tees teesi teesi." Ella recalled a day when she and Charlie were ten years old. They walked home with Jennie and Cyrus. Birds sang that day, too. Someone had dropped a book on the path. Not by accident, the owner had stomped it into the dust.

Jennie stepped around it.

Charlie stooped to see. "It's *Uncle Tom's Cabin*. A book everyone is talking about. People cringe at its depiction of slavery."

Ella leaned in. "Let me see—"

Charlie hid it behind his back.

"Charles Henry Dickey, let me see."

He put the novel back on the ground. "Leave it for someone who is poor in spirit."

Ella had grabbed for that book, too. "I heard it portrays slaves as people just like us."

Charlie put his foot on top of it and refused to budge. "A dangerous book. Folks who never thought about it before now have a reason to oppose slave power."

Ella left the novel but ran back later to get it. His behavior didn't make sense. Charlie loved books. When he had a book in his hand, he became dead to the world. Then, when she read *Uncle Tom,* she realized Charlie had given her a compliment—Ella didn't need a book to make her want to help suffering humanity. The way things turned out, *Uncle Tom* became the most dangerous book of their generation. It hardened both sides. Afterward war came. Nearly took Charlie, as it took hundreds of thousands of men.

When she asked to read Charlie's journals, what did that do? Had she broken their bond? His last journal entry confirmed his passion for Leah. Like General Pemberton, who deserted his northern roots, Charlie was ready to abandon his home, family and friends for a woman. He asked himself, 'can I ever stop? Or let her reform me? Will we meet somewhere in the middle?' Had Leah refused to change? Were they still corresponding?

What power did Leah have over him? She found slavery appealing. Yet he loved her. Did she make slaves of men? Charlie "longed for a woman to write love letters to," meaning Leah. She evoked passion. That much was certain. He wanted that woman, so badly he didn't care about her loyalty.

Ella shuddered. How could Charlie treasure anyone like that? The answer thrust Ella out of her room. She knew where to find Charlie.

Chapter Nine
Charlie Dickey, May 1865
Ottawa, Illinois

The wind whistled up the north bluff behind the Dickey residence. The property his father owned now included a large graveyard. The sun shone and made it a mild day. The quiet of being outdoors suited him. The quietude of the cemetery did not, yet he came to the edge of the ravine and visited the family burial plot every day. Mother was here. Will was here, and Cyrus had joined them. Father had not rested until he brought Cyrus home. To another hero's welcome.

Charlie knelt on the ground. *Chastised on Earth, God tried him and found him worthy of Himself.* He found it hard to bow his head and pray. As far as the living were concerned, neither side had conquered the effects of war. No matter what politicians said, the hatred of a house divided still lingered. Charlie gazed up through bare branches. Trees towered above. No broken tops, no splintered trunks. When a glint of steel caught his eye, Charlie turned immediately toward it. Someone on his right flank. Not a saber or a gun, but a shears. A woman cut greens.

It looked like Ella. She had a special way of working, fingered each plant, assessed its value, brooded over its health, smiled if a stem fit well in the arrangement. Admired it and passed on, if it didn't.

Were other people out walking, too? Or had she come alone? He coughed to announce his presence.

Her eyes lit up, and her boots rustled the grass. "May I join you?"

"Folks will say it's not proper."

Ella shrugged that off. Then turned toward the graves.

The way she bowed her head sent tremors through him. Not just anyone stood next to him, but a woman with knowledge of everything. He didn't have to tell her, 'Here lies...' They looked down at the headstones together. Didn't have to say a word. The world rolled on. A train whistle wailed in the distance. The moment was unthinkable and yet it was shared.

After a long while, Ella reached for his hand. "It would be proper for the two of us to walk alone if we were engaged."

He clutched her gloved fingers.

She searched his eyes.

"My journals didn't scare you away?"

"Just the opposite."

He wasn't sure he heard correctly.

She pulled him forward. "Come with me."

He let her guide him down the hillside. Before they got two steps inside her home, Ella blurted, "Father, we have company." She rushed into the parlor, dragging Charlie along. To his amazement she cried, "Charlie and I want to be married."

Diary Entry — 1872
Charles Henry Dickey
Mississippi Cavalry (African Descent) Reunion

Veterans from both sides gathered 15 miles from the Mississippi River. As I left the steamboat, the earth shook, and the roar of artillery made me duck. Instinctively my hand reached for the bugle—but, of course, I no longer played battle calls. The blast had come, not from cannon, but from quarrymen clearing rocks from a railroad bed. In 1861 I enlisted unconcerned about danger. Now I shiver at nothing. I have many concerns and danger hovers. The sulfur scent of explosives found me. I pray I've heard artillery clamors for the last time—pray to God to make it so, for I cannot bear the shriek of grape, crash of shells or retort of muskets. Never want to witness a charge, horses screaming in pain, the rebel yell as men rush in, or a long-sustained northern yell, both inhuman and ruthless. No more charging toward musketry, no more columns of smoke above artillery batteries and, God help me, no more groans from wounded. I pray the nation never again has cause to fight.

I shouldn't have come to the reunion. I started to turn around and go home, but Randall Johnson and Lieutenant Cook spotted me and waited for me to join them.

I had come this far and decided to continue. Johnson, Cook and I headed for the campground. William T. Clark, Assistant Adjutant-General, welcomed veterans. "Men of the cavalries, I salute you. I hope you are enjoying the peace you bravely fought to obtain. Looking out over the crowd, I cannot help remembering skirmishes like the one at Bayou Bluff, where rebels fought fiercely but could not dislodge colored soldiers or the white cavalry with them. You fought hand-to-hand—"

Clark gave a rousing speech, it's true, but before he got far into his talk, I eased away from the crowd. I felt on edge. Clark stood tall. "Credit must be given"... "conduct excelled" ... "could have held until the last man was shot."

A man nearby shrieked, and I froze. What violence was this? The man waved his hat in the air to show support, not violent at all, and yet my body tightened into knots. I had not served at Bayou Bluff, by then I mustered out. How fortunate to stand among these men, see survivors again, commemorate their sacrifices. They deserve all the honor government can bestow and all the respect mankind can give, but I felt cut off from them.

252

My thoughts froze. Though all eyes focused on the dais, I blinked rapidly. I could not listen to Clark's speech. Could not be a party to the reunion, not yet. His ardor covered my retreat.

Generals do not agree on why battles were won or lost. I am not a professional military man and cannot say. Whatever historians decide, I have a deep respect for soldiers, South as well as North. But now, today, I could not listen. Maybe years from now, I can attend a reunion. By then I may respond differently to the thoughts stuck in my head. I know things I cannot admit to others. It is hard to admit to myself that fear infected me, not in a panicky way, but like harmful vapors, making me sick. Sorrow darkened and deepened after I quit fighting. Sorrow is the new enemy. It has to be attacked and beaten or declared the winner. Can I rush headlong into a battle of emotion? I fear not. I fear General Sorrow will win the war.

To get home Rhoderic trekked over poorly signed trails, down steep slopes and through forests. He has traveled better trails and worse. This Rhoderic did not go to war. He enjoys wild land, but I allow no exploration of places along the way. We passed through villages without stopping. Even the most beautiful inland towns cannot hold me. I ride up the hill, shaded by tall oaks, to the gated entry of Father's old house with its childhood memories of Mr. Lincoln. I do not take the path to the door. Someone else lives there now. Cyrus, Will and Mr. Lincoln all rode there. The house brought us together in good times. Breeze drifted through open windows, carrying the scent of the Illinois River and damp foliage from the forest. The family's sideboard held Mother's biscuits and chicken. I do not wish to go inside, preferring instead to remember the house as it was.

Ella waits for me in our home. No time to dally.

On our wedding day she wore a dress with multiple layers and looked like a sugar confection. Her fingers reached for mine at the altar and refused to let go. I don't remember the ceremony, except a church lit with candles and the delicate taste of her kiss. Then the bedroom, her body all whiteness, I could not believe she was mine to touch. I stood for a while and could barely breathe. The whole night I never took my eyes off her but watched her sleep.

Ever since, if nightmares stifle the air and missiles hiss, she holds me. I tremble in her arms, reliving the carnage. Fears deepen at night. I blow "Boots and Saddles" and climb on the first Rhoderic's back. Soldiers ability to kill one another improved continually, at the outset of fighting men

253

carried inaccurate smooth-bore muskets, then rifled muskets with deadly accuracy and toward the end deadliest of all, repeating rifles. We thought war amounted to nothing more than a ninety-day frolic. How wrong, how wrong. How I wish I could recall war differently. Deny what happened. Resurrect those who died. Without prompting victims invade—a widow's sorrowful face, Dick making coffee, a black child running behind the column, Charlie McKennell cringing at the taste of sassafras tea steeped three times. Events written down in my own hand cannot be denied but, more than anything else I've tried, finding just the right words somehow eases the pain.

I should have no regrets. A soldier does his duty. Through trials, sickness, wounds, the Union continues.

My shoulder aches, at times pain stabs. The bullet severed nerves and has not healed. When a storm comes, the entire arm burns brightly. My left hand remains weaker than the right, never grips as tightly as it should, my souvenir of war. I know my left hand is likely to fail and plan accordingly. I am fortunate—the bullet passed through. A constant reminder, except for the timely arrival of a surgeon, I could have bled to death.

I don't have to lead Rhoderic home. He knows the path. Our house is modest. Our lives full of labor but not hardship. Our perils casual. Ella turns a house into a haven. Inside it is clean and well-ordered. In the yard she nurtures lobelia and other wildflowers, offspring of flowers she planted during the War. She harvests and sows succeeding generations of seed, waters and makes it possible for new flowers to take root and grow. Her garden rivals that of great southern houses. The Honey Locust tree looks brighter, greener than when I left for the reunion.

When I enter, she is making bread, not hardtack, but soft, yeast bread. The back of her dress ripples as her hands knead dough. The smell of yeast perfumes the kitchen, alive and warm. Our youngest son, Will, toddles beneath the table with unsteady steps. When he falls, the hard floor surprises him, and he hollers.

She scoops him up. "Are you hurt?" Flour-covered fingers turn him side-to-side for examination.

Dimpled arms clutch her neck, and he nuzzles his mother.

Cyrus is two years older, and he craves Mother's attention, too. Ella stops for hugs and kisses. The way she touches our sons stirs me. My chest bursts watching the sight. We named the boys to honor brothers who died. However, we conceived boys unlike their namesakes. Our little

Cyrus is a new creation, unlike either brother we lost. He takes after his mother, fair, thin with startling blue eyes. Will does not favor Will Wallace. Instead he is the image of his Uncle Cyrus, so much like Cyrus at that age people swear heaven sent a replacement for the man lost in war. I hope so, sincerely hope little Will grows up to be the kind of man Cyrus was, never questioning duty to family or country. The best man who ever served.

When they are older, I will teach them everything a man needs to know about horses. Cyrus already shows promise. His fourth birthday present from his Grandpa Dickey was a pony. Cyrus took to the saddle and knows instinctively what took me years to learn—that a horse reflects his owner. A horse serves a man well or poorly, as he deserves.

Someday a time will come to send Cyrus and Will to school in the South. To learn about southern ways, what was lost and what may be gained. The southern code men died for is different from ours, and the boys need to understand the distinction. Need to know southern men firsthand, not just rely on accounts in periodicals or books. Great accounts have been written about the War Between the States, but none of the authors have captured it all, not the way it was.

The boys wiggle free of their mother's grasp. Though she wants to hold them close, Ella releases them. "Your father is home!" The morning sky covets Ella's blue eyes. "Home early because he hates to leave."

I start to tell Ella about the melancholy feelings the reunion brought. Seeing those men unnerved me, it felt like watching a chaplain close a dead man's eyes. But I keep silent because she smiles warmly and doesn't need to hear the horror, anymore than I need to tell it. Ella wipes her floury fingers, but I capture them and bring them to my lips. To me, she is still the beautiful girl John and I rescued in our childhood games. Back then we were musketeers. I no longer lust for adventure. I lust for her. Her chest rises in a breath. Her lips part, and I imagine her undressed.

I am pathetic in my need, but this is well and good, for her body is strong. A few more freckles adorn her nose than when she was a girl. Her waist is not as thin, but softer.

At the end of the day, I suck her flat against me, tell her nothing. Get as close as two people can, breath to breath. Her hands hold on, fingertips dig in as I carry her to bed. I grab urgently with the good right hand, the bad hand clasps her fingers for security. A mole occupies the space between her breasts and I graze it with my middle finger. I wash her face, arms, neck with kisses. Savor the salty, sweet taste of her. My ardor grows

255

unruly. I have to pull back or affection becomes too rough, but Ella does not protest. Instead she wraps arms and legs around me. She knows I have a thousand reasons to hold her. When I enter her, there is comfort. She loves me every way a woman can. The difference between us disappears, together we erase separation of flesh. The war almost cost me this great joy, but now love binds us. Love flows, warm, unrestrained. I have no need to explain.

Acknowledgements

Readers interested in nonfiction accounts of Charles Dickey's Civil War service should consult his autobiography: *Memories of Charles Henry Dickey*, by Charles Henry Dickey, Bennett & Morehouse Printers, Oakland, 1926. Dickey indicates family and friends asked him to write the story of his life, but he did not write for general publication. His small book was intended for people who knew him. He writes, "I have been privileged to live in a very remarkable period of the world's history and especially of the development of the United States." Many other Civil War veterans and civilians echoed his sentiment. People understood their participation in America's Civil War shaped history. Soldiers wanted to place themselves in the great campaigns. Generals wrote articles and memoirs, promoting their version of events. Dickey's autobiography is only 56 pages long, and he devotes just 16 pages to his service during the American Civil War, severely limiting the amount of detail. For example, he describes General Halleck's advance and capture of Corinth in two paragraphs. Yet his slender book inspired me.

When Charlie was growing up, Abraham Lincoln visited the Dickey home. Charlie witnessed Lincoln's first 1858 debate against Stephen A. Douglas. He indicates his father, T. Lyle Dickey, supported Lincoln's opponent, Stephen Douglas, during this senatorial race, but that Charlie liked Lincoln better. As a novelist, I wanted to flesh out a boy's first impressions of Abraham Lincoln and Lincoln's rise to the pinnacle of power. Charlie's position during the War also provides a compelling story, bridging the gap between officers and enlisted men. He served as Sherman's bugler and part of Grant's escort, witnessed these generals firsthand, but also performed guard duty and skirmished behind fencerows. This position in the middle, between headquarters and enlisted men, intrigues me and allows the story to depict commanders as well as privates.

The characters of Ella, Leah, and Jennie are not based on real people. They are strictly the product of my imagination and do not resemble real people living or dead. These female characters are meant to reflect women caught up in war's upheaval.

I want to acknowledge the Illinois Historical Society. Their bibliography of holdings led me to the Wallace-Dickey papers held at the Abraham Presidential Library in Springfield, Illinois. The Library's Manuscripts collection had yet to catalog the Wallace-Dickey papers when I read them.

257

However, the Presidential Library made these documents available in the Manuscripts Reading Room.

Despite months of research and substantial efforts to write a story that accurately represents Civil War campaigns, I probably misrepresented some details. I sincerely hope any misstatements do not detract from heroic men and women on both sides of the conflict, who struggled through these great events. My admiration for the participants grew deeper with each campaign I studied. I hope the story reflects my appreciation for their dedication and bravery.

Georgiann Baldino
November, 2013

Sources and Suggested Reading

Anderson, Nancy Scott and Dwight, *The Generals Ulysses S. Grant and Robert E. Lee,* Alfred A. Knopf, New York, 1988

Carter III, Samuel, *The Last Cavaliers,* St. Martin's Press, New York 1979

Civil War Letters From Home, Camp & Battlefield, Bob Blaisdell, Editor, Dover Publications, Mineola, New York, 2012

Corrick, James A., *Life Among the Soldiers and Cavalry,* Lucent Books, San Diego, 2000

Davis, Williams C., *The Fighting Men of the Civil War,* Gallery Books, New York 1989

Dickey, Charles Henry, *Memories of Charles Henry Dickey,* Bennett & Morehouse Printers, Oakland, 1926

Faust, Drew Gilpin, *This Republic of Suffering,* Alfred A. Knopf, New York, 2008

Girardi, Robert I., "Illinois' 1st Response to the Civil War," *Journal of the Illinois State Historical Society,* Vol. 105, No. 2-3, Summer-Fall, 2012, p. 167-172

Harris, William C., *Presidential Reconstruction in Mississippi,* Louisiana State University, Baton Rouge, 1967

Illinois Reading Room, Ottawa Public Library, Clippings and Photos, Cabinet 1, Drawer 1 and 2

Kellogg, Mary E., Compiled, *Army Life of an Illinois Soldier, Letters and Diary of Charles W. Wills,* Southern Illinois University, Carbondale and Edwardsville, 1996

Kohl, Rhonda M., *The Prairie Boys Go to War, The Fifth Illinois Cavalry 1861-1865,* Southern Illinois University, Carbondale and Edwardsville, 2013

Lowry, Thomas P., M.D., *The Story the Soldiers Wouldn't Tell, Sex in the Civil War,* Stackpole Books, Mechanicsburg, PA, 1994

Marten, James Alan, *Children and Youth during the Civil War era,* New York University Press, New York, 2012

McBride, Earnest, "The Battle of Milliken's Bend Black troops made the real difference," 1996 *The Jackson Advocate,* Jackson, Mississippi

Miller, Jason, "To Stop These Wolves' Forays, Provost Marshalls, Desertion, the Draft, and Political Violence on the Central Illinois Home Front," *Journal of the Illinois State Historical Society,* Vol. 105, No. 2-3, Summer-Fall, 2012, p. 202-224

Patterson, Benton Rain, *The Mississippi River Campaign, 1861-1863,* McFarland & Company, Inc., Jefferson, North Carolina, 2010

Porter, General Horace, *Campaigning with Grant,* William S. Konecky Associates, Ind. New York, 1992

Raymond, Steve, *The Civil War Service of the 78th Illinois Volunteer Infantry Regiment,* Globe Pequot Press, Guilford, Connecticut, 2012

Simon, John Y., Edited with Notes and Foreword, *The Personal Memoirs of Julia Dent Grant,* G. Putnam & Sons, New York, 1975

Simson, Brooks D., Editor, *The Civil War, The Third Year Told by Those Who Lived It,* The Library of America, New York, 2013

Smith, Timothy B., *Corinth 1862, Siege, Battle, Occupation,* University Press of Kansas, Lawrence, 2012

Stillwell, Leander, *The Story of a Common Soldier of Army Life in the Civil War, 1861-1865,* The Project Gutenberg ebook

Townley, Wayne C., *Two Judges of Ottawa,* McLean Country Historical Society, Volume 7, Egypt Book House, 1948

Waldrep, Christopher, *Vicksburg's Long Shadow, The Civil War Legacy of Race and Remembrance,* Rowman & Littlefield Publishers, Inc., Lanham, Maryland, 2005

Wallace-Dickey family papers, Manuscripts Section Lincoln Presidential Library, Illinois Historical Society, 4th Cavalry, Box 2 and 3, Springfield, Illinois

Wallace, Isabel, *Life and Letters of General W.H.L. Wallace,* Southern Illinois University Press, Carbondale, 1909

Wallace, Lew, "The Capture of Fort Donelson, Part II," *The Century Magazine,* Vol. XIX, Dec., 1884,

http://www.rugreview.com/cw/cwe2.htm, November 27, 2012

Whitman, Walt, *Complete Poetry and Collected Prose,* "Specimen Days" 1882, The Library of America, New York, 1982